# SPOTREPS

## A MAELSTROM RISING ANTHOLOGY

Edited By
## Peter Nealen

# Table of Contents

# Foreword

## Peter Nealen

This collection came together thanks to a couple of things. One goes way back to the beginning of my writing career. In a way, it could even be said that this entire book is Dave Reeder's fault.

I sent Dave a copy of *Task Force Desperate*, in the hopes that he'd review it on Breach-Bang-Clear. He did, and the review was pretty glowing. Over the next couple of years as the *American Praetorians* series advanced, his enthusiasm didn't wane. In many ways, I'm indebted to Dave as a perpetual source of encouragement as an action thriller writer.

He also brought up the possibility of writing in one or another of my series. When the idea for the *Maelstrom Rising* series came to me, I initially worked up a little promotional graphic, a black and white photo of a raging fire on a street, with the following text:

> *Most of the pundits are calling it World War*
> *Three, though a friend of mine says it's really*
> *more like Five or Six. Others are calling it the*
> *Great Global Breakdown, or the War of All*
> *Against All.*
> *We Triarii?*
> *We just call it work.*

1

Dave immediately wanted to know what he had to do to play in *that* sandbox. And as the series got larger, that idea stuck around.

The final idea for this anthology came at *Life, The Universe, and Everything*, a writer's conference in Provo, Utah, back in February, 2020. The series' scope was getting bigger and bigger as I continued to map it out, and even with the POVs split between Matt Bowen and Hank Foss, there was going to be a lot going on that the main books didn't cover.

So, starting with Jim Curtis, I asked if others who enjoyed the series, and/or were pretty good action writers themselves, wanted in. A sidebar conversation, completely separated from the panels and official meetups, had turned into a major project.

The end result is the book you hold in your hands.

The authors have brought their own perspectives and styles to events scattered all around a world going to hell in a handbasket. They've hopefully shed a little light on things going on well outside of Matt's or Hank's perspective.

It might take a lot for some people, particularly those who are used to a comfortable, relatively stable existence, to stand up and fight. It might take losing everything. These stories are mostly about those people. People who stand up and fight, because there's no other choice left.

Join us as we venture back into the maelstrom of the next war.

# Beware an Old Man

## Peter Nealen

Joaquin Santiago had never been the image of "an officer and a gentleman." Now that he was pushing sixty, he was even less so.

His craggy, pockmarked face had more of the Indio than the Spanish in it. The deep crow's feet around his black eyes had been permanently embedded there by a squint that never quite went away, and were only accentuated by the permanent scowl that his face naturally settled into. Full sleeve tattoos on both arms were starting to blur as he got older.

His physical appearance hadn't been the thing that had made him too rough for many of his peers, though, as much as he looked like a Mexican gangster having a bad day. His gravelly voice, burning, unblinking stare, and utter disregard for couth language and polite euphemism had made it a minor miracle that he'd earned his eagles even after almost thirty years.

Those pitiless black eyes were watching the graffiti-covered barricade shutting off the street about two hundred yards away through binoculars. "Any word from the state cops yet?" It was almost dark.

"Nothing yet," the human mountain standing next to him rumbled. Barry Tomlinson stood a full head taller than Santiago, and probably outweighed him by a hundred pounds. "The Threepers are champing at the bit; I think Wallace is about ready to start kneecapping a few of them to make sure they stay put."

"If they start pushing in, he has my permission." Santiago's rasp was ice cold. "Whether it's before or after he gets the 'Go.'"

He hadn't taken his eyes from the binoculars. The PRA thugs manning the barrier were as brash and confident as they'd been ever since they'd repulsed the Carson City police department and firebombed the mayor's house.

*They're still stupid, wearing black in Nevada in July. And they're not quite so confident to stand around with guns and pipes with their faces uncovered. Pussies.*

Three of the People's Revolutionary Action operatives were standing brashly at the barricades, all dressed similarly in black hoodies, black jeans, red or black bandanas covering their faces. One had a bicycle helmet on and sunglasses, despite the dying light. That one had a Kel-Tec Sub2000 in his hands; the second was carrying a bare-bones AR-15 with the carrying handle. The third was just holding a two-foot length of pipe.

He'd long since stopped considering these three "activists." He knew there were still some of them in there; the PRA always kept a bunch of loud, dumb, ambulatory meat shields around. But not many of them were the armed ones.

A lot of them were becoming hostages, and from his boys' recon reports, they were starting to figure that out, the more that the actual PRA operatives brutalized them inside the "Independent Revolutionary Commune of Carson City." Two of them had tried to escape the night before, and been shot in the back as they ran.

*Same old story. Happened in Seattle a few years ago, happens in Detroit and Chicago on the weekly. Try to get away from the thugs and they'll kill you for it.*

What bothered him was how fast Mayor Kreef had bent the knee. It wasn't as if there hadn't been plenty of examples of where this sort of thing led, going back over a decade. The "Independent Revolutionary Commune of Carson City" was hardly the first no-go zone to have been erected in an American city.

It was just the one that he'd decided was the final straw.

He'd been keeping his ear to the ground since before he'd retired. Nearly thirty years in the military tended to lead to a pretty wide-ranging web of contacts, and while he might be considered by a lot of the ladder-climbers to be a brutish, sour, angry man, he'd gathered a considerable network of like-minded officers and Senior, Staff, and regular NCOs.

Once the murders had started in the IRCCC, and the Mayor's already neutered response was repulsed and answered by firebombings, he'd decided that it was time to put that network to use.

He didn't even live in Nevada. But he'd been watching the disorder spread for years. And there comes a time when a man has to draw the line and say, "Enough."

Lowering the binoculars, he checked his watch. "How long since we contacted the Highway Patrol and the Sheriff?"

"Coming up on twelve hours." Tomlinson was still watching the barricade through the window, his meaty arms crossed over his chest. "Even the photo recon from Roe didn't get any movement. They're not deploying."

Santiago's scowl deepened. "Then it's up to us. I'm done waiting for more kids to get murdered and girls to get raped. Those quaking fucks have had almost a month to clean these cockroaches out." *Not to mention a week of extremely detailed intel and targeting coming out of that pesthole, thanks to us.* He picked up the gray BCM Jack carbine that had been leaning against the wall, set the binoculars down, and headed for the door. "Give the boys the 'Go' signal."

He clattered down the stairs toward the bottom floor of the three-story office building, joining three more men in plate carriers and carrying rifles at the door as he heard Tomlinson's voice crackle over the radio. "Execute, execute, execute."

The three men waiting for him were almost all getting long in the tooth to be gunfighters, except for the tall, black-haired man at the door itself, his green eyes burning. They were also all considerably younger than Santiago himself, but he'd be damned if he stayed upstairs and oversaw things from a safe distance. He'd despised TOCroach commanders before, there was no way in hell he'd become one now.

A few sporadic gunshots echoed from somewhere inside the IRCCC. Through the glass doors, he could see that none of the thugs on the barricade even flinched or looked around. Those noises had become regular background noise over the past month.

The explosion that shook the ground and rattled the windows around them wasn't something they'd gotten used to, though.

The three thugs twisted around, staring in shock at the fireball boiling up into the sky from about three blocks up. At the same time, Santiago and his fire team stormed out onto the street.

They split as they hit the street, the three in the lead going to the right side while Santiago and Tomlinson took to the left. Leonard Neal, the black-haired former Recon Marine, paused just long enough at the corner ahead to barricade on the building and fire six shots.

Six shots, six hits. He'd just double-tapped all three PRA thugs from eighty yards in seconds. They weren't all dead; at least one of them was already screaming bloody murder. But they were down.

The five of them sprinted toward the intersection and the barricade. The jersey barriers weren't their concern; they had human obstacles to remove.

Most of that gunfire, Santiago knew, was from his boys. Some of his two and three-man recon teams had gotten into position with concealed weapons and enough "party favors" to pull the kind of sabotage that had diverted the three PRA thugs' attention. Most of the assault teams, however, had been waiting outside, geared up with their personal kit and weapons, waiting for the word. Most of those gunshots had heralded the deaths or incapacitation of the border guards like Neal had just dropped.

They sprinted between the barriers, careful to slow and check the cross-street. Rifles spoke behind him as he and Tomlinson cleared the west. When he glanced over his shoulder, he saw several dark shapes slumped on the street in front of the bookstore on the corner.

"Roll right." The street in front of him and Tomlinson was clear. Push the immediate threat. He didn't want to hook around the west side of the mall just to get shot in the back by more thugs coming from the east.

Neal took point as they crossed the street and dashed to the driveway that was the only opening in the low cinderblock wall that bordered the parking lot. It took a second to clear the opening, and then they were sprinting toward the corner of the massive, whitewashed brick mall while Neal and Hyde crossed the driveway to hold the corner and provide some cover deeper into the parking lot.

They didn't pause for long at the corner; Tomlinson barricaded to cover the parking lot to the north, while Foret covered the lane to the west, just long enough for Neal and Hyde to collapse in on them.

As soon as the fire team was back together, they started up the ramp to the loading gate.

If recon hadn't confirmed that the gate was still open, they would have found another breach point. But the IRCCC savages had looted just about everything in sight, starting with the mall that they'd made their headquarters, and they weren't particularly good at fixing what they'd broken.

The loading dock's rollup doors were jammed open, and the place had, predictably, been trashed. Smashed-open boxes were scattered across the concrete floor, and it smelled like someone had used the place as a latrine.

It also wasn't guarded.

Fortunately, thanks to Neal's recon, they knew roughly where they were going, so they wouldn't have to sweep the entire mall. Santiago led the way, trying to ignore how hard his heart was pounding in his chest and his knees were creaking just from that short sprint.

*Not a young man anymore. Maybe Barry was right, and I should have stayed back to coordinate.* But it was too late by then, and the burning hatred for what was being allowed to happen was going to have to keep him going.

They moved toward the stairs. There were two cargo elevators heading up to the back of the mall, but Santiago didn't trust elevators, especially not under these circumstances.

He bypassed the ground floor. There were targets down there, but not the one he was after. Neal and Tomlinson were right on his heels; in fact, they could probably easily have gotten past him, but neither one wanted to cross the Old Man.

He did pause at the door leading onto the second floor. He fought to get his breathing under control as he put a hand on the door handle, ostensibly waiting for the rest of the stack, but they had all kept up.

Pushing the door open, he moved out onto the hallway, carbine up and scanning.

There was no doubt where his targets were. They weren't exactly being quiet.

The shrill female voice was so high, loud, and fast that he couldn't make out what she was saying. It just sounded like angry screeching. The deeper male voice was more comprehensible, but the stream of invective, threats, and particularly vile profanities weren't any more useful, except to confirm that whoever was up there really deserved what was about to come to them.

Tomlinson was on the other side of the door, his weapon held at high ready, one hand on the handle. He looked at Santiago, who nodded. *Don't let the boys see how tired you are already. Fatigue doesn't matter. It didn't matter in Mitrovicë, it don't matter now.*

They eased the doors open. There were too few of them to go fully kinetic; if they alerted the enemy now, they might just run into a wall of lead when they came around the corner. The voices were too attenuated to be right outside the door.

The hallway was deserted, the chintzy clothing stores mostly dark. The shadows hid most of the destruction, but the smashed windows, cracked mannequins, and overturned displays. Most of the clothing near the entrance had clearly been taken.

Unfortunately, the layout meant that there weren't a lot of solid walls between them and the hallway. They moved to a point just behind the corner, Santiago peering through the cracked glass and jumbled remains of several displays to see if he could spot the bottom feeder who called himself Leader DK.

There he was, right in the middle of bitch-slapping the short, thickset black woman who was still screaming at him. The slap silenced her for a second, with a ringing *crack*, but two other girls, who were down on their knees with a couple of DK's "entourage" holding them with their arms twisted behind their backs. Both of the young men—no, that second one was a woman—wore the same pseudo-uniform of hooded sweatshirts and black or red bandanas over their faces.

"I said shut the fuck up, bitch, before I decide that you're *all* enemies of the people!" Leader DK's voice was deeper than his rangy build might have suggested. Unlike his cronies, his face was uncovered, and if not for the hammer and sickle on his shirt, he could easily have blended in with the peckerwoods who had made the grievous mistake of trying to intimidate Tom Wallace a few months before. Pasty pale, narrow-shouldered, and sunken-cheeked, it didn't surprise Santiago in the least that he was beating on women while hiding in a mall.

The scrawny "leader" leaned in close. "You saw what happened to Tonya when she tried to undermine what we're doing here. You want me to give you to Viktor? Or maybe to Cindy?" He ran a finger down her jawline as she whimpered. "Oh, yeah, she likes the darker girls."

Santiago had heard enough. So had Tomlinson, who was already lobbing a flashbang around the corner with all the strength of his massive arm.

Flashbangs usually weren't easy for civilians to get their hands on. Which was why Santiago had connections.

The bang went off with a brain-rattling *boom* and a brilliant, blinding flash, before the last syllable was out of DK's mouth. Gray smoke billowed up as the four-man team came around the corner, having paused just long enough that they weren't going to eat the concussion.

There wasn't enough smoke to obscure their targets, not at barely twenty yards. Santiago's trigger finger was already taking up the slack as his sights settled on DK.

Gunfire thundered in the hallway as three of the four of them opened up almost at once. Santiago hammered three shots into DK's upper torso before transitioning to one of the thugs holding one of the girls, blowing the burly woman's brains into another PRA thug's face before chopping that one down with another three shots.

It was all over very quickly. Every one of the armed PRA operatives was down. Two of them were still gasping out their last breaths with awful, blood-choked gurgles. The four of them spread out, weapons still leveled. The three young women who'd attempted to confront DK were screaming in terror.

Santiago swapped magazines as he looked down at "Leader DK." The kid was dead already, the hammer and sickle on his chest soaked with blood, his eyes staring glassily at nothing. Santiago felt nothing as he looked down at the corpse. He'd seen enough over the last week's worth of reporting to know that the little Communist shit had died a lot faster than he'd deserved to.

The thickset young woman whom DK had been brutalizing looked up at them and screamed. "What the fuck?! Why did you do that?" She immediately launched into a screaming, incoherent tirade, at least until Santiago pivoted to point his weapon at her.

"I didn't come here for you," he growled. "As far as I'm concerned, you're every bit as much of a problem as he was. But as long as you keep your hands where I can see them, you won't have to pay the same price he did."

For a moment, he thought that she might just be stupid enough to try something. He could see the hatred mingled with the fear in her eyes. But the fear won out, as she stared at the still-warm rifle muzzle trained on her forehead.

"What do you want to do with them, boss?" Tomlinson had his own weapon covering the two screaming girls who'd been held on their knees. None of the four of them had moved to deal with the last two gasping their lives out. One had already fallen silent.

"Secure 'em, just so we don't get shot in the back on the way out." He had no intention of trying to hold this area. They had their targets, and they'd prosecuted them. He'd wanted Leader DK for himself.

It took moments to get the three screaming, cursing young women on their bellies and zip-tied. They didn't bother to gag them, as tempted as he was to order it. They were noisy and unpleasant, but that wasn't something they'd need to worry about for much longer.

He glanced down at the rapidly cooling corpse that had been a would-be dictator only a few moments before, and keyed his radio. "All Trench Knife elements, this is Knuckle Duster. Objective complete, falling back."

\*\*\*

"Well, it took two more days of chaos, but the Carson City PD finally went in." Wallace sat down in the patio chair and accepted the cigar that Santiago handed him. If Santiago could have blended in with any *narco* cartel or *barrio*, Wallace could have disappeared into any East African city, except for his Georgetown accent. "The mayor was still scared shitless about it, or so my contact in City Hall says, but they really didn't run into any resistance. The criminal elements that survived our sweep must have been even more scared."

"As long as they were waiting for the other shoe to drop, that's fine." Santiago rolled the smoke around his mouth and blew it toward the full moon. "I'm still pissed that it took those scared little *pendejos* so long to follow up."

The targets his friends had hit had been carefully calculated to break the IRCCC, without needing to occupy the area. They'd wiped out the worst of Leader DK's enforcers, killed or otherwise brutalized the up-and-comers who might have

11

replaced them, destroyed most of their supplies, and blown up or disarmed several of their contingency charges. There hadn't been much left for the cops to clean up after that.

Wallace didn't respond as he lit the cigar, rotating it in the match flame to get the coal nice and even. "You know, boss, this isn't going to be the last place this happens."

Santiago puffed contemplatively on his stogey. "No, it isn't." He wafted another cloud skyward. "There's been too much lawlessness, political bullshit, and general breakdown over the last couple of decades. It's only going to get worse." He drew in deeply, making the coal glow bright orange in the Arizona night. "Unless…"

"Unless?" Wallace made it a query, but his tone still suggested that he knew full well what direction Santiago's thoughts were going.

Santiago made his decision. "I'll start putting out feelers in the morning. We'll have a meeting out here in…say a week." He looked over at Wallace with a sardonic half-smile. "Stick around, Tom. I think you're going to like this."

Wallace's grin was ghostly white in the darkness. "Oh, I'm sure I will."

# Calling in the Note

## Brad R. Torgersen

It was 1:00 AM when Burrito Lamanchez showed up at the Alki Beach pier. Extracting him from the strip club near Pike Street Market had been no easy task. There's a really pretty blonde with big fake tits in there who always gives Burrito a good time. He'd bitched up a storm on the club's analog land line—funny how we've had to go back to those, with all the shit going down around the world—but I'd insisted it was important, and name dropped Marlon Sorroti for emphasis. That had shut Burrito up. He still owed Marlon for bail the last time Burrito found himself in the King County lockup. If Marlon was calling in the note, Burrito knew better than to let extracurricular activities interfere.

A light misting of rain slicked the wooden planks of the pier. I pulled the hood of my fleece-lined jacket down over my brow, watching Burrito's shit-ass clunker Camaro rumble into the mostly-deserted parking lot—his bass speakers blasting mariachi music. Local PD didn't like it if you were on the beach at this time of night, but that had been back before everything got crazy. Now the local PD didn't come out of their barricaded holes unless the mayor ordered it.

A great time to be alive, for guys like Burrito and me. Assuming the Russians, or whoever the boogeyman of the month was, didn't start air-dropping into the city.

Burrito got out of his car and staggered over to me, clearly above the legal limit.

"Where's fucking M-Day?" he asked, looking around.

"Nice to see you too, Carlos," I said with a smile.

"Bullshit with that," Burrito growled, his breath painting my face with what smelled like Jack and Coke. "Candace was fixing to give my hammer a polish in the private room when you called the club manager. If M-Day isn't here, I'll break your goddamned face."

"Relax," I said. "I'm here at Marlon's request."

"And?"

"And he's got a proposition for you. Well, both of us, really."

"I 'aint got all goddamned night, *ese.*"

"Sorroti's got someone with a trailer full of weapons and ammunition that he wants on a boat by tomorrow night."

"How much is, 'a trailer?'"

"Not sure. It's enough that M-Day doesn't trust his usual guys to get it up to Elliot Bay from Lewis-McChord."

"The shit's *military?*"

"Apparently so."

Burrito's scowl gradually lessened. Now it was beginning to sink in why one of the Puget Sound's more colorful crime bosses couldn't use his usual crew. M-Day needed prior service personnel for this particular job—people who could drive onto the largest joint installation in the region and act like they owned the place.

Which was partially true. Burrito had been stationed there in the late teens, before getting out. And I'd been there as recently as oh-five. Neither of us had current military ID, but that was easily remedied. Especially under the present circumstances. The trick was going to be getting in, getting the load, and getting out without Military Police or the rent-a-cops at the gate being any the wiser. Nobody was sure how much control Washington D.C. still had over the Army and Navy assets in the area. But it was a sure bet the post commander would still have security manning the gates.

I told Burrito this in as few words as I could manage—I knew he was still badly chaffed over the idea that his favorite stripper was grinding on someone else's lap, not his.

"So I'll be in the black?" Burrito asked. "M-Day calls it even?"

14

"He told me to tell you it was as good as done. We get the merchandise to the port before 10 PM tomorrow night, and the books are balanced."

Burrito thought about it carefully, his face grown wet with water droplets glistening in his tightly curled black hair.

"What's in it for you, Kyle?" he asked.

"You're not the only one who owes Sorroti."

"Cut me in for half of what you get, and I'll do it."

"Whoa," I said, holding up my hands. "M-Day is offering you a clean slate, compadre!"

"And you wouldn't have called me if you didn't need my help, so either I get half of what you get, or I am getting back in my fucking car and you can find someone else."

I dropped my hands. Burrito had always been a blunt bargainer. Zero bullshit. It's why I knew once I had him onboard, I could trust him straight through.

"Okay," I said. "Done."

"When do you want to meet?"

"Tomorrow," I said. "11 AM sharp. Right here. We'll leave your car and go in my truck. It's got a full hitch rig on it and a diesel engine. Shouldn't have any problems with even a heavy trailer."

"What about uniforms? I tossed all my shit when I discharged."

"Also handled. OCPs are easy to get. You can change into the new uniforms I bring you—in the public restroom, before we go. I even got First Corps patches and Velcro name tapes and stuff."

"You must have been pretty sure you'd get me," he said.

"Of course," I replied, smiling. "You're a reliable man."

"Fuck you. Okay, give me the cash now, and I'll see you at 11 AM."

I fished in my pocket and brought out five hundred. People were starting to talk if paper money would last the decade. But with so many electronics being fried or down, five Benjamins was a hell of a lot better than credit or gift cards.

"Enough for tonight," I said. "You get the rest as we drive out the gate with the merchandise in tow."

He slowly took the five one-hundred dollar bills, and stuffed them into the front pocket of his oversized, baggy shorts. We looked at each other.

"If you hurry," I said, "I'm sure Candy Dandy would be happy to catch you on the rebound."

"Her name is _Candace,_" Burrito muttered, then turned and walked quickly back to his car, which re-roared to life, tubas and trumpets thumping through the damp night air.

I watched him pull out and speed southeast along Harbor Avenue, towards the on-ramp for the West Seattle Freeway bridge. I sighed, breath clouding in the mist-laden air, and watched the Seattle skyline's dark, looming buildings glower over the face of the water.

*** 

To my surprise, Burrito was ten minutes early.

And he'd shaved. And cut his hair too. A genuine high-and-tight. His wraparound rainbow-mirror sunglasses sparkled as he got out of the Camaro and slammed the door, checking to be sure that both the driver's and passenger's sides were locked securely. Then he walked towards me, his muscled jaw working on a wad of gum. If he'd gotten further smashed the previous night, it didn't show. His gait was solid and his movements alert. The clouds had mercifully parted in the early morning, allowing Alki a taste of warmer weather to come. A crowd already teemed along the extra-wide sidewalk that ran the length of the beach, and scads of pedestrians, bike riders, rollerbladers, and other citizens enjoyed the dry while it lasted.

Funny, really. The world was gradually coming down around peoples' ears, but they still went out and played like nothing was happening. Better than being locked up at home, I guess. All of us had gotten way too tired of that shit back during the pandemic.

I threw a gym bag at Burrito when he got close, which he caught securely in one hand.

"Everything's in there," I said.

He stopped and put the bag on the hood of my truck, unzipping it and pawing through the contents. When he got to the

16

plastic baggie containing the velcro name tape and fake ID, he looked at me.

"Sergeant *Jesus* Rodriguez?"

"I didn't come up with the name," I begged, hands out.

Burrito dumped the baggie back into the gym bag and muttered something in Spanish about white folk, then he and I both strode off down the sidewalk—steering through the press of people—until we got to the public restroom. A family in sun hats exploded past us as we walked to the door to the men's portion, the odor of stale piss filling our nostrils. He beat me to the handicapped toilet, and I cursed him under my breath as I squeezed in next to him in one of the much smaller, regular stalls.

Putting on the uniform in a cramped, stinky toilet felt just like rolling on a condom—it was second nature. How many times had I done this in my cut-short Army career?

Civilian clothes stuffed unceremoniously into my gym bag, I stepped out of my stall. Burrito was already standing in front of the cracked public mirror, checking himself. Unlike the old uniforms of our youth, the current ones had nothing sewn onto it. For the first time I realized I couldn't remember if the name went on the right and the U.S. ARMY went on the left, or if the name went on the left and the U.S. ARMY went on the right. Looking from Burrito's chest to my chest, I saw that we were mirrored.

He reached out and began fixing me.

"Army always goes over your heart," he said, switching my tapes with a couple of quick rips.

"Thanks," I said.

"How did you remember I was in Syria?" Burrito asked.

"What?"

Burrito tapped the Velcro patch under his flag brassard on his right shoulder.

"Oh, I dunno. When I was in the uniform supply shop in Tillicum I just scanned the wall. Snagged the two patches that seemed most familiar—one for you and one for me. Rank too."

"Didn't you make E-7?"

"I wasn't able to board before they chaptered me."

"That sucks."

"Yeah it does," I said, and meant it.

We turned back to the bathroom mirror, each of us staring at an otherworldly version of ourselves—the men that *might* have been, if things had gone a little differently.

Burrito finally scowled and, spitting his gum into the nearby trash, said, "Fuck this, come on, let's go."

I followed him out into the sunshine, pausing just long enough to fix my patrol cap on my head. Burrito donned his smoothly, as a matter of course.

I noticed civilian eyes darting to us as we walked back to my truck. In the time since I'd been out I'd forgotten that not everybody in Seattle was a friend of the military. Especially not now, with so much being uncertain. A uniform—any kind of uniform—potentially marked us for trouble. Assuming we stuck around long enough for the local street enforcers to get tipped. That Aztlan shit from Southwest had its tendrils in all the local Hispanic gangs. Prepping the soil, as it were.

I thumbed the button for my Chevy 2500's remote lock, and Burrito climbed into the passenger side while I got in on the driver's. We threw our bags into the back seat of the extended cab and I cranked the engine, which rumbled generously. Seattle's classic rock station—classic being broadly defined now as anything originating between eighty-five and oh-five—piped through the speakers. Burrito frowned, adjusting his wraparounds, and I chuckled.

"No barrio music for you, *cholo,*" I said.

Burrito slugged me in the shoulder hard enough to hurt.

I kept laughing, and pulled out, taking pains to avoid the many cars cruising slowly along the Avenue en route to the best beach sand in Seattle. We rolled past Burrito's Camaro, checking just to be sure it was unmolested, then settled in as I took us over to the on-ramp, onto the West Seattle freeway bridge, and eventually merged onto south-bound Interstate 5.

When Burrito's frown didn't go away, I relented and turned the radio off.

We cruised in silence for awhile, until I experimentally cleared my throat—around the same time we passed Boeing Field. Which was conspicuously empty of aircraft these days.

"How's Lupito doing?" I asked.

Wrong question, as the frown became a grimace.

"Rita won't let me see him, since I went to jail. Judge awarded her full custody and she took him back to live with her mother in California. Which is a hell of a place to have him now!"

"Sorry, man, I didn't know."

"You wouldn't. You haven't talked to me in two goddamned years."

"Hey, life has been busy."

"Yeah," he said, still grimacing—but offering nothing further.

I knew Burrito had had some shit luck lately, but I hadn't known that it went so far as his only son. Little Loopy, as I liked to call him—hell, little, the boy was probably a teenager now—had always been Burrito's pride and joy. And though Rita had divorced while Burrito was in the pen for the first go-round, I was suddenly and profoundly put out to learn that she'd since extended her hard feelings to include leveraging their son.

Thank God I'd never gotten married, or had kids.

The whole mess seemed like nothing but trouble.

Silence dragged, Burrito staring out his window and me watching the I-5 hardball rolling south. Washington State Patrol had cleared most of the major pile-ups. You could go a good distance now without taking detours onto surface streets. A few clouds on the horizon told me that our spot of dry wasn't going to last the day, which meant I'd need to take it extra careful coming back up if the freeway was wet and we had a heavy load in tow.

Burrito surprised me when it was he who spoke next.

"So who exactly are we meeting at JBLM?"

I popped the arm rest and pulled out an older-model, use-worn cell phone. The ancient flip kind. It hadn't been zapped.

"Don't know names. Got this in a bike courier pouch from Sorroti. I know where we're supposed to be, and when, and we'll know someone's coming to meet us when this rings."

"Money?"

"M-Day said he already put some cash down. Said that once the trailer was on the back of the truck and I'd inspected the contents sufficiently to be sure that it contains what it's supposed to contain, I was to call him on this little piece of shit, and give it to our person on the inside, at which point they'd handle the rest between them. We drive away."

"Sounds simple," Burrito said, "which scares me, Kyle. I didn't bring heat because if the PD catches me with an unlicensed weapon in my car one more time, I am done. You got any firepower in this rig somewhere?"

"Reach in the pouch behind my seat," I said.

He did. And recovered a well-oiled M1911 semi-auto. With three full magazines.

"Old and slow," he groused. "You got a permit for this?"

"In a manner of speaking."

"Damn, *ese,* the gate cops search us—"

"They won't search us," I said, reaching out and tapping the ID cards on the arm rest.

"Bullshit. Force protection is going to be robocopped. M240s sandbagged at the gates and everything. You think we can get on with just a couple of fake CAC cards?"

"We've got better," I said, and fished some printed papers out of one of my breast pockets.

Burrito whistled. "These look like official orders. Who do you know that can get you this stuff?"

"I know a lady who works at the Coast Guard station down by the ferry docks," I said.

Burrito just looked at me.

"She's got a gambling problem," I continued. "It was easier for her to cut me these items than it was for her to cut me back the thirty-five-hundred she's owed me since Christmas."

Burrito took his ID out, running a thumb over the glossy finish that covered his photo.

"Where did you get the pic? Looks like me in '12."

"It is you in '12."

"Oh," he said. "Think anyone can tell I'm not that young anymore?"

"You're as fresh-faced as the day you signed up," I said, smiling.

The corner of his mouth cracked upward, if only just a bit, and I immediately began to feel better about how the rest of the drive was going to go.

As we passed Federal Way I went into a bit more detail about the plan.

Once we were in the gate—timed for the lunch rush, when the lines would be longest and the gate guard would be least likely to give us a close look—we'd head for the one place on Lewis-McChord where nobody ever went: the post Army museum, closed for renovations until further notice. There we'd wait until the cell rang, at which point that was our five minute warning that our cargo was near to arriving. I'd do all the talking and be out in front, with Burrito at the driver's door to the truck—open, ready for him to dive in. Or pull the M1911 from the door pocket and unload, if whoever we were meeting decided to get creative on our asses.

But if that happened . . . well, both of us didn't need to say that we hoped that wouldn't happen. Getting back off-post with one of us hurt or bleeding, or gunshot damage to the truck, was about as likely as Burrito suddenly being into gay bar music. I had to hope that Burrito's funny sense for things—which had come in handy on more than one occasion prior—would tip him soon enough that he'd drop our greeter before said greeter could do us any great harm. Then we'd have to run like becalmed hell for the underpass from North Fort to Main Fort, and wend our way quietly—whistle, whistle, nothing to see here—to one of Main's several exit points.

The museum was a ghost town, yes, but if something went down, even that relatively remote location wouldn't protect us if someone heard and reported weapons fire away from the ranges, or worse yet, actually drove past the museum while activities were in progress.

Passing through Fife, I began to get that familiar tickle of nervous tension in my stomach that I always got as I approached the decision point of a job. Technically, as long as we didn't pass through the gate, there was still time to turn around, head back, call Sorroti and call the whole thing off—beg some kind of excuse, and hope Sorroti wasn't butt-hurt about it. Which was unlikely, given the haste of this particular movement.

But once we were inside, it was game on.

Burrito must have felt it too, because the grip he had on the passenger side ceiling handle was like a boxer's fist. His wraparounds concealed the emotion in his eyes, but the slack, almost stoic expression on his face was familiar: the time for surety was near, and that was when he'd be shedding all hesitation and doubt.

Tacoma was its usual gritty self. The most noteworthy thing about the hollowed-out downtown district was the fact that it was the location of the Pierce County jail house—a facility I was more than just a little acquainted with. All the real businesses had since spread out to the suburb side of town, which was on the other side of us, headed towards the two bridges that spanned the Narrows; one new and one old. If I felt like our return flight path up I-5 was too risky—for any reason—we could always jump off onto 16 and bury ourselves like ticks in the Olympic Peninsula. From the cops. From the Army. And from Sorroti, if it came to it.

One thing about me, I'd not managed to make a living in my current avocation without having several backup plans in the floor of my mind. Just in case shit didn't transpire per expectation. And sometimes it didn't.

Tillicum wasn't so much a town as much as it was a shabby, oversized strip mall. We flashed through it until we got to the double-branch off-ramps: one feeding towards the Main gate, and one feeding towards North. Rolling up on the guard shack at the North entry point, Burrito and I both sat up a little straighter as we noticed Air Force Military Police—not rental cops—manning the station. And Burrito hadn't guessed the half of it. Not only were machine guns sandbagged at the entry point, there were a couple of goddamned Strykers poised to watch over things as well.

"What the fuck . . ." Burrito said under his breath.

Those eight-wheeled armored fighting vehicles were a bad sign.

"Damn," I said. "Well, just be cool, bro. Be cool."

We waited patiently in line, floating forward one or two car lengths every thirty seconds or so, until a Senior Airman with a Beretta on his hip walked up to my window and waited for me to extend both my false ID and Burrito's, along with our papers. He looked at the cards and the documents, turning them over in his gloved hands a few times—emotion concealed behind his own pair of wraparound sunglasses—then looked at me and nodded, smiling, handing the cards and fake orders back to me.

I breathed a long, slow sigh of relief and handed Burrito his card, then approximated my own smile and nodded at the Senior Airman, advancing forward through the checkpoint as two Army MPs watched passively from their sandbagged position.

Well, time to see how much had changed since either Burrito or myself had graced the place. If I'd not known Burrito better, I'd have thought he was getting wistful, swiveling his head around as he took in all that was new. Civilian traffic was less than I remembered, but Humvees with squad gunners in the turrets, rolled by occasionally. I turned left off 41st Division and onto A Street. Which led past a crapload of older industrial structures before A Street blended into South Drive, which eventually intersected with Pendleton Steilacoom. Yeah, I was taking the long way to get to the museum, but it was the way I was most familiar with. Now that we'd cleared the first, most nerve-wracking hurdle, I was feeling much more relaxed.

Burrito must have too, because he started humming something and tapping his hand in rhythm on the outside of the cab—window still rolled down so as to allow the sweet spring breeze to fill our nostrils.

God, the son of a bitch *was* wistful.

Well, couldn't blame him really. This place represented an altogether better time for he and I both. Before things had gotten all fucked up, and we'd gone down certain inexorable roads. If Burrito wanted to enjoy a little trip in his own personal wayback machine, who was I to resent that?

When Pendleton Steilacoom split, I went left, curving around onto Main, and observing the museum with a beautifully deserted parking lot—lots of plastic on the windows and construction dumpsters out front, sans contractors. As had always

23

been the case, the museum was last on the post commander's list of things that needed fixing, so whatever schedule this project was on, it was currently stalled. And small wonder. JBLM had far more to worry about these days.

Only a set of train tracks separated the museum from the southbound lanes of I-5, which was just fine because to virtually everyone on I-5 headed south—cops included—everything north of the train tracks was effectively invisible. A bunch of old Army crap. Who gave a damn about that, especially when it was all ripped up? My pickup would look like the foreman's.

I pulled into an empty spot where one of the dumpsters would partially occlude us from Main Street, and turned off the engine. A gentle pattering and the splash of water on the windshield told me that we'd lost our sunshine for the day. Burrito kept the window down just long enough to enjoy a few more breaths of country air, then reluctantly hit the switch and rolled up his window, the water beating down steadily.

"We just sit here and wait?" Burrito said expectantly.

"Yup," I said, holding the old-model cell phone in my hand to examine the display and make sure it still had charge. The little digital clock on the phone said it was 12:36 PM.

***

At 3:15 PM, we began to get pissed.

Clouds had rolled in, gray and thick, and the rain beat mercilessly on the truck's hood. We'd cracked the windows a little so that they wouldn't fog up too bad, but Burrito had gone back to silent scowling, and I could sense that if something didn't happen soon, he'd demand action.

Theoretically, I could call Sorroti and do a big giant WTF.

But the boss would be annoyed by that, especially since he'd said nothing else mattered, as long as the load arrived back in Seattle and was on the dock by 10 o'clock that night.

"You bring any lunch?" Burrito asked.

"No," I admitted.

"I'm getting hungry. And this is a goddamned circle jerk."

I couldn't argue with him on either point.

24

Looking at the cell, I scratched the display thoughtfully with a thumbnail. Maybe there was no sense sitting here when the fish weren't biting?

I turned the engine over. "Feel like a Double Whopper meal? I'm buying."

"Damn right you're buying," Burrito said, still scowling. Just not quite as much as before I'd offered to buy him some grub.

We re-traced our route back to the intersection between A Street and 41st Division, pulling into the shoppette where a few cars were parked under the awning, getting gas. I was about to pull into the drive-thru when Burrito told me to pull it into a space.

"Gotta use the latrine," he said.

I pulled into an empty parking spot in front of the new rectangular building that was part gas station, part convenience store, part clothing and sales, and part fast food joint. Going into a public building like this wasn't exactly on my hasty OPORD for the day—if at any time anyone took a close look at us and didn't like what they saw, we could be in for a world of hurt. But Burrito was right. When nature called, nature called. And I had a feeling we'd both feel a little less grouchy if we got some hot food in us.

We got out of my truck and quickly headed inside—rain still falling fast—Burrito heading to the male latrine door and me standing over by the feeder line for the Burger King's cash register. Like at the beach, people seemed to be proceeding in as normal a manner as possible. Despite everything going on around the globe. Posted at the register was a positively pubescent boy, bored like nobody's business, and the air was thick with the smell of fryer oil and broiled beef hamburger patties.

"What the hell are you doing here, Senninger?"

I whirled around at the familiar voice.

*Holy goddamn . . .*

The only thing that had changed about Mike Buford was that he'd been promoted. The little rank square on his chest now showed three stripes and two rockers, not three stripes and one rocker. Otherwise he had the same bitch-ass superior attitude I'd learned to hate him for when we'd been in Baghdad. His nasal, redneck drawl still made my skin creep.

"Excuse me?" I said, feeling sweat spring out instantly across both palms.

"I heard they chaptered your butt," Buford said, poking a finger accusingly at my chest. "What's with the new name tape, *Goulivier?* You get married and take your wife's name, like a little cunt?"

"Sarn't," I said, playing it innocent, "I think you might have me confused with someone else,"

"Like hell, they should have busted you down to ee-nothing and sent you to Leavenworth."

I just looked at him, not sure what to say.

"So which loser unit got stuck with you? It's Saturday. Don't tell me you went *Reserve* of all things?"

Shit. *Uhhhhhh . . .*

"Yes, I'm Reserve."

"Which unit?"

I thought furiously. Fuck it, whatever.

"Two One Two Two," I said.

"Bullshit," Buford said. "That unit got torn down years ago. It's a maneuver Brigade now. And your patch—" he pointed to my shoulder "—says First Corps. You wouldn't be <u>lyin'</u> to me now, would you *Kyle?"*

My fists began to ball. This was all going very badly very quickly.

"Actually," I said, working very hard to restrain myself, "which unit I'm with isn't really any of your business."

The formerly bored teenager at the register was now staring at us, mouth half open, while everyone else behind the counter had stopped to watch.

"We'll see about that," Buford said, then directed his attention to the boy at the register. "Hey kid, lemme use your land line. I gotta check something."

My mind began to go blank with panic. I'd not anticipated running into someone I'd previously known, much less someone who'd hated me. Of all the piss-poor, lousy, goddamned bad luck. I wished loudly and with much passion that I'd told Burrito to simply *hold it,* and that we'd gone through the drive-through.

"Is there a problem here, Sar'nt?"

Burrito had come out of the bathroom and approached us soft-footed.

Buford looked at Lamanchez, and nodded his head at me. "You with this scumbag, Sergeant Rodriguez?"

"That's *Staff Sergeant* Goulivier," Burrito said, tipping his head to me. The too-calm expression on Burrito's face told me that he was just moments from violence. He knew we were in deep shit.

"Sar'nt," Burrito said, "I think we need to deal with this outside, so we don't do Army business in front of civilians."

Burrito had turned on a heel and was already headed for the door. I followed suit.

"Get back here!" Buford commanded.

We ignored him and kept going. Right out the door and towards the truck.

I heard Buford coming out the door behind us.

When his hand grabbed my left shoulder and yanked back forcefully, I did something I'd wanted to do for many years: I whirled around and drove a fist directly into his jaw as hard as I could. The pain in my hand was worth it, seeing Buford sprawl on the pavement, out like a light.

Burrito looked at me, surprised.

"We need to get the fuck out of here," he said. "Shitcan the op."

"No, wait," I said. "Pick him up and put him in the back seat. I can handle this."

I put on my patrol cap, then calmly walked back into the Burger King. The staff watched me, wide-eyed.

"Sorry about that," I said to them all. "We're going to take him back to his unit. I'd appreciate it if nobody says anything about this. I wouldn't want him or me to get in needless trouble over something silly. MPs have obviously got their hands full pulling perimeter security right now. We can get him home, and the Sergeant Major will handle it. *Hooah?*"

I looked hard at the manager, who was older, black, and looked like he might have been in at some point. Our eyes held for a minute, and he slowly nodded.

I smiled my best, most winningest smile, thanked him, and walked back out.

Burrito already had Mike Buford, eternal asshole, stuffed into the back seat.

I climbed in and Burrito glared at me as I started the engine, backed us up, then rolled us out.

"Fucking hell, Kyle, they'll *still* call the MPs."

"Maybe," I said. "But if we get out of here fast enough, the MPs won't know who to look for, or where. So far as those people are concerned, it was just some NCOs working out their differences."

I rapidly re-traced our route back to the museum, while Buford snored in the back.

"What do we do with this *pendejo?*"

A very good question. I looked at one of the construction dumpsters.

"There's some nylon rope under the seat in the back," I said. "We gag him, tie him, and throw him in."

"And what about our *pickup?*"

As if by design, the well-used phone in my pocket began to jingle.

I smiled at Burrito—half bravado and half relief—and pulled out the cell.

"Where are you?" I asked.

"We're ten minutes out," said a low voice, thickly Louisianan, probably black. "Where the hell are you?"

"We're right where we're supposed to be," I said. "Just get here fast. We need to move the hell out."

The line clicked, and the signal dropped. I took that as an acknowledgement.

***

It took Burrito and I five minutes to hog-tie the unconscious Buford, gag him, and heave him over the lip of the construction dumpster. He made a loud crunch at the bottom, and I hoped very much that he broke bones. If the fast food guys had called in the heat on what had happened in the parking lot, nothing seemed to have come of it yet. The scene at the museum was still very wet, and very deserted.

Eventually, an ancient deuce-and-a-half five-ton truck grumbled into view, pulling up alongside us. Where in the hell on post had they managed to find *that* ancient monster?

Per plan, I got out and Burrito waited at the driver's door, within reach of the .45 pistol in the door pocket.

"I was told there would be a trailer," I said to the large black youth in issue OCPs who climbed down from the passenger side of the deuce.

"It's on the way," he said. Another large, black youth in OCPs and covered helmet sat nervously at the wheel, keeping the old truck's diesel engine running.

I shot a look at Burrito, whose face had once again gone too-calm, and looked back to the first soldier. I noted that his name tape had been strategically ripped off.

They didn't appear to have any weapons, but that didn't mean weapons weren't present. I couldn't see the seat of the five-ton from where I stood, but I wagered there was something up there that Burrito and I didn't want to get acquainted with.

For four minutes we stood silently, getting very wet in the May rain, until a second truck—civilian, Ford—motored into the empty lot, towing a beat-to-shit custom built trailer that sagged badly on its wheels. A heavy tarp was stretched and tied across what appeared to be a series of rectangular objects on the trailer bed. There were two more youngish soldiers in the Ford's cab, though this time they were in civilian attire—only their haircuts gave them away. They pulled to a stop three car lengths away and climbed out: one white, one latino.

The latino kid immediately went back to begin unhooking the trailer, while the white kid waited near the driver's door, his eyes somewhat concealed behind a soiled, purple and gold Lakers team cap.

Four to two. And the drivers looked spooked.

Adrenaline was pumping heavily into my veins when the Latino kid, finished with jacking the trailer up off the Ford's ball hitch, peeled back the tarp to reveal numerous plastic-wrapped wooden crates.

I carefully walked towards the trailer, making sure my hands were in sight at all times, nodded silently to the Latino kid, and examined the crates. I bent and picked one up one of the smaller ones, experimentally shaking it until I heard the tell-tale brass rattling of the rounds inside the cardboard boxes inside the crate. It weighed about what it should have, and I set it back down, realizing it had been too long since I'd handled that much mass. My back would be pissed at me in the morning.

"You have something for us," said the white kid in the Lakers cap.

"Yeah," I said. "After I am sure this is everything, and the trailer is secured. Move your Ford out of the way so my partner can back us up and I can hitch us on."

Lakers Hat complied and got the Ford clear, while Burrito—not needing to be told—climbed into my Chevy and expertly backed it up to the trailer. I lowered the trailer arm down onto the ball hitch and secured it, taking up the winch jack in short order, while Burrito got out and resumed his watch from the driver's side door.

The two black kids hadn't said a word since the other truck's arrival.

Undoing several bungee cords, I peeled back the tarp almost entirely, quickly counting the visible, stacked crates and guesstimating a number. By my reckoning, the load looked right. I stepped onto the trailer and peeked between the ammo boxes to be sure the middle of the crate stack wasn't dummied, then hopped off and pulled the tarp back on, re-doing the bungee cords.

I pulled out the used cell phone and held it up, glancing around at the four youths to see who wanted it. The first kid—who'd climbed from the five-ton—walked over and snatched the phone from my hand.

"Your unit won't miss this stuff?" I said, half smiling. "Arms room security's going to be pissed when they do inventory."

"Fuck you," the kid said, turning away from me.

I raised an eyebrow, then shrugged, knowing it was a sign that the kids were even more nervous than Burrito and me. Amateurs. Didn't matter to me anymore where they'd stolen the rounds and weapons from. It was time for me and Burrito to clear off the objective.

30

The kid with the phone had it in his ear as he walked back to the five-ton and Lakers Hat and the latino boy waited near the Ford.

Which is when Mike Buford, the eternal asshole, chose to make his presence known.

A muffled groan issued from the nearby construction dumpster, following by a clattering of debris and a loud clang against the metal.

The kid with the phone jumped so high, he could have skied over LeBron for the dunk, and began running for the five-ton, screaming and waving a hand signal to the driver.

"IT'S A SETUP!" the kid yelled.

Lakers Hat and the Latino ducked behind their respective open doors, and emerged with what looked like M9 pistols in their hands.

Everything became a blurred chaos.

Young men screaming. Burrito, screaming louder. The five-ton blasting black smoke as it ponderously tore a wide circle around the lot, seeking freedom. The loud cracking of several pistol shots as I dove for my truck, the passenger door hanging wide open. I leapt inside and crashed into Burrito, who'd already climbed in and slammed his door, my body almost lurching to the floor as he cranked the engine, slammed the gas, slammed the brake, slammed the gas, then peeled jerkily for the road. I peeked over the top of the dash to see Lakers Hat lying in a wide pool of blood while the latino kid was nowhere to be found.

The deuce was headed back into the warren of North Fort.

Burrito looked like he might aim to go back out the North Fort gate.

"No!" I yelled. "Like we planned, man, take the underpass and let's go out a different gate!"

"Fuck you, *ese,*" Burrito grunted. It was then I noticed his right hand clutched over his thigh, which bled dark red through his fingers and down the leg of his OCP trousers.

Fuck, fuck, *fuck.*

"Shit, man, pull over, I can drive."

31

"No time," Burrito said, his brow dripping rain and sweat and his eyes sharp as knives as he drove—just barely under control.

We kept on Pendleton and cleared the underpass—not far from the museum—and Burrito began making his way across Main Fort, past block after block of old brick Army construction which now looked very, very imposing. Our only real blessing was that rain meant there were few pedestrians out and about. Fewer people to have possibly heard the shots, seen something, and reported it.

The MP station was somewhere near. I scanned rapidly for anything that looked even remotely like an MP patrol car. Thankfully, none were around.

Burrito kept it right at the speed limit as we approached the intersection with 41st Division, the main road which would take us out the main gate and onto the freeway.

Two cop cars, lights on but sirens off, flashed past the intersection towards the gate.

"Fuck," Burrito said, his face snarled up into a permanent expression of pain.

I pulled his hand away from his thigh and saw the hole, and the blood.

"Shit," I said.

"It went through," Burrito said.

"If it hit an artery . . ."

"I'd be dead already," Burrito replied

"Let me drive so you can wrap something on that," I said sternly.

"No."

"Carlos, you motherfucker, this is no time to—"

"No, Kyle. Not until we're clear!"

He'd shouted the last words so loudly my ears rang.

The light was green at 41st Division, and we kept right on going. Past the airfield on the right—Blackhawks and Chinooks tied down on the gloomy tarmac—and the intersection with 4th Division, where Pendleton turned into Jackson. Past the NCO Academy, past the Rangers, until Jackson curved around the Madigan hospital campus. Burrito was obviously headed for the

Madigan gate, which would turn into Berkley Street overpass, and an on-ramp to northbound I-5.

A hunch hit me.

"Turn at Filmore," I said.

"What for?"

"There might be MPs waiting at Berkley," I said.

"Where the hell else are you planning to go, man?"

"Take Filmore and head for the logistics gate. It's small. Less of a chance someone notices or stops us."

He glared at me, but complied, again keeping the truck and trailer barely at the speed limit as we bounced down the curving road, past trees and into a block of ancient warehouses. I kept looking behind us, expecting to see lights, but saw only the gray, rain-soaked pavement, empty and relieving.

When we got to the logistics gate, Burrito brought us to a dead stop.

It wasn't manned, but it wasn't open either. Chain link stretched across the road, barring exit or entrance.

The peel of obscenities that Burrito unleashed at that point was too hot even for me to describe, but I lifted my eyebrows and popped my door, slapping him on the shoulder.

"If you can walk, get out and switch sides." I reached into the back and pulled out a large bolt cutter that I kept in the truck just for situations like this. You never knew when you'd have to snap a piece of steel chain. Especially in my improvisational line of work.

When it was clear Burrito could not walk unassisted, I went around the cab and put his right arm under my shoulder, praying nobody saw us as I helped him limp—bloody and shaking—from the driver's side to the passenger's side. Then I threw the truck's under-seat med kit in his face and ran to the gate, cutting links and pushing as hard as I could to get the gate open.

I ran back to the truck and froze, hearing the distant sound of police sirens.

Burrito had heard them too.

"Let's go," Burrito pleaded. I threw the bolt cutters in the truck bed, ignored the blood all over the driver's seat and floor, climbed in, slammed the door, and moved us down the last length of road, towards the gate, and out.

Trees greeted us on the left side of 150th, while cheap off-base commercial housing went by on the right. The rain fell heavily, and the sky was unforgiving and gray as I sped us towards the on-ramp. I thought I caught a glimpse of flashing lights in the mirror just as the gate slipped out of sight. Ideally, I'd have had time to go back and re-chain the gate, to slow them down, but was now desperate to reach the freeway.

Ignoring the rain and the speed limit, I punched the diesel engine and kept my hands clenched to the wheel. Burrito meanwhile was cobbling a pressure bandage together using lengths of ace wrap, several sterile cotton bandages, and one of my old t-shirts that had been in the back seat since last week's run to the laundromat. He worked quickly, but his hands shook badly and his ordinarily olive face was growing pale. Based on how slippery the floor felt and how the wetness on the seat was soaking through to my skin, Burrito couldn't be so sure about the bullet having missed the artery. I guessed that if he wasn't seen soon—very soon—he'd be at the edge of death.

There was a guy I knew in the Seattle Soho district who could patch Burrito up: a paramedic with a coke habit who knew a bit about sewing substantial wounds, for the right price. If we could get to Seattle in time . . .

I almost took the on-ramp on two wheels, the trailer slewing dangerously behind me and several crates almost shifting out from under the numerous bungees holding down the tarp. Neither Burrito nor I said anything as I floored it down the on-ramp, merged aggressively into northbound lanes, then let my breathing begin to slow as my heart rate gradually wound down to something approaching normal.

Burrito kept both hands—hopelessly bloody—pressed on his wrapped and red-soaked leg as I drove. My mind began to figure out how and where I was going to stash the truck until I could get it deep cleaned. We'd have to burn the uniforms. I reached under the dash and flipped the switch on my jury-rigged police scanner. Highway patrol chatter was muffled and difficult to make out, but I reasoned it wouldn't be too long before the state troopers got wind of what was going on at Lewis-McChord.

Would they pursue? Or would they—as the Seattle PD was prone to doing these days—chalk it up to a case of anything not presenting an immediate and major threat to many lives and much property, simply not care?

Minutes passed, and we hit Tacoma. The scanner didn't seem to indicate much, only that the state troopers were now aware of the fact that, "a vehicle" of uncertain description carrying, "suspects," had broken out of the logistics gate and was believed to be somewhere on the Interstate headed north.

When we got past Fife, I made a decision.

"What are you doing?" Carlos said weakly as I got us off the freeway.

"Pacific Highway," I said. "Ninety Nine. If they think we're still northbound on the Five, we need an alternate route up to town."

"And a doctor," Burrito said.

"That goes without saying, compadre. I know someone. I'll make the call on the way. Just keep the pressure on that wound and don't fucking pass out on me!"

***

Burrito had passed out on me.

We were parked behind the hulk of a recently-closed grocery store, somewhere south of Boeing Field.

The clock in the dash of my truck said it was 7:38 PM.

I reached out and put two fingers on Burrito's neck—he had been slumped against the passenger side door for at least twenty minutes—and felt a thready pulse.

The cab stank of sweat and congealing blood.

The cokehead paramedic was at least 45 minutes behind schedule. I looked at the little flip phone and considered calling and chewing my paramedic out again, but figured that wouldn't make the tardy bastard move any faster than he already was. He'd said he was coming from Northgate, and that could mean he was either almost on us, or still twenty minutes away, depending on what traffic in the Seattle metro area was like.

Not for the first time, I considered just rolling into the nearest Emergency Room portico, opening the passenger door, pushing Burrito out, yelling for help, then taking off. With a little luck, they'd save the man's life, but you don't just show up unconscious at a hospital with a bullet wound in your leg without the cops—overtaxed and outmanned as they were—asking questions once you're awake. Burrito could plead the 5th all he wanted, they'd bust his nuts just the same, and I wasn't entirely sure he wouldn't rat me out in the process if he felt like I'd betrayed him by dumping him. Which I was positive he would.

So, we waited. And the last of my friend's life slowly leaked out of him onto the floor of my truck.

I'd done what I could to adjust the bandage on his leg, but short of putting it in a full tourniquet, didn't really have any options. Here again I was pretty sure Burrito would cut my head off at the neck if he lost the leg unnecessarily. So, I gambled on the paramedic to be as good as his illicit reputation said he was.

A beat-up For Escort wagon rounded the corner of the grocery store and rolled slowly towards the truck. Recognizing it, I stepped out of my truck cab and semaphored my arms wildly.

The Escort stopped, and I ran up to the driver's window, which had rolled itself down in the spattering rain.

"Did you get shot in the ass?" said the paramedic, who absently wiped at his nostrils with a nervous hand.

I looked down at the blood all over the seat of OCP pants.

"Not me, idiot. Get your ass over here, or my partner will die."

Paramedic—who had never given me his name, for understandable reasons—cut his engine and his lights, exiting the vehicle. He went to the hatch back and popped it, pulling out his huge paramedic's toolbox, then pointed into the car and told me to grab the other, smaller box, which I did. We walked quickly back to the truck and I pointed inside, where Burrito was still slumped against the passenger door, eyes shut and mouth slackly open as he breathed shallowly.

"Fuck," said Paramedic, "he needs a hospital."

"He'll go to jail," I said.

"Better than being dead."

"I called you for a reason, asswipe," I said furiously. "Now where's the damned saline? He's lost a ton of volume."

"We need to get him somewhere I can look at him."

"Your wagon got room in the back?"

"Hell no."

I looked around quickly, seeing the padlocked cargo dock door of the vacant grocery.

Thirty seconds later, I had the padlock cut and the door pushed upward. If the derelict store was alarmed, I didn't hear anything. In this part of town, probably nobody cared enough to keep the place wired anyway. Paramedic and I grunted as we muscled Burrito's too-heavy dead weight over to the dock and gently pushed him up onto it. Then we brought the boxes, a mag light, and a smaller tarp I'd had in the pack of my truck, unrolled the tarp, and put Burrito onto it so he was out of the rain. I grabbed the saline bags Paramedic had brought, poked my friend's arm as well as my rusty Combat Life Saver skills allowed, and watched as the fluid began to drain into his veins while Paramedic cut off Burrito's trousers with a pair of old surgical scissors.

Shining the mag light so that Paramedic could see, I watched as he examined the impossibly bloody makeshift bandage on Burrito's leg, tested it with gloved hands, then looked back up at me with alarmed eyes.

"I'm not kidding, man," Paramedic said, "he needs a goddamned hospital. Now."

"Not going to happen," I said. "Carlos isn't doing another round in the pen. He'd sooner die first. And I'd sooner cave your skull in than let him die without you at least trying. You owe me for settling that powder debt with your pusher. Consider this payback."

Paramedic stared at the bandage indecisively.

*"Now,"* I snarled.

"Okay," Paramedic said, "but it's freezing on this dock. We need to get him somewhere warm."

I stared into the blackness of the empty grocery's dock.

\*\*\*

We moved Burrito to an abandoned store office, his torso and good leg wrapped in packing blankets as I stared at

37

Paramedic, who tugged and pulled at the inside of Burrito's leg, using instruments inserted through the hole the bullet had made in the front.

One thing Burrito had been right about, the bullet had gone clean through.

Well, not exactly clean. Paramedic had extracted a fair amount of cloth, and we'd had to temporarily roll Burrito onto his stomach while Paramedic sutured the exit wound.

The entry point was more difficult to sew, as Paramedic was positive there was a nipped artery somewhere, which continued to bleed far too much for either of our tastes. Electricity for the grocery was out, so my mag light was all we had, and I waited impatiently, shining it where Paramedic directed as I held up the second bag of saline draining into Burrito.

Carlos's breath came in short, rapid draws and his skin on his face had become so pale, he might have passed for Caucasian. If he felt any pain, he couldn't say it.

"How much longer?" I said.

"I dunno," Paramedic said. "You got a date or something?"

"Burrito and I had a certain place to be, before this," I said. "It's almost Nine."

"It takes as long as it takes," Paramedic said, continuing to work. "This blood vessel won't close itself. What I need is some suction, and he needs a transfusion, and we need some goddamned better light, and . . . Well, it takes as long as it takes."

I made myself look into the wound as Paramedic worked. I'd seen my share of blood and gore, but somehow this time it was worse than usual. Those other people, they hadn't been my friends. A low, slithering bit of nausea circled my stomach as blood continued to fill the hole in Carlo's leg—blood which Paramedic had to swab away periodically with a fistful of cotton gauze.

I looked at my watch.

There was no way I was going to make it.

Rage swept through me then, the hot kind of instant anger that used to get me into trouble when I was younger. My instinct to pick up something heavy and throw it, was quickly replaced by the knowledge that not only was Carlos most probably going to die, but I wasn't going to make the time Sorroti had set for me at the docks, and then all of this—every bit of it—would be for naught.

I hung the bag of saline on a coat hook on the wall of the office and stood up.

"Where are you going?" Paramedic asked with irritation. "I can't work unless you hold the flashlight!"

"I'm not going anywhere, I need a hand free to make a phone call."

The abused flip cell opened, showing low bars for the antique service which hadn't been fried, and I called up the number I needed—hesitating briefly before punching the green button with a thumb.

I put the phone to my ear. Waited.

"Are you at the docks?" said M-Day's voice.

"There's been a complication," I said.

"I don't like hearing about complications."

"No shit. Look, one of my crew got hurt."

"Yes, the news has leaked from Lewis-McChord. What's happened to your crew is not my concern. You have approximately fifty-five minutes to have the delivery to the designated location, or you and your crew are on your own."

"Listen," I said, trying to sound urgent without being too demanding—Sorroti didn't like demanding—"I can get the shit to the docks in time, but my man needs help. Real help."

"I trust you to handle your own internal affairs, Senninger."

"He needs a doctor. And extra blood. And antibiotics. And a place to rest. Or he'll die."

The connection was silent for a few seconds.

"These things go far beyond our agreement," M-Day said coolly.

"I know."

"We were going to be even, you and I. Mr. Lamanchez was going to be even with me, too."

"I know."

39

"You will both owe me considerably," he said, apparently tasting the possibilities.

*Fuck.* I wanted to throw the phone. But what else could I do?

"Yeah," I said simply.

More seconds of silence.

"Very well, give me your friend's location."

I relayed it.

"There will be people there in thirty minutes."

"I can't wait that long," I said. "I need you to call whoever it is at the docks, and tell them to give me more time."

"That I cannot do," said Marlon Sorroti. "You have exactly one hour. I suggest you use it wisely."

"But what about Carlos—"

"Leave him. If my people find him alive, they will do what they can. If they find him dead . . . Then he's not your concern anymore, either. But you will still owe me."

*Bastard son of a bitch.* I gritted my teeth and pressed the phone into the skin of my face. "Fine, fine, just send help, I am gone."

I hung up before I said anything I might regret.

"What the hell, you're just going—" said Paramedic.

"Yes," I said, handing him the flashlight. "Stabilize Carlos and keep the wound packed. Someone is coming."

"I'm not going to sit here—"

"Shut your mouth, coke brain, you're goddamned well sitting here until someone comes for Carlos, and if I hear later that you left him—"

"Okay, okay, shit, Jesus," Paramedic said, a bloody, gloved hand patting the air down between us.

I realized I'd had a fist raised, as if to crack him.

I lowered it. Then stooped near to Carlos's head, running a hand along his sweat-drenched scalp. *"Vaya con Dios, muchacho,"* I whispered in his ear, then stood up and trotted for the exit.

***

It was 9:49 PM when I rolled between the stacked cargo containers.

Rain had stopped, but a fine mist still hung in the damp air.

The huge cranes of Seattle's commercial shipping district dominated the sky, their black silhouettes offset by the red glow of their aircraft warning lights.

Six men greeted me at the end of the pier where I'd been told to go.

Well, greeted wasn't exactly the word. They stoically waved me forward, told me to stop the truck, then three of them were unhitching the trailer before I could so much as turn off the engine, which I didn't do because something told me I wouldn't be here long enough. I rolled down the window as one of the men approached, clad in work overalls and a wool turtleneck. A massive black mustache dominated his upper lip, and I couldn't quite tell if he was Hispanic, or Slavic, or somewhere in between. He and his compatriots nattered at each other in a language I was sure I'd never heard before, while he simply stared at me through the window of my truck.

I felt the trailer unlooked from the ball hitch.

The man just continued to stare.

I opened my mouth to say something, but he made a quick slicing motion across his throat, and I kept my trap shut.

More voices from the trailer as the tarp was peeled back.

At 10:03 PM, the man in overalls with the mustache leaned close.

"Is expected delivery," he said in not-too-bad English. "We will give our regards to your boss. You go now."

"Just tell me that stuff's not going to wind up in PRA hands," I said, exhausted.

The guy with the mustache suddenly bellowed laughter.

"Hardly. Community Watch," he said, then closed his mouth.

"What?" I asked.

His arm shot out and indicated a coil of hawser on the pier, around which I could (barely) drive my Chevy 2500 in a circle.

"Go. Now."

Fuck it.

I motored forward—the truck much quicker, now that it was free of the trailer—and made the maneuver, only just missing the edge and avoiding a plunge into the Puget Sound.

By 10:20 PM I was out of the docks and back on the road, this time towards Tukwila, where I could stash the blood-soaked Chevy, get into some clean clothes, then go find out if Carlos had made it or not.

***

Local news didn't give many details, other than that JBLM reported the death of one soldier, the apprehension of three more, and a pending investigation into the matter. Assuming they got information out of Buford, they'd have an eye witness on both Carlos and me, but since he didn't know Carlos's real name, and since I hadn't been registered under my real name in four years, unless Buford somehow identified us face-to-glass in a lineup, there wasn't much chance he'd be a danger. He had no photos to run through recognition software—any which still worked, that is.

I'd wrapped up my hand—swollen since that afternoon—and felt a little satisfaction in the fact I'd cold-cocked the fucker at least once in my short life.

The Saturn, one of three used cars I kept stashed strategically around the greater Seattle-Tacoma area, got me back to the closed grocery just after midnight. There were no cop cars in the area—nothing to indicate that anyone had been any the wiser to the earlier compromising of the store's loading dock. I found it still open, in fact, with my mag light and tarp and Carlos and Paramedic and all of Paramedic's shit gone. Hell, the floor of the dock and the interior office appeared to have been wiped clean. The place smelled of bleach water and disinfectant—Marlon's boys were thorough, I gave them that.

I went back to the open dock door and began to pull it down to shut it, when I noticed a little envelope rolled into the slot where the pad lock had once gone.

I took the envelope out and opened it. There was a note, to me.

No money, of course. Doubtless M-Day had simply deducted my expected five thousand from whatever expenses were now incurred against my name—and Burrito's—for the effort it had taken to retrieve Carlos and patch him up.  If they'd been able to patch him up.

I shut the door and went back to my car, where I found a text on the old flip phone.

It was from Paramedic of all people.  He was back in Soho.  Carlos would make it.

I leaned against the open door of the Saturn, and felt tremendous relief.

There was a second text also, not from Paramedic, telling me to expect a new message on Tuesday night.

Marlon Sorroti had another job for me.

I sighed and flipped the cell closed, listening to it snap before I dropped it into my shirt pocket.

Then I slipped into the Saturn and turned the engine over, pulling out from behind the closed grocery and setting a course for my apartment.

# By Any Means Necessary

## Steven Hildreth, Jr.

The timer sounded off, and I made my way to the oven. After I donned a mitt, I cracked the oven open and removed the baking sheet from within. The sweet aroma of honey filled my nose, and I smiled. I'd first tried *karumeyaki* from a street vendor in the Namba district of Osaka, during a little R&R. The first crunchy bite was probably the closest I'd come to falling in love, and I made it my mission to master the recipe and chase that first-bite moment.

I removed my mitt, blew on a piece to cool it off, and then picked it up between my thumb and forefinger. I gave it a couple more preparatory blows, took a bite, and savored the taste. It'd taken me quite a bit of trial and error, but I was pretty sure I'd mastered the recipe. I knew too much of the *karumeyaki* would fatten me and wreck my teeth, but a treat every now and again never hurt anybody.

"Mmmm, baby, that smells good."

The voice belonged to my mama. Once I'd gotten the recipe down pat, she and my pops were my control group. My mama, the hardest working woman I knew, somehow found time between shifts as a clerk at the school district records office to put in the work as a housewife. Part of that work involved being a master confectioner. You could say she was partly to blame for my being bullied before my 6th grade growth spurt. A steady stream of peanut-butter M&M cookies and Texas brownies has that effect. If it was sweet, she had a tongue for it.

When Mama fell in love with my *karumeyaki*, I knew two things: I'd gotten it down pat, and that I was her child. Now, I made it for her every now and again, in-between making her the same cookies and brownies she'd made for me growing up, along with a few other treats I'd picked up along the way.

On the other hand, when my pops had eaten his first, he gave a muted nod of approval and returned to perusing the news on his tablet. That was about par for the course. It wasn't that he didn't love me or my mama. He wasn't one of those aloof, detached patriarchs who are the staples of broken backgrounds. If there was a way to describe my pops, the word I'd pick would be...tired. A workload as an AP history teacher, a football defensive coach, and a baseball head coach kept him busy.

At home, he was busy grading papers or studying film. We'd get a two-week summer vacation if money had been good to us, and then he'd be right back to preparing his curriculum and his playbook. If he wasn't working, he'd be quietly reading the news while Ella Fitzgerald, Nat King Cole, or Duke Ellington played on vinyl in the background. When you factor in working your way up from being the school's custodian to holding an Ed.D, it makes sense that he seemed to be on autopilot all the time.

Pops worked right up until the day he died. He'd gotten back from a baseball road game, spent a few minutes with my mama, and then went to work grading papers. When he didn't come to bed a couple hours of later, my mama checked on him. Heart attack in his sleep. I'd been taking care of her since then. She'd exceeded the life expectation after a spouse's passing, and she showed no signs of slowing up.

"Jordan, baby," Mama called again. "Bring me one, will you?"

"Yes, Mama," I said with a smile.

They'd cooled to the touch. I grabbed a paper towel, dropped two morsels in it, and made my way to the living room. The sound of Bird Parker's "Salt Peanuts" filled the living room.

Mama sat in a recliner, bundled in blankets. She might have been a fiend for sweets, but you couldn't tell by her willowy frame. Her hair was barely gray, though she required thick glasses to be able to see. A warm smile adorned her handsome face as I lowered the pair of *karumeyaki* to her. She plucked one from the napkin and popped it in her mouth. Her smile grew wider as the taste rolled over her tongue.

"You got your daddy's brains," she told me, "but thank the Lord you got my cooking touch. God rest your daddy's soul, but that man could burn water."

"He was a fine grill man though," I pointed out.

"Baby, it don't take much to grill," Mama said. "Hardest part's getting the marinade right, and you can figure that out with enough trial and error. After that, just comes down to sitting back, drinking beer, and checking the meat every now and again. Put that man in the kitchen and he was utterly *lost*."

I bobbed my head as I shrugged. "That's fair."

Mama's eyes turned to the television. It was Fox News, and it was thankfully muted. If you listened to them, you'd think that Negroes and Mexicans were the sole cause of America's problems. If they weren't focusing on individual knuckleheads or the Modern Black Panther Party for Equality and Justice, they'd beat the drum on the cartels and La Raza. With demographics changing, Fox had stayed in vogue by capitalizing on white folks' fragility.

Then again, being fair, if you switched the channel to MSNBC or CNN, you'd figure that the only problem America had were the Fourth Reich genetic rejects. Of course, the answer was somewhere between the two. Stupidity and a propensity for violence weren't exclusive to a single demographic, despite popular arguments to the contrary.

Mama shook her head as she studied the headline along the bottom of the screen. "Things are getting crazy out there, baby."

Coming from my mama, that was saying something. Between student debts and a barely middle class income, Jackson

Ward was one of the few neighborhoods we could afford to live in growing up. I'd come of age during the tail-end of the reign of drugs and gang violence. I'd suffered more than my share of beat-downs at the hands of bangers. As I was on my way out of high school, gentrification had taken hold, and slowly my family became one of the last black holdouts on the block. While that presented its own set of problems, not having to stress over hooliganism or a gunfight breaking out down the block was nice, and with all the work my mama and my pops put into the house, it held a nice bit of equity.

That was beside the point, though. Point was, Mama and Pops had grown up in Jackson Ward. Their parents had, too, as had every generation of Mitchells and Durands going back to the end of the Civil War. They'd been raised on the stories of Jackson Ward being a hub of black commerce, and how that had deteriorated after the Civil Rights Movement and the advent of the Drug War. They'd lived through the Crack Epidemic and the gang wars of the '90s, had seen the worst of it.

So, for Mama to say things were getting crazy held some weight. Though I didn't have her experience for perspective, I was inclined to agree just on my own observations.

I sighed and shook my head as I reached for the TV remote. "Mama, that stuff will rot your brain. You shouldn't be watching this."

My mama gently slapped my hand to keep me from changing the channel. "The news ain't always pleasant, but that doesn't absolve you from your civic responsibility to stay informed." She grabbed the remote from my hands and returned it to its place on the right armrest. "But you're right, baby. Watching *only this* would rot my brain. That's why I check *all* the news and read between the lines. You know this."

I did know that, and Mama knew that *very* well. She'd earned her B.A. in Political Science from Lincoln University, and she'd had aspirations to pursue a law degree. Meeting my pops and conceiving me had forced her to shift her priorities. Though she was about filing papers during the day and cooking and

48

cleaning at night, Mama's mind never dulled. Like I said: the hardest working woman I knew.

I checked my watch. "I gotta be leaving for work soon, Mama," I said. "Promise me you won't stay up too late watching that stuff."

"I'm just about done," Mama said. "You promise me you'll be safe tonight at work."

"Of course," I said.

"Gimme a kiss, baby."

I leaned in and pressed my lips to her cheek as she did likewise. She cupped my face and stroked my cheek with her thumb. "I'm proud of you, Jordan. Your daddy was, too. He wasn't the type to voice it, but he *was* proud and he *did* love you, as I do."

I smiled. "I love you too, Mama." I gave her one more kiss before I rose and made my way to the kitchen. I checked my lunchbox, made sure my meals were prepped and I had my utensils, then slung the lunchbox across my chest. As I made for the door, I paused in the kitchen doorway and looked at my mama as she relaxed in the recliner. She sang along softly to Bird Parker, only stopping long enough to enjoy the other *karumeyaki*.

My smile widened.

The world might've gone crazy, but as long as I had Mama and she had sweets and jazz music, it'd be all right.

***

"Violence erupted at a demonstration by the Modern Black Panther Party in downtown Richmond today," the bland-voiced talking head said through the ambulance's interior sound system. "A spokesperson for the Richmond Police Department confirmed that upon the arrival of counter-protesters, both sides clashed and shots were fired, though they have been unable to ascertain which side fired. One Panther protester was wounded, and several dozen were arrested on a variety of charges.

I tuned out the news update and kept my eyes firmly locked on my phone. The Kindle app was open to a page in Michael Twitty's *The Cooking Gene*. The radio station was set to what used to be called the "oldies" station—which was now a blend of the '80s, '90s, and '00s—but the crazier the world got, the more the updates seemed to compete with the music.

It was of no consequence. I turned the eBook's page with my finger and continued to read. I'd keep my ears open for music or a dispatch call, but beyond that, I was focused on finishing the book tonight.

"Dispatch to Medic 1-4," a dispassionate female voice said, competing with the talking head for volume.

Garber—the driver—reached to turn down the talk radio and grabbed the business radio headset. "Go for Medic 1-4."

"Police request medical response," the dispatcher said.

"10-4," Garber said. On cue, Vickers—who sat shotgun—flipped on the lights and sirens. Grievous bodily harm always warranted a Code 3 response, even though most of these calls ended with us simply jotting down a time of death and waiting for the Medical Examiner. Garber continued by asking, "What's the address?"

"519 West Clay Street, Unit #1."

My blood chilled in my veins and my eyes bulged from their sockets as my head whipped to face the front. "That's my mom's place," I said, my voice deathly quiet.

Garber and Vickers glanced to me, and then to each other. Their training kicked in. Every first responder shared the nightmare of being dispatched to a loved one's location. Vickers floored the gas while Garber keyed up the handset.

"Medic 1-4, en route."

My heart thundered in my ears. It was only a four-minute drive from our current location, but each second ticked down slowly. With each passing moment, I delved deeper into my thoughts. Mama was something of a pacifist, and she'd never liked having firearms around the house. Pops had always been more of a pragmatist, and he had known that whether it be set-tripping morons or sheet-wearing shitheads, it was better to have a gun in the house than not. He'd trained both my Mama and I for as long as I remember, and made Mama promise him she wouldn't just

50

sell it the moment he passed. I'd reinforced that when I left the Army and moved back in with her. There was a chance that the dead body wasn't my Mama, that it was the intruder and Mama had plugged him in the chest, just like Pops had taught us.

*You know that's not it, Jordan*, the voice in my head said, the small one that assumed worst-case scenarios, that had gotten me through hairy scrapes in A-Stan, Iraq, and the Philippines. *Brace yourself.*

I clenched my teeth. *Shut up*, I told the voice. *Shut the fuck up.*

I saw the lights before I saw the black and whites. I squatted in the back of the ambulance and moved to the door, ready to leap out the moment we reached the police line. I felt the ambulance lurch to a halt, and I grabbed the door handle. A resounding *clang* echoed against the ambulance body as I threw the doors open and hit the pavement on both feet. I turned the corner fast and sprinted towards the police line.

A baby-faced blond officer held his hand up and squared his feet. "Sir, you need to stand back. We're not ready for meds yet."

"That's my Mama's house," I said, wide-eyed and frantic. "I need to get in there."

The look on the cop's face softened, and he faltered a little. "Sir—"

"I need…"

My voice trailed off. Motion had caught my eyes from above, and I followed it to its source.

The tree had been there as long as we'd lived there. It was the de facto boundary line between the Durand household and our neighbors. A spotlight shone about 15 feet up, to the lowest branch.

Her hands were limp at her side. Both eyes were swollen shut, and dark pools of blood stained her pink nightgown. Her mouth was locked open, her head held up by the noose around her neck. A slight breeze swayed her body from side to side. One of her slippers barely clung to her foot, and the momentum was

51

enough to knock it free. I watched the slipper fall to the ground, collide with the pavement, and then fall with the sole up.

I don't remember the tears streaming down my face, or collapsing to my knees, or the scream that erupted from my throat and flew past my lips. I don't remember the officer, Vickers, and Garber struggling to hold me up, or how they kept me from rushing the police line and going to my mother's side. I can't remember Garber sticking me with a sedative to knock me out, afraid that I'd start swinging on people to cross the line.

The only thing I remember before things went dark was the slipper on the sidewalk and my mother's body swinging from a noose above it.

***

The following week was a collage of flashes.

I remember corpse identification at the medical examiner's office. I remember the interview with the lead homicide detective. My mother had no personal enemies. She stayed in the house and kept to herself. I did all her shopping, and I took her to all her medical appointments.

Official cause of death was blunt force trauma, corroborated by the massive pool of blood in the living room. That made the motive pretty fucking obvious to me, and the routine questions all the more infuriating. But, I was numb. I took the questions in stride, answered them, and got the detective on his way.

My boss couldn't give me a leave of absence, but he told me if I resigned, he'd guarantee an immediate rehiring once I was ready to return to work. I quit on the spot and made my way to an Extended Stay America near Bon Air. I couldn't stay in the house, even after it was cleaned. Too many memories. My parents had made it home. Now, it was nightmare culture dish.

Aside from funeral arrangements, there was a long stretch of nothing. People tried to call and give their condolences. I let those go to voicemail. I was only looking for one phone call. After the 48th hour passed, I knew the call wasn't going to come. Yet, I waited another five days. I didn't sleep much. When the fatigue overwhelmed me and I was forced to close my eyes, all I saw was my mother swinging from the tree, her slipper on the sidewalk. The worst treatment I'd endured at Camp Mackall during SERE was paradise compared to replaying that image in my head until my body could jolt awake from the nightmare.

The fifth day was my breaking point. On a whim, after waking up from another replay, I remember grabbing my phone and delving into social media. A post announced a Modern Black Panther Party rally on Wednesday, two days from then, at a community center a few minutes from my parents' place in Jackson Ward. I copied the address to my phone's note pad.

Wednesday evening came around. In my flat-billed cap, sweater hoodie, jeans, and Jordans, I blended in with the crowd. I'd arrived 15 minutes early. Conversations buzzed around me. I tuned it out, one part because I wasn't interested in what the others had to say, and one part because I was solely fueled by caffeine and slow-burning rage. The nightmares hadn't stopped, and I could count on one hand how many hours of sleep I'd had that week.

"Brother and sisters…Chairman Jerome Willis."

The applause popped out the gate and grew in crescendo, snapping me out of my haze. The community center director, Gary Reynolds, stepped away from the podium and applauded as Jerome Willis approached. He was an imposing figure, and looked to be about the same height and build as me. The Modern Black Panthers adopted the same uniform as the OGs: blue shirt, blue jeans, black boots, black jacket, and black beret. A group of men and women stood at the back of the stage, similarly dressed.

On the crowd's perimeter were several other Modern Panthers, some concealed carrying, others carrying what appeared to be civilian-legal Type 56 AK rifles. The unique slant of the weapon's buttstock identified it as Chinese rather than Russian or otherwise European, and my mind thought back to how Norinco had greased Congressional palms, gotten their import ban lifted, and then flooded the market with their products.

A holstered pistol peeked out from beneath Willis's jacket as he clasped hands with Reynolds and then embraced him. Once he took the podium, Willis held up his right hand in a clenched fist, a gesture rapidly emulated by the crowd.

"Power to the people!" Willis bellowed, his deep bass voice carrying considerably, even without the microphone.

"*Power to the people!*" the crowd echoed. My fist was up, but I only mouthed the words. I wasn't convinced.

"Power to the people!" Willis repeated.

"*Power to the people!*"

When the echo died down, Willis continued, "Rest in power, Gladys Durand!"

"*Rest in power!*" Another in the crowd shouted, "*Preach!*"

Willis slowly lowered his fist, then gripped both sides of the podium and leaned forward. "Brothers and sisters…Brother Gary is 100% right. These *are* troubling times, and there *is no* coexisting with the white oppressor." After sporadic affirmations from the audience, Willis continued.

"It has been said that history doesn't repeat itself, but it does rhyme," Willis said. "One only needs to study the history of the Original Black Panther Party for Self-Defense and compare them to the origins of the Modern Black Panther Party for Equality and Justice. Blacks had migrated from the south during World War II, hoping to attain the illusion of the American Dream. Over 20 years, they protested peacefully, believing they could change the hearts of their oppressors.

"When that failed, a pair of visionaries realized that their action must be more direct," Willis continued. "They realized that capitalism was not a system in which all could equally pursue opportunity, but rather a mechanism of the Caucasian hegemony designed to oppress the other. They'd studied the works of Marx, Lenin, and Mao, and saw the power that lay available to the proletariat, and realized that the only language those oppressors understood was the means of force."

I noticed movement in my peripheral. Another Panther approached, an attractive dark-skinned woman with a stack of leaflets in her hand. Her afro was held back with a hair tie, allowing her to wear the Panther uniform beret. She handed me a leaflet and gave me a slight smile as she looked me over. I forced myself to smile and nod as I accepted the leaflet, then returned my eyes to Willis and he continued.

"Africans armed with firearms, knowledge, and a determination to pursue equal *human* rights," Willis said, "not the *American* rights afforded only to the white man. That is what Brothers Bobby Seale and Huey P. Newton envisioned with the Original Black Panthers. They let the slavecatchers with badges know they weren't afraid. They let the whites that benefited from the privileges of their oppressor status know that they would not take that oppression lying down. They let the white capitalist class know through the Ten Point Program that Africans would claim their freedom, through armed revolution if necessary."

Willis held up a finger, his eyes honed into a death glare. "The oppressor saw the writing on the wall. They knew if they continued to openly hold down Africans, they would lose their hegemony. So, they engaged in a brilliant bit of maneuvering. They removed the explicit language from the law that made whites superior, initiated the drug war—by their own admission, a ploy to legally lock up Africans—and perpetuated the damage done by Jim Crow. Simultaneously, they promoted the myth of a 'post-racial' world, allowing those guilty whites to delude themselves into thinking that because that racial language had been removed from the law, all was well, and anyone who said otherwise was a radical.

"It worked until Barack took office," Willis said. "That's when we thought, 'Finally. A brother has ascended to the high offices. Perhaps he can bring about the change needed to heal our wounds and finally deliver equality.' What nobody knew was that Barack was not the savior for which we hoped. Whether he was contained by the white man's system or corrupted by it is irrelevant. *Nothing* changed." More agreement shouts from the crowd. "The whites didn't care that nothing changed. They saw us speak up and knew their kingdom was in danger. They *knew* that if we kept up the pressure, eventually, we *would* put someone there that *would* change things.

"White supremacy and white nationalism reemerged. Police slave hunters continued to murder us with impunity, and all the peaceful protest in the world has failed to deliver justice and equality. That is where I recognized that, much like Brothers Bobby Seale and Huey P. Newton before us, we needed to arise, armed, and seize our freedom, by force if necessary. And this time, we cannot be content with symbolic gifts. They will either give us what we are due, or we will *take it*."

The crowd erupted into another wave of applause. I took the opportunity to slowly edge towards the door and make for the center's exit. The Panthers at the door gave me strange looks as I moved past them, but didn't say a word. I didn't look like a cop, and I'd mustered my best poker face, so they filled in the blanks with whatever they wanted to see.

Once I was out of sight of the center, I opened the pamphlet and skimmed through it. It was the kind of bullshit I'd expected. On paper, the Ten Points sound great. Freedom, employment, education, housing, and due process, all cornerstones of a civilized society. It was in the fine print where you see that those aren't the end but the means to the end.

Past the Ten Points, the Modern Panthers didn't even try to hide their leanings. If I were to get specific, "Maoist" wouldn't be as accurate as "Marxist-Leninist-Maoist." One could write a dissertation on the differences between Marxism, Leninism, and Maoism, but the simplest explanation is that Marxism was specific to the Industrial Revolution, Leninism to the Bolshevik Revolution, and Maoism to the Chinese Revolution. Marxism-Leninism-Maoist tries to strip away the geographically specific elements and apply it globally.

Reading through the pamphlet's bullet points, I not only identified the MLM thought, I saw Beijing's guiding hand in the verbiage. One particular phrase stood out: "We must be committed to a protracted people's war against the white capitalists. Every revolutionary attempt fought through conventional means has been successfully crushed, and we must adapt and evolve if we are to destroy the white capitalist hegemony."

My previous knowledge of the PRC making in-roads with separatist groups aside, that phrase struck a horrifically nostalgic chord with me.

It was about halfway through my stint with Group. We were on a 90-day rotation in the Davou del Sur Province, advising the Lion Heart Battalion in their ongoing counterinsurgency against the Beijing-funded New People's Army. We'd been spun up as the QRF after a bombing in the Dawis *barangay* of the city of Digos, near where we'd set our FOB.

The target had been an open-air market. I'd been responsible for triage, and my Pinoy counterpart and I'd immediately established a casualty collection point. I wouldn't say that you eventually learn not to care when you've treated enough casualties that don't make it, but you do build a wall that allows you to compartmentalize and push forward. It's the only way you can do that job. It's hard enough being a soldier and knowing you might not return with everyone with whom you rolled out. Without that wall, that plus the additional burden of being responsible of patching up the wounded would be enough to break strong men.

For some, even with that wall, those burdens are fatally crushing.

The Dawis bombing was almost my breaking point. A nine-year-old boy had caught shrapnel to his stomach in the blast. His mother had run as fast as her legs would carry her to the CCP, eyes reddened from the tears that streaked her face. My partner and I had immediately set to work, setting him up with an IV, bandaging the wound, and doing what we could to stabilize him for transport. I got into it with my team lead, demanding we CASEVAC the boy because he was urgent-surgical.

57

When I was overridden, I'd gone back to check on the boy. He was awake long enough to stare up at me, his glimmering eyes pleading with me to do something to bring him back from the brink.

A second later, his eyes rolled into his head.

I'd felt something gently touch my thigh, and I looked down. It was a pamphlet, caked in dust but relatively serviceable. I have no idea what possessed me to pick it up and read it rather than brush it off and continue my triage. It took me a moment to mentally translate the Tagalog, but when I had, the phrase was eternally seared into my psyche.

"We must pledge a war of the people against the ruling class. Every revolutionary attempt fought in the conventional way has been successfully defeated, and we must adapt and change if the proletariat is to destroy the bourgeoisie."

The boy wasn't the only one whose life had been forfeited in the pursuit of a utopia, both that I'd personally witnessed or in general history.

That didn't stop me from directly associating that phrase with the look of a boy whom, not even hours before, had likely daydreamed of reaching adulthood and making his way in the world, only to come to a sudden and premature comprehension of life's fragility.

What was worse was that the bombing motive wasn't even congruent with the NPA's aims. A couple weeks after the bombing, our SOT-A attachment intercepted a transmission that indicated that the bomb's target was a shop owner who'd refused to pay tribute to the local NPA cell. He'd been declared an enemy of the people and targeted.

Remove the political veneer and you'd get exactly what that was: criminal extortion.

The Modern Panthers wanted to bring that bullshit to American soil. That reduced the difference between them and the Fourth Reich to not fucking much.

I crumpled the pamphlet in my fist and dumped it in a bus stop receptacle as I made my way back to where I'd parked my vehicle.

The justice system had failed Mama. There was no choice but to pick up arms and go to war, but I wouldn't do it with a group so far disenfranchised that they opted to fight one atrocious ideology with another.

I was going to have to fight my own war.

As I reached my car, an ironic point emerged in my mind. Despite his inclinations towards socialism and disdain for capitalism, I admired Malcolm X. That was primarily because I figured that if I'd been born in that era, I'd have opted for his approach over MLK's peaceful strategy. I don't regret that admiration because Malcolm's primary focus wasn't forcing an economic utopia. His aim was captured in my favorite phrase of his, which was on a poster I had of him peeking out a window, M1 carbine in hand:

"We declare our right on this earth to be a man, to be a human being, to be respected as a human being, to be given the rights of a human being in this society, on this earth, in this day, which we intend to bring into existence *by any means necessary*."

The Fourth Reich had stolen my Mama's right to exist peacefully, her pursuit of life, liberty, and happiness. The government, through incompetence or malfeasance, refused to hold her murderers accountable.

I fully intended to exact justice the same way Malcolm demanded it: by any means necessary.

\*\*\*

Reconnaissance is a thinking man's game. It is what separates the blunt instrument from the precision weapon.

Reconnaissance requires the patience to collect and develop the information, as well as the critical thinking to translate the raw intelligence into bullet points in an action plan.

It took another fortnight before I got my first break. Once I identified my target, it was as simple as developing a pattern of life and finding the weak point. That was only slightly harder than actually snatching him off the street. If you know what you're doing, you can snatch a mark in broad daylight with the bystanders none the wiser.

Ask me how I know.

Now came the hard part.

I sat in the darkness, watching the target. He was stripped to his skivvies, fastened with hinge cuffs to a chair I'd bolted to the floor. His feet were in a tin pail that I'd half-filled with water. A camera was positioned off to the side, constantly recording.

The target couldn't stop shaking. One part of that was nervousness. He was clearly in decent shape, which wasn't too common with people of his age and occupation combined. By this point in his career, most of them had let themselves go and relied more on brainpower than physical strength.

That was a shame. Were he a weaker man, I might have broken him before that night.

Admittedly, I was outside my lane. I was a shooter and a medic, not an interrogator. I'd watched a few interrogations done abroad, some of them above-board and others questionable. For the most part, I remembered the interrogations that had produced the most actionable intel and did my best to emulate those. No leading questions. Keep things open-ended. He needed to tell me the truth, not what he thought I wanted to hear. If I kept my aims opaque, he'd be more likely to break.

I told myself that the only reason the rubber hose, car battery, and jumper cables were involved was because the man needed to know this was no law enforcement operation, that there'd be no holding out for a lawyer, that only the truth would end the pain and set him free.

Maybe if I lied to myself one more time, I might actually believe it.

I checked my watch. He'd rested long enough. I stepped out of the shadows, letting my boots echo on the empty warehouse's concrete floor. A shudder gripped the subject's body, the sound of my pending return a sign of more pain to come. His light brown hair had touches of gray in the temples. There were fine creases around his eyes, which one could tell were blue only because both eyes hadn't swollen shut. Bruises and electrical burns adorned his torso, and a dark spot on his briefs marked where he'd soiled himself. His legs tremored as he fought to meet my eyes.

"Officer Maske," I said, my voice flat and emotionless. "Are you ready to start again?"

Colton Maske, duly sworn officer of the Richmond Police Department, stared at me, but for the first time throughout the 19-hour interrogation, he said nothing. No threats of what would happen when it came out that I'd kidnapped and tortured a peace officer. No racial invectives. No personal threats on my person. Maske was clearly struggling to put on a valiant front, but he was nearing his breaking point.

I pulled up a folding chair, turned the back towards him, and copped a squat, my arms resting on the back. "You know I didn't grab you by accident. We *both* know you're not an honest cop. I've got enough hard evidence of your association with the Fourth Reich that IAD would have you riding the pine pony until they decided to cut sling load, even in this political environment." I sat up straight and sighed. "Why not spare yourself more pain? Tell me about the Fourth Reich, and this ends."

Maske drooped his head, his breathing labored. "What's the point?" he muttered. "You're gonna kill me either way." A weak chuckle fell from his lips. "You don't think I know who you are, Jordan Durand? You're out for blood. Take your pound of flesh and get it over with."

I pursed my lips as I deliberated. The thought of death being on the table struck me as a useful tool, but if he had no hope of surviving and was resigned to his fate, then the interrogation could drag on longer. I'm sure if I hurt him long enough, hard enough, his focus would shift to a quick end to his pain, but that presented a whole other batch of problems.

I rolled the dice. "I'm going to let you in on a secret, Officer Maske. I actually have every intention of letting you live if you talk."

Maske snorted. "Bullshit."

"Think it through," I said. "If you know who I am, you've read my file. I'm not some revolutionary looking to make a point. If my goal was to kill you, I *definitely* wouldn't waste my time grabbing you. Trust me, I had *plenty* of opportunities. But, killing a cop brings heat, even if he's dirty. The best way to deal with you is to air your misdeeds, incense the public, and worry the pols. The system will do the rest."

"Letting me live would be the dumb play," Maske said. "I know who you are. The moment I get free, no stone would be unturned. Not even your Special Forces training would save you."

"True," I conceded. "That's why I'd keep you here while I verified your intel, and I'd keep your little powwow with the Fourth Reich as leverage." I paused a beat. "I can see the wheels turning in your mind, Officer. Feed me a line of bullshit, send me on a goose chase, buy yourself time to break loose."

I leaned forward for effect. "I snatched you on the first day of your three-day weekend. You work four 12-hour shifts per week. You're single. You've got an ex-wife that would probably give me a gratitude blowjob if I disappeared you, a couple of kids that realize they're pawns for you to spite the ex, and no steady girlfriend of which to speak. I've got a little over 52 hours before anyone notices you're gone, and it'll only take me a few hours to vet whatever you give me. I've also disabled your smart watch and phone, so even if we eclipse that window, nobody will be able to trace you."

Maske retreated within himself. He was shook. I would be, too, if somebody had been able to lay out a brief, detailed, and accurate snapshot of my life. In his situation, it got the point across: I *owned* him, and there was nothing he could do to improve his conditions until he compromised the Fourth Reich.

He was right on the edge. I just had to push him.

Deliberately, I rose from the chair, and picked up a red plastic bucket from behind Maske. Within was some tap water and a sponge. I submerged the sponge, removed it from the water, squeezed it half-dry, and then began to gently pat it along Maske's chest and abdomen. He sucked air through his teeth, the pain from the bruises and burns aggravated from contact. Maske had learned over our time together that the sponge bath would help the electricity conduct better through his body.

"So, the only thing remains, Officer Maske," I said as I wrapped up the sponge bath, "is the decision before you. I've got nothing but time. This pans out, I leave you be to go after the Nazis." I set the bucket down, dried my hands on my jeans, then took a knee and connected the alligator clamps to the car battery. "If not..." I turned around, a clamp in each hand. I touched the clamps together, and a sharp *crack* filled the room as the current sparked, eliciting a flinch from Maske. "Well. You're the only Nazi on hand, and I'm *itching* to get my Aldo Raine on."

We stared at each other for a long interval. He waited for me to back down, show some sign that I was bluffing. I waited for him to break. When he didn't break, I lunged forward with the clamps open and inbound to his chest.

"*Stop! Stop! STOP! I'll talk! I'LL TALK!*"

His eyes threated to pop from their sockets, and his voice had skyrocketed octaves. I held the clamps inches from his skin, tempted to give him a jolt anyway. Colton Maske had betrayed his oath and the Constitution because he didn't like people with more melanin than him. I had no doubt that he'd abused the powers of his office to harm "the other."

I was positive that if he didn't have a hand in my Mama's death, he was covering for someone who did.

Slowly, I stepped back from Maske and set the clamps on the ground, separated and within easy reach. More importantly, they were in Maske's line of sight, an unspoken reminder of what awaited him if he jerked me around. I spun my chair to face him, took a seat, and clasped my hands on top of my leg.

"Go on, Officer. I'm listening."

\*\*\*

"Jordan, what the *fuck?*"

Granger Brown's voice was normally on the nasally side, but the pitch was raised a notch as he watched the video on my phone. His doughy exterior was deceptive. We'd gone to elementary and middle school together before he'd moved away, then reconnected at Sand Hill for infantry OSUT. We hit Airborne together after that, and a few years later, we were in the same Ranger School class. He'd seen combat in both Afghanistan and the Fourth Balkan War as an 4th Brigade, 25th Infantry paratrooper, got out around the same time I did, and went right to working for Richmond PD. One might think he'd gained the extra weight post-ETS, but the truth was, Granger was always a little doughy. He still managed to run a 6:30 pace for five miles and could crank out push-ups, sit-ups, and pull-ups like none other.

It was our historical and military bonds that compelled Granger to help me. He'd been the one that identified Maske as a police officer when I ran my surveillance photos from a Fourth Reich rally past him. He'd subsequently gathered all the pertinent details I'd needed to snatch and download Maske. Now, watching the video as he sat across from me in the Fan District Waffle House, I got the feeling that Granger was regretting those decisions.

Normally, Granger looked like Soap from *Punisher: War Zone*: a goofy-looking white boy with strawberry blond hair, blue eyes, and a cheerful demeanor. At that moment, there wasn't an ounce of cheer in Granger's face. He'd dropped the English muffin slathered in grape jelly he'd been chewing on before watching the video, and seemed to pay no mind to the eggs, bacon, or waffle on his plate.

"He wasn't going to talk any other way," I said.

"This isn't going to hold up in court," Granger insisted.

"I don't need it to hold up in court," I growled.

"Well, I do!" Granger hissed. He tapped the table with his finger. "You know what kind of position you've put me in, Jordan?"

"I do." I let out a long breath. "I also know that you know this is a problem and that it didn't pass the smell test. You wouldn't have agreed to help me otherwise, our history notwithstanding."

Granger rubbed his chin slowly as he stared at the video's final frame. "Be that as it may, I still can't make this hold up in court. That's the important thing." He handed the phone back to me, then interlaced his fingers and twiddled his thumbs nervously. "You tortured a confession out of a police officer."

"A *dirty* cop, one that had a hand in murdering my mother, lists other officers who are in the employ of Erik Baum and the Fourth Reich, and has provided a treasure trove of intel on the Reich."

"Which I can't do anything with." *Unless I bring you in,* Granger didn't say.

"He provided the cloud link that had his insurance file," I said pointedly. "You saw it. He corrupted the video files for the traffic cameras that would put the killers at the scene at the time of death. He has the originals in the cloud. You saw the group chat transcripts where Baum gives Maske the order to cover the hitters' tracks, along with a lot of other fucked up shit. You've got them and him dead to rights."

"Fruit of the poisonous tree," Granger responded. "Any lawyer worth their salt's gonna have it thrown out, and we're right back to square one."

I took a sip of my coffee. "Let's lay the cards on the table. You do nothing, the dirty cops keep supporting the Nazis. They'll continue to justify the crap coming out of the Panthers' mouths. The city's half-black. You thought counterinsurgency in Pristina was hard? If even five percent of the population decides to align with the Panthers, you're gonna have a war on your hands.

"Option #2: you bring me in. Good-faith exception allows you to admit what I've developed into evidence. You'll definitely bounce the dirty cops off the force, but as far as stopping the Fourth Reich, it'll be hit and miss.

"Option #3: parallel construction. You've seen enough that you can develop this information on your own and produce evidence against the bad cops that will hold up in court. You can't take it to IAD. The Reich's got people there. Build your case, take it to DOJ, and let the system do the rest. That doesn't work, I'll leak the files to the press and force the issue."

Granger eyed his mostly-untouched plate as his thumbs continued to work nervously. "What about the Fourth Reich? What about Baum?" He looked up to find me staring at him, a blank expression on my face and hardness in my eyes. "Ah. Right. I probably don't want to know." He hung his head again and shook it slowly. "How'd the world get this fucked, man?"

"World's always been this fucked, Granger," I said quietly. "It's just boiling over now. Been a long time coming."

Granger stared out the window. My eyes followed his. It was a slow hour. Cars lazily rolled along Route 250. Across the street, a black father and a white mother pushed their child along in a stroller as they walked in the direction of a shopping center to the northwest. The skies were clear and the sun hung high in the sky, shining brilliantly.

"You know," Granger said, "normally I'd remark what a gorgeous day it is, even despite the world going to Hell in a handbasket." He shook his head. "Now? I can't shake the feeling that the tranquility's a mirage. Sooner rather than later, it'll be impossible to find a scene like this, a day like this."

I removed a USB drive from my shirt pocket and slid it across the table to Granger. "Then build your investigation. Clean up your house. Leave the Fourth Reich to me."

Granger looked me in the eye, his tone low and serious as he spoke. "All right, Jordan. We'll do it your way. But from here on out, you've got to work on your own. I can't be involved with…" He waved his hand erratically. "…whatever it is you're going to do."

I nodded. "Understood."

"Be careful," he admonished. "The path you're going down…once you're committed, there's no turning back."

"Yeah." I lifted the coffee cup to my lips and paused before taking a sip. "I know."

\*\*\*

The trailer park was a stone's throw south of Goode Creek. It was about what you'd expect: unimproved dirt roads, beer cans and other litter interspersed on the ground, weeds growing in what passed for yards, and a whole lot of lemons for vehicles. My hackles were on end as I approached. I couldn't see anyone, but I could feel I was being watched. Places like these were highly insular. In that regard, it was no different from the hood: you knew who belonged and who didn't. I was decidedly an outsider. Fortunately, the dusk lighting helped to obscure my skin tone. A red-checkered flannel, boot cut jeans, Salomon boots, and the Ford ball cap on my head would hopefully give me a little extra breathing room.

I wasn't going to drive up to the front door. I'd stashed my vehicle in a 7-Eleven parking lot down the street, out of sight of the cashier, and made my way in on foot. There was no telling how long it'd take Granger to get DOJ on the case, and the last thing I needed was some skinhead calling his buddy with a badge and bringing my little war to an end before it really kicked off.

The messenger bag slung across my chest and resting on my left hip had all the tools I'd need. It was a bit heavy with everything I'd stuffed within, but it wouldn't earn more than a passing glance. One would have to look close to notice I wore clear vinyl gloves. I'd leave no fingerprints. Again, for all intents and purposes, until I received the all-clear from Granger, I was up against both sides of the law.

I saw the address number mounted to the right of the door. I'd committed that number to memory. It was the place. It was unlike the other trailers in that the Chevy parked out front was pristine, well maintained. Whoever lived here had some extra money to throw around.

It wouldn't surprise me: my open source analysis of the Fourth Reich indicated that the movement's stance on black market trade varied between cells. Some were firmly of the belief that criminal enterprise was beneath the white man and relied on member dues and donations. Others had no problem with gun running and protection rackets, leaving only prostitution and drug running to us colored folk. A third faction figured that anything done in the name of the master race was *erlaubt*, as long as it wasn't marketed to whites.

My guess? This was the third case. Maske had an extensive file on the target, largely due to the target having a Virginia DOC register number and arrest record. Benny Ralston was Erik Baum's logistics guy, managing the beans and bullets. He'd gone to Coffeewood on a robbery charge, then had been transferred to Red Onion because he'd demonstrated an assaultive tendency towards staff. Red Onion was a real gladiator academy, the worst of the worst. He also developed something of a reputation as a procurer, having compromised female staff and used them to mule cell phones, cigarettes, dope, porn, and anything else the Brotherhood desired. Apparently, it was a natural role transition on the outside.

Ralston's Chevy was perfect. Sleek black, tinted windows, lifted. It wouldn't take long to lure them out. I reached into the messenger bag and removed an aluminum fish bat. It was small enough to fit in the bag, yet sturdy enough to do the kind of damage I needed. I took the bat in both hands and swung with an intensity that would have made Barry Bonds jealous. The bat connected with the windshield and it spider-webbed. The truck alarm sounded off, and I watched for movement on the periphery as I continued to go to work on the pickup. Windshield. Body. Side mirror. Any spot I could find was kissed by the bat.

"What the *fuck* is going on out there?" a heavily accented voice barked from inside.

Almost showtime. I did my best Matthew McConaughey. "That's the last time you sleep with my little sister, *Jethro!* Girl's only 17, you *perv!*" I wouldn't win any talent shows, but it kept the bass from my voice and gave them the impression it was a brother white.

The inner door was thrown open, immediately followed by the slamming of the screen door against the trailer. I shifted the bat to my left hand, my right hand reaching my shirt to my belt line. There were three of them, all of them shirtless and sporting

Swastikas, Iron Crosses, and shamrocks ink. One of them had a rifle and the other two brandished handguns. The one in the center was taller than the other two, lanky with a bit of a paunch around his midsection. He got a good look at me, and his eyes popped from their sockets.

"A fucking *nigger*...you got a death wish, *boy*?"

That was the target. Benny Ralston, in the flesh.

I smiled as my right hand slipped into my bag and grabbed hold of a flashbang.

This dumb Nazi fuck was a few seconds away from a dirt nap and he didn't even know it.

I tossed the bat forward, drawing their attention in that direction. I ripped the flashbang from the bag, yanked the pin free with my off hand, then tossed it in the bat's direction as I ducked behind the front driver's side wheel.

Anyone who's been hit with a flashbang knows it sucks, and that's if you know it's coming and have eye and ear protection. The average flashbang emits 12 *million* lumens of light and 180 decibels of sound. If you're unfortunate to feel its effects unprotected, there's a good chance of lasting permanent damage.

I had electronic ear pro jammed in my ears, and I squeezed my eyes shut as I screamed to balance my equilibrium. The ground thundered as the flashbang did its thing. A split second later, I emerged from behind the Chevy, my FNX-45 Tactical extended in both hands. I lined up the Vortex Venom's red dot on the closest man's chest, a Swastika covering his sternum. My finger twitched three times, and the Belgian hand cannon thumped in my hands. The Speer Gold Dot 185-grain .45ACP hollows tore effortlessly through his bare chest, no doubt shredding his aorta and puncturing his lungs.

It was Ralston's turn. He was doubled over, his Glock dropped at his feet, his hands clutched at his face. A pair of .45 slugs tore through his abdomen, and a third ripped through his left pectoral. Ralston stood a second longer before he collapsed to the dirt, blood gushing from his wounds. From the way he writhed on the ground, he was alive, but I'd fix that in a moment.

69

The final Nazi was fighting through the flashbang's effects and trying to raise his rifle, some sort of AR knockoff. I emptied the remainder of the magazine from his sternum, up his throat, and along his face. The slide locked to the rear as the final round ripped between his eyes, gray matter spilling from the gaping exit wound in the back of his head. That guy's strings were cut, and he crumpled next to his comrades.

I removed a spare magazine from a pouch beneath my shirt, exchanged it with the empty one, and stuffed the latter in my back pocket as thumbed the slide release to put the FNX-45 back in battery. I paused a moment, watching the door for additional threats. When none presented themselves, I scanned my surroundings. I saw a few bent blinds in windows, but I didn't hear anyone rushing to avenge Ralston. That was just as well.

Only then did I advance. I reached my first victim, leveled my pistol with his face, and put a round between his eyes. Didn't hurt to be careful.

Ralston struggled to look at me, his eyes dilated and his skin paling fast. He didn't have long. His hands had gone to his abdomen, trying to keep his fluids in his body. Ralston managed something resembling a sneer as he met my eyes.

"Y-you'll p-p-pay for t-this, n-n-ni-nig—"

I hadn't realized I'd raised the FN from my side and squeezed the trigger until I felt the recoil. The Gold Dot cut through his brains and shut him up.

I holstered the FNX-45 and retrieved the finishing touch from the messenger bag. Part of my prep for tonight had been to buy a six-pack of wine coolers, empty the contents in my hotel sink, and fill the bottles with kerosene. I'd then stuffed a rag into each one, flattened it, and then covered it with Saran wrap and held the whole thing in place with a rubber band. That last part was to keep the kerosene from leaking into the material.

One by one, I uncovered my Molotovs. I lit one, then hurled it as hard as I could through the window. The second went through the front door. I alternated between window and door to spread dispersion. Once the blaze had a good hold on the trailer, I turned and briskly made my way to the park's entrance. It wouldn't take long for the whole thing to burn down.

I moved quickly. I felt eyes on me. It was a noisy diversion, necessity notwithstanding. It wouldn't be long before somebody called the cops or decided to take matters into their own hands.

I made it to the entrance without incident. I button-hooked right and broke into a jog. As I ran, I ripped the flannel open and peeled it off. The hat was balled up with the shirt, and both went into a trash can. My black undershirt was baggy enough that I could untuck it and conceal my hardware. Within four minutes, I was behind the wheel of my car and on my way out of Windsor.

One target down. Three more to go.

***

Eighteen hours later, I sat in my car downtown, across the street from Baum Used Motors. I sipped a Rockstar, my fifth in as many hours. My body demanded rest, but I had a long way to go before I could oblige.

I'd pushed the pace after the trailer park. My second target had been a printing press in a Chesterfield County strip mall. It'd gotten hairy—my entrance was compromised and it turned into a gun battle—but I adapted and overcame. When it was said and done, there were seven more dead Nazis to my name.

Target #3 had been a pub out by city limits that was popular with the Fourth Reich. It was the trailer park hit refitted to the terrain. Their bikes and pickups caught Molotovs, and when they came out to investigate, I mowed them down. It was right at closing time. I racked up another eleven bodies. I firebombed the pub and *di di mau*'d off the objective.

That was three hours ago. My hair and clothes reeked of cordite, and it hurt to keep my eyes open. My stomach growled, having received nothing but energy drinks and a Snickers bar over the past twenty-four hours. Yet, my focus was laser-sharp. This was the prelude to the end game. I couldn't lose sight of the goal now.

The pattern of life I'd developed on Baum showed he arrived at the dealership at 05:30 prompt and departed at 19:30,

71

without fail. Between those two hours, his movements were unpredictable.

I could have ambushed him at either time, but that wasn't the objective. Cutting off the snake's head would be satisfying, but it wouldn't be a crippling blow. Beneath him, Baum had several capable and intelligent deputies, any of which would be eager to ascend to command.

While sitting back and watching the Nazis eat each other alive would hurt their movement, it wasn't enough for me.

The Fourth Reich needed to die.

It required perfect timing. Baum needed to be close enough to the dealership to get rattled, but not close enough that he'd be maimed or killed. Preferably, I'd need the streets relatively empty to minimize the risk of collateral damage. I didn't want anyone beating Baum to the dealership, either. I had no idea if the Baum Dealership's workers were privy to their employer's ideology. Without that positive identification, I wasn't going weapons free.

Ideally, I'd do this kind of job with shaped charges. I was a medic, but cross-training was an ongoing deal within the ODA. I knew enough about explosives to get by in a pinch. I also knew that adequate explosives were tightly controlled, there wouldn't be enough time to get the necessary certifications to obtain them legally, and stealing them outright presented its own risks.

What was easy to obtain, on the other hand, were the materials needed for homemade napalm, a couple of cheap burner phones, and some electrical wiring. Run the wires between the charges and connect one to a cell phone, and you had yourself a poor man's daisy-chained IED. The call would light up the phone's circuit board, and the electricity would travel through the wiring, igniting the napalm.

I sat in my car across the street. My thumb gently caressed the call button, the detonation phone number already displayed on the screen. I watched through my binoculars as the Chevy pickup made its way down the street. A quick glance at the bumper confirmed it was Baum's truck. I waited until Baum was about 50 meters from pulling into the dealership before I thumbed the button.

It wasn't out-and-out explosion. Napalm has incendiary qualities, but it doesn't rip things apart on its own. However, it does ignite *very* quickly and it sticks to damn near everything in the vicinity. By the time Baum was 25 meters from the entrance, the flames had grown considerably, and Baum brought his Chevy to a screeching halt. The majority of the lot would be engulfed in flames by the time the fire department arrived. It'd cost him millions in property damage, and in turn would cost the Fourth Reich millions in operational funds.

I'd cracked down my window just enough to edge the directional microphone out of the window right after ignition, and I'd heard Baum make calls to 911, one of his dealership subordinates, and what I assumed was his corporate insurance. It took him an hour before he made the call I was waiting for.

"Gather everyone," Baum said. "Emergency meeting at the ranch, tonight at 7:00." There was a pause. "No, you fucking idiot. Not on the phone. Just make the calls."

That was check. I had a pretty good idea where that meeting would take place. I just needed to nudge them into congregating.

That set the stage for checkmate.

***

I couldn't shake the eerie feeling that I was being followed as I left Richmond city limits. It was an even stretch of highway with light traffic, so anyone attempting to tail me in a vehicle would be burned. A couple of times, I pulled off to the side of the road, made as if I was stretching after a long drive, and scanned the skies. Civilian drone usage had picked up over the past decade, and its use by law enforcement had also expanded. If it was a drone, then either the operator was smart and knew to keep it out of my visual range, or it was a government operator running a high-altitude model. A quick sweep of my car revealed no tracking devices.

I dismissed it as paranoia and got back in my car. From there, it was another 15 minutes to the Baum farm, which was located between Williamson Farms and Varina. It was an expansive estate, located at the low ground between three small hills. I parked my vehicle and got into character.

I wore a combat shirt and fatigue trousers, both in ATACS-FG. A skull crusher mounting an AN/PVS-14 went on top of my head and round my chin, and I put my boonie cap on top of that. My FNX-45 was transferred once more from the concealment holster to the Surefire suppressor holster. I'd had to dig through duffel bags to find my custom SAW gunner chest rig that I'd run on my first A-Stan deployment. I slipped into that before donning my Compact Assault Ghillie. It wouldn't be as good as a dedicated suit, but it'd help break out my outline at a distance.

I took a few minutes to apply a quick camo paint job to my face. Dark green for the high points, light green for the low, and brown to fill in the spaces between. Once I was satisfied, I cleaned my hands, slipped on some gloves, and made for the *pièce de resistance*.

The base Fightlite MCR followed all NFA laws and regulations. It was a semi-automatic AR platform that accepted both box magazines and belt drums. What made this illegal was the bumpstock I'd acquired from a dark web vendor. With a little practice, it gave me a squad automatic weapon that would help balance out the force disparity. I'd attached an EOTech optic and a Steiner DBAL-I, both of which would make me more accurate. With my gear ready, I shouldered my assault pack, lowered my NODs in place, and made my way up the hill.

It didn't take long to crest the hill and overlook the farm. Several cars and pickup trucks were parked on the west side of the property. The main house looked unattended, while the barn was well-lit. I could see a couple of sentries posted outside at the entrance, rifles held at the low ready. I raised my NODs and took a peek through my binoculars. Neither Nazi sported night vision, which was to my benefit.

I scanned the surrounding area. The final part of my plan started to form. I walked slowly until I was about fifteen meters from my selected kill zone, at which point I transitioned into a slow high crawl. The soil was loose enough to manipulate with my hands. I set to emplacing seven napalm charges in a loose L-shaped formation. I daisy-chained them and connected one to a cell phone. That number was on redial, as there likely wouldn't be time to stop and dial it on the fly, nor did I want to risk premature detonation with a pocket dial. I grabbed loose foliage and lightly concealed them. If they took time to stop and look, they'd see something was off, but it was the best I could do with the time available.

With that set, I crawled forward about 15 meters. From my position, the door sentries were about 50 meters or so from my position. I thumbed the button on my Grip Pod to deploy the bipod legs, rested them on the ground, and slowly rotated the selector switch from SAFE to FIRE. I peered through the EOTech's screen, lining up my reticle with the closest target. It was around that time that I realized that there was a sound system in place, and the familiar voice of Erik Baum carried through it. I paused as I listened.

"The mud people have finally found a competent monkey amongst them," Baum said, his baritone voice dripping with captivating magnetism. "Rather than target innocent, hard-working white folks attempting to make a living beneath the oppressive boot of multiculturalism, they have identified our movement of white freedom fighters and have lashed out directly *at us*."

Grumbles filled the dead space. One voice with a thick country flavor shouted, "*Fuck them niggers!*"

"That is fine," Baum's voice continued. "We *welcome* this fight. History is full of epic tales of European champions conquering unclean heathens. The only time the unclean have managed to secure victory has been through propaganda designed to make our race feel guilty for our accomplishments and our superiority. The irony of that is that propaganda was historically engineered by white people and Jews aiming to tear this nation apart at the seams." He snickered. "They can't even do *that* properly without taking cues from a white man."

"*Sieg heil!*" a voice shouted.

"*Sieg heil!*" the rest bellowed in unison.

"It's no different for whomever has brought the fight to us," Baum said. "They are using tactics and techniques developed by white men, techniques which have won victories for white men. Their natural inferiority means they *will* crumble. It means that we *will* do what our forefathers failed to do: eradicate the Negro scum from our country with a cleansing fire and make it pure once more!"

"*Sieg heil!*"

I'd heard enough.

Applying forward pressure to the Grip Pod, I squeezed the Fightlite's trigger. A six-round burst stitched the Nazi sentry from hips to chest. As he folded, I drove my reticle left, resting it on the chest of his companion. The Fightlite spoke again, another burst of six ripping through intestine, stomach, lungs, and heart.

"*We're under attack!*" a voice yelled from within a barn. Give the man a gold star.

"*Let's get 'em!*" another shouted.

"*Go!*" Baum hollered. "*Go, go, go!*"

The first wave of four rushed towards the barn entrance. I held the trigger down and swept the muzzle from left to right, cutting them down in their tracks. A couple of them lay still, while others writhed and moaned as blood spurted from fresh wounds. One peeked his head out, and I let loose with another burst, the rounds impacting inches from his head and forcing him to duck back behind concealment.

Now came the risky part.

With a grunt, I forced myself to my feet and bolted in the direction of my kill zone. Within five seconds of my rush, I felt a round *snap* as it flew past my head. I threw myself to the ground, going as flat as possible as I frantically crawled forward. Rounds impacted around me, chewing up the dirt. I was still a bit short of the kill zone, but my luck wasn't going to hold out. Eventually, one of those rounds was going to tear through my flesh, and that was going to put a damper on my plans.

I spun onto my back with my knees bent, half-sat up, and shouldered the Fightlite. I sprayed a 15-round burst toward my pursuers. That kept their heads down long enough to go to my chest rig for a smoke grenade. The civilian models wouldn't burn as long as their military counterparts, but it'd give me a few more seconds to fall back to my secondary position.

I yanked the pin from the grenade and threw it as hard as I could. It'd already begun to spew thick, white clouds of smoke as it made its flight, and obscured the Nazis' vision. I scrambled to my feet, ran just past the edge of my kill zone, then turned back and went to a knee. With the Fightlite in my shoulder, I began laying down six- and seven-round bursts. Judging from the occasional shout or yelp, my rounds had either found some targets or come close, but I was under no impression that my fire was accurate. I just needed them to follow the breadcrumbs.

As the smoke dissipated, I spun and sprinted for the hilltop. Along the way, I flipped the feed tray open, cleared it off with the back of my hand, and ripped the mostly-expended nutsack from its mount. I fetched a fresh one from my chest rig, snapped it in place, and laid the belt on the feed tray, brass to the grass. I slapped the tray cover shut, racked the charging handle, and ran another five meters before I turned back, hit the ground, and shouldered the Fightlite.

"He went this way!" a voice shouted. They were in a ragged line, bunched up. More than a few of them were winded from the chase. I'd be lying if I said I wasn't winded, but I was also carrying a total of 800 rounds of 5.56, a sidearm, and a chest rig full of kit. All of these guys were in civilian clothes, and only a few of them had chest rigs. It wasn't just the fatbodies, either. A couple of skinny Nazi pricks were also having trouble humping up the hill. As the first one reached the bottom edge of the kill zone, I knew they weren't going to catch it in time.

With my off-hand, I dug into my pocket for the Nokia burner, unlocked the keypad, and brought up the speed dial. I pulled down my PVS-14 and peered through it. I counted 15 bodies in pursuit. Baum wasn't in the front, which didn't surprise me in the least. The point man—a chunky guy with a scraggly circle beard—huffed and puffed his way to the front of the kill zone. I let him walk right past it. I estimated I'd probably catch about half of them. I gambled on letting the front half past and dealing with them after detonation.

Finally, the tail man entered the kill zone. I thumbed the call button.

The fire roared as the charges ignited, napalm spraying in both directions and sticking to clothing, weapons, and flesh. The grass was also caught in the blaze. Those whom I'd allowed to walk past the kill zone turn around, predictably dumbfounded.

"What the *fuck?*" one of them shouted.

They were still mostly in a line when I pulled the trigger. I held the trigger down, making only slight deviations to make sure each Nazi in the stack caught his fair share of lead. It only took me five seconds to cut them down. I paused a beat, scanning ahead of me for any stragglers. The only movement I saw was from the kill zone, and I doubted they'd pose any threat until I was up close.

I rose from my position and backtracked down the hill. The stench hit my nose a few steps in. It wasn't the first time I'd smelled charred flesh—the Dawis bombing immediately rushed to mind—but it was a scent that never left you once you'd smelled it. The difference between Dawis and here was that I didn't feel an ounce of sympathy for the burn victims this time.

They'd wanted cleansing fire, and I'd given it to them.

They'd at least had a fighting chance, which was a hell of a lot more than they'd given my mother.

As I walked amongst the bodies—gunned down and charred alike—I gave each of them a burst to the skull from point-blank range. There wasn't any mercy behind the action. I just didn't want any of these Fourth Reich shitheads finding a second wind and trying to take me to Hell with them. I checked each face before I fired, looking for Baum. Not a single one matched his description, though most of the bodies in the napalm blast were too crispy for positive identification.

A faint sound from the barn's direction reached my ears. I looked up to find a man sprinting from the entrance in the direction of the trucks. I dropped to a knee, shouldered my Fightlite, and gauged his direction and travel speed. I gave him a little bit of a lead and let out an exhale as I squeezed the trigger.

The lone figure ran right into the six-round burst, or at least enough of it that it chopped through his legs and laid him flat on his face.

I jogged towards the runner until I was within 10 meters of him, at which point I slowed to a brisk march. He'd managed to drag himself forward a few feet in the time it took me to cross the distance. When I reached him, I gave him a boot to the ribs and turned him on his back.

Erik Baum glared at me, his facial expression a grotesque blend of excruciating pain and disgust. There was enough ambient light that he knew who I was, or—in his terms—*what* I was, even with the camouflage paint.

"So much for the master race," I growled, unslinging my Fightlite and setting it on the ground, out of Baum's reach.

"You won a battle," Baum growled through clenched teeth. "Big deal. You're outnumbered. More and more of my brothers and sisters are taking the red pill. In time, we will annihilate you."

I reached into my chest rig's utility pouch and removed a folded piece of paper. The idea had come to me between the trailer park and the printing press. All I'd needed was a few minutes at a Kinko's and I'd created plausible deniability.

"Their own leader couldn't be bothered to take point," I said. "I think my people will be fine."

"You're nothing," Baum rasped. "You're less than nothing. You're a *nigger*. I will die as a proud martyr of my race. I'll be a rallying cry for other to follow, and you'll still be a fucking *nigger*."

I showed Baum the flyer. It bore the logo for the Modern Black Panther Party for Equality and Justice. "I waffled on this," I said. "I really didn't want to give these Maoist shitheads credit for something they didn't do. End of the day, though, it's a net benefit. Your inbred Nazi homeboys realize you were done in by a *nigger*, and it starts a vicious cycle between you and the Modern Panthers." I paused a beat. "Who wins when Nazis and Maoists kill each other? Everyone else. That's who."

I set the flyer on his chest and smoothed it out. Baum's face twisted as he ginned the energy for one last outburst. "*Fuck—*
"

He never saw the Cold Steel Tanto race from its sheath on my chest rig, and he only felt it once it punched between his ribs and pierced his aorta. I stared him in the eyes as the life rapidly faded, the blood from the puncture seeping through the flyer and staining it red. I gave the knife a twist for effect, and leaned in, making sure he'd hear me before he passed.

"*That's* for Gladys Durand, you son of a *bitch*."

Checkmate.

***

There was no time to rest. If I'd covered my tracks properly, then I needed to use the space I'd bought myself to skip town.

If I hadn't covered my tracks, that only added urgency to the action's necessity.

I'd wiped off my face the best I could, changed back into civvies, and driven back to the extended stay. All of my gear was safely in a duffel bag, save the FNX-45, which was back in its concealment holster. I made my way to my room via a side entrance, swept and cleared the room, then immediately stripped down and headed for the shower.

It was a quick and thorough shower, scrubbing all the dirt and grime from my body while hitting the hot spots. Just enough that I wouldn't smell myself. The FNX was propped at the back of the shower, ready for action. Thankfully, I didn't need it, and I finished the shower without incident.

I don't know why I'd brought the underwear with me into the bathroom, but when I stepped back out of the bathroom, I was glad that I had.

There was a white dude sitting at the table. He looked a little on the heavy side at first glance, but you could tell it was mostly muscle, particularly by the way his arms fought against his polo's sleeves. His blond hair was neatly combed and trimmed in a way that screamed to me, "I'm military trying not to be military." He had dead blue eyes and a permanent scowl on his face.

The guy was a meat eater. No doubt about it. No idea what tribe he was with, but he'd spent some time outside the wire.

I kept the FNX at my side. The meat eater kept his hands interlaced on the table. Very slowly, I said, "If you were with the man, you'd have come knocking with a SWAT team and a warrant. If you were with the Fourth Reich, you'd have popped me in the shower."

"Astute observations, Mr. Durand," the man said, his voice gravelly.

"I'm guessing you're armed."

He smirked. "Crazy times out there. Goddamned right, I'm armed." He shrugged and pursed his lips. "Of course, I don't have to tell you that. I saw the mess you left at the Baum estate."

I fought to maintain my poker face. My instincts were right. I *had* been followed. "I don't know what you're talking about."

The meat eater leaned forward, his palms flat on the table. "Mr. Durand, I'm gonna ask you two favors."

"Which are?"

"Don't bullshit me. You already know I'm not a neo-Nazi and I'm not a fed."

"And the second?"

"Put some fuckin' pants on. I don't wanna have this conversation while you're half-naked." He must have seen the shift in my facial expression. "I'm gonna keep my hands just like this. You keep your eyes on me, and we'll have this talk like gentlemen."

I considered it a beat. "All right." I didn't like being that exposed any more than he liked seeing it.

It took me about 90 seconds to pick out a polo shirt of my own and a pair of jeans. I kept the FN within reach and faced him as I got dressed. Socks and shoes could wait. I wasn't going to give him an opening, even if he seemed trustworthy enough to take him at his word. Once I was dressed, I picked up the FN, kept it at my side, and sat across the table from him. He leaned back, his hands still in plain sight.

"Who are you?" I asked.

"Call me Hartrick," the meat eater said. "I represent an organization concerned with the direction this nation's taken."

My eyes narrowed. "An organization?"

"Jimmy Tubbs told us about you," Hartrick said. "We were going to reach out a few days ago. You had us spooked for a bit when you went to that Panther rally. Thought maybe the Panthers were stepping up their game by recruiting a SOF veteran. So, we started following you. Lost you briefly, but picked your trail back up right after you hit the Fourth Reich's printing press. When you blew up Baum's car lot, that was when we got a warm and fuzzy on your motives. Our organization could use someone like you."

"That's the second time you've gone with 'our organization,'" I said. "Who do you represent?"

"The Triarii."

"The Triarii." I pursed my lips and drummed my fingers on my thigh. "You mean, the right-wing militia."

Hartrick visibly bit back a response. He paused a moment. "You believe in the Constitution, Mr. Durand?"

"The ideals embodied, sure, when they're equally afforded to everyone."

"Judging from your jacket and the way you stormed out of the Panther rally, you're not fan of the ChiComs."

"Not at all."

"And you're definitely no fan of the neo-Nazis," Hartrick said. "Congratulations. You're a right-wing militiaman."

"I just get a little wary when I hear folks talk about 'preserving the nation,'" I said as evenly as I could. "For a while, that's been code for, 'Make America White Again.'"

"Not here," Hartrick said. "We've got no room for racist shitheads of any color, just as we've got no room for Commies. You aware of the history behind the name?"

"Decisive troops of last resort in the Roman Republic," I said. "Usually the oldest and wealthiest, with the best equipment. Often not employed because the front ranks would win the battle, but were the make-or-break troops in the heavier battles. Inspiration behind the phrase, *res ad triarios venit*."

"'It comes down to the Triarii,' or until the bitter end," Hartrick said. "And that's where we're at right now. The bitter end. Foreign influence fanning dissident groups. Weakened infrastructure giving up entire neighborhoods, cities, and sections of states to violent non-state actors. The Republic's in danger, Jordan."

"The Republic's made a lot of avoidable missteps that's led to this situation," I said.

Hartrick bit his tongue again. I had the feeling somebody had told him to play nice. "And now it's up to us to right the ship before we're done in."

I had a feeling he and I wouldn't see eye-to-eye on what those missteps were. How could he? He hadn't walked in my shoes. That said, things were gonna get a lot worse if full-on collapse set in.

"Why me?" I asked. "I'm sure you've got plenty of skilled people on your payrolls."

"We do," Hartrick said. "It's not enough. We're evolving. Gonna need to take things to the next level. Sure, we could pool what SOF veterans we have, but the fact of the matter is, we don't have enough. We need a larger base to develop the curriculum and then expand the program." He shrugged. "Plus, I have a feeling your war with the Fourth Reich's not done."

I shook my head slightly. "Not by a long shot."

"You pulled off a one-man blitz on an entrenched enemy. Bravo. How long do you think your luck's gonna hold out? You join us, you've got a much better chance of winning your war. Your war becomes our war."

"I wouldn't go that far, Hartrick," I said, a chill to my voice. "But I understand your meaning." I stood, slid the FNX into my waistband, and extended my hand across the table. "I'm in."

Hartrick slowly rose and took my hand. He had a firm, dry grip. He met my eyes as he spoke.

"Welcome to the Triarii."

# Gorgeous George Goes Home

## David Reeder

**Amos Lovell, Torre Angelini (Angelini Tower), Maracaibo**
**Separatist Zulia State**
**Bolivarian Republic of Venezuela**
**-10° 34' 00" N, 71° 44' 00" O**
**03h14L**

Amos Lovell was nothing if not handsome. His smile had dropped panties from Tucson to Tehran. More insouciant than was appropriate for a "fighting" NCO, Lovell been the natural sworn enemy of any protective father, brother, boyfriend, or husband damn near since his balls dropped. A smug Jean Val Jean meets Tyler Rake looking sonuvabitch, any sane man hated him on sight.

He was all but nondescript stood up next to Jorgé Federico Gutierrez, though. Even homely. That motherfucker, they used to joke, was too pretty to be allowed to live. Him and his jawline, those perfect fucking Photoshop-white teeth, and Rocco Siffredi cock. Gorgeous George, they called him, for damn good reason.

Used to call him anyway. The joke wasn't funny anymore. Gorgeous George was gorgeous no longer. In fact, he was scarcely recognizable. Amos wasn't even sure he was breathing.

His face was broken and bloody, most of his incisors shattered, both lips were all but shredded. It looked like someone had been trying to carve a map on his face with razors. Which in a way they had been.

Lightning from out past the bridge over la Lago de Maracaibo—Maracaibo Lake—threw gory shadows across the room. A cold wind from across the water whipped hanging plastic sheets into a frenzy. They were doing a half-assed job of covering what ought to have been the east wall, but wasn't, allowing glimpses of a horizon far beyond the strait and the city of Santa Rita, across the water. The fourteenth floor was a pain in the ass to reach if you were climbing up. It would have given them a superb vantage point overlooking the water, the strange local lightning above it, even the visiting Chinese flotilla out past the bridge had they been interested in such a view.

They weren't. Neither was Lovell. But the eerie Catatumbo lightning on the lake was distracting the men who weren't fixated on Jorgé's torment.

That did interest him.

When Amos followed a pair of nine-bangers through the door it took the men who'd been cutting on Jorgé a few heartbeats to react. That proved they were better torturers – or sadists, anyway – than they were soldiers. But then, few of the men hired to help suppress the Zulianidad separatists were as professional as they were cruel. The latest Presidente de la República Bolivariana de Venezuela was far less concerned with recruiting quality thinker-shooters than we was getting as many boots on the throat of the Zulia state's would-be secession as possible.

In some places that would have been a terrible strategy. In what had been Venezuela's largest state, however, quantity and brutality had a quality all their own.

Lovell registered the look of shock on each distinct face inside as he crossed the threshold. He muttered "Pericula ludus" under his breath the way some men might murmur a Paternoster, cataloguing each man he needed to kill in staccato freeze frame sequence.

A single camping lantern threw wan light across the room and dragged their shadows longwise toward the gaping hole where once there'd been a balcony. There was blood pooled darkly on the floor—not all of it Gutierrez's thankfully, and only a portion of it new—though there was plenty enough of that, and sufficient light to see.

Flashbang strobes vied with the continuously flickering Catatumbo lights as Lovell started shooting. Muzzle flash immediately became part of the visual bedlam. Happily, just his muzzle flash at first.

He brought his rifle down from high port, out and back into his shoulder, killing the closest gunman in an effortless fashion that bespoke of long practice. It was the only thing to do – and what Jorgé's uncle would have expected anyway.

He was many things, was Amos Lovell, not all of them good or even pardonable. But he was a good soldier.

A very good soldier.

Thankfully the mercenaries holding Jorgé were not. They were dark-skinned Essequibo hired guns from Guyana, likely from one of the many smaller PMCs operating west of the Carretera la Montaña, and all were at least half stoned. Had they been some of General Reverol's hired Guatemalan Kaibiles or a part of the so-called Chilean "Colonel" Urzúa's Compañía Escorpiónes they'd most likely have gotten him once he was fully in the room. Certainly before he'd put more than a couple of them down. Happily, they weren't. Lucky, that.

Only the dead man had been paying any semblance of attention. But though his rifle had been at the low ready, his eyes had been fixated on the burgeoning drama between a multi-tool and Jorgé's face...

...which was of course why he was the dead man. Or the first dead man anyway.

It was a helluva risk, trying to clear whole apartments by themselves. But with only shitty local fuel available, Henk's helicopter could only carry four, and even that was iffy. And it's not like it was an official Soldats Sans Frontières or sanctioned 8th SFG operation anyway.

Amos was nothing if not a gambler though, and Henk had flown far scarier runs with AvTEG, Air Branch, and 36 FTA. Plus, the crusty pilot was bored. So, the battered old Kiowa with the maroon and white Lone Star guidon on its nose and a massive number 12 on the door took them up and dropped them off. They unassed the bird on the wreck of what had been the twenty-ninth floor and began clearing toward the ground. Each took one floor at a time individually. They leapfrogged their way down.

It was blind ass luck he'd heard Jorgé's screams through the gag, the doors, and the storm out over the city, but Amos Lovell was nothing if not lucky. Nearly as lucky as he was pretty.

Except of course for when he wasn't. The next few moments would be interesting.

There were five targets in the room, at least that he could see. He'd prioritized them before the second burst of the flashbang started and was shooting them before the fourth ended.

One — center-punched three times in rapid succession by 77-grain open-tip match grade rounds. A fourth round through the throat. He dropped back as though doing the rucksack flop, tilted halfway back on his ass in an improbable lean, then slumped over sideways. The boneless drop made it clear he wouldn't be getting up again, but by then Lovell's attention was elsewhere.

Now for the others.

Two — was the bug-eyed fucker standing so close to the hole in the wall that the plastic sheeting was flapping against his leg. Type 63 rifle, no sling, Amos thought. Looks scared shitless.

Three — was big, swarthy fucker with a porn mustache, likely an Arawak hired gun from Suriname given the colors of the roundel on his hat. He was standing in a doorway, likely to a bathroom, entranced by Jorgé's torture. There was a white stripe painted across the bridge of his nose. Tondar TD MPT-9 sub-gun, Amos noted diffidently, been doing business with the Iranians maybe?

Wait. Did that mother-fucker have an erection?

Four — was the one leaning over Jorgé with a multi-tool. He'd thrown a hand up over his face at Lovell's entry, knocking a toquilla straw hat awry. That's probably his FAL leaning against the moldy bookcase over there, he thought, recognizing also that if they were still torturing him then Jorgé was probably still alive.

Five — was the man standing next to Three. He was black as wet coal, probably a Garifuna tribesman, and flinching back from the nine-banger that rolled practically between his feet. Another FAL, Lovell processed, folding stock, slung nearly all the way around behind his back, no pistol in view.

He started out intending to kill them in the order of threat they presented.

Number Three.

He dropped the Arawak next, shooting him twice with a hammer pair through awful brown teeth and forever banishing the sight of that hideous mustache. A third bullet, almost certainly redundant, punched through the white stripe—more likely an affectation than genuine—and the nose it crossed. The big man tottered backward, turned in an obscenely dainty pirouette and pitched forward onto what was left of his face, legs rigid and arms straight down at his sides.

Sorry 'bout your hard-on you sick fuck.

The carbine's voice seemed even louder than normal, confined as it was within the apartment's bare walls. Amos was using one of several GAU-5s the Boss had bought from the Barranquillans before the rest of l'Escadron arrived. It had been a wise decision. As soon as it became clear this was to become an actual shooting war, the Policía Nacional shut down the airport and all formal border crossings to interdict supplies, weapon shipments, and all unapproved "advisers."

Almost simultaneously the Bógédá Shān (a Chinese Navy Type 075 amphibious assault ship) and ironically named Ürümqi (a PLAN Type 055 cruiser) had helped the Sahand class Simón Bolívar block the Tablazo Strait as well. These helpful actions came, apparently, at the request of the "rightful" government in Caracas.

Subsequently, all personnel arriving by official channels were relieved of their weapons before ever deplaning. United Nations UNMOs and Organization of American States peacekeepers were forced to abide by those restrictions same as all visiting NGOs.

The Boss, thankfully, had other plans entirely for Soldats Sans Frontières, which had far more latitude of maneuver than did any of the "official" regardless of nationality or organization. And the Boss had far less inclination to abide by the rules anyway.

Though nearly 3/4 of a century old and bought sight unseen off Colombia's questionable black market, all the GAUs had been thoroughly loved on by 1er Escadron de Chasseurs à Pied's armorers. They now functioned flawlessly. The barrels were less than ideal, but they served well enough for close-in work.

Number Four.

Number three's brains hadn't even begun sliding down the wall before Amos was breaking the trigger on Number Four. He was the one busily doing something vile to Jorgé's eye with a multi-tool, which he dropped just before Amos walked a series of bullets across his chest. Crimson blossoms stitched a line from one side of his garish yellow shirt to the other, giving it a vaguely Hawaiian look. Lovell should have been killing Number Two next, as Four didn't have a gun in hand and Five's was slung, but...Four had been the one been carving on Jorgé's face for fuck's sake.

That shit had to stop.

Jorgé slid sideways as far as the ropes holding him would allow, head lolling back on his neck. The torturer's stupid hat fell in Jorgé's lap as he lurched backwards a step, lifting a cautionary finger as though about to object. His eyes were blinking in near comical surprise the whole time, a clown shot to pieces in a bloody kids show. The follow-up shot blew the man's eye through the back of his skull and a piece of tooth or bone hit Amos in the face hard enough to snap his head sideways and start his eyes to watering.

"And that's why you wear eye-pro," he muttered, though he wasn't actually wearing any and no one in the room could hear him - himself included.

Gunfire thundered suddenly and it wasn't his. The concussion of a nearby muzzle pounded his ears.

Jorgé was choking on blood. A bullet plucked at the hem of Amos's shirt. Another plowed through the brand new pouches on his left side, shattering through three rifle magazines before crashing off course and dragging a searing line across his upper leg. Sharp bits of plastic and metal bit into his belly. He staggered at a hammer blow like a mallet smashing his hip.

Somewhere an FN FAL was roaring.

Blood began to run down Amos's leg and into his crotch. It felt like he'd pissed himself in a pool, only creepier.

He turned. I should have dropped the folding stock FAL next, he thought ruefully, then stumbled and nearly fell when two bullets hammered into the front plate of his armor. He gasped and staggered, eyes watering so badly he couldn't pick up his sights. He felt the urge to puke and didn't, but wasn't able to suppress a moan.

Number Two

The man by the big damn hole in the wall hadn't changed position, he'd just started shooting. He wasn't very good at it either. Amos tried to pivot, GAU barrel following his eyes, but his legs weren't working exactly right so it was more of a controlled bumble. Regardless, the GAU was barking and he didn't miss. Two heartbeats and a handful of meat-slap noises later, Number Two was gone. Something far less graceful than a Peter Pan dive took him plunging out into the Maracaibo night.

That left...

Number Five.

The black man with the folding stock FAL was now moving and shooting; Amos caught the shift through the tears and grit in his eye, felt more than heard the snap of rounds bracketing his head. He threw some courtesy rounds back, none more than perfunctorily aimed, then transitioned to his Browning-like Zamorana pistol when the GAU's bolt locked back.

That fucking FAL was loud at a range of less than ten paces, but Amos's ear pro was the best money could buy and the black guy was wearing none. He cringed while jerking the trigger, clearly unprepared for the din. And cringing was actually the last thing he did, unless you count dropping to the floor dead or shitting himself while becoming a corpse.

It was a difficult series of shots, hitting a moving target both above and below a presumed plate carrier while half-blind with pain and blood from a split cheekbone with part of a tooth stuck in it. But Amos Lovell was nothing if not good with a pistol.

Number Five's end was a graceless sag that left him face down on the ground. The remaining rounds in the Zamorana punched into his back between his shoulders as an encouragement to stay there.

Clear.

Gorgeous George was, for the moment, safe. Rescued even.

It wasn't until after Amos had reloaded and given each of the five dead mercenaries a courtesy round with the GAU that he realized he'd been shot. One of the bones in his lower leg was broken, and he was bleeding. He was bleeding a lot, bright red little squirts in sync with the hammering heart in his chest. He could thank the pale shard of his fibula spearing out of his leg for that. Good thing he'd somehow wound up leaning against the wall.

"Mother fucker," he swore, not that anyone was listening, and sat down hard.

The venerable IFAK on his battle belt was wrecked, but the secondary tourniquet on his belt, a late-gen CAT, was still intact. He looped it around his leg high above the knee, cinched it down tight and turned the windlass until he felt his pulse pounding on the band of nylon. His leg felt like it was being crushed in a vice. In fact, it fucking felt like the skin was going to split apart like clay under a wire. He wanted to punch somebody but no one was close enough. And anyway, they were dead.

On a good note, the bleeding stopped. On a worse note, he threw up, little chewed up bits of Twinkie-like double-chocolate strawberry-filled gansito in a froth of bile on top of the blood already pooled on the floor.

It wasn't the least incongruous thing he'd seen during a fight, nor the first time he'd vomited after one, but it was close.

"I think maybe I'm going to pass out," he told Jorgé, who was still blissfully unconscious, but breathing, which was better than the alternative.

Jorgé moaned.

"I know, right?" Amos agreed amiably, rolling onto his ass and gasping. Pain spiked white and blinding through is leg, worse than it had been before.

He hadn't thought that was possible. He laid there for a few heartbeats, staring up at the ceiling and breathing. There was puke in his beard.

"I think maybe I also shit myself," he gasped.

Jorgé seemed to gargle back, and although Amos couldn't understand him, he waved weakly to acknowledge whatever the hell it was he'd said.

"Look," he said to Not So Gorgeous Anymore George, waving vaguely toward the hole in the wall. "That's some Michael Mann shit right there."

The Essaquario he'd shot by the hole in the wall had apparently not actually taken a dive. The flapping plastic curtain had wrapped around him as he went over the edge. He was hanging there upside down, just his lower legs visible. One of his boots was half torn off and a piece of rebar has speared him through the meat of his calf. Upon further consideration, Amos though that might have as much to do with him hanging there inverted as did the plastic.

Jorgé's eyes rolled. He hacked bloody drool into his lap and Amos nodded in agreement.

"You're right," he said, patting himself down in search of additional holes. "Fine. Not Michael Mann then. Michael Bay. What the fuck ever. Goddam ingrate."

Then it was time to move.

It was more than a little fucking hard, dragging himself across the floor to the wall where he could watch the door for more Essequibos, Tupamaro militia, or worse, SEBIN hitters from the Bolivarian intelligence service. Making that move wasn't as hard as slamming the auto-injector of anesthetic into his calf, though. That time he did pass out, and puked again, though this time without any bits of Twinkie-alike. He was only out for a few moments, however, and by the time he came back around the articaine-epinephrine and methamphetamine cocktail had started to take effect. He awoke to discover he'd been able to stuff Celox gauze in the hole in his leg and wrap the exposed bone with an Izzy bandage.

"Look at that shit," he told Jorgé drunkenly, pointing at his handiwork. "Did that shit in my sleep."

It took three attempts to get through to the others and call them in on his and Jorgé's location. It took two more to reach Henk, who was, judging by the background noise, rocking out to The 20/20 Experience with the rotors turning. The former CW5 had been waiting on a helipad at the Venezolana de Cementos, in a pro-Zulianida portion of the city controlled by Wayúu tribal militia. So, barring the unlikely interference from Z-10s off the Bógédá Shān, he and his piece of shit, absurdly painted relic of an OH-58D were just a few minutes out.

Then the most important comms.

The video call from his Hamsa went straight through to Alexandria. It was a direct line.

"Go for Godine."

Amos winced when something moved in his leg, blinked tears from his eyes, fought the urge to let his bladder go and just piss there on the floor.

"It's Lovell, sir," he said.

He started to slide sideways down the wall, righted himself. He was feeling pretty drunk, which only made his typical relaxed drawl sound even worse. After further consideration he went ahead and let his bladder go. It didn't seem like he was going to be able to stop if for very long anyway.

"I've got him. I have your godson."

"Is he alive?"

Amos nodded.

"He's alive. He's fucked up like a cyclops with Down's Syndrome, but he's alive."

A long exhalation echoed from the tablet.

"That's good news," the massive former armor officer said grimly. "You keep him that way. I'll tell the Colonel his nephew's alive."

Jorgé's uncle, his dad's brother, was a storied infantry officer, also retired, with friends in interesting places. His old man had been killed in the Maghreb. Another uncle, his mom's brother, had lost a leg in the Šar massif.

"Well done, young man," said another, taller man, leaning into the camera's eye. His suit was worth more than Amos made in a month. Maybe several months. But there was a hard edge to the politician that Amos recognized and respected.

"You're going places, corporal," he said. "You're going places indeed."

Gosh, he thought, not while my leg's fucked up like this. And I really enjoyed that gansito. Except for maybe the strawberry part.

"Thank you, sir," he said. "Did you know that Ürümqi is the farthest city from the sea anywhere in the world?"

A lighter flared as a cigar was lit. Godine's expression recaptured Lovell's drug-addled attention.

"Senator Boorstin's right, young Caporal," Godine growled. He even pronounced the rank correctly. "We have a job for you, if you want it. And you do. I've already spoken to Bruno."

The call ended, though Amos couldn't remember who'd ended the connection to whom. Bruno was Lovell's boss. The Boss. Commander of the best of the several successor PMCs that followed the dissolution of the Légion Étrangère.

Lovell was well aware of the close connection between combat veteran officers who'd deployed together. Even some of those from different countries. Sometimes especially those from different countries, if they were among the "fighting officers" being systematically marginalized or replaced by their respective governments. His own Chef d'Escadron, Marcel Saint Raspéguy — "Bruno" to his face by a very select and dangerous few, and behind his back to his soldiers — had been awarded the Légion d'Honneur after the Kordofan Intervention. Godine had received the same award at the same time, in the same hospital.

But that was before Amos's time. And before the Legion retired its colors rather than be subsumed by the European Defense Corps.

His eyes jerked open suddenly. "Fuck me, says I," he muttered to the dead Essequibo in the excruciating bright shirt. "Sorry. I think I might have passed out there."

The narcotics were now separating his voice from his head in surreal detachment so it sounded like he was talking to himself from across the room.

He stared at the corpse for a few minutes trying to decide what color the flowers on its shirt had been before being soaked with gore.

"I could wear that," he told the dead man. "And I'd make it look good too."

Even shot up and bleeding out he sounded like a surfer straight out of Central Casting.

Then Jorgé coughed. So, Amos coughed in solidarity. Amos groaned, so Jorgé moaned too. Then Henk came up on the net to advise he was three minutes out. Justin Timberlake was blaring in the background.

"I'm gonna need to get myself cleaned up, Jorgé," Amos told the disfigured young 8th Group officer. "Gonna meet me a Senator."

He flicked a chunk of something out of his beard and wiped the back of his mouth with his hand, then tore a pocket off his shoulder to wipe the blood from his hand off.

Amos Lovell was nothing if not fastidious.

And Gorgeous George was going home.

# Breaching the Spider's Parlor Door

## Peter Nealen

It was the third day of riots, and nobody was showing any sign of calming down.

We had to move carefully, skirting around the "Red Zone" around downtown Baltimore and avoiding the cops at the same time. Not that they were looking for us; from the flickering firelight downtown and the sounds of sporadic gunfire, they already had their hands full. But they were already twitchy, and with the drones in the sky around the Red Zone, all it would take would be one wrong glimpse of guys in plate carriers and carrying weapons for the red and blue lights to come swooping down. Especially given just how illegal the short-barreled rifles we were carrying were.

Of course, the cameras on every traffic light and corner were a problem, too. Especially since Scott suspected that our target was more tapped into the system than the cops were. We just had to hope that he wasn't expecting us to come looking for him.

I paused at the corner, staying back in the shadows of the alley, and peered up and down the street. It was deserted; the riots had generally stayed away from this part of town, though the stores that lined the street hadn't exactly gone unscathed. There were shattered windows where they hadn't been covered by steel bars. Several of the streetlights were out, but the cameras bolted to just about every building didn't necessarily need visible light to record.

"This place looks like fucking Syria," Dwight whispered from behind me. He was a big dude, and pushing fifty, but Dwight was quiet when he moved; I hadn't even heard him get close. "Never thought I'd see this kind of shit Stateside."

I just shrugged fractionally as I continued to scan the street, looking for a way across that wouldn't expose us to too many cameras. I'd seen a couple of minor skirmishes during my time in the Marine Corps, but they had all been dealing with little jihadi brushfires in Africa or the Philippines. I'd never seen Syria.

But at the same time, I'd seen enough to know what he was talking about. The chaos wasn't everywhere, not yet, but the US wasn't what it had been.

And the powers that be seemed at best content to fiddle while Rome burned. Which was where we came in.

It wasn't the time for woolgathering about how bad things had gotten, though. I had seen our opening. When I'd first looked, I'd seen at least three drones overhead. It was getting hard to say whether they were private or police-operated, though there was a thinner and thinner line there in recent days. But as a thunderous detonation shook the ground and echoed across the city, and a fireball went up somewhere downtown, all three drones arrowed off toward the riots. There were still the stationary cameras to worry about, but they should be easy enough to either dodge or, in extremis, to shoot.

"Moving," I whispered. Stepping out into the street, my 5.56mm PDX held down by my side so that even if the bad guys were watching the camera feeds and noticed me, despite the disruption of the blast downtown, it wouldn't necessarily look like I was carrying a weapon, I started to cross.

Every nerve screamed at me to run, to dash to the next covered and concealed position. But one thing I'd learned in the Grex Luporum Selection Course was that if you're going to infiltrate in an urban environment, it works best to act casual and look like you belong there.

So, I kept my gait to more of a stroll, my shoulders slightly hunched, my rifle tucked in such a way that hopefully it just looked like I had my hands in my pockets. I still felt exposed as hell, even though I knew that Dwight had me covered from the alleyway.

The rest of the team wasn't with us; another thing that Brian Hartrick had beaten into our heads was that on an urban infiltration, footprint matters. If we looked like a hit team, we weren't going to get close before either the cops took us, or the quarry ran for it.

I got across the street and slipped between the buildings, dropping my PDX back into both hands as I scanned for more cameras. Of course, there were two, but it was simple enough to keep a dumpster between my weapon and the one that was pointed my way, as I turned to watch the street and cover for Dwight.

He didn't follow me, not precisely. He waited for a couple of minutes before moving out, and when he crossed the street, he aimed for the next alley over. It meant that we were separated and couldn't quite directly support each other for a few minutes, but we had to assume that we were being observed, especially this close to the target building. The more random and disconnected we appeared, the longer we'd have before everything went to hell.

As soon as he was out of sight, I turned, tucking my weapon back under my arm, and continued down the alley. I kept my head down as I passed the cameras. No point in giving the target any more info than necessary, if he was tapped in. Which he probably was.

I keyed my radio. "Five minutes," I called.

"Roger," Dave replied. He and Chris were sitting in a van three blocks away, waiting for us. They were our extract, but more than that, they were running direct support.

I heard the buzz behind me, but didn't break stride or look back. After all, one quadrotor sounded much the same as another, and if the bad guys had drones patrolling, then reacting was probably going to tip them off.

A small, dark shape whizzed overhead and down the alley toward the warehouse at the far end. "Going dark in thirty seconds," Dave called out.

I didn't acknowledge; neither did anyone else. Instead, I reached into my chest rig and powered my radio off. Just in case.

The drone got to the end of the street and blew up.

It was a muted explosion, especially compared to the bomb that had gone off a few minutes earlier. It probably wasn't audible more than a quarter mile away. But then, the whole point wasn't physical destruction. We had breaching charges for that.

The fact that the handful of lights around the warehouse went out at the same time the drone blew up told me that it had worked.

I broke into a run. The EMP's effect wasn't going to last; the target had to have backups. Our window was a narrow one, and it was closing fast.

Dwight came out of the next alley over, his rifle in his hands. Phil, Jordan, Scott, and Greg were ahead of us; Phil was already cutting the padlock on the cyclone fence gate with a pair of bolt cutters, while the rest covered down on the openings we could see.

Inside the fence, the warehouse was dark, a hulking, two-story block of cement, cinderblock, and steel. Rollup doors flanked the front entrance, which was shadowed by a narrow awning.

It looked innocuous enough, but if our intel cell was right, looks were deceiving as hell.

The padlock parted with a sharp *snap*, and the ends of the chain holding the gate shut swung away with a faint jangle. Only the noise of the riots, sporadic gunfire, and the wail of sirens almost drowned it out. Phil grabbed the gate and pulled, opening a gap just wide enough for two of us to go through. Weapons up, Jordan and I went in.

It was a short dash to the warehouse wall, and we crossed it in seconds. But instead of immediately breaching, we slowed down and took stock once we were under the awning.

We had good reason to. The target had already demonstrated just how dangerous he was. We weren't going to do anybody any good if we went charging in where angels fear to tread and got our heads blown off.

Now that we were off the street—and the mask was at least partway off; the EMP would have tipped him off that *somebody* was coming—we could afford to get a little more high-profile. Almost at the same time, Jordan and I pulled our thermal fusion goggles out of their pouches and pulled them over our heads. In a moment, our surroundings turned into a brighter image, the phosphor tubes lighting everything up in grayscale, thermal signatures outlined with brighter lights.

Through the NVGs, it became immediately obvious that trying to run right at the breach would have been a very bad idea.

The door had pressure sensors top and bottom, and unless I missed my guess, they were wired to some sort of IED. It fit the profile. The People's Revolutionary Action had gotten quite adept at making bombs lately. Given the upper middle-class background most of them had, and their antipathy for military service, one had to wonder where they were getting the expertise.

It was a long list of suspects.

I kept my rifle pointed at the door when Jordan tapped his chest and let his own PDX hang on its sling. Swinging the backpack off his shoulders, he dug into it and came out with a taped coil of det cord. It wasn't as big as a classic flex-linear charge; we didn't have the resources for it, and Jordan didn't have the room in his pack. But it should be enough.

I stood back, scanning our surroundings as he peeled the backing off the tape and affixed the charge to the seam between the doors. It wouldn't blow them all the way open, but it would hopefully do enough to set off any booby traps that the target had set.

It took a couple more seconds to prime the charge, and then he pulled the igniter and we started moving back.

*Well* back. We moved clear to the corner, though I turned and popped around to make sure we weren't about to get shot in the back before we took cover. We didn't exactly have a bomb blanket with us, and who knew how much boom was behind that door. The rest of the team had moved to a covered position behind a container at the corner of the loading yard.

I just hoped that wasn't booby-trapped, too.

We'd barely gotten set when the breaching charge went. The sharp *crack* of the flex linear was almost immediately drowned out by the more considerable *boom* of the IEDs going off.

The entire building and the ground shook as the doors were ripped off their hinges with a flash and an ugly black cloud of smoke and debris. Fragments whickered past and tore through the cyclone fence.

Jordan and I were moving before the dust had settled. He's a little taller than I am, so he got to the breach a split second before I did, his rifle up in his shoulder, tracking through the smoke and dust. The rest of the team was right behind us, closing in from their shelter behind the container.

The entire doorway was just *gone*. I didn't know what kind of explosives they'd used, but the IED hadn't just taken the doors; it had taken out the frame and a good chunk of the cinderblocks around it. Footing was treacherous going in, but we got over the rubble and inside the opening, weapons up and tracking to clear our corners before we turned our attention and our muzzles toward the rest of the warehouse interior.

If we'd been expecting an open warehouse, or even the shelves that were more standard in working facilities, we were in for a surprise.

We were in a sort of entryway, maybe five meters deep. Facing us was an almost solid wall of cargo containers, stacked two high.

It had clearly taken a great deal of work to get them inside and lined up like that; there were two rollup doors in the walls to our right and left, but the arrangement would have required one hell of a crane and a lot of time.

The containers around us were scorched and riddled with holes. What looked like a dent had been hammered into one nearest the IED. There were no lights; our own IR weapon lights provided the only illumination, showing up starkly in the phosphor tubes of my NVGs.

Aside from the creaking and groaning of the structure in the aftermath of the explosions, there was no sound. It only made me more paranoid.

"Well, well," a voice crackled from a speaker somewhere nearby. I was somewhat proud of myself; I hadn't flinched, while Jordan had, his PDX twitching hard toward the sound, his finger awfully close to the trigger. "You must be somebody special. The average SWAT pigs would have been pink mist from the IED." The voice chuckled, though it was more of a high-pitched titter. "That's fine, though. I've got *plenty* of other surprises in here."

I was pretty sure the voice belonged to our target. The general cadence was right, though he'd used a voice distorter in all of his manifesto videos. He tried to lower his voice, but it sounded like he was about to cough. "Let's play a game!" He tittered again, and the speaker went dead.

None of us moved for a moment. My IR light shone down the narrow corridor between containers ahead, revealing only that the corridor turned sharply to the left only a few feet inside.

I moved forward carefully, trying to scan every inch of floor, wall, and ceiling before I passed it. Clearly, our target had expected company, and the IED at the entrance was only the beginning. And given what our intel had already told us about him, he was about as sadistic as he was clever.

Facing the mobs and bombs downtown might have been preferable to going into that warehouse.

Jordan started moving to join me, several steps later. Out of the corner of my eye, I thought I saw him shake himself, as if he'd been momentarily paralyzed until I started toward the corridor.

I didn't see any pressure plates or tripwires, or even any laser sensors. The fusion goggles should have picked anything like that up, though I was still a little nervous, just in case he was using some sort of new tech that I hadn't heard of before. Of course, I realized as I started toward the corner, anything he might be using that was that advanced would probably have been too fragile to withstand the blast when the IED at the doors went off.

I slowed as I neared the corner, though I wasn't exactly rushing before that. Part of me was thinking that if we'd been smart, we would have pulled off the target as soon as he started talking to us, but I also knew that we probably weren't going to get another chance.

And as long as he thought he was safe in his little web, he wasn't running.

Easing around the corner, I flashed my IR light down the passage ahead. It was almost as short, terminating in another

103

corner. The part that raised my hackles was that the passage was formed by another container, rather than a gap between containers. The opening ahead gaped like a maw, and I really didn't want to go in there. But that was the only route toward our quarry.

That alone was dangerous. This guy had clearly set this up, *expecting* us to come for him. Or at least he'd been expecting *somebody* to come for him. This felt like sticking my head into a lion's mouth.

But short of calling in an airstrike on the warehouse— which wasn't exactly an option; never mind the fact that we really *did* have the capability, Colonel Santiago wasn't ready to let the country at large know that yet—we didn't have an option. This guy had to go down, and that meant going into the spider's parlor.

So, I moved in, stepping around the corner, my muzzle tracking across the opening as I cleared the threshold.

The container ahead of me was empty and dark, except for the camera mounted in the corner ahead. Its red light glowed balefully, as if to remind us that we were being watched. I was sorely tempted to put a bullet in it, but I didn't think that was going to do much good. He knew we were there, and even if we wrecked every camera we saw, he was going to be able to track us by following the cameras going dark.

I slid closer to the far wall, giving Jordan space behind and beside me to get his own weapon into the fight, while giving me a bit better angle on the next turn ahead. I glided forward, my footsteps ringing on the metal floor beneath me. Jordan moved up with me, and we closed on the next corner, Phil and Dwight behind us.

I was just short of the corner when I heard Dwight snarl a particularly vile curse behind me, and then somebody slammed into me from behind. I lurched forward, into the corner, throwing my foot forward to try to catch myself as I swung my PDX toward the opening passage ahead. A moment later, the container rang with an earsplitting *bang*.

Even as I was thrown into the L-shaped intersection, I saw movement ahead and snapped my weapon toward it as I hit the far wall just under the camera. The impact was jarring, but it probably saved my life.

If the noise a moment before had been bad, the shotgun blast in that enclosed space was like getting slapped in the face with a Mack truck. The thunder was a physical force that rattled my brains, and I could *feel* the buckshot as it whipped past my shoulder and slammed into the wall behind me. The range was so short that the *crack* of the impact was lost in the bone-shaking report of the shot.

I had my IR light on, tracking my weapon toward the muzzle flash, but there was no target there. I was on the verge of panic as I dropped my muzzle, the circle of infrared illumination pinning the source of the shot in a circle of light gray in my fusion goggles a fraction of a second before my finger tightened the rest of the way on the trigger.

The *cracks* of 5.56 out of a short barrel didn't seem as loud as the shotgun blast had been, but that might just have been because my hearing had already been deadened by the catastrophic noise.

The bullets smashed into the small, six-wheeled vehicle squatting in the center of the passageway, shattering plastic and throwing the glorified remote-control car sideways. The short-barreled shotgun mounted to the top of the chassis pointed toward the wall as the impacts slewed the drone around.

Jordan moved up and kicked the thing over, then raised his own weapon to cover down the corridor again. "One-shot setup," he muttered. "Means there's more."

I glanced at the wreckage as I joined him, my heartbeat thudding in my ears and my palms sweating against my weapon. That had been way too close.

It didn't take a detailed study to see that Jordan was right. The shotgun had been a simple break-action, single-shot job, sawed off and affixed to the top of what might have started its life as a kid's toy, only with a complicated mount that had wires going into the action. It must have been reworked for electronic firing.

"Lucky," the target's voice said from hidden speakers. "Don't worry; I've got plenty more of those. And some other surprises, too. This is going to be fun."

"He sure sounds confident," I growled.

"No reason why he shouldn't be," Phil said, sounding more rattled than I'd ever heard him before. Phil was usually confident to the point of being obnoxious. "He's got us right where he wants us."

I glanced back at that, since Jordan had the forward area covered. That was when I saw what that initial *bang* had been.

A door, or barrier, had been affixed to the ceiling as we'd come in. Once the four of us had penetrated a certain distance inside the container, it had fallen like a mousetrap, and was now blocking our way out. It had also cut Scott and Greg off.

"Weeb, Deacon," I called.

"We're okay, Deacon," Scott replied. "It's going to take some doing to get through this, though."

"Do what you can," I said. "We're going to push on." I still had four shooters, and in those close quarters, that might be enough. Especially if the target was going to actively try to take us out, staying put was not going to be a good idea. "If you can't breach it, let me know before you pull off, so we can find another way out."

"Roger," he replied.

If we hadn't been committed before, we sure were now. There was no way out but through.

"Hold what you've got for a second, Jordan," I said. We needed to reassess real quick. Close quarters combat usually called for speed, surprise, and violence of action, but this wasn't your usual hit. We were in a maze, and there were going to be more booby traps and ambushes ahead of us. If we just pushed the fight, we were going to get slaughtered.

"This is going to slow us down, but we've got no choice," I said. "Keep close, watch your step. Check everything before you move forward into an area that hasn't been cleared. There could be pressure plates, IR lasers, tripwires, you name it." I thought for a second. "You see a camera, you smash it. You see a motion sensor, shoot it. Every corner gets pied off before we go around it."

"This is high-tech Sangin, man," Dwight grumbled. "And we never really cleared that place out, either."

106

"This bastard's in here somewhere," I said, even as doubts started to rise in my mind. Was he? Or was this all an elaborate trap, and he was somewhere miles away, surrounded by monitors and computers, laughing his ass off? "Doesn't matter how many toys he's got; as long as we can get past 'em, we'll get him."

"Very confident," the voice said. I scanned the walls, but couldn't quite see where the speaker was. "We'll see how long that lasts." He sighed loudly, the noise scratching over the PA system. "This really is kind of inconvenient, you know. I'm trying to orchestrate some chaos elsewhere right now, and you're kind of disrupting my disruption." He tittered again. I was really starting to hate that sound.

Jordan hadn't taken his eyes or his muzzle off the next turn while I'd spoken. Stepping closer, I took my hand off my weapon just long enough to thump his shoulder. "With you."

He stepped out at an angle, keeping back from the corner itself and clearing down the corridor as he went. Together, we started down the narrow, darkened passage.

There was no light except for the occasional lurid red glow from one of the cameras, that seemed to be mounted *everywhere*. I found myself wondering just how long it had taken the target to set this up, and how much it had cost. Of course, like most of the PRA, he was filthy rich, so the cost probably hadn't mattered that much to him. Presuming he hadn't simply stolen the funds or gotten the materials through cyber fraud. All of which were strong possibilities.

As we neared the next turn, I got closer to the camera mounted on the wall and lifted my weapon to smash it. I hesitated for a second; what kind of booby traps and failsafes might the target have built into the cameras? His own little personal labyrinth was already dangerous enough.

But fearing a trap in every square inch of the place was just going to paralyze us. I lifted the PDX and smashed the buttstock into the camera's plastic casing, though not without wincing a little as I did so.

There was no explosion, no sudden electrocution, no poison gas leaking into the corridor. The casing cracked with the first blow, then shattered with the second, the light going out as the lens cracked in half.

Jordan waited for me to finish, keeping his weapon trained on the passage ahead, scanning ceiling, walls, and floors for anything out of place. Only when I came up and brushed against his shoulder with my elbow did he continue forward.

There was a four-way intersection ahead, and he slowed further. Decision time.

I was trying to map out the maze in my head. I generally have a pretty good sense of direction, but being in this man-made dungeon made it hard to keep my bearings. I thought that we were still heading roughly toward the back of the warehouse, if slightly offset from the center.

"Push forward," I murmured. Jordan didn't say anything, but as he got to the intersection, he started moving through it, covering down on the right-hand passage as he passed it. I followed, the two of us almost side-by-side as we crossed the opening, only I pivoted to cover down the left-hand passage as I went. It was dark and empty, terminating less than ten feet away with another T-intersection.

We had just gotten across when a trap door in the ceiling ahead swung open and something dropped out.

I don't know what prompted me to do it. But I grabbed Jordan and threw myself down at the deck, dragging him with me, just before the little quad-rotor drone hovering at eye level blew up.

The *bang* reverberated down the metal corridors, and fragments sleeted through the air overhead. I felt a sting on the back of my neck, just as Jordan and I hit the floor with bruising impact. It knocked some of the wind out of me, and I was pretty sure I was bleeding, but I was still alive. The frag must have been somewhat directional; he was probably hoping to take somebody's head off with the drone.

Given that this was the guy who had chopped up a cop's family to make a statement, that kind of fit his character.

I lifted my head and my weapon, in case he had some other nasty surprise coming in the wake of the exploding quad-rotor. For the moment, it was clear.

"Everybody good?" I asked, raising my voice past the ringing in my ears. I wanted to look behind me to see if Dwight and Phil were still breathing, but I'd taken the corridor, and giving it up to look behind me might be a very bad idea.

"We're alive," Phil replied, though he sounded a little pained.

Jordan grunted as he pushed himself to his feet, getting his weapon up. He was fine; Jordan might have had a fifty-ton chip on his shoulder most of the time, but he'd been a Special Forces Medic. If he'd been badly hurt enough to need treatment, Jordan would have said so.

I got to my feet, keeping my weapon up and trained down the corridor. The walls were pocked with fragmentation impacts, and there was smoke drifting in the air near the ceiling. A quick glance around confirmed the damage went all the way around the intersection; the target had had four of those damned things waiting.

Which probably meant that there were more.

"Keep moving," I said. I had a bad feeling that if we got bogged down too long, he was going to send more remote-control cars with shotguns, or something nastier, after us.

I wasn't wrong, either.

The ringing in my ears from the blasts meant that I didn't immediately hear the buzz of the drone rotors. But as Jordan and I pressed down the corridor ahead, our IR weapon lights splashing bright circles ahead in our NVGs, movement in the dark alerted me even before I caught the faint whirring whine.

I'd been halfway expecting another drone or two. Instead, it looked like a swarm of six or more coming around the corner, out of the dark.

By that time, I'd reached the conclusion that nothing in those corridors was going to be either human, or innocent. Movement meant it got shot. That was what gave me the momentary advantage that probably kept us all from getting turned into chunks.

My first shot smashed right through the first quad-rotor's vitals, killing the power and sending it flipping backward at the same time it started to drop. It struck the one behind it, sending it spinning into the wall as I transitioned to the next one. I was shooting fast, and it was moving, so the next round went through an armature, snapping one of the rotors off and sending the drone into a wobbling spin.

Then one of the ones in back detonated the small, boxy payload hanging beneath its fuselage.

The explosion slammed me back into the wall, and I thought I felt a rib crack just before I blacked out.

I came to crumpled against the wall. For a moment I couldn't see, and with something close to panic, I reached up, to find that my NVGs had just been knocked askew. They still worked, and with some adjustment, I could see the corridor again, cast in shades of gray and black.

I had no idea why we were still alive. My head throbbed, and as consciousness returned, along with a desperate urgency to get up, to get back in the fight, before another drone, or a PRA terrorist, came around that corner and finished me off.

It hurt to move. I tasted blood in my mouth, and when I tried to shove off the wall and get my feet under me, a stabbing pain in my side just about made me pass out again.

Groping around, I found my rifle, and, breathing and moving carefully, I got up on a knee. Smoke was still swirling in the air, and there was wreckage scattered across the floor; plastic crunched under my boot as I moved.

We were alone for the moment. I was briefly afraid that I had been the only one to survive, but then Dwight rolled over with a groan. Jordan was stirring. Only Phil was still motionless.

Scanning the corridor in front and behind us, I stepped over Jordan to check Phil. He was still breathing, if somewhat laboriously. I shook him slightly. We didn't have time to wait for him to come to on his own.

For a moment, I half expected the target to start cackling over the loudspeakers, but then I remembered that the blast had probably knocked out any cameras or speakers he had installed in that part of the maze.

Phil had fallen flat on his back. He squinted up at me, but his NVGs had been knocked off, so he couldn't see anything. "Easy," I whispered. Or tried to. My ears were ringing so bad, and my hearing was so deadened, that I could barely hear myself. "Easy," I repeated, somewhat more loudly. "Your NVGs are on the floor behind you."

He groped around for them, then pulled the skullcap over his head. Jordan and Dwight were back on their feet by then, and I held out my hand to help Phil up. He grabbed it and I hauled him upright.

"How are we still alive?" Jordan asked. His voice was slightly too loud, but to my brutalized ears, it still sounded like he was speaking underwater.

"Somebody's looking out for us," I replied. "Plus, I don't know how big those charges were, but I probably triggered the explosion farther out than they were supposed to go off." My head was pounding, and it hurt to breathe. "My guess is that he wasn't expecting us to be able to shoot the quad-rotors in the dark."

"Doesn't matter," Dwight growled. "Let's push and get this little bastard."

Nodding, I turned back toward the front, running my hand over my weapon, checking by feel for any damage that might have put it out of action. The NVGs didn't focus all that well at varying distances, and I didn't want to fiddle with them, particularly after that shock. I was just grateful they were still working.

Everything seemed to be fine. Hefting the SBR, I moved up next to Jordan, who was posted up on the corridor ahead, and clapped him on the shoulder.

He started forward, with my muzzle just over his shoulder. There wasn't a lot of space in that corridor, but we had to make do with what we had. Two guns were better than one.

The turn ahead, that I had thought was another right-hand corner, turned out to be a T-shaped intersection. Jordan paused just short of it, and I muttered—or tried to; my voice was louder than I wanted it to be—"Left."

That put me on point. I went left, while Jordan stepped to the right to cover my back. Soon I was moving to the next corner, with Phil right at my shoulder.

As we moved forward, stepping carefully and scanning for more booby traps, I started to think I was hearing a strange, buzzing, whining sound. It was getting louder as we moved forward, muffled by the ringing in my ears.

I took the corner and found myself facing a short, empty passage with yet another blind corner ahead. The whining was coming from around that corner.

Phil and I advanced on the corner, and I eased around it, leading with my weapon.

There was another six-wheeled drone on the floor, tipped over on its side, its wheels still spinning. This one didn't have a shotgun mounted on it, but what was there still made my blood run cold.

There was a bottle attached to a sprayer clipped to the top of the chassis, with wires running to what looked like a complicated mechanism to activate the sprayer. I didn't know what was in that bottle, but I doubted it was silly string.

The plan was clear. The exploding quad-rotors were supposed to incapacitate us, and then this thing was supposed to roll over and poison us to finish the job. He didn't risk too high-order an explosion so deep inside his lair, and still killed anyone coming for him. Except that his drone hadn't worked quite right, or hadn't had the right pathfinding.

I backed up. I didn't want to risk shooting that thing, because I didn't know what might spray out of the bottle if I did. "Backtrack," I said. "We'll take the other passage."

Jordan had turned to cover our six o'clock as soon as we'd stopped, so he simply waited for Dwight to tap him, and took point. That was why we trained to be able to fill any position in the stack. There were no set positions; you had to fill, flow, and go.

Having already cleared the passage, it was a short trip around, or it felt like it. We weren't letting our guard down and running through; the target's use of drones meant that he could be bringing all sorts of vicious little surprises up behind us.

We hooked around the corner on the far side from the tipped-over poison drone. I was still leery about it, even with the sprayer pointed away from us.

We'd reached the end of the line. The corridor we stood in simply connected the two passages we'd cleared, with a blank wall beyond. On the inside of the square was a door. Unless I missed my guess, we were at the far end of the warehouse. Unless he'd been *really* clever, there wasn't anywhere else he could hide. So Jordan stacked on the door, Dwight pushed past him and got into position near the door handle, and Phil and I got into place behind Jordan. The whole little dance took barely five seconds.

Dwight donkey-kicked the door. The jamb cracked and the door slammed inward. Jordan plunged through the gap, and Phil and I followed, our muzzles dropping level as we went through the opening.

The place was a den. The three of us filled the narrow entryway, which was strewn with cables and plastered with computer monitors. The floor was also almost ankle deep in trash, mostly soda cans and fast food wrappers.

There was just enough room in the small space for Jordan and me to advance on Thom Bevo with our weapons up. Phil had to step behind the two of us, his own weapon lifted toward the ceiling.

Bevo was sitting in front of a bank of laptops and monitors, his hands flying over the keys with a sort of frantic energy. He didn't turn to look at us as we stepped closer.

"Hands on your head, Bevo," I snarled. He just typed faster.

I got a glimpse of what he was typing, and altered the angle of my rifle slightly. I shot the laptop in front of him, the *snap* of the bullet passing by his ear making him flinch violently, possibly even more than the harsh, thunderous bark of the weapon's report in the small room in the first place. The screen was shattered by the impact, smoke curling from the jagged bullet hole in the LCD display.

"Let's finish this nice and quiet-like, shall we?" I rasped, as I took another step toward him, though not without taking a glance down at the floor to make sure I wasn't about to step on a pressure plate or something. Our profile on Bevo didn't suggest that he was hard-core enough to want to become a suicide bomber—he was more the type to manipulate other people to do that, often without ever meeting them in person. But it never paid to get complacent, especially not in this nightmare funhouse.

113

"It's too late," he said. His voice was nasal and high-pitched. He was skinnier than I'd expected, even given the profile we had on him. Still just as pale and pasty as I'd suspected he'd be, though. "I've already got bots spreading all sorts of inflammatory news about what's happening here across half the city. By the time they get here, my people will be ready to tear anybody who looks like a cop to pieces."

"Well, then," Jordan growled, "it's a good thing we're not cops, huh?"

Bevo turned around to face us. For a pencil-necked geek who specialized in spreading terror by technological proxy, he was remarkably calm when faced by three big, hard-faced men with weapons.

"You've already lost," he said, folding his arms across his chest. He wasn't an impressive specimen from the front, either; his chest seemed sunken, in keeping with his hunched shoulders. But he was still defiant, even looking down the muzzles of three 5.56 rifles. "I don't know where you think you're taking me, but if you were going to kill me, you'd already have done it when you came through that door." His voice did falter slightly when he'd said "kill," and in that instant, some of his façade slipped, ever so little. He was still desperate.

It didn't change the fact that we were still going to have to get out of there with him intact. "You can't stop what's started. The Revolution is here. You can't put the genie back in the bottle." He looked at Jordan. "You can get with the future, or you can be stepped on. That's the truth of it."

"That's the same thing every mass-murdering piece of shit like you has said for the last hundred years," Jordan replied. He stepped forward suddenly, and Bevo flinched backward but couldn't avoid Jordan's darting hand. An ebony fist knotted itself in Bevo's shirt and Jordan hauled him bodily out of his expensive computer chair and slammed him on his face on the floor. "It was bad enough fighting assholes like you in Africa and the Middle East," he said. "Fuck you for bringing this home."

Jordan wasn't gentle as he dropped a knee onto Bevo's back and hastily zip-tied his hands. "Now shut up or I'll tape your damn mouth shut," he snapped. Apparently, Bevo had either had the wind knocked out of him, or he believed that Jordan would do it. He didn't do much more than moan.

I had stepped back, letting Phil and Jordan handle Bevo. I keyed my radio. "Peanut, Deacon. Target secured; we're coming out. Be advised, more opposition is expected from outside in the next few minutes."

"Roger," Dave replied. "We'll be out front in thirty seconds. And we've got some surprises waiting for anybody wanting to crash the party already. We needed to move, anyway, so we've been circling the block."

I grinned tightly as I looked down at Bevo. He might have expected otherwise, but we'd had contingency plans for mobs. "Weeb, Deacon," I called.

"This is Weeb," Scott replied. "We're through the mousetrap. You can come out."

"Roger that," I answered. I looked around at the rest. "All right," I said. "You heard the man. Let's go."

Jordan hauled Bevo to his feet, thrusting an arm between his flex-cuffed arms and up onto his shoulder, while the other held his weapon ready. He had complete control and could move Bevo wherever he needed to.

Dwight led the way, retracing our steps around the opposite corner from the poison drone, which was still spinning its wheels. I didn't know if Bevo had set it up for bot control or remote, but if the latter, there was a switch still being pressed somewhere.

There is an old saying, "Speed is security." Dwight embraced it, dragging us through the dark, rapidly moving back through the corridors we'd cleared. With Bevo in tow, and presumably no longer in control of the traps, we could at least be somewhat confident that we weren't heading into any more pressure plates, tripwires, or motion sensors.

Of course, he could have failsafes set up, but if he really had mobilized the "revolutionary" mobs, we needed to get out fast.

Scott and Greg had pried the trap door open and Greg was holding it up over his head. We slipped through, Scott taking point, and then Greg let it drop with a resounding *clang* as he fell in behind Phil.

In what felt like a fraction of the time it had taken to navigate the labyrinth in the first place, we were back at the opening blasted in the front of the warehouse. The van was already outside, with Chris standing next to the open side door with his own PDX in his hands. What looked like smoke drifted in front of the headlights, but I caught a faint whiff of the acrid smell of tear gas.

"Let's go," Chris barked. As we came out and closed in, I could see his eyes watering slightly. So, one of our little surprise packages had already been triggered.

"He called in the mobs before we breached," I told Chris as I came to a halt beside him. Jordan pushed past us, shoving Bevo into the van. The murderous hacker had the good sense to keep his mouth shut. "The usual." We'd seen this sort of "crowdsourced" mob violence before.

"We know," Chris said. "Jubal's on it. He's muddying the waters as best he can." He pointed. "There was a bunch of about six coming down that alley, but they tripped one of the tear gas canisters we dropped. They didn't want to stick around after that."

I nodded to acknowledge both bits of information. Jubal was one of our best info-war guys. He had gotten pretty good at mirroring the "provocateur bots," and doing it in such a way to send the would-be rioters chasing their tails all over town. He could do it to the cops, too, if the situation warranted it.

Phil and Dwight rushed past us and into the back of the van, the shocks compressing noticeably when Dwight hit the floor. I clapped Chris on the shoulder. "We're up," I said. "Let's move."

He nodded and clambered into the passenger seat, while I followed Dwight inside the back and slid the door shut.

Moments later, we were leaving the smoke and fire behind. We'd gone into the spider's parlor, and, unlike the fly, we'd come out with the spider in our grasp.

116

# Blood on the Sand

## LawDog

I had just gotten laid when the son of a bitch tried to kill me.

Damn it.

It was one of those lovely Mediterranean nights on the northwest coast of Morocco, with a gentle breeze coming in from the Atlantic side of the Straits of Gibraltar to put a chokehold on the heat coming out of the Maghreb. I was full of a really good supper and a glass of wine. Her sweet perfume lingered, bringing a smile to my lips, when the elevator stopped at the 8th floor and a Berber got on.

He was from a deep-desert tribe, the skin of his hands roughened by the desert, a faint smell of smoke clinging to his *djellaba*, dark eyes intent in the depths of the hood.

It was the last part that saved my life. I had noticed that the robe was white with red stitching – not the brown of a bachelor male. I idly wondered what a married deep-desert man was doing in a very expensive Tangiers high-rise condo 300 miles from the desert, when the fact that he had the hood up smashed through my "Hail-fellow-well-met" mood like a rhino in combat boots.

I was coming off of my lean against the elevator wall when the glitter of the blade driving in at my abdomen – I never saw him draw it – sent my forebrain shrieking for the rafters, and my left forearm driving against his. As I evaded the thrust meant to eviscerate me, I unconsciously darted to my right, away from the blade I had parried to my left.

Unfortunately, I had never practiced "Getting Off The X" in an elevator, and I bounced off the control panel and into the son of a bitch. Usually you don't feel a stab, but I felt the sudden electric burn in the love handle on my left side. As I slapped at it, my left hand grabbed his wrist, immediately followed by my right hand, holding his forearm like a baseball bat. I locked out my arms, pushing the blade out of my side, keeping that length of steel away from my tender pink hide, driving my forehead into the hollow between his chin and collarbone, and used my legs to push the shorter, lighter man into the other wall of the elevator as hard as I could.

He grunted as we hit, and I felt him punch at my head with his left fist, but all he got was my shoulder and back, and as I concentrated on driving his knife arm away from his body I felt his hand sliding along my face, going for my right eye. I risked letting go with my right hand to drive my right elbow into his jaw, and paid for it with another electric burn just below my breastbone as his jaw snapped shut and he went – just for a second – boneless.

It was enough. I grabbed the back of the blade, drove my knee into his wrist, pulled/twisted – and then I was the one with the knife. He tried. He really did, but as he grabbed for my wrist, I drove the top of my head into his jaw using my legs, and when he went wobbly, I went full Singer Sewing Machine.

He gave one convulsive shove, and I was off-balance enough that it sent me into the far wall of the elevator. Then it was over as I watched him die.

The 'Ding!' of the elevator door opening yanked me out of his eyes; I took a deep breath, and darted into the lobby, crouched, knife low, expecting to see his buddies, but the lobby was empty.

Warm sloshy wet in my underwear region drew my attention to my unknown assailant's handiwork. The laceration across my abdomen looked nasty, but what worried me was the through-and-through puncture just below my left floating ribs, which was leaking through my tailored silk shirt every time I moved. I tucked the knife into the belt in the small of my back, and buttoned the dark blazer all the way, hoping it would cover the blood, then staggered out into the Tangiers night, looking for a taxi, the adrenaline making me mutter darkly about my ruined silk shirt.

***

Two hours later, after a quick story about an unfortunate scooter crash, numerous shots, and a politely disbelieving eyebrow from the doctor packing the puncture and stapling the laceration, I was pulling on my stiffening blazer when a man who could have been Jean Reno's bigger brother ambled into the room, and perched a haunch on the counter.

*Fuck,* I thought to myself, *Secret Police. Just fucking great.*

"Well, Scooter," he said, in an accent right out of Georgetown, "You've had an interesting night."

I paused, my own eyebrow climbing towards my hairline, "US Embassy?"

He grinned, "Oh, no. Private citizen," he held out a hand, "I'm Bob. Good to meet you."

I looked at his hand, shrugged, and tried to get my right arm into the blazer without pulling anything loose, "No offense, Robert, but I've got a roast in the oven, and a new Vespa to buy, so if you don't mind …"

He held up a hand, "Your dancing partner is in the bay. The elevator is clean, too." He snickered, "Vespa."

My hand slid under the sheet on the bed where I had hidden the knife, and I tried to loosen my shoulders without looking like I was, "Do I know you?"

"We've met. A long time ago. You wouldn't remember me." His other hand came up beside the first one, and he showed me the palms, and the backs. This was supposed to relax me, but fat chance of that. "I'd like to apologize for all of this." He gestured at my midsection. "That's kind of our fault."

I felt my eyes narrow, and he made the *calm, calm* gesture with his hands. I wondered if he's actually spent that much time in the Maghreb, or if he was just pulling my leg, as he went off on a non-sequitur: "You been following recent events lately?"

"The world is about to go south. Just like the world is always about to go south. Just like the world has been going south my entire life. What's that got to do with the price of tea in China?"

119

"Funny you should mention that." He didn't look amused. "China is about to go hot. One month, two at the outset, and the States will be at war with the People's Republic of China."

I felt a chill that had nothing to do with the anesthetic crawl up my spine. I'd heard whispers … "So?"

"There's a group of folks who think that maybe the little yellow bastards shouldn't win. However, we don't have the blessing of a government, or the budget of a government, so we're kind of having to wing this one."

I made a rolling gesture with my hand. He grinned, again, teeth bright against a dark face, and pointed, "What's 40 klicks east of here?"

I blinked, "What?"

"Tangiers-Med. Not only a deep-water port, but the largest port, period, in all of Africa; with Beijing pretty much the quiet majority holders."

"Ok?"

"Of all the resources and assets held by the Chinese on the Western coast of Africa, what percentage passes through Tangiers-Med on the way to the Suez Canal and home? Resources, I add, that would be vital to any sort of war effort?"

Oh.

"If you ask our little yellow buddies the unofficial official word is 40%." He clenched a fist, "We estimate that the actual number is closer to 90% of West African resources passing through that port. 95% of Nigeria's petroleum output. Iron and titanium from Sierra Leone. Cobalt, zinc, and copper from the Congo and Eritrea. And that's the start."

"Interesting," I said, as a suspicion began to flower in the pit of my stomach, "But what's that got to do with me?"

"We suspect that some mid-level functionary in the Ministry of State Security is bucking for a promotion, and fingered you for a slam order. We figured that he decided that a retired US Diplomatic Security Service agent, who cut his teeth on the 'muscular diplomacy' of the Reagan and Bush years, and spent his entire, short career banging around the Mediterranean basin might get a case of the hips towards Beijing once the bangs start going off."

120

Crap.

"Now, although we didn't run you out there as a stalking horse, while the little yellow bastards are chasing you around, they're not looking for us. And anything we do will get blamed on you." Again with the grin. "Sorry about that."

"No, you're not. What am I supposed to do?"

"The pool is strongly on you disappearing, and the Chinese spending a shit-ton of money trying to find you. Your little playmate was publicly put on a plane to New York just now, by the way. The guy who bought the ticket happened to leave a US Embassy card. And your medical bill was paid in good American dollars."

I looked at him, as he smugly unwrapped a stick of gum, thought firmly about the knife by my fingertips, and sighed, "That's it?"

He popped the gum into his mouth, "Pretty much. Good luck. Have fun."

I snorted, "The pool is on disappearing, huh. Which way did you put your money?"

He smiled while chewing, eyes crinkling, "Our Communist buddies are going to find their dead hitman come sunup." He opened the door to the cubicle, paused on the way through, "You might want to scoot."

***

Every decent sized city in Africa has a gentleman whose official business is selling mobile phones. Used to be jewelry and gems, or carpets, but these days it's phones. Unofficially his job is information, services, and privacy. In Tangiers you're looking for Suleiman bin Suleiman in the *medina*.

As daylight peeked, I sat in a small coffee shop just inside the wall that separates the *medina* from the newer parts of Tangiers, sipping Moroccan coffee thick with cinnamon, cardamom, and milk, trying to pretend that the feelings in my stomach were butterflies and not something worse.

Across the narrow street sat Suleiman and Sons Carpets, Jewelry and Phones, its narrow entrance set way back under cover from the sun, colorful carpets swaying gently in the morning breeze. One of his sons had come out and raised the ordnance-

121

quality crash gate that protected the front of the shop at the sound of the *muezzin* calling the Faithful to prayer just before sunrise, but I waited until a European couple entered the shop and left, the woman exclaiming over a piece of jewelry, snuggling closely against the arm of her husband.

I drained the dregs of the coffee, stood up, nodded to the proprietor and ambled across the street, just another European tourist. Even this early in the morning, the difference between the muggy heat outside and the coolness inside the shop was shocking.

Behind the counter, Suleiman bin Suleiman smiled genially at me, a portly Jewish gentleman who looked more like Santa Claus than someone whose family had been, he had told me over wine and *tagine* one evening long ago, providing gray and black market services to those in need of such since before the Roman Empire had moved in. Something he still took personally.

"Greetings, my friend," He boomed at me, "How may this humble shopkeeper be of assistance?"

I nodded heavily at him – as close as my stiff neck came to a bow – and murmured gently, "My friend, I have a gentleman's need of discretion."

"Ah!" so saying, he lifted a section of countertop and bowed me through. Gesturing to one of his innumerable sons and nephews, he led me through a curtain and into a room in the back of the store, and waved me towards a comfortable pile of probably priceless rugs. I sat, cross-legged, sideways to him with a low table beside us. A much younger male relative came in carrying a tray with tea and dates. I watched quietly as Suleiman poured two cups of tea, chose one. I waited courteously as he took a sip of his own, selected a date, and bit into it.

I sipped at my cup and made appreciative noises until he set his aside, fixed me with serious brown eyes, and rumbled, "So, my friend. The desert and the *medina*, they bring me news of my friend, Jackson, son of Raymond."

I bit into a sweet desert date, and cocked an eyebrow at him, "Is this so? What do the sands and the Old City have to say about me?"

He sipped, "I am told that the children of the Middle Kingdom have taken an interest in my friend."

"Oh. It is a pity, then, that I have decided to take a holiday far away, and will not be available to talk to them."

"And you come to Suleiman for assistance in your travel affairs? You are wise. How may this humble servant assist your travels?"

"A ticket, my old friend, quietly, to Marseille; and my safe box."

He regarded me levelly, as he rung a small bell. The kid who brought the tray padded in, and Suleiman whispered to him, sending him off.

"I have a friend with a yacht, who owes me favors. I think a relaxing fishing trip from here to Tunis would be an excellent way for one such as yourself to start a holiday. Once in Tunis, I am sure a ticket will be waiting for you at the airport."

The boy brought in an iron lockbox, probably older than me, and set it on the table between us. Suleiman reached into a drawer under the table, pulled out a key, opened the box and turned it to face me.

Inside were my spare passports, money in various denominations, two pistols, and a small metal cylinder, anodized red, with a caduceus engraved on the side. I reached in for the money, and found myself picking up the Walther .22.

On one hand, if I cut and ran to France, I'd be safe in a beach villa somewhere with warm water, warmer women, cool evenings; the Chinese none the wiser. On the other hand, Europe was on fire, and while the ancient port cities had operated under their own rules for more than one empire and countless conflicts, if the Chinese were about to kick-off a hot war, things might be more spicy in my old haunts than I might like.

On the gripping hand: my left hand traced the line of staples across my abdomen. Those motherfucking Mongolian mud-pimps had royally fucked what had been a really good evening.

I looked across the table into the wise eyes of Suleiman bin Suleiman. He slowly grinned.

Ah, hell.

***

Ten days later I sat at a coffee shop catty-cornered across the street from the Lux Mall, just after noon in the full humid glory of the day, sipping spiced coffee and watching a white Range Rover SUV parked down the street. The driver leaned against the fender and chain-smoked Turkish cigarettes. Nasty habit.

The Range Rover actually belonged to a non-Chinese shipping consortium whose very Chinese employees did the lion's share of business on behalf of the People's Republic of China in Tangiers. Today it was the assigned transport for one Shi Zhaohui, whose official job title was Assistant Paymaster. While not as glamorous a job as his boss, Shi Zhaohui was the guy who kept track of bribes paid, bribes owed, who got the bribes, when the bribes were due, and other payment services of the type that don't usually appear on the corporate yearly Profit/Loss statements. One of those things was probably "Assassins Hired", but that wasn't why I had a case of the ass at him today. No, Shi was about to Have A Very Bad Day because he seemed to be the kind of guy who 1) Probably didn't keep records in writing; B) Wouldn't help business efficiency if he Went Away; and iii) Probably couldn't be replaced all that quickly or cleanly.

I took another sip of coffee, reached into my pocket and pulled out a keyring with a red pill box hanging next to some random house key. Smiling at the waiter, drowsing against the bar, I unscrewed the lid, and dumped three gel capsules into my hand. I knocked one of the pills back and washed it down with a slug of coffee, glancing at the kid bussing tables. As I looked, he turned a fan more towards him, waving a sheaf of napkins at his face in an effort to cool off.

Under this cover, I popped the other two capsules between my thumb and forefinger, emptying the contents into the cylinder, then screwing the lid firmly shut. Holding the pill container in my left hand in my lap, I licked my thumb and forefinger. Mm. Krill. Yack. I reached back down, took hold of the part that connected the bottle to the keychain and unscrewed the connection, revealing a threaded hole that – coincidentally – matched the thread on the extended barrel of my Walther TPH. Covered by the table, I pulled the tiny pistol out of my robe, and attached the silencer.

It's another ten minutes or so of coffee sipping before the guy standing beside the Range Rover abruptly fumbled with his pocket and brought out a cellphone. As he answered, his upper body rocked a couple of times, and he dropped his cigarette to the street.

Ah-hah. Batter up. I sat the coffee down, grabbed the white paper sack of *m'hanncha* pastries and set it in my lap, then reached up to adjust the face covering of my *shemagh*. I stood and started across the street, deserted in the heat of the day, to the Lux; pistol in my right hand inside the sack, thumb clamping the small white sack against the slide of the pistol, just one more local on the way home with sweet pastries for his wife.

A couple of seconds after I got onto the sidewalk, the Range Rover pulled into a diagonal parking spot in front of the high-toned luxury shopping plaza, between a white Rolls Royce Corniche and a beige Mercedes GLA. *Perfect,* I thought, as Shi Zhaohui and a shorter, rough-looking dude, stepped out of the mall and strolled along the sidewalk to the car. Rough Dude was the bodyguard, and since Zhaohui was carrying the sacks, probably a pretty good one who knew better than to let the principal bully him into carrying the junk.

But he wasn't that good. I waited a breath after they disappeared between the two vehicles, and stepped around the front of the Mercedes, thumb releasing the bag of pastries, Walther coming up to eye level, and he made one of the classic fuck-ups: he let himself believe that where he'd just been was safe. His back was to me as he held open the door of the Range Rover for his principal, and I put two .22 Long Rifle solids into the base of his skull.

Still moving forward as he dropped, I tracked the sight a skosh left, catching the puzzled left eye of Shi Zhaohui, trying to figure out what was happening, until two rounds into that eye dropped him. Another step, I swung the pistol to my left, left hand meeting right, and the two final rounds went through the open window and into the driver's ear canal.

I looked around, left hand going into the pocket of my robe, coming up with the spare magazine, left thumb hitting the magazine release at the base of the grip, slapping the replacement

125

home, then over the top of the pistol to cycle the slide. As to be expected, anyone awake at that time of the day was either inside under air conditioning, or dozing somewhere in the shade, so I didn't expect witnesses, but it never hurts to check. I smacked two more rounds into the driver and the bodyguard – always pay the insurance -- the pistol went into my robe pocket, and I dropped to a knee, turning Zhaohui over, bringing out the distinctive Berber knife that someone tried to kill me with earlier, and ice-picked the blade into his open mouth as hard as I could, leaving it there.

Taking a deep breath, the smell of fish oil and unburnt powder from the silencer mixing unpleasantly with the normal smells of violent death, I stood up, straightened the *djellaba*, and tried to nonchalantly amble towards the door of the Lux Mall. Not as easy as you would think, post-murder, but easier under the desert robe, with a *shemagh* and dark glasses covering my face. I shouldn't have worried – no one in the luxury shopping mall looked askance at another Berber wandering through, especially not when I turned down the service hall to the restrooms.

Halfway down the hall I paused beside a door and looked both ways. No one coming, and no surveillance cameras. I slid a plastic card out of my pocket and shimmed the door, slipped into the mop closet and closed the door firmly but quietly behind me. The people who shop at this kind of place don't believe that cleaning people exist, so anyone who would be bothered to walk in on me wouldn't be in until after the mall closed.

The *shemagh* went into the mop sink first, followed by the *djellaba* and the slippers. Under the robe I wore the standard uniform of Tourist (European, One Each) of tan linen slacks and white button-up shirt. I unscrewed the silencer, wiped it, the pistol, and both magazines thoroughly with the cloth of the robe, and dropped them all onto the pile. I untied the desert boots from my belt and slipped them on, eyes scanning the shelves.

Once the shoes were on, I took two bottles of chlorine bleach, poured both over the pile of clothes and murder tools, turned the faucet on "Low", and let the water gradually fill to the over-flow slot.

I went to the door, opened it, checked for pedestrians, and pulled the door firmly locked behind me as I strolled down the hall to the restroom, where I washed my hands a couple of times, trying to get the shaking to stop as I dried them. I donned a star-struck expression as I went into the main mall, pretended to window-shop, bought an over-priced straw hat and left the mall through the doors on the opposite side from my crime scene.

Hailing a taxi, I went to the train station, grabbed the carry-on luggage I had previously stashed in a locker, and took another taxi to a popular tourist hotel, checked in using a bogus British passport, then sat in a chair in my room and tried not to shake until sleep snuck up on me sometime just before dawn.

The afternoon call to prayer woke me with a start. I halfway expected shadowy figures in the room with me, but I was alone. I staggered into the bathroom and took a much too long hot shower, before taking a taxi to Old Town.

Suleiman bin Suleiman looked even graver than normal, and I paused, scanning the shop for anyone looking official or thuggish. Other than two of his sons, we were alone, and Suleiman raised a hand to me before lifting the counter and ushering me to the back room. The tea was poured, sipped, the dates nibbled, before he looked at me with sad brown eyes, "My friend, have you heard of the news?"

Feeling a bit twitchy, I responded, "I have heard that a shipping company has suffered a loss …"

He waved a hand, a copper bracelet marked with Hebrew letters sliding along the skin. That was new. "Yes, that, too. No, Jackson, son of Raymond, I speak of the tragedy after *Isha* prayer, when helicopters struck a Berber camp in the desert."

I blinked, "What?"

"The desert whispers that the children of the Middle Kingdom have become displeased with a tribe of Berbers with whom they enjoyed a brief alliance. The tribe was chastised in the night."

I took a slow breath in through my nose, and out through my mouth, "I grieve for those whom the Amazighs lost. It is a terrible thing."

Suleiman bin Suleiman looked at a fig, eyes distant. I cleared my throat, gently, "However, my friend, I wish to speak

127

with you about my holiday. I have decided that Rome would be comfortable this time of year."

His eyes didn't stray from the fig, and his voice was very soft, "They used phosphorous."

When I was getting paychecks from Foggy Bottom, I had toured sites where white phosphorous had been used, usually against civilians. The smells and the horror frequently showed up in my nightmares. After a moment I opened my eyes; and across the table, Suleiman was looking at my hands. He glanced up at my face, and I saw a decision flash across his tired eyes. I looked at my hands, and was mildly surprised to see that both knuckles were bone-white from the clenching. A deep breath, and I consciously relaxed, wiggling my fingers.

The kid had appeared, Suleiman whispered quietly and shooed him away, "My friend, I have a favor to ask."

I paused in mid sip, cocking an eyebrow at him.

"I have old clients who have come to me seeking advice. They have a problem which requires the counsel of one who is wise to the world, but is young enough that his blood burns. I merely ask that you listen to their problem, give your thoughts, and your humble servant will have you on your way to Rome. Nothing more."

I found myself running my fingers along the pile of the carpet I'm sitting on. It was soft, and felt good. I looked at Suleiman, took a deep breath, and nodded once. He nodded in return, and rung that bell. At the sound, one of his elder sons brought in two men. Deep desert, if I had any guess, but the smell of campfires clinging to their clothing had an ... odd, almost industrial smell. They're brothers, I thought, or some close kin. Hard to tell with the ... and I realized that I had seen their eyes before. In a younger face, on an elevator. I had watched the light fade from identical eyes.

Crap. I tried to relax, mind racing, as two kids brought in a low, wide round table and set it in the middle of the four of us; placed a tea set, along with a tray of *m'hanncha* on the top before scuttling out the door. Murmuring soft pleasantries, Suleiman poured four cups of the strong Moroccan tea, and allowed the two kinsman to pick their cups; I grabbed one of the remaining two

128

cups at random, he raised the last to his lips and took a slow sip. In turn, I took a sip, for once not noticing the super-sweetness, and the two guests took polite sips of their cups.

Suleiman broke a section of the outer ring off of the pastry and bit into it delicately; normally the filo pastry stuffed with almond paste was one of my favorites, but this time I barely tasted it, as I tried to figure out how Suleiman and his family would react if I had to kill one of his guests. Both of the tribesmen also seemed to have something on their minds, as they took enough of a bite to satisfy courtesy, no more.

Suleiman bin Suleiman dusted powdered sugar off of his hands and cleared his throat. Addressing the men across the table, he murmured, "Here is the man of whom I spoke."

Choosing my words carefully, "My old friend, there are issues …"

"We know who you are." The younger Berber's English had an American flow to it. Either the internet, or some study Stateside, I guessed, "We know what you did." He turned his upper body to the right, towards the desert, and raised his hands, palms open and out, "I swear on the heads of my sons that we have no quarrel with you."

I blinked; beside me, Suleiman did the same.

The older Berber took his tea-cup in both hands, raised it in my direction, and took a ceremonial sip, "You have given no offense, Jackson bin Raymond, this I swear. Will you listen to our plea?"

His English was a little rougher than the younger guy, and more British accented. I looked at them for a moment, raised my teacup for a sip, set the cup on the table, and made a palm-up gesture.

"Our brother took gold from the Chin. Our brother, not us," the younger man's voice had the toneless metallic cadence of someone trying to keep his emotions under tight wrap, "He did not succeed in his task," Both of them nodded in my direction, short, sharp nods, "This happens. You responded to the insult of the Chin by striking at them. This is proper." He paused for a deep breath, eyes sparkling with rage, "The Chin, instead of …" Another pause, and his brother rested his hand on his arm, and looked at

129

me. In his careful British-accented English: "The Chin do not hold our oath, do you understand? We have taken no gold from the Chin. Only our brother, who is dead, took gold. We did not. Do you understand? We have *nothing* with the Chin."

Younger brother snarled, throat tight, "They came in the night, and brought fire upon us from the sky. They sat in the sky, and rained down fire upon us, us who had done nothing to them! They brought fire to our women, and our children, and our possessions – for what?!"

He stopped, audibly grinding his teeth, and the brother faced me squarely, "You have been insulted by the Chin, and you answered them. Their insult to us *must be answered.* You understand this. You know the yellow man. Show us how to answer them in blood and fire."

I took a deep breath.

On one hand, this really wasn't my business, I like Rome, and even though Europe was half-a-step from Balkanizing completely, there was a pretty good chance I wouldn't get shot at there. On the other hand, if you're looking for a distraction, winding up a horde of berserk desert barbarians and turning them loose on a vendetta is a guaranteed distraction.

On the gripping hand: I could feel the baffled rage coming off of the kid; in my mind I could hear the thumps and hiss of white phosphorous rockets, and screams of children tearing across the still desert night.

Ah, hell.

***

It took a week and a half for Suleiman to get the information we needed, and another four days of simple simulations of what I needed the Amazighs to do. After ninety-six hours of repetitive drilling, I was fairly certain that at least half of the six two-man groups would probably get their jobs done without getting caught. Maybe.

I pointed, and the driver pulled the maroon panel van into a parking spot on an overlook commanding a view over the Atlantic off Cape Spartel. I had the passenger window open, enjoying the crash of the waves on the rocks, and drawing deep breaths of the cool, crisp sea breeze. The rocky limestone hills behind us were nicely lit by the full moon, and it looked to be a lovely night for an assassination. I grabbed the backpack sitting between the front seats, and grinned tightly at the driver. He grinned back, gold tooth glinting in the dome light, and we got out of the van; back doors opening to let the other four wiry tribesmen out.

It hadn't taken long to select targets that met with the Berbers' approval. Most of them were connected with Mayaguez Shipping and Logistics, Ltd, the most-definitely-not-Chinese shipping consortium whose entire upper command staff just happened to be Chinese nationals, and who just happened to have an influence at Tangiers-Med Port all out of proportion to the size of their company.

The one target not (openly) associated with Mayaguez S&L, Ltd, was currently inside a *riad*, about 300 yards up the hill from the road we were parked on.

I shrugged on the backpack, looked both ways along the road, not expecting to see anyone out at 4:00 AM, jogged across the road followed by my shaggy ducklings, and began the hike up the hillside towards the yet-unseen *riad.*

Fifteen wheezing minutes later, I was tucked behind a boulder beside the flagstone side road that led around the ancient Moroccan villa, eyeballing the front door. Typical of the kind, the *riad* was a broad two-story stone cube with the only windows showing on the second floor. Ground side, there was this door, a smaller one on the north side, and a three-car attached garage on the south side. On the top of that garage was a generator.

Slipping my backpack, I flipped open the top and pulled out a Czech 9mm submachine gun, twisted a silencer on the muzzle, inserted a magazine, and ran the bolt. My light jacket was dropped onto the backpack, revealing armor, and three more magazines went into the front of the armor carrier.

Around me, the tribesmen were doing the same, and then one of them looked at me expectantly. I nodded, and he shouldered his subgun, took a long time aiming at the electrical transformer on the pole down the street, and then the *blap* of the round was eclipsed by a God-awful electric buzzing and eye-searing blue arc.

The *riad* was currently being used for a romantic weekend getaway for the Junior Minister of Trade and Culture for the Chinese Mission to Morocco, one Bei Rui-gan and his Moroccan mistress. Since Junior Minister Bei was noted for being the only Chinese underling diplomat to have an office in Tangiers—three hours away from the Moroccan capital of Rabat—his cultural duties involved a great deal of time with the seedier and thuggier elements of Moroccan culture and no time at all with, you know, cultural things; and given that he ran around with a pack of Chinese knuckle-draggers who almost managed not to march in step, we figured him for the Ministry of State Security HMFIC in the area.

Goodness.

I counted slowly under my breath, and hit seventeen before the generator on the roof of the garage belched a cloud of black smoke, and then I was on my feet, sprinting for the front door before the raspy roar reached my ears.

Suleiman's coin to several cleaning people had revealed that our little yellow buddies had installed one hell of an advanced video surveillance set-up in the villa. Motion-sensors, infra-red, the whole enchilada, hooked up to a battery back-up that provided seamless, uninterrupted transition during the frequent power outages.

Unfortunately, the battery back-ups only powered the surveillance system. And nobody wants to cough up money for a getaway just to sit, baking in the dark. So, the owners of the *riad* had installed a very good generator. And when that very good generator kicked on, it inevitably hard-restarted the computer running the surveillance. Which meant the People's Liberation Army commo specialist running electronic security had to wait for the computer to restart, click on the system icons, and enter each password.

We had, I figured, about fifteen seconds, plus or minus fat-fingering the keyboard, before we showed up on multiple monitors in glorious Technicolor.

The door was a tall studded wood affair inside of the classic arched doorway, with an iron key-plate in the center of the right half, and I crouched to the left, stock extended on the little gun and tucked into my shoulder. Gold Tooth skidded to a stop just after I did, fumbled in his pocket for the key a whole bunch of Berber money had paid for. Waited, waited, before the door swung open, and I was inside a narrow, arched hallway. Nine quick steps, and the hallway gave way to the classic open center courtyard of a *riad*; white tile and paint glowing softly in the moonlight, blue accents drawing the eye to geometric patterns. A shallow fountain burbled happily in the center, and orange trees in full blossom scented the air with that distinctive jasmine/citrus/honey perfume.

There were intricately-painted doors into the courtyard on every wall, the second floor a covered walkway which extended the entire circuit, also with doors leading off into rooms, and I moved as fast as I dared to my first objective: a small door tucked behind the spiral staircase in the back right corner. The entire trip across the courtyard, my shoulder blades clenched at the amount of uncleared space behind me, expecting a shout, or a shot at any moment, and I was at the door. One quick breath, and I opened the door like I was good news.

Inside was a mass of computers and monitors, with a slender male sitting with his back to me, holding a cup of something hot with his left hand and typing on a keyboard with his right. Three *blaps*, and he wasn't typing anymore. Someone not Gold Tooth hurried past me, and started yanking power cords out of the wall, but that wasn't my issue as I slipped out the door and up the staircase, muzzle covering the door at the far end of the second floor. At the top, I paused, crouched, scanning as much of the periphery of the courtyard as I could, clear, I'm up and stalking down the walkway, footsteps muffled by the thick red and gold carpeting, Berbers breathing heavily, excitedly behind me.

Third door down, the intricate painting on its face of a garden absently noticed, I glanced behind me. Gold Tooth grinned at me, eyes wide in his face, two of his kin right behind him. Quick breath, he opened the door, and I buttonhooked into the room. The shaven-headed man punching the power button on the desk never knew what turfed him to hell, and I continued the pivot, hammering another guy mid-yawn sitting at a table in front of a suite of cards. Shouts came from behind a door on the back wall, and two Berbers went through, followed by the chatter of silenced 9mms.

Not my problem. I ripped the magazine out of my gun— I've no idea how many rounds I'd fired—jammed it into my back pocket, yanked a replacement off my vest, into the gun, chamber check, and then Gold Tooth and I slipped out the door, scanned the periphery, turned right, and moved as quickly as we could down to the door at the end of the hall. I heard sleepy noises downstairs as the house staff stirred.

I was almost at a sprint when I slammed my boot into the door just to the right of the lock, to reveal a huge bedroom. There was a feminine shriek altogether too close, I tracked the dot of my sight, came off the trigger when I saw the C cup rack, and darted right, trying to find a Chinese spymaster.

He solved the issue for me, with a muzzle flash from the howitzer in his right hand, I tracked the dot across his torso and he twisted slightly, I was driving the dot up to his face when the third muzzle flash out of that fucking sewer pipe in his hand cranked my sight down and to the left. Snarling in frustration I drove it back up, and he dropped out of my sight picture. Taking another step to the right, I found him lying on his side, his upper half on a priceless blue carpet, and I put an insurance round through his brain stem.

A deep breath and I scanned the room. Gold Tooth was covering the mistress, I noticed that my shins were cold and clammy, and there was an oily nausea feeling pooling up from the pit of my stomach. Shit, I got tagged. Right on top of the barely-healed stab wound. God damn it. I slid my left hand under the armor, and across the scar, looked at the fingers. No blood. God bless armor.

Taking deep breaths, the world started to come up to normal speed around me; I staggered over to the dead guy, and realized that he was wearing body armor, socks, and a grimace; the body armor having a nice three-shot group of my bullets dead center.

I swear to God, what kind of inconsiderate, paranoid bastard wears *body armor* on a romantic weekend with his mistress?! I slammed a vicious kick into his giggly bits. Honestly, some people don't have any couth.

"*Si?*"

Gold Tooth looked at me a little oddly, "Are you well, *Si?*"

I nodded. The brief spurt of anger had driven the nausea back down out of notice, and Gold Tooth smiled, apparently relieved, "It is good, *Si*. Come, we must go."

***

When the *muezzin* sounded the *Dhuhr* call to prayer, I was two alleys down from the shop of Suleiman bin Suleiman at a table under the shade of a fig tree, wolfing down chicken *tagine* and Moroccan bread served up by a tiny, smiling little old lady sitting behind a charcoal-fired oil drum stove. I wasn't particularly surprised when Bob Reno traded a handful of *dirhams* for a bowl of the stew, some bread and a glass of tea, brought them over and sat down across from me.

"Whoo," he said, spooning a chunk of preserved lemon into his mouth, chewing contentedly, "Tangiers is getting sporty these days."

"Do tell," I muttered, squidging a chunk of bread through the gravy. Heaven.

He grinned at me, "Berbers riding around on motor scooters, one driving and one firing a rocket launcher. And, boy howdy, do they have a case of the ass at Mayaguez Shipping and Logistics. Blew up their headquarters, the homes of the CEO, the COO, the security bunkhouse, and a couple of veeps."

I savored a sip of heavy, spiced milky coffee, and shrugged eloquently, "It's the desert sun. Drives them mad."

"Coincidentally, the same time the Berbers were going nuts with heavy ordnance, someone shot a Chinese diplo-schmuck and his security team to doll rags."

I grabbed up the last olive, chewed meditatively, and grunted.

He chortled happily, "Sweet Jesus cinnamon titties, Scooter, but you don't do things halfway, do you?"

"If you're going to be a boogeyman," I showed him my teeth, "Be a Bandersnatch."

135

More chortling, and he applied himself to the stew. I eyed my own bowl, considered licking it clean, and settled for leaning back in my seat and sipping my coffee.

Halfway through his bowl he opined, "Three different ships are in a holding pattern out in the Atlantic, because of this kerfuffle in Tangiers. A little birdie tells me that the investigation of all that restlessness is going to turn up some recent naughty behavior on the part of our little yellow dance partners that will embarrass His Majesty." The smile he gave was feral as all hell. "For the near future, the Royal Government of Morocco will make things difficult for Chinese shipping. Not impossible, but difficult."

I contemplated my coffee, "Near future, huh?"

He waggled a hand, "Beijing will publicly, and with great fanfare, arrest six or seven officials. A couple will wind up with their organs shrink-wrapped, the rest will be punted into a re-education camp. The trials will take less than six months, and things will improve in Tangiers-Med. Ish. Meanwhile, that's loads of cobalt, uranium, bauxite, crude oil – all the goodies that keep a modern Communist society on its feet – running weeks and months late."

He belched happily, and wiped his lips with a napkin, "And it's a big enough problem that Beijing is going to have to divert people and resources away running proxy wars in CONUS, to smoothing things over in Morocco. Damn fine work."

I shrugged, finished my coffee, and cocked an eyebrow at him, "You never did mention which way your money went regarding me vanishing."

"Scooter," he winked, "Pool isn't done yet. I will note, however, that my bourbon collection has become world-class." He fished in a pocket, slid a paper tube across the table to me. Krugerrands. A full tube of one-ounce gold coins. My other eyebrow headed for my hairline.

"While you and your desert buddies were getting your rave on, stuff may have been added to various Chinese property out at the port, and some things might have fallen out of shipping containers," he pointed at the roll, "Nine of his buddies were delivered to your carpet selling friend to hold for you."

"What are you trying to buy?"

"Buy? Nothing." He stood up, dusted off his hands, and turned to wander off down the alley, paused, "Most people could disappear like champs with that much money."

My voice was dry, "Most people?"

The grin was huge, "Good luck, Scooter. Have fun."

***

I nibbled on a chunk of *baklava*, sighed happily, and looked at Suleiman bin Suleiman, "My old friend, I think I have put off my holiday in Barcelona long enough."

He gave a benevolent Santa Claus smile, "As it so happens, I have a friend with a mistress in Gibraltar. He intends this very evening to pay her a long-overdue visit, and would welcome the company of a man with discretion and courtesy aboard his yacht for the trip. It is fate."

"Fate, indeed," another sip of the tea, "I think, my friend, that I will not need your assistance to get from the Rock to Barcelona. The Spanish countryside is lovely this time of year, and I will make my own way."

"As you wish." He sipped his tea, slowly, three times, "Before you go, there are some who wish to pay respect."

I gave Suleiman the hairy eyeball, but he imperturbably rang that damned bell, and one of his sons immediately bowed three people through the curtain. The first one was my buddy Gold Tooth, behind him was a gentleman old enough to be "distinguished," but young enough to be cornbread hell in a fight. From his silk suit, I guessed he was an elder in the tribe. Behind the men was a younger woman, I figured junior wife, or—based on the outfit—more probably a younger cousin.

The ritual drink and food was taken with a certain amount of cheer, and the elder fixed me with an assessing gaze, "Jackson, son of Raymond, you have our thanks for your assistance."

I almost said 'My pleasure' but that might be a little off, so I inclined my head, "Thanks are not necessary. I understand debt."

The gaze from the woman kneeling beside the elder was making me nervous for some reason, and I looked at Gold Tooth, "I am worried, my friend, to see you still in the *medina*. The police

137

will be annoyed, and I feel you should be far from this place, and quickly."

Gold Tooth snorted, eloquently, and the elder smiled, "There is a valley in the mountains, where the cool wind blows through the cedars, and the water runs cold. We have taken to the desert, and will meet there on the next full moon. Idrissa merely wished to make sure you were well before he left."

"Idrissa, friend, as you can see, I am well. How fare the others from last night?"

"Rahim and Issam fell at the shipping security compound. One of the dogs was lucky with rifle fire. We will bury them with their fathers."

Damn. I sighed, and thought of the weight of the gold coins in my pocket. Fuck.

"Were Rahim and Issam married?"

"Yes."

"Did they have sons to carry their names?"

"Issam does. Rahim has a daughter."

I placed two stacks of krugerrands on the table, three coins each. A year's salary in Morocco. "For the wives of Issam and Rahim, so that they do not have to take the first man to husband who offers."

The surprise from the Berbers was palpable. Beside me, Suleiman bin Suleiman grunted softly, approvingly. I put a single coin behind the second stack, "This is for the daughter of Rahim, to go to her bride-price when she is of age. I will not have her be embarrassed when she looks for a husband."

The woman nodded contemplatively. I look at the elder, "What is the name of the man I fought in the elevator?"

He looked at me for a long time. "Maleek."

A stack of three coins joined the first two, "For the widow of Maleek."

Another long look, and the elder nodded, stood up, and Idrissa swept the gold into his hands. Suleiman and I stood.

The elder nodded to my old friend, looked at me, "Suleiman, son of Suleiman knows of the valley of which I spoke. He can tell you how to get there."

I hoped my surprise wasn't visible, as the elder and Idrissa walked to the doorway, where they stood and talked softly.

I looked at the woman, she held out her hand to me, and I helped her to her feet. There was a lot of French in her gene pool.

"Tell me, Jackson, son of Raymond. Do you have sons?"

Her eyes were really big, and really blue. I smiled, gently, "No, Princess. I have nieces and nephews, but no children of my own."

"Ah. When you come to the valley, there will be good food, and laughter; the men will tell lies of their exploits, and I will dance for you."

"I'm afraid I must go into hiding from the Chin in Europe."

Her laughter was soft. She reached up and took a comb from her hair, put it in my hand, then walked to her kinsmen. She knew how to walk, that one, and she looked over her shoulder at me when she reached the curtain, "That's my favorite comb, Jackson, son of Raymond. Do not forget it when you come."

Then they were gone, Idrissa's gold tooth winked at me in a huge parting grin.

Suleiman gave me a benevolent uncle smile.

"Don't say anything."

The smile became a grin.

On one hand, I could disappear into Europe and no-one would shoot at me until those coins ran out. On the other hand, if China and America were really about to go at it, I could be a fairly significant pain in the ass in Morocco.

On the gripping hand: the comb was warm in my hand, and under the creamy scent of sandalwood, I could smell the perfume she wore in her hair.

Ah, hell.

139

# ACTApedia Entry – Chinese Liminal Warfare

## David Reeder

### China – United States Relations
*From ACTApedia, the other free encyclopedia. Publicare et Propagare*

*[This article needs to be **updated**. Please update this to reflect recent events or newly available information.]*

*This article is about relations between the United States and China, whose United Nations seat is occupied by the People's Republic of China. For relations between the Republic of China and the United States, see Taiwan–United States relations.*

China–United States relations (simplified Chinese: 中美关系; traditional Chinese: 中美關係; pinyin: Zhōngměi Guānxì), also known as U.S.–Chinese relations, Chinese–U.S. relations, or Sino-American relations, refers to relations between China and the United States since the 18th century. The relationship between the two countries has been, until recent years, quite strong, complex, and even somewhat positive in various respects.

The United States thinks of war as Tomahawk missile and Reaper strikes, special operations raids and the use of air power to destroy hostile targets. China considers such "kinetic" measures to be just one small part of warfare.

This is why so very few people in America recognize that while the US may not actually be "at war" with China, China has been very much at war with the United States since at least the late 90s. It is long term, liminal warfare to be sure, cloaked in economic deals and massive humanitarian expenditures all over the globe, but warfare it is: *liminal warfare.*

[Heightened Tensions and Liminal Warfare – Main Article: US-China Conflict]

Beijing strategizes long term, albeit not always effectively. Washington D.C. does so, at best, in eight year, two-election cycles.

Despite its inarguable size and strength, China has long known that despite the decreasing disparity in the two nation's military strengths, it would not fare well in a "shooting war" with the United States – certainly not an extended one. Indeed, the fact that Beijing holds over 30% of American national debt (over 1.5 trillion U.S. dollars) makes out-and-out open warfare extremely unlikely.

So, China wages war on multiple, frequently ambiguous, and plausibly (if just barely) deniable, levels.

> "It is becoming obsolete to automatically consider military action the dominant means and the other means supporting means in war . . . As the arena of war has expanded, encompassing the political, economic, diplomatic, cultural, and psychological spheres, in addition to the land, sea, air, space, and electronics spheres, the interactions among all factors have made it difficult for the military sphere to serve as the automatic dominant sphere in every war. War will be conducted in non-war spheres..." *Qiao and Wang, Unrestricted Warfare*

This particular manner of waging war, which has been used by the Chinese with varying degrees of success since men were wearing metal armor and killing each other with sharp objects, has been very effectively honed over the last three decades. The 11th century "Six Secret Teachings" counsels several ways to undermine a target nation through the corruption of its officials, leaders, and heroes. They call this the Civil Offensive.

As mentioned in *Unrestricted Warfare*, the very definition of "war", at least in Beijing's view, has changed. It is no longer "...using armed force to compel the enemy to submit to one's will", but rather "...using all means, including armed force or non-armed force, military and non-military, and lethal and non-lethal means to compel the enemy to accept one's interest".

Thus the Chinese use investment, financial disruption, currency manipulation, cyber warfare, ecological warfare (including wildfires and biological "interventions"), foreign assistance, humanitarian aid, and canny exploitation of crime (such as smuggling and narcotics trafficking) and the savvy use of black markets to augment traditional land-sea-air-space-cyber elements. Stock market crashes, infrastructure computer hacks, innuendo, and social media-fueled scandal may not be as obvious as the clatter of tank treads and the scream of jet engines, but they're no less effective when disrupting the solvency and stability of a nation.

These methods are not a substitute for armed conflict, whether traditional-conventional or asymmetric-SOF focused. They are simply, to the Chinese strategist, a logical (and pragmatic) extension of the norms of waging war.

The goal, as propounded by Qiao and Wang, is to use "...all means whatsoever—means that involve the force of arms and means that do not involve the force of arms, means that involve military power and means that do not involve military power, means that entail casualties and means that do not entail casualties—to force the enemy to serve one's own interests."

Note that *to serve one's own interests* is not necessarily the same as *to be victorious on a military battlefield*.

> "The fundamental difference between the Chinese and Western approach to strategy is that the Western approach is aimed at the capability of the other side; the Chinese is aimed at the psychology of the other side. So, they pay a lot of attention to intangibles of hospitality, forms of dealing with the interlocutor." *Henry Truman*

This is not to say China has not been developing and improving a traditional military – it has, particularly in a maritime capacity. China's borders are vast. It has more than 9,000 miles of coastline (and 14,000 miles of land border) along with one of the largest surface areas on the planet. To defend those borders, and to sustain the trade necessary to keep the largest population of any country in the world happy, is no easy task.

Security along its landward frontiers is less difficult than it shoreline. Formidable geographic barriers (consider the Central Asian desert and the virtually – militarily – impenetrable Himalayas) see to that. But its shoreline is less naturally well-endowed for defense, and its economy relies heavily upon maritime commerce.

In addition to building a blue water fleet to expand its ability to defend itself and, just as importantly, to project power into both the Pacific and Indian Oceans, Beijing has for many years been building areas of (seemingly) militarily innocuous strategic influence all over the globe.

Sun Tzu said, "Attaining one hundred victories in one hundred battles is not the pinnacle of excellence. Subjugating the enemy's army without fighting is the true pinnacle of excellence."

Chairman Mao later echoed this advice almost verbatim.

The famous Chinese strategist isn't the first to recommend such mechanisms for prevailing. The "Six Secret Teachings," which are believed to date from the 11th century B.C., include several points on undermining a target nation (in this case believed to be the Shang dynasty) through the corruption of its officials and leaders. It is referred to in the "Six Secret Teachings" as the "Civil Offensive."

**Warfare is the Way (Tao) of deception.**

China is *very* good at it.

> "The seemingly effortless defeat of Saddam Hussein's large, Soviet-style army by a numerically smaller but technologically much more advanced Western force had spooked Chinese planners, showing them the primacy of precision over mass. The unprecedentedly low American casualties and the almost unbelievable speed of the Iraqi collapse prompted debate within the Military Commission in Beijing and intense discussion in the war colleges.
>
> Chinese analysts were well aware that Iraqi forces had relied on a strategy of mass—using quantity to offset technological inferiority, much as China had done in Korea, India, and Vietnam—and had failed utterly. At the same time, Chinese technical intelligence officers, who had examined Iraqi tanks and aircraft captured by Iran during the Iran-Iraq War, were well aware that Saddam's military technology outclassed their own.

The two inescapable conclusions were, first, that China was at risk of attack by external aggressors now that the end of the Cold War had rendered it the sole remaining major Communist power and, second, that the PLA would be immensely outgunned in a future conflict.

Chinese military thinkers began focusing on a dual-track strategy of peaceful economic and political engagement with the West (seeking to postpone or entirely avoid any possible conflict) while simultaneously accelerating their development of new military..." *David Kilcullen, The Dragons and the Snakes, Oxford University Press*

## SUSPECTED LIMINAL WARFARE ACTIVITY BY REGION/TARGET OF INFLUENCE

### • European Defense Council

### NATO, the EDC (Council), and the EDC (Corps)

"As the leader of the EU, Germany has said that Europe should take charge of its own security. It is also a brand new world security situation now, as both China and Europe would want to hedge their risks in dealing with the US." *Wany Yiwei, European Studies, Renmin University of China, in an article on Business Insider*

The relationship between the European Defense Council and China is a far better one than that of *NATO* and China. This is due to a number of things, including a desire on the part of major "Old Europe" players (particularly France and Germany) to dominate what is being called the "New Europe", which includes former Warsaw Pact countries. Nowhere is the contrast between the EDC and NATO more obvious than in the individual relationships of certain member states. As an example are the rapidly increasing tensions between Greece (which China continues to woo with economic aid) and Turkey (which recently severed diplomatic relations with Beijing). Another obvious example is that of the United States and China (which are frenemies at best), but another, less obvious one is the growing antipathy between Norway and China (which have been at odds over exploitation of the Arctic Circle).

Despite issues with some of the less influential countries, China is now firmly embedded in many EDC (Council, not Corps) territories, particularly the Mecklenburg-Vorpommern region. Chinese business interests purchased the Gnoien-Warbelow airfield near Trollenhagen outright, Chinese scholars comprise a substantial minority of the faculty at Hochschule Neubrandenburg, and local Chinese ex-pats are even the source of substantial support for the Neubrandenburg Philharmonic Orchestra.

These developments could mean a lot or nothing. Given Neubrandenburg's proximity to the presumed headquarters of the nascent EDC (Corps, not Council) First Division, however, Chinese interest in the area is worrisome (at least to observers in the UK, US, and Canada).

Of additional concern, at least to those with an antipathy toward increased Sino-EDC cooperation, are the inclusion of small numbers of PLA troops in heretofore exclusively European exercises like Celtic Uprise and Dynamic Front, the expansion of joint exercises like those of EU NAVFOR and Combined Aid, and the sudden invitation to certain PLA, PLAAF, and PLAN officers to the French and German military institutions like the *Centre de Préparation des Force* and even the *Führungsakademie der Bundeswehr* on "exchange programs".

• **European/NATO Ports and facilities**

In 2016 COSCO Shipping (China Ocean Shipping Company) purchased a 51% controlling interest in the Port of Piraeus in Greece. A few years and $750 million USD worth of investments later, that amount jumped to 70%.

The commercial advantages are undeniable – the port is the largest commercial harbor in Europe, in a location central to the shipping of three continents. Just as importantly, however (perhaps more so), it is home to Greece's largest naval base, a hub for NATO Mediterranean maritime operations, and the home port to at least one of US 6th Fleet's permanently attached squadrons.

COSCO soon also owned majority ownership of the largest container terminal at France's third busiest port, Dunkirk, and Belgium's Zeebrugge harbor. It likewise gained significant influence at Noatum Port Holdings in Spain, the Port of Rotterdam in Netherlands, and many other economically and militarily strategic ports.

Dunkirk, for instance, is not only a massively important European entrepôt, it's just a stone's throw from the British coast – not to mention the new semi-permanent home of the latest iteration of China's Task Group 150. A three-ship flotilla is hardly going to gain naval supremacy in the Strait of Dover, as France's President was heard to tell the British PM in a decidedly scornful tone, but the Royal Navy is well aware that even a handful of YJ-91 missiles could effectively shut down the English Channel – to say nothing of second-generation ASBMs that could easily be concealed in bulk freighter's or under the cover of port facilities.

Control of such critical infrastructure is achieved in a number of ways, from outright mercantile purchase to technological assistance and even trade. Rotterdam was reckoned to be the most automated port in the world even before the UK and Italy withdrew from the EU, all thanks to Chinese cyber-tech...technology which Chinese companies still service and upgrade.

Beijing has taken additional steps under the guise of "private" tourism-economic ventures.

A significant example of this: Roslea Hall, a four-star hotel on the shore of Gare Loch, was purchased by investor Tom Xu for an unknown amount of money. Roslea Hall is certainly a good purchase for someone wishing to enter the UK's hospitality market, but it's also a superb acquisition for anyone wanting to keep an eye on Faslane, also known as His Majesty's Naval Base, Clyde.

HMNB Clyde, located just about four miles from Roslea Hall, is one of three Royal Navy bases in the UK. In addition to being the Royal Navy's headquarters in Scotland, it is also home to about a dozen RN submarines - including all five of her nuclear subs. It is also home to No. 3 Commando Brigade of the Royal Marines.

Any submarine sortie from Faslane must pass between the town of Rosneath, on the west, and Rhu, on the east. The transit is a narrow channel barely the length of a football field.

Roslea Hall looks right over it.

Signals intercept and monitoring ship traffic to and from the Atlantic are (rightfully) the primary concern of His Majesty's intelligence services at Faslane. However, it is by no means an exaggeration to note that a proficient hostile actor could easily hit a transiting vessel with something as small as a handgun, to say nothing of an RPG-30, *Nashshab* (بي جي نشاب), or even higher tech man portable missile.

• **The Arabian Sea**

Beginning a 40-year lease with the government of Pakistan, Hudong-Zhonghua Shipbuilding recently took effective control of Gwadar Sea Port. The harbor at Gwadar is an expansive deep water port close by the PNS (Pakistan Naval Service) Jinnah Naval Base. The port facility is at the heart of a 2300-acre "special economic zone" with a new international airport under construction.

The advantages of this maneuver are many, including:

• Positioning friendly security elements stationed there just a stone's throw from Iran. This puts them in an excellent position to access and influence the Gulf of Oman and from there, the Straits of Hormuz. Should (or when) the expected Saudi-Iranian cold war turn hot, Chinese forces would be in a position to assist Iran, interfere with the Saudis, US, and likely coalition partners, or simply to "intercede" as a peace-keeping entity. Such a choice would depend upon how Beijing read the situation, but the precedent for such peaceful third party interference was long ago set by a number of countries – in particular the US.

• Anchoring the "far end" of the China-Pakistan Economic Corridor, thus linking China to the Arabian Sea. This allows China to utilize Pakistan for energy transport by land (bring Iranian and Caspian Sea oil overland), thereby bypassing the choke point and constraints of Strait of Malacca (though steps have been taken to control that area as well).

• Providing a foundation from which to counter anti-Iranian, arguably pro-American activity by Saudi Arabia in a mostly-Sunni region. This region historically extends from what is now Pakistan into the Sistan-Baluchistan province of (predominantly *Shia*) Iran. Small parts of Afghanistan's Helmand,

Kandahar, and Nimruz provinces are also considered to be part of Balochistan.

▪ Further weakening US-Pakistan relations. China is already Pakistan's largest military supplier and has a vested interested in counterbalancing or marginalizing American influence in Karachi.

▪ Providing de facto "insurance" by virtue of economic influence with the Baluchi people. Geographically, Balochistan comprises a little less than half of Pakistan, home to just 4.5% of it population, but its economic significance is immense —not least because the preponderance of Pakistan's natural gas and mineral wealth is there. It is also a restive and frequently volatile region, with a simmering autonomy movement. The presence of strong Chinese- and Chinese-contracted security forces combined with that economic influence give Beijing substantial weight in local affairs and would continue to do so even in the unlikely event that Baluchistan became independent (though Saudi Arabia has been supporting the restive autonomy movement there for at least a decade).

▪ Establishing cover: the presence of such security elements at Gwadar Sea Port and the airport provides excellent cover for Chinese liminal warfare operations across the region, but particularly in the littorals of the Gulf of Oman, Arabian Sea, and Gulf of Aden.

Note: Among security elements maintained by HZS at and near the port facility are several "commercial" fast attack craft virtually identical to the PNS Azmats, crewed by a mix of veteran sailors (including a large number of Bangladeshi navy SWADS operators), the Sri Lankan Rapid Action Boat Squadron, and (predictably) "retired" officers and NCOs of the PAPCGC. It is reliably assumed, though yet to be proven, that several senior "security officials" helping protect Beijing's interests are in fact serving PLA and PLAN general officers who have been deniably reassigned or "retired" to ostensibly civilian employ.

As of this writing, ground elements and light to medium armor capability have reached at least 25,000 personnel. Most are provided by a number of PSCs, including Hua Xin Zhong An Security Services and, barely a decade after the independence of South Sudan, the surprisingly competent *Juba Garang*. The latter company is a South Sudanese PSC originally recruited by the state-owned China National Petroleum Corporation (CNPC).

These former militiamen, trained by (and having close ties to) successive CHNBATT elements (see Chinese activity in China, below) number about the same as a light battalion. Ironically, much of this unit's equipment was purchased with funds from the US State Department's Africa Peacekeeping Program (AFRICAP) and issued from the DynCorp-built South Sudanese military GHQ at Bilpam. Many of the African security personnel are veterans of the Nuer White Army and/or the SSPDF 1$^{ST}$ Division.

• **Oceania**

Beijing's activity in the South Pacific is very similar to its actions in the Arabian Sea. Consider the extensive construction and investments that have been made in and around Darwin.

HMAS Coonawarra (the Darwin naval base), Robertson Barracks (home to Australia's 1st Brigade and 1st Aviation Regiment), and RAAFB Darwin (home to Australian air squadrons as well as US B1-Bs, B-52s, and F-22s) are all immediately adjacent to the Port of Darwin. So too is a USMC Air-Ground Task Force (MAGTF).

These interconnected military installations and critical joint US-Australian infrastructure have been significant in US Far

East strategy, but also in Australian operations in East Timor, Papua New Guinea, and other locations.

Controlling interest in the Port of Darwin is owned by China's Shandong Landbridge Group, and has been for years. Similar investments have been made at the military-proximate ports of Townsville and Queensland.

Elsewhere, though "nearby" in a strategic sense, China has gained control of several harbors in Malaysia and another in Sri Lanka. The latter facility (at Hambantota) was taken as a debt-for-equity swap when the Sri Lankan government was unable to repay the millions of dollars it had borrowed from a Chinese consortium to build the actual port in question.

No one who can read a map should wonder why China would wish to position itself in either of those countries, nor why the Malacca Strait is important.

*One quarter* of the world's traded goods pass through this tiny channel every year, including more than 20 million barrels of oil per day. Much of that oil, of course, comes via the Persian Gulf through the Strait of Hormuz in tankers that must first pass Gwadar, in Pakistan (q.v. below), and then Sri Lanka before reaching the Malacca Strait. Hundreds of millions of tons of additional gross tonnage travels toward these waters through the Bab-el-Madeb Strait as well. See *Camp Lemmonier* below, for the significance of that.

## • The Persian Gulf

Several years ago Beijing began eight modified diesel-electric submarines and coastal patrol ships to Pakistan; originally four of these were to be built in Pakistan and four in China, though eventually this was increased to six and four. The first two of what was eventually to be 10 Type 39B *Yuan* class vessels delivered had active duty PLAN (中国人民解放军海军) advisors aboard "for the foreseeable future" for training. Intelligence sources report that many of those advisors have never left, or if they did return to China did so only after being relieved in place.

Additional rumors indicate that most of the crew members on the half dozen most effective vessels are contracted Chinese "civilians" with former service in the PLANSF, outnumbering those who are actual serving Pakistan Navy personnel. There has been some (warranted) speculation that at least two of these patrol ships are effectively a maritime PMC, with a completely foreign (to Pakistan) crew complement, paid for by Beijing but flagged by Islamabad.

The first Chinese-built submarine was delivered under escort by the Kilo class sub *Yuan Zheng 68 Hao*, the same one thought to have stalked the USS Ronald Reagan.

These 10 boats (12, really, see below) substantially improved Pakistan's A2/AD (Anti-Access/Area Denial) capabilities, a fact which is of great concern to the navy of India. So too is Beijing's ever cozier relationship with Islamabad – particularly since at least four of the new submarines were in service *before* the long delayed INS Vikrant ever started her sea trials (and long before her sister ship's keel was laid). The PNS submarines and their attendant facilities represent a significant force multiplier for Chinese military interests in the Arabian Sea, freeing similar PLAN vessels up for other duties (or, at need, potentially operating in conjunction with them).

Interestingly, it is later discovered that two older vessels, PNS *Abu Dujana* and PNS *Abu 'Amr* had been previously purchased outright by the Pakistan National Shipping Corporation and based in secrecy in parts of the Gwadar Sea Port. Both of these vessels are Song class subs thought until discovery to have still in use by PLAN.

Masked by construction equipment, bulk freighters, and the bustle of other shipping, these two additional submarines were not identified until joint training maneuvers and crew transfers were necessitated by sea trials for the more modern boats.

The PNKC deal is found to have been brokered by the (state-owned) Pakistan Maritime Security Agency and paid for with a loan by the Sonali Bank of Bangladesh (also state-owned). According to news releases, the submarines, allegedly disarmed at the time of purchase, are intended for use as "unarmed ISR platforms" by PNS merchant marine concerns in counter-piracy operations.

## • The California Coast

The world-renowned Hotel Del Coronado, once declared one of the top 10 resorts in the world, was quietly purchased by the Anbang Group from the Blackstone Group for a sum estimated to be well in excess of $1 Billion USD. The sale was made and considered complete until formal finalization was blocked by the US government.

Anbang Group was a private Beijing-based holding company at the time of purchase, though later it reverted to Beijing's control.

The significance of Hotel Del Coronado is one of geography and proximity. The resort is close by Naval Air Station North Island, Naval Amphibious Base Coronado, Silver Strand Training Complex South, and San Diego Naval Base. It *directly* overlooks Point Loma.

The significance of this is manifold.

- Point Loma is home to the USN's Fleet Intelligence Command Pacific, its Space and Naval Warfare Systems Command, *and* Submarine Squadron 11.

- San Diego Naval Base is home to CSG-9 (Carrier Strike Group 9), flagged by the USS Theodore Roosevelt and one of the most powerful formations in the United States navy.

- NAS North Island is home port to another of America's 10 nuclear carriers, the USS Carl Vinson and CSG-1.

- Naval Amphibious Base Coronado is not only where West Coast SEALs are trained and headquartered, it is the location of United States Naval Special Warfare Command (NAVSPECWARCOM).

- Silver Strand Training Complex South (SSTC-S) is one of the most comprehensive training facilities for Special Operations Forces in the country, used not just by SEALs but by all elements of USSOCOM. It is used as both a ship systems testing area, MOUT/urban warfare training and littoral operations, and all Naval Special Warfare (NSW) UAV and USV development.

It is a fairly simple matter to see what an excellent surveillance platform the Hotel Del Coronado is (in addition to being a very profitable business concern).

Anbang Group was run in part by Mr. Chen Xiaolu before his death. Chen was a former Red Guard and retired PLA Colonel and his father none other than Marshall Chen Yi. Chen Yi was a Mao Zedong contemporary, a PLA Commander, and later the Chinese Foreign Minister.

The attempted sale of the resort was blocked <u>by the Committee on Foreign Investment in the United States</u>, whose job it is to review acquisitions of American businesses by foreign investors and concerns for possible threats to national security. Shortly after the finalization of the deal was prevented, Anbang Group was "nationalized" by Beijing.

By the time the government intervened, however, a substantial portion of the staff had been hired and trained at the behest of what were to be the new owners (i.e., the Chinese, via Anbang Group). Renovations in some areas of the resort, *including those set traditionally set aside by the "Hotel Del" for the use of high-ranking local military personnel and their spouses*, were completed by Chinese-owned construction companies.

This lead at least some to question whether surveillance tech might not have been installed during the work, but such speculation was denounced as conspiracy theory and Sinophobia.

Blackstone Group retained ownership over the hotel. However, over the next decade and a half at least 15% of the (multiple) billion-dollar company's voting shares were gained by Chinese nationals. By the time of the Fourth Balkan War Chinese investors all but managed the place.

## • East China Sea

Japanese intelligence assets claimed in late 2016 that China was providing aid and advice to the Kariyushi Club (Ryūkyū Independent Party) of Okinawa. Events in the years to follow lend at least some credence to this assertion.

Okinawa and the Senkaku Islands have long been considered a part of Japan (by the Japanese, anyway), but China makes claim to the area as well. Fearing Beijing might co-opt the independence movement, organizations like the Yuimarle Ryukyu no Jichi" ("autonomy of Ryukyu"), began publicly calling for independence from Japan *without* Chinese involvement.

However, there is ample evidence to believe that other groups have been rather less concerned about the possibility of losing autonomy to the Chinese should independence be gained – which could be accurate or could be gross overconfidence.

The Chinese, publicly unwilling to set a precedent that might affect their claim to Taiwan, repeatedly and contemptuously dismiss allegations of such involvement. They do, however, continue to contest Japanese sovereignty over the Ryukyu Archipelago and Senkaku Islands and have carefully (if very quietly) fomented trouble for the Japanese by dint of the U.N. International Covenant on Civil and Political Rights for self-determination.

More overt actions, including several violent ones, are suspected to be China-backed, if not entirely China-planned and – executed, though none have been proven sufficiently to allow the Japanese more than public posturing. Among those action were the loss of an MV-22 from MCAS Futenma over the Jungle Warfare Training Center to an Anzi Mk II MANPAD, the destruction of a Japanese National Police Agency (NPA) Special Task Force Type 87 ARV by an EFP in the "Soapland" district of Naha City, and the unsolved rape, murder, and disfigurement of five young Okinawan women on Mibaru Beach.

The so-called "Mibaru Beach Massacre" became the catalyst of protests every bit as riotous as those that followed the King Center (Martin Luther King Jr. National Historical Park) Bombing in at Atlanta. In addition to a great loss in lives and property, it drastically affected the forward deployment of US military assets to the region.

Although the Mibaru Beach Massacre was allegedly perpetrated by off-duty US military personnel ("three fit white men with very short hair", according to a witness) who purportedly carved white supremacist iconography into the girls' remains, there is little to support such allegations. All American troops were restricted to base on the night of the attack due to preparations for a simultaneous USAF MCCRE and USAF ORE.

Casting further doubt upon the matter was concurrent activity by the Defense Intelligence Agency. The DIA was at the time investigating a small group of Serbian nationals who'd traveled to the island from Alaska, ostensibly for a scuba-diving trip, on suspicion of terrorist ties to *Salar* and Uyghur groups.

None of those men returned to Juneau, though the unidentifiable remains of one man who *might* have been from that party were recovered on Uotsuri Island a few days later. [Recall that Beijing has been wooing Belgrade for many years. In fact, in the earliest part of the last decade, Serbian President Aleksander Vucic – before his assassination and the chloropicrin-cyclosarin attack on Novi Sad – kissed the Chinese flag in gratitude for Chinese help during the COVID-19 virus and sponsored pro-Chinese billboards throughout the city.]

Regardless of proof or arrests, civil unrest among Okinawans following the Mibaru Beach Massacre had a huge impact. In addition to several deaths and much property loss on and off the various DoD installations, it ultimately forced the withdrawal of the 12th Marine Regiment to Hawaii and the transfer of the 67th Fighter Squadron (half the air superiority strength of Kadena AB) to Australia.

## • East Africa

When the African Union (AU) held its biannual summit in 2012, it does so in a brand new headquarters. The thoroughly modernized structure, which cost an estimated $200 million USD, is paid for entirely by China and given to the AU as a "gift to Africa". Accusations that China was (and continues) directly monitoring every type of communication to, from, and within the AU Office Center and Conference Complex are widely dismissed. Despite this, China remains extraordinarily well informed about AU matters thereafter.

## • The Horn of Africa

When ships of the PLAN's Zhanjiang South Sea Fleet arrived at the Horn of Africa years ago to formally open the "Chinese Peoples Liberation Army Support Base, Djibouti" (CPLASBD). It was the China's first overseas base, from which Chinese warships were to sally into the Red Sea and the Gulf of Aden (across which travels some 15 percent of the world's maritime trade) to support counter-piracy operations.

It was also used as a materiel support hub for the 5,000 (now over 10,000) Chinese troops deployed in peacekeeping missions across Africa (several times as many as were there as recently as 2019). PLAN "Blue Helmets" are stationed in Sudan, South Sudan, Liberia, Mali, the Democratic Republic of Congo, and other places.

China (which owns over 90% of Djibouti's national debt) locates its base immediately adjacent to the Doraleh container terminal, which has been operated by the state-owned China Merchants Port Holdings since Djibouti nationalized the facility.

The base, and PLAN presence therein, has expanded every year since.

The CPLASBD is an excellent location for commerce and a strategic location, situated as it is by the Bab-el-Madeb Strait, which separates the Red Sea from the Gulf of Aden. It looks across the Arabian Sea to the Gwadar Sea Port in Pakistan and is positioned to control approach to the Suez Canal from the Indian Ocean side.

More significant to US national security interests, it is located immediately adjacent to the bases of several allied militaries (Italy, Japan, France) and their counterterrorism efforts – including *Camp Lemonnier*. Camp Lemonnier, formerly a French Foreign Legion facility, is the most important US base in the region, and the only permanent US facility in Africa. Camp Lemmonier is home to the Combined Joint Task Force Horn of Africa (United States Africa Command), and now it is effectively "just across the way" from America's greatest geopolitical rival.

By the time of the Fourth Balkan War and the ensuing drawdown from deployed US military personnel, the equivalent of a reinforced Chinese combined-arms battalion was permanently stationed. The unit's role is to serve as a QRF for Chinese and Chinese-backed peacekeeping units (in particular Burmese, Bangladeshi, Sri Lankan, and Pakistani formations).

The disingenuously named 1st Independent Coastal Defense Brigade (Chinese: 独立海防第旅) is in fact the equivalent of a heavily reinforced Chinese combined-arms battalion. In addition to the traditional elements of the PLAGF combined-arms battalion, the unit can call on one, sometimes two, permanently stationed (though rotating responsibility) *Jiaolonng* "Sea Dragon" commando platoons, as well as a "guest" Jianjiji J-18 STOVL fighter squadron, multiple organic People's Liberation Army Naval Air Force (PLANAF) helicopter squadrons (attack and transport), and other supporting elements.

It wasn't too long after the base's establishment that Chinese soldiers assigned to #1 ICDB were attending the *Centre d'entraînement au combat d'Arta Plage* (French Desert Desert Commando Course) alongside French, German, Slovakian, and soldiers of other nationalities (notably *not* those of the United States, Canada, or Turkey) at Arta, Djibouti.

In fact, during the Relief of Mayotte (q.v.), the far more numerous Chinese STOVL fighters and tanker aircraft based in Djibouti flew far more CAS missions than did local French aircraft for the French relief force (itself comprised of 5eme Regiment Interarmes d'Outre Mer (5th Overseas Combined Arms Regiment or 5eme RIAOM).

Later, when Chinese troops air-assaulted into to relieve South Sudanese "constables" under attack there, a large number of AMX-10RCs of 3rd Squadron, 5eme *Regiment Interarmes d'Outre Mer* (3/5RIOM) were in the armored reinforcement column alongside an equal number of Chinese VN1 APCs.

• **Elsewhere in Africa**

Zimbabwean leader Robert Mugabe was overthrown in a very strange coup in late 2017. No coup in Africa is completely improbable, though this one was more unexpected than some.

The ouster, ostensibly done at the behest of powerful political influences led by veterans of the "independence war" that saw the end of Rhodesia, was carried out by elements of the Zimbabwean Defence Forces (ZDF). The ZDF was led at the time by Gen. Constantino Chiwenga.

Although there was obvious rancor between (then) Vice President Emmerson Mnangagwa (himself a former commander of the ZDF who was backed by most of the armed forces) and First Lady Grace Mugabe (the former president's intended successor), this was almost certainly not the sole cause of the conflict.

Chiwenga returned from a visit with the Central Military Commission of the Peoples Republic of China just days before the

162

coup. In fact, his early return from China, prompted by warnings from Chinese Intelligence that Mugabe intended to have him arrested, was nearly a violent one. Members of the ZRP Support Unit (a Zimbabwean paramilitary police unit) were at the airport to seize the general but were overpowered by Chimenga loyalists.

The official line at the time, repeated by the UN and most news outlets, was that the coup resulted from conflict between Mnangagwa and the Mugabes. Democracy activists in Nigeria, South Africa, Guinea, and the South African Development Commission however told a different story – as did several African intelligence services.

Zimbabwe is home to numerous and *very* lucrative mining ventures. Virtually all are co-owned by the ZDF and shell companies run by the PLA. Zimbabwe's Central Intelligence Organization, or CIO, was previously the demesne of Vice President Mnangagwa. Zimbabwe Security Forces have often exerted economic control over the country. In this case, several Zimbabwean police organizations also held a large stake in those mining enterprises (among others), most of which are a massive (and strategically significant) source of rare-earth metals, diamond, gold, and platinum.

Robert Mugabe had been in the process of nationalizing those concerns, and indeed had nearly completed the process. This would have made them the property of the Zimbabwean government – which was Robert and Grace Mugabe – and cut the CIO and assorted police units off from their revenue.

Within a week of the coup, all nationalization of joint PLA-ZDF mining ventures was reversed and a number of accidental deaths were recorded. Tremendous wealth continued to flow, though none was ever used to mitigate record levels of high crime and internal dissent.

163

Little was heard about the matter from the African Union in its China-built headquarters complex, though any transition of government on the continent (much less an overthrow) should have been the focus of scrutiny and comment. Perhaps even armed intervention (as happened after the declaration of the Islamic Emirate in North Sinai by the purportedly IRGC-backed *Ansar Bait al-Maqdis*, and later in the Republic of Zangaro).

Less than a decade later Mnangagwa and his retinue were killed in a VBIED attack allegedly conducted by supporters of the aging Grace Mugabe, who was said to be in hiding in Nigeria. General Chiwenga became the new President.

Approximately a month after Chiwenga's inauguration, Beijing propped up his administration by underwriting loans from the International Monetary Fund, which had previously ceased working with Harare. It also "loaned" Mnangagwa a large training cadre of its Peoples Armed Police (including several units that had been responsible for securing the Winter Olympics in Bejijing) to train a new *Gendarmerie* style branch of the ZRP Police. This new element, the Police National Constabulary subsumed the contemporary Police Protection Unit, the Presidential Guard, and some specialty units from the Army.

Additional training and support came from Pakistan's (Sindh) Rangers – transported to Bulawayo by massive PLAAF Xi'an Y-20 *Kunpeng* transports. The Pakistanis are still there.

### • Baja California

#### ▪ Competition with US Pacific Ports & Influence in Mexico

The Barrio Chino based Chinese Consolidated Benevolent Association (CCBA) took control of numerous dominant structures and significant local businesses in and around Lázaro Cárdenas, Michoacán, including controlling interest in several parts of the harbor itself, without anyone really noticing. Indirectly financed by Beijing and several prominent Chinese-Mexican businessmen (including Zhenli Ye Gon), the move included steps to ensure substantial influence of over local infrastructure, particularly the railways.

The Port of Lázaro Cárdenas is a major deep-water seaport well positioned to move massive amounts of materiel (mostly via the Transportación Ferroviaria Mexicana or *TFM*) into the United States toward Houston, Oklahoma City, Kansas City, and Chicago.

Because of ongoing congestion at such major American ports as Los Angeles and Long Beach, the city quickly became home to one of the largest and busiest container ports in the world. It was soon an economic challenge to ports all along the California coast and directly impacted San Diego's economy sufficiently that state and local officials began seeking legislative reform to fight back.

In fact, its proximity and capacity may well be why Littoral Combat Ship Squadron One was left in San Diego instead of deploying to NSA-Souda Bay (Crete) as was originally intended, though that delay was rescinded upon accusations of anti-Mexican racism and even Sinophobia.

▪ **Regional Muscle**

After the Banco Azteca Massacre and so-called "Zaculeu Intervention" (when Mexican military forces crossed the Guatemalan border and established the euphemistically named "Huehuetanango Security Zone"), there were numerous terrorist attacks on the Mexican rail system — though curiously hardly anywhere else. These attacks, allegedly backed by Guatemalan security services and members of the resurgent Zapatista

Insurgency, resulted in several security companies being contracted to provide security for the TFM.

The largest of these formidable organizations were the La Chinesca based *SRD* (Servicios de Respuesta del Dragón, or "Dragon Response Services), a PSC comprised almost entirely of Chinese-Mexicans, and Operaciones Estoicas (OE, in English *Stoic Operations*).

OE is of course the often controversial PMC thought by the *Procuraduria General de la República* (PRG, the Mexican Attorney General's Office) *Centro Nacional de Planeación, Análisis, e Información para el Combate a la Delincuencia* to be connected at several levels with the Abarco-Cruz Cartel narco-terrorist group.

SRD was founded by Oscar Arturo Murrieta Navarro, a former *Fuerza Especial de Reacción* operator and veteran of the operation to capture Javier Torres Félix. Forced to retire after unproven allegations of ties via a cousin to the sicarios for the Caro Quintero group), Navarro spent several years as Chief of Security for Zhenli Ye Gon's company, *Unimed Pharm Chem México*. Leaving Unimed Pharm and backed by his former boss's substantial resources, he used his considerable network of friends within the Mexican Special Forces community to build what was to become perhaps the most successful PSC/PMC in Latin America.

For its part, OE, headquartered in La Mesa, was actually under active investigation by several Mexican intelligence agencies. Given the demands of dealing with the insurgency to the south, however, little was done with it. That investigation was later completely dropped after several dozen police officers were murdered and a series of assassinations effected. Those assassinations began with federal judge Uriel Villegas Ortiz, then Supreme Court Justice Arturo Zaldívar Lelo de Larrea a few

166

months later, and Finance Minister Arturo Herrera (among others) the following year.

The murders of Representative Duncan Hunter of California's 50th Congressional District and Vinci Police Department detective Raymond Velcoro are thought to have been one of several other killings related to OE activities.

## JUMP TO TRIARII COUNTER-INSURGENCY OPERATIONS, LOUISIANA

## JUMP TO 36TH INFANTRY DIVISION "FREE TEXAS ARMY" BORDER OPERATIONS

# Cowboy Up

## JL Curtis

Ranger Enrique Sandoval sat in his black Tahoe at the burnt-out remains of the Love's Truck Stop on I-40, just east of Amarillo. He fiddled with the radio squelch and volume, making sure it was high enough to hear over the wind, then turned the AM radio down as he looked at his watch. *I hope Austin knows what they're doing. Sit out here and wait for a radio call from Leroy Jenkins, then meet with… Hell, I don't even know who these people are that I'm supposed to meet. Triarii? Some kind of quasi-military group? And they're running a convoy of supplies. What supplies? From where to where? And I'm not to ask questions or try to pull them over or let anybody else in law enforcement know about it. This is fu…*

The radio suddenly came alive on the Rangers' tactical frequency. "Lone Star, Leroy Jenkins. Lone Star, Leroy Jenkins, how copy?"

Enrique keyed up. "Leroy Jenkins, have you Lima Charlie. I am at the designated meet point. Black Tahoe."

"Leroy Jenkins is ten out. One vehicle will break off to rendezvous with you. It will be a green M1117. How copy."

"Roger." *What the fuck is an M1117? Some kind of… TAC vehicle?* Enrique never heard of them in the Army when he was in, nor was it anything in the Rangers' inventory.

Eight minutes later, he saw some kind of angular, four-wheeled armored personnel carrier trundling down the access road as a long line of semis led by another couple of those things continued westbound down I-40. He stretched and got out, squared his cowboy hat, and walked to the front of the Tahoe, then watched as the TAC vehicle turned into the parking lot. He saw the top of a head in the turret as the gun swung in various directions. It crossed the parking lot and came to a stop twenty feet away. A hatch opened and a geared up little guy in tan BDUs got out, an AR pattern rifle across his chest and a pistol in a thigh rig on his right side. Incongruously, he had a blue courier pouch in his right hand. "Ranger... Santiago?" he asked.

Enrique shook his head. "Yeah, that's me. Leroy Jenkins? Really?"

"I'm Hartman. I didn't come up with it. I accept no responsibility. Hate to ask, but can I see an ID?"

Pulling out his credentials, Enrique showed them and asked, "Satisfied?"

Hartman glanced at them and smiled ironically, then said, "I just do what I'm told." Then, "Mind if I use your hood?" Enrique waved him toward it magnanimously, and Hartman dug out a key and unlocked the courier bag, pulling out a folder of documents, a CD, and a thumb drive. He reached in and found one more document, then pulled a pen out of his shoulder pocket, "Sign please, then we'll be out of your hair."

The Ranger looked at the sheet and was startled to note that it was basically a military standard transfer document, listing the items on a multi-part form. He signed it and handed it back as Hartman was sticking the items back in the bag. Hartman handed him the bag and the key, ripped the back copy of the form off, and handed the rest of the form to him. "Ranger, this is... there is some serious shit heading for Texas. This is all the intel we have. I know you have to get it to Austin, but I'd recommend you copy it onto your computer just in case. Now if you'll excuse me, we have to catch up with the convoy."

Hartman trotted back to the TAC vehicle, as soon as the hatch closed, it started moving back toward the interstate. The gunner waved, and Enrique waved back distractedly, shoved the form into the bag, and got back in his Tahoe. Drumming his

170

fingers on the steering wheel, he looked at the bag, then pulled out the thumb drive. *Should I? It's not like I know he's telling the truth, but… Fuck it, I've got a spare computer at the house if I blow this one up.* He moved the files over, quickly scanned the directory and opened the file that said RAIL. His eyes grew wide as he scanned it, and he started thinking about where the trains ran in his area. *Fuck me, no wonder they want this to get to Austin!* He pulled out the thumb drive, slid it back in the courier bag, locked the bag, and headed down US 287 to turn it over to the next Ranger south of him.

Twelve hours later, Colonel Grant, the commander of the Texas Rangers, was reading the cover documents and shaking his head. As he read each page, he handed it across to Major Martin, his deputy. Grant said, "This is… it fits what Company E is reporting. We need to get this out to every Ranger, either by courier or computer if we can."

Martin shook his head. "Networks are still down. Hell, everybody is on backup generators, but they're running out of gas. Speaking of gas, we're getting pretty low, too."

Grant took his glasses off and rubbed his nose. "Dammit. Okay, send copies out with F troop. Tell each Ranger who receives it to copy it and pass it along. Coordination with the locals is authorized if they think it's safe."

"That's a sad commentary, Bill. What about Garber, Daniels, and Sandoval? They got it here."

"Find out if they made copies. I'm betting they did. Tell 'em the same thing. I gotta go see the governor."

"What about DPS?"

"Make a complete copy, and I'll deliver it to them on the way to see the governor. We need to move on this."

***

Twenty-four hours later, Rangers Jim Garber, Ed Daniels, and Enrique Sandoval sat in Wise County Sheriff Danny Richie's conference room in Decatur, Texas, along with Sheriff Jesus Ortega from Montague County and Eric Lynn, the police chief of Decatur. It was an interesting group, to put it mildly. They all

171

knew each other but seldom all got together. Garber, big and burly, with a salt and pepper mustache, sat sipping a Fresca as Ed Daniels poured coffee for everyone else. Daniels looked more like a banker or preacher, quiet, small and slim, peering through thick glasses. Sandoval and Ortega could have been brothers and conversed quietly in Spanish. Eric Lynn still had the high and tight haircut he'd worn as a Marine for twenty years, along with a permanent scowl. Sheriff Richie walked in apologizing. "Sorry, got hung up." He could have posed for the Marlboro ads back in the day. An archetypal cowboy, he was lean and wiry, had a brushy mustache and did, in fact, own a ranch outside Alvord.

He flopped down in the chair at the head of the table and sighed, then said, "I guess we need to get this started. Who wants to kick it off?"

The three Rangers looked at each other, and Sandoval took a sip of coffee, then set it carefully on the table. "I guess it's on me. First of all, I'll be having another meeting this afternoon with Sheriff Bell over in Clay County and Sheriff Hamlin up in Wichita County. I'll schedule meetings with the others up my way in the next few days." He pointed to the other two Rangers. "We've talked, and what we 'think' is going on is that the gangs will start branching out from Dallas and Fort Worth. Apparently this is already happening down in Houston and Austin. Jim's got some info on Dallas and Fort Worth."

Garber grimaced. "There are at least three main gangs that are fighting over Dallas and Fort Worth: the Fourth Reich, *Soldados de Aztlan*, and a fairly new group comprised of the splinter group comprising former Bloods, Crips, and Black Lives Matter members. That bunch calls themselves BLACK: Bloods, Black Lives, and Crips Krew with a K, and they are fighting the established gangs for control and food. It looks like SdA is the main player. Based on a CI we've got in place, two sicarios from *Los Zetas* cartel, Jose Garcia Maldonado, aka 'Zafado', and Jesús Peña Garcia, aka 'Loco', are running the show in Dallas and Fort Worth. They're getting guns and drugs from Mexico and the Chinese. Thanks to some intel we have, it appears a lot of both

172

food and guns has been coming in by rail. Also, they're starting to run out of food, because less of their convoys are moving in the hood. Which means they're going to start going further and further afield looking for more. I think the guns will just be a bonus."

Sheriff Richie scratched his jaw and asked, "Has been? Nothing's moving since the power went out. If they start looking around we're going to be the target, but that would mean convoys of trucks…"

Ed Daniels nodded. "And that's a big part of the issue." He reached down and pulled a photo out of his briefcase, then shoved it across the table to the two sheriffs. "Enrique and I have pretty much driven 287 from Amarillo to Decatur, and Jim's covered the area down toward Saginaw. There are eleven trains stuck that we've seen. At least four of them are bulk transport with Conex boxes or semi-trailers on them. See those two Conex boxes in the center of the picture?" The two sheriffs bent over the picture, and Sheriff Ortega said, "The ones that say GCC?"

"Yep. They filmed those in San Diego. When the Marines took back the port, they popped some of them open. The blue ones had aid supplies in them, but the red ones had weapons, ammo, and a bunch of other stuff. The four trains we've seen have had both colors on them, nine blue ones for every red one."

Ortega leaned back and put his hands behind his head. "Seen a few of them. I just… well, honestly haven't been paying a lot of attention to that, because I have plenty of other problems. Sounds like I now have another one."

The others commiserated with him, and Richie finally said, "So, what are we supposed to do?"

Garber cocked his head and said, "Well, I'd suggest breaking into them. The cartels have already emptied the ones down in Saginaw. And it's not like these others will move soon. Hell, the cartel guys are running around in up-armored technicals, DPD and Fort Worth PD have pulled in their horns, especially after the cartel blew up and burned the central maintenance facility, which housed all the spare cars, TAC vehicles, fuel and tires. DPD won't even go into the barrio or Southside anymore.

Most of the time they just sit in their stations, if they even come to work. They have pulled DPS out; now they're only working the interstates."

"Speaking of that, why isn't there a DPS rep here?" Richie asked.

Sandoval said grumpily, "We invited them."

Daniels interjected, "On the bright and shiny, the governor allowed the guard to, quote, work independently with local authorities, unquote. He didn't allow opening the armories, but you should be hearing from them if any of them are in your counties."

Richie and Ortega both smiled and looked at each other. Richie said, "Dunno about Jesus, but I've got about seventy guard guys, a good number of ranchers and ranch hands, and a bunch of veterans who have already contacted me. We've been putting a militia together already – started doing that the day after the power went out."

"What have they got for weapons?"

Ortega laughed loudly. "I don't think you want to ask that question. Let's just say 'well-armed' is not a misnomer. Hell, the three gun stores in Montague sold all of their guns and ammo within forty-eight hours of the power going out."

Richie chuckled. "Same down here. As far as comms, damn near everybody has those personal radios and CBs, and a few have sat phones. We've got a warning net, ranch to ranch, since most of the ranches have some kind of power, either solar or gensets. Most of the ranches have five hundred- or thousand-gallon tanks of fuel and plenty of horses. Basically, my deputies are comms links back here, and I've doubled up in dispatch, making them the operations center."

Ortega grinned. "And I've done the same. We could use some better weapons, though. I don't have any automatic weapons, just shotties and ARs in the cars."

Sandoval said, "Well, according to the intel, the Conexs contain plenty of full-auto rifles, both Norinco AR copies and

174

Type 56 AKs, ammo, some big guns like W85s, which are the equivalent of a Ma Deuce, and a lot of RPGs."

Garber grumbled, "The SdA technicals down in Dallas and Fort Worth are running W85s up top."

Richie replied, "Well, we've got a few technicals, if you will. Some folks on the ranches have been… busy. And some vets have been helping them out."

Ortega chimed in, "Same, same with us. I've got a few folks building them out, and we're moving them down toward 287, because if they come, that's the way they will do it. And I've got one up-armored D-11 Bogle has built."

Daniels grinned. "Old man Bogle, the one with the feedlot and ranch up by Bowie? For some reason that doesn't surprise me. And his feedlot would be a target too, considering all the cows he's got up there."

"Yep." There was laughter around the table at that.

Garber nodded. "DPS is watching the highways. Hopefully, we'll have at least an hour or two of lead time if anything kicks off. And we've got a deep cover in the SdA, if – big if – he can get a message out safely."

The Rangers pointed out the train locations they'd seen and which ones they believed might have weapons, aid, or both on them. They were all north of Alvord and easily visible from Hwy 287, prompting a long discussion about what could happen if the cartel started looking for more food and guns. They decided to use one as bait, check the other ones to out, and to mitigate the vulnerability of Bogle's operation. Two hours later, with a basic plan to counter various cartel excursions, communications plans were laid out, and they broke up with agreements of mutual support.

Richie caught Chief Lynn by the arm, saying quietly, "Eric, wait a minute." When the others had walked out, he whispered, "I know you don't like it, but I want your folks to maintain your patrol patterns here in town. We're not trying to cut you out, but if Alvord and north is where we think they'll go, I'm going to have to pull my folks up there."

Lynn grimaced. "They're not going to like being left out of the fight."

Richie shrugged. "I know, but y'all will be it in the south end of the county if this goes down and anybody else shows up."

"Okay." His shoulders slumped, Lynn walked out shaking his head and mumbling.

***

Johnny Wade picked the red GCC container off the train sitting eight miles north of Alvord and carefully set it on the shoulder of 287, then climbed out of the crane cab. The two sheriffs were standing by as he cut the locks and customs tags off the Conex, then swung one door open.

Sheriff Richie chuckled as he saw the pallets. "Jesus, I don't think you'll have any more issues with not having enough weapons." They swung the other door open, and Johnny trundled the forklift up to the doors and pulled the first two pallets out, then set the top one on the shoulder next to the bottom one. He popped the bands holding it together, and they opened the top to see boxes full of magazines with spam cans of ammo underneath. The other pallet held Type 56 AKs in crates, and Sheriff Ortega said, "Mine, mine, mine!" He laughed, then said seriously, "Eight per case is forty-eight per pallet. If I could get three or four of those…"

Two hours later, they had divided the 38 pallets, then split the aid pallets from one of the blue Conex boxes. Johnny loaded his flatbed with the Conex for Sheriff Ortega and said, "I'll be back in an hour or so. I'll get Mack to bring his crane down to the sheriff's office and drop it there. As soon as we get that done, I'll come back and pick yours up."

Richie nodded. "Sounds good. We'll get you the diesel to get the other Conex boxes full of aid packages moved, too. We'll split them equally."

Johnny grinned. "And I get a pallet or two of aid packages to take care of my folks?"

The two sheriffs looked at each other and Ortega said, "He's got you, Danny. I'd pay that bill, if I were you."

They all laughed as Richie nodded.

176

*** 

Sheriff Richie walked into the former administration office, and Brent Fisher looked up. Richie asked, "Got anything new, Brent?"

The grizzled old man shoved one earphone off and waggled his hand. "Shrimp says Bogle got the cows moved down to the feedlot by the highway as bait. HF is sucking hind tit today, so we're doing everything on CW, taking a bit longer, but these PRC 150s are working."

The sheriff's radio went off. "Sheriff, Ranger Garber says there's movement. Two armed cartel convoys are coming north, ten miles apart. One is… ten stock trucks, looks like they are after cattle, and one is ten box trucks going after a train, just like we thought. Trooper Eckert is a mile ahead of them and says they've shot at him."

Richie keyed his radio and responded, "Get the alert out. I think this is the real deal." He started to tell Fisher to pass the word, but saw that Fisher was already on his headset and furiously tapping the butterfly key. The sheriff ran by dispatch, yelling, "I'm on my way to Alvord." Not waiting for a response, he banged out the back door and jumped in his Tahoe. As soon as he started it, he heard Rangers Garber and Daniels discussing the situation on the radio and listened patiently as he drove north, calculating how to react. He finally broke in. "What I'm hearing is we should let the first convoy through, since it's portable barnyards, right? And we'll try to take the second convoy?"

Daniels replied, "Yes, that's what I'd recommend."

Garber said, "Concur. The second convoy is just now getting to Rhome. I'll drop in behind them and call the locations to y'all."

Daniels replied, "I'm coming into Bowie now. Ortega is mobilizing his folks, and Bogle is prepping their explosives to blow the road into the ranch if necessary."

Richie exited 287 and pulled in behind the Valero station at FM 1655, sliding to a halt as a big Chevrolet pickup pulled a boat up to the diesel pumps. A string of cars and trucks and a couple of horses continued to trickle in as three men worked over the boat. The fire chief pulled into the lot with a pumper, backing carefully into a corner of the lot away from the pumps.

***

Sheriff Ortega rocketed down the highway, heading for Bowie and the Bogle ranch, cursing the beautiful weather as Shrimp hung on for dear life. "Dammit, Sheriff, I'd prefer not to die until we get there. I don't have any damn legs to brace with over here!"

Ortega slowed down and glanced over at the little wizened man in the passenger's seat. "Sorry, Shrimp. But I need to... Shit!" He swerved wildly, barely missing the big Black Angus steer standing in the right lane. He grabbed the mic and keyed the radio, barking, "Daisy, call Bergstrom and tell him his damn cows are out again. If they're still out when I come back, I'm gonna shoot the sumbitches."

"Dispatch copied, Sheriff. Be advised, Bogle is activating their folks now."

"Roger. I'm headed for the hotel on 59. I'll meet our folks there."

Ranger Daniels added, "I'm ten away, coming south. Meet you at the hotel parking lot."

At the feedlot, the cowboys and veterans were finishing the preparations they had been working on for almost a week. Pruitt, the Segundo, was passing out Type 56 AKs and the Norinco clones, along with bandoleers of magazines for each, to the cowboys who were spreading out down the side road. Becky, Pruitt's seventeen-year-old blonde-haired, blue-eyed granddaughter, her AR slung over her back, was handing out canteens full of water and getting teased by various cowboys. Joe Littlebear, Victor, his son, and Little Joe, his grandson, rode up, and Joe bowed graciously to her. "Thank you, Miss Becky. I will treasure this water prepared with your own hands." He smiled wolfishly at her, and she laughed.

"Why the paint on your face, Uncle Joe?"

Joe thumped his chest, then chuckled. "I am Comanche; it is appropriate to wear war paint when one goes to war!"

Becky sighed. "It just looks like you got black paint on your hands and smeared your face."

"The paint is a sign that I have triumphed in hand to hand combat." He pointed to his forehead, saying, "This is for power and speed."

Victor Littlebear shook his head. "That was a long time ago, Dad. Come on, Little Joe." The three of them rode out of the yard and across the road, then cut across the field to a copse of trees near the frontage road. "Are you sure about this, Dad? You think you can do something with those Molotov cocktails?"

Joe grinned, his bright white teeth contrasting with the black war-paint on his wrinkled face. "You shoot, I ride. I've seen what these can do. Comanche warriors were once feared; now they will be again."

Lisa Boone came trotting up to them, an AR slung over her back, a personal radio in her hand. "Uncle Joe, I'm your communications link."

He nodded as he rode into the trees, then got down, loosened the girth on his horse's saddle, and lay down, pulling his hat down over his face. "Wake me when they get here. Us old folks need our naps."

Lisa looked at Victor, who just shook his head. Little Joe checked his rifle yet again. Then she threw up her hands and laughed softly as she rode up beside Little Joe. "He is something else, isn't he?"

Little Joe nodded, twirling his finger at his temple. "That he is. But I've never seen a better horseman."

Ortega and Daniels met the veterans at the hotel, and the sheriff passed out Type 56s to any that wanted them from the back of his pickup. Once everyone was armed, he gathered them around. "Okay folks, we're going to be the backup for Bogle. That's a tight area down there, and he's got plenty of cowboys ready to go. Also, if the trucks come this way to go back down to the feedlot, we're going to try to stop the big rigs and take out the

179

back technical. Now remember, Bogle's folks will shoot this direction, so be prepared to get to cover if you hear rounds start popping off. Questions?"

***

Richie's radio crackled as Ranger Garber reported, "Fifteen miles out of Alvord. I'm guessing they are blowing right on through Decatur."

Deputy Menendez, hidden up a driveway well off 287, responded, "Lead group is through Decatur. Looks like they're running about sixty. Technical in the lead, big gun in the back and at least three guys in the back. Armor is… cab is armored, looks like the front end too. Back is armored about as high as a stake bed truck. Five… pickups behind it with… five or six shooters in them, no armor. Some in the cab, some in the back." A minute later he added, "Ten cattle haulers, and another full-up technical as tail end charlie."

The sheriff keyed up, "Thanks, Miggy. Dispatch, have Fisher pass that to his contact in Montague County. Tell him we will let the first bunch through."

"Dispatch copies."

He hopped out of the Tahoe and walked over to the diesel pumps, making sure his radio was off before he got too close. The 17-foot runabout on the boat trailer was pointing the wrong direction, with the bow at the back of the trailer, and was missing its engine and drive. Inside, it had been gutted, and they had secured one of the three-hundred-gallon plastic tanks in place of the seats. The old man pumping diesel into the plastic tank was giggling, and Sheriff Richie shivered. "Bert, are you sure this will work? We've got about twenty minutes."

The boy at the pump said, "That's four gallons, Grandpa."

Shutting the nozzle off, Bert handed it down to his grandson. "Thank you, Ethan. Now go with your gram, if you would."

"I can't stay and watch?"

Bert cracked his neck as he climbed nimbly out of the boat. "Maybe from a ways back, but not up close." He turned to the sheriff. "Danny, I did this shit for twenty years in the military, and another fifteen as an on-call EOD guy. This ain't my first rodeo. It will work. We goosed the ANFO mix a bit, and I got six sticks of dynamite mixed in, along with aluminum oxide and sugar." He pointed to the box strapped onto the cage that held the plastic tank. "All I need to do is hook up the wires and we're ready to go. I just need to be within a hunnert yards to make sure it goes off."

Richie bit his lip. "This is going to blow a hole in the road, isn't it?"

Bert giggled again. "Most probably, and a few windows out. Ain't like many folks are using 287 anyway, these days."

Alton Morrow walked up, chewing on a piece of straw. "Done, Bert?"

"Yep, other than the final connection."

"Sheriff, I scoped out the area here, and talked to the chief. I think a straight shot out of the parking lot from here is about right. That's the steepest slope down to the road. Chief says he'll wet it down as soon as that first bunch goes through."

Deputy Parker slid to a stop in his Tahoe and jumped out. "Everybody is in position along the frontage road down to the park. Spears is tail end charlie. He said he'll take care of the last technical. He wanted a radio check. And Amanda has her unit over behind the hotel, pulling ground security for the snipers." A young Hispanic kid sat in the front seat of the Tahoe, smiling as he waved at the sheriff.

Richie waved back and asked, "Is the box truck blocking the exit?"

"Yep, Felix parked it like we discussed, made it look like it'd run out of gas."

Derrick Shack, the bank's security manager, laid his map out on the hood of the sheriff's Tahoe, pinning it down with magazines he pulled from his pocket and said, "I got that. I'll start now." He turned on his personal radio and started calling people as he pulled a pencil out and checked off names.

Shack leaned over and said, "Trooper just went by Spears."

Richie yelled, "Heads up, first convoy is coming by in a minute. Everybody stay back from the road!" He looked around and asked, "Where are Brien and his spotter?"

"They're on the Budget Motel roof, Sheriff."

"Lemme see your radio." Derrick handed it to him, and he keyed it, saying, "Brien, this is Sheriff Richie. How copy?"

"Five by, Sheriff."

"First convoy is coming through in a minute. Let them go. The second convoy is about ten minutes behind them."

"Rog."

He started to key the radio, then he heard Spear say, "Convoy passing now. Technical up front, big gun in back, with a front shield only, manned and looking. Five crew cab pickups following that thing, looks like four in each cab, two or three hunched down in the back. All the ones in the back appear to have weapons. Look like AKs. And barnyards. Looks like two in each cab. And... apparently the shotgun riders have AKs, too."

He keyed the radio, "Got it. Assume the second convoy will be about the same." He heard a double click, then silence. He turned to Parker and asked, "Did you make sure the folks on the west side of the highway know to stay inside and low?"

Deputy Parker nodded. "They got the word; Price was taking care of that. They're sitting over there with shotguns, rifles, and pistols in case anybody runs that way."

"Okay," Richie said. He keyed his radio, saying, "Dispatch, have Fisher pass to Montague the convoy is fifteen minutes out from Bowie."

"Dispatch copies," came over the speaker as they heard the first convoy go by.

A minute later, he heard Brien say, "First convoy is clear. Confirm I'm to start the ball game."

Richie nodded to Shack, who keyed the radio and said, "You are cleared to start the ball game." He watched the fire department pumper back across the road and run two short hose lines out, spraying the side of the embankment down, getting it as wet as they could, as Morrow backed the boat in line with the firetruck. Morrow got out and unstrapped the boat from the trailer as Bert finished hooking up the wires, and the sheriff shivered as he saw a red light come on the box strapped to the tank. *I hope to God Bert is right and this works. This shit is really going to happen. We're going to preemptively kill God knows how many people in just a few minutes.* He shivered again, then looked around, hoping nobody had noticed. The firetruck snorted and pulled away, and Morrow backed up until the boat was right at the top of the embankment.

The radio broke Richie's reverie, and he said a quick prayer as he heard Brien's spotter say, "Got the convoy in sight. Technical, five pickups, a… damn… a Caddy convertible, a bus, and… ten semis pulling box trailers."

Richie ran over and grabbed the radio Shack was putting to his mouth. He keyed up and said, "Don't shoot the bus. We don't know who is on it. Everything else is fair game. Repeat, do not shoot the bus!"

The boom of Brien's MK-82 50 cal snapped Richie's head around. Even as he motioned, Morrow was already stomping on the gas, and the trailer started tipping down the bank. Morrow slammed on the brakes and then roared forward, pulling the empty boat trailer back into the parking lot. Brien's spotter said, "Boat is in the right lane. Technical is still coming. Gunner is down."

Richie looked at Bert, then nodded. Bert, now deadly serious, flipped two switches and they found themselves on the ground, being pelted by dirt and gravel, their ears ringing. The veterans and cowboys that had been crouching by the gas station were running across the road and throwing themselves down at the top of the embankment as he heard the MK-82 fire twice more.

As the back of the convoy slowed, Spears braced himself against the tree he'd chosen to support the old 30-06 and shot the gunner in the rear technical and watched him fall as he mumbled, "Stupid, stupid… Now let's see if I can clear the cab with these old AP rounds." It took three rounds, but on the third one, the

183

technical jerked forward into the back of the semi-trailer directly ahead of it. He yelled, "Reloading, watch the bed of the—"

He ducked as rounds sprayed through the trees, and splinters hit him in the face. "Fuckers," he grumbled as he quickly loaded another five armor-piercing rounds into the old bolt gun and put all five of them into the bed of the technical. The veterans opened up on the three pickups left in a flurry of well-aimed rifle fire and quickly suppressed the few rounds coming back from the pickups. The firing died off quickly, except for one shotgun round.

Shack's voice came over the personal radios. "Cease fire, cease fire. Everybody safe your weapons. Sheriff's folks will go take a look."

Sheriff Richie, the deputies and some veterans, guns at the low ready, walked slowly down the embankment. As they did, the sheriff heard, "This is Garber. I've got one down back here."

Richie keyed his mic and said, "We've got a bunch more down up here. Where are you?"

"Half mile back. Coming up, this one isn't going anywhere. It's a Bravo Mike, mid-twenties."

Deputies Parker and Price approached the bus carefully, both with rifles up. Amanda Price yelled out, "Open the door!" as she pointed her rifle at the stunned driver sitting in a welter of broken glass from the windshield that had exploded into his lap when the ANFO went off.

The door hissed open, and Parker said, "I'll make entry. Cover me from here." Price nodded at him and he stepped aboard, then quickly back out. "Bus is full of black males, looks like there are a few cut by the glass flying around. Gonna bring them off and line them up on the road." She nodded again, her M-16 still pointed at the windshield. Parker stepped back in and said, "Starting from the rear of the bus, get up, hands behind your heads, walk slowly to the front, then down the steps and lay down on the ground. Hands behind your heads, feet crossed."

The stunned blacks, forty-five of them, were soon on the ground. One of the older ones said, "Man, we ain't got no guns.

We... we was up here to get some food. Ain't no call for what you done."

A single shot sounded by the trucks, and everyone jumped. One of the veterans waved and yelled, "Sumbitch tried to shoot me, but I got him first."

They lined another nineteen men up on the road, nine of them segregated when the sheriff got down there. Spears said, "These nine were riding shotgun, literally. There were ten, but that last one didn't want to come out."

Richie hunched his shoulders, then said, "Thirty-eight dead in the front. Thirty in the pickups, five in the technical, and three in the Caddy convertible."

Spears smiled. "Five in the back technical, too. And no survivors."

Garber rolled up in his Tahoe, a bullet hole in his windshield, and got out grinning. "Looks like the plan worked like a champ, but I didn't expect a bunch of prisoners."

Richie chuckled grimly, "Neither did we. And I don't have any place to hold fifty-four prisoners, guess we can ship them up to Wichita. Oh, and one of the dead is a Chinese major. He was in the back seat of the third pickup with this guy." He flipped the IDs to Garber, saying, "Make of that what you will, but this pretty much confirms everything those other guys gave us on intel."

Garber walked up to the Caddy, looked in and laughed. "Well, well, well. Puddinhead Smith." He thought for a second, then added, "That means the other one has to be Rat Face. Leaders of the Bloods and Crips in the same car – will wonders never cease? Now, if I can just find someplace to get a new windshield."

Brien and his spotter were looking at the remains of the flipped over technical as the sheriff walked up. Richie watched curiously as Brien wrenched the driver's door open, spilling out a burnt corpse. Recoiling, he asked, "What are you looking for?"

Brien said, "Just checking the penetration on the Raufoss rounds I fired. Looks like it went all the way through the plate, the driver, and out the back of the cab armor. I was hoping it rattled around a little bit, but at least I got the driver." He turned and

185

looked back at the hotel, now missing most of the windows on the third and fourth floors. "Hope you know you damn near blew us off the roof. A little warning would have been nice."

Richie shrugged. "Sorry about that. I wasn't sure how much damage we would get." He pointed at the technical sitting upside down on top of the first pickup in line. "I really didn't expect this, or all the windshields blown out, but it worked to keep the return fire down."

"Did we lose anybody?"

"Yeah, Ray Carter took a ricochet in the face, and Tom Stiles got hit in the top of the head, never even got a round off."

"Damn."

***

As the first convoy rolled north, Zafado looked out the window nervously. "I do not like this. I see a lot of horses and riders."

Schneider, the Reich leader sitting in the front seat of the first pickup behind the technical, laughed, "Bunch of redneck cowboys," lifting the Type 56 AK in his lap he patted it., "This tops anything those punks have. This will be a piece of cake, don't you worry."

Zafado smirked. "Hopefully, they are as dumb as the cows they herd."

The Chinese radio sitting beside Zafado on the back seat went off, and they heard rapid Spanish from the technical ahead of them. "We see cows. But the road does not have a ramp."

Zafado grabbed it and hit the mic key. "Can we cross with the technical and pickups?"

"I think so."

Zafado made a quick decision. "We cross. Jose, you are in the lead truck. Take the big trucks up to the next crossover and come back down to the cows. Felix, take the technical across the median."

"*Si*, Zafado," came over the radio.

Zafado reached down and fondled the pearl handled, chromed 1911 in his waistband, smiling. "Maybe they have some pretty girls up here."

***

Joe Littlebear tightened the girth on his favorite horse, rolling his lit cigar in his mouth as the first technical started slowly across the median, and said, "We let all of them go by; the back one is ours. Are you ready, Victor?"

Victor looked up at his dad and answered, "Yes, I'm going to move forward so I'm ready to shoot. Little Joe, you stay with papa."

Little Joe nodded, eyes wide as he looked at Lisa. Lisa keyed her radio and advised, "Uncle is moving into position." She heard a double click back and blew out a breath as her horse stamped nervously. The first technical went by, then the pickups straggled by, and finally the last technical pulled up just past them and stopped. Victor shot the man behind the W85, and that kicked off everything. Joe kneed his horse and burst from the copse of trees almost at a gallop as he lit the wick of the Molotov cocktail in his right hand. He let out a ululating Comanche war cry as he charged up to the technical and lobbed the Molotov cocktail into its bed. He quickly reached for the other one, lit it and threw it into the pickup truck in front of the technical, then kneed his horse around while bullets cut the air around him. Victor and Little Joe were firing from cover into the pickups as men jumped out trying to escape the flames.

More gunfire sounded up the ditch toward the feedlot as the other cowboys started firing. The first technical had just turned up the dirt road to the feedlot when Bogle's D-11 came roaring around from behind the first barn. The gunner on the technical stopped swinging his gun toward the ditch and frantically turned back to the front, firing at the dozer as it trundled down on them, its U-blade raised.

The W85 rounds were bouncing off the armor over the front of the big dozer, so the gunner lowered the gun to the blade. A ricochet came back and took his head off just as the D-11 got to

187

the technical. The u-blade went under the front end, and old man Bogle jerked the blade up, standing the technical almost on its tailgate. Cowboys ran around the sides of the dozer and fired through the underbody until he dropped it back on its wheels. Pruitt ran up and stuck the barrel of the Type 56 in the slot in the driver's side window and emptied the magazine into the interior.

Zafado had dropped to the floor of the pickup as soon as he heard the first rounds fired. He frantically reached up and opened the back door away from the gunfire. He crawled out of the pickup and down into the ditch, then crawled toward the feedlot gate, cursing softly in Spanish as the gunfire shredded his and the Reich's gunnies. He hid in the grass by the gate until he didn't hear any more firing. Only then did he risk a look back at the other trucks, but all he saw was the last two on fire and no one moving in any of the others. He heard laughter up by the first technical and peered around the cross tie that held the fence up, his temper flaring.

He reached down and jerked his pistol out of his waistband and started to shoot the cowboys standing by the technical, but just then they moved around in front of it. He cursed again, then bent low and crept up to the back wheel, then to the front wheel. Just as he started around the front end, Becky Pruitt started coming the other way. He chuckled, causing her to look up, and he said, "*Hola, chica.* Come here."

Becky stopped short and shook her head, and he added, "*Tal vez te haga mi puta.* Come here!"

She took a step back, and he raised his pistol. "Come here, or I kill you." He saw something flash in front of his face, and he was suddenly being dragged backward, losing his pistol. He tried to get up and only went face down. His loose pants slid down his legs to the tops of his boots as he was dragged backward. He heard female laughter and lost it, screaming curses in Spanish at the top of his lungs, even as he flopped onto his back. Lisa backed her horse up to keep him from getting up. Pruitt led the charge of men around the technical and stopped short, first snickering, then laughing outright.

Becky looked up at her grandfather, "That… he was going to make me his whore or try to."

That stilled the laughter, and one cowboy said, "Well, since his pants are down, we can cut him right now."

Somebody else said, "Let's brand his ass, too… I'll get the iron going." A couple of mumbles were heard, and two cowboys strode off, one coming back with a long extension cord.

The other cowboys, Victor, and Little Joe came back leading Joe's horse, with Joe across the saddle. Lisa, tears in her voice, said, "I was coming to tell you. Uncle Joe got shot. He… was dead before we could get to him."

Becky bowed her head, tears rolling down her face. Grimly she glared around, then said, "Somebody give me a pair of gloves and the tools." She put her hands over her face for a few seconds, then added, "Victor, Little Joe, I'm so sorry. I didn't know."

Pruitt looked down at her. "What are you going to do?"

"I'm going to turn him into a steer for what they did, Grandpa," she looked around and said, "Y'all hold his ass down."

Four cowboys grabbed his legs, spreading them and sitting on them, while two more put their knees on his chest. Another cowboy brought a pair of gloves, the Newberry knife, and a spray bottle of Champion Seal.

Becky knelt and rudely shoved the knife into position. Smiling through her tears, she said, "*Desde hoy, tu vas a ser la puta. Pinche joto!*" She clamped the knife closed, and Zafado screamed, and then passed out. She finished the job, sprayed the area with Champion Seal, then got up and ran for the barn, crying.

Pruitt took the branding iron, checked to see that it was hot, and looked at old man Bogle. Bogle nodded and Pruitt said, "Flip his ass over." Two of the cowboys did, and he applied the brand just as Sheriff Ortega and Ranger Daniels walked up.

The sheriff blew out a breath and said, "Do I want to know?"

189

Bogle said, "Joe Littlebear is dead. He took out the two trucks on fire. This sumbitch tried to grab Becky."

"Is he still alive?"

Ranger Daniels noticed the blood between his legs. "Turned him into a steer, didn't ya."

Pruitt glared at the two of them. "You got a problem with that, I'm your boy."

Ed Daniels stepped back, raising his hands, a little smile on his face. "Not from me. I don't have to deal with him in jail."

The sheriff's face fell, and he mumbled, "Aw, shit. I gotta put up with his ass. Literally. Him and the other ten we took out of the trucks." He glanced over at the old man, "Mr. Bogle, you got any use for ten cattle trucks and drivers?"

Old man Bogle laughed. "I think we can find something to keep them busy."

***

Rangers Garber, Daniels, and Sandoval once again sat in Sheriff Richie's conference room, in Decatur along with Sheriff Ortega, Chief Lynn, and one new attendee, Ranger Major Len Martin, from Austin. Sheriff Richie strolled in and shook hands with the major. "Welcome to our humble abode, Major."

"Call me Len. Y'all have done one helluva job up here, but there is going to have to be an investigation."

Richie pursed his lips. "Whatever. We did what we had to do to protect ourselves, but we had a lot of help from veterans, ranchers, cowboys, DPS, and your folks. We took some losses, too. We lost two people: Ray Carter and Tom Stiles. We still got two in the hospital, Jesus lost one, and Wichita has a bunch of extra prisoners to feed because we didn't have any place to put them."

Ortega added, "Joe Littlebear. Damn Comanche charged the technical and one of the pickups with Molotov cocktails and got both of them... but they got him."

Martin bowed his head for a few seconds. "I heard. I'm sorry for that, but between you two and your folks, you effectively gutted the leadership of the major gangs in Dallas and

Fort Worth. This might give DPD and FWPD a chance at regaining control, but there will be splinter groups and the remnants of the major groups reforming. The question will be which ones get it together first. From what I hear, y'all have plenty of weapons now to deal with most anything that comes your way. But there will—"

Sandoval interrupted, "Major, I've already done the investigation." He slid a thumb drive across the table. "Here are all the witness statements, the district attorney's inputs and statements that they will not file charges. My investigation indicates all the shoots were good, as they did not fire first."

Martin cocked his head and looked at Sandoval. "You… already investigated… and got DA statements. He looked at the thumb drive like it was a snake, then sighed, picked it up, and put it in his shirt pocket. "The colonel… ah, screw it. I'll go with what you said."

All of them chuckled at that, and Sandoval continued, "We've allocated the weapons and food supplies where we think they will do the most good up here, and we still have half of a Conex full of weapons. All of my counties now have militias or are forming them."

"That's another thing I wanted to discuss. We'd like to get some of those weapons out to the various Rangers in the field." He glanced over and saw Garber hand a grinning Daniels a twenty-dollar bill and shook his head. "Let me guess, you knew this was coming?"

Daniels laughed. "Hell, Major, we've already been passing them out. Rangers are showing up with horse trailers and we load 'em up. I figure we've already taken care of most of North and East Texas already. There should be at least a pallet or two down by College Station by now, and a truck from El Paso is supposed to be here tomorrow. Everybody is getting M4 clones, AKs, RPGs, and a Whiskey-85 apiece."

Martin shook his head, mumbling, "Why did I even bother…"

Richie chuckled. "We even saved a few for you and the Colonel."

# Think of the Children

## Chris Hernandez

"God dammit," Rodriguez muttered. "They're comin' agin."

Nunez groaned in silence. Rodriguez's warning had come through Nunez's feigned sleep, and even though Nunez had been more or less conscious behind closed eyes he wished more than anything else that he didn't have to wake up. Not to this. Not again.

Nunez forced his eyes open. For the first few seconds he couldn't see through the fog of fatigue, wisps of smoke, his headache, and what looked like actual fog. But the haze gave way to semi-sharp focus, and he was able to make out Rodriguez's eyes, staring downward from a hanging head. Further down the trench, soldiers grudgingly forced themselves through the motions: checking rounds in chambers, wiping dirt and dew from optics, checking magazines, settling feet and elbows into hollows and divots for stability even though they had plenty of time before anyone would fire a shot.

Except for Rodriguez, their faces looked blank. Or, Nunez thought they did. Nunez couldn't quite focus yet, he couldn't really tell.

Thirty yards down the trench Lieutenant Waldron wiped his face, put his helmet on, and got to his feet. His expression, and every motion of his body, screamed *Fuck this, I hate this, I'm done.* He looked at Nunez, shook his head, and slogged away through the ankle-deep sludge to wake up the handful of Joes who'd been allowed to sleep. Waldron took care not to nudge the bodies, or piles of parts, pushed against the back wall of the trench; the poncho- or woobie-covered bodies he avoided out of respect, the mud-covered corpses out of disgust. Disgust, and the slight chance that one of them just might be wrapped in a live vest.

Nunez pushed his upper body off the trench wall he'd been leaning against and tried to stand. His put his left hand down for stability, and whatever it happened to land on shifted. He looked down and could barely discern the faint outline of a forearm and hand, just under a layer of liquid grime and blood. He stared at it, then put two fingers on it and gently forced it further under the mud. Whether it was Persian or Arab, or both, he couldn't tell. And he wasn't about to dig it out and look.

"How many, Rodriguez?" Nunez asked.

"Forty, maybe," Rodriguez said, without looking up. "Or sixty. Who fuckin' knows. I don't wanna look."

Nunez didn't even think about bitching Rodriguez out. He was surprised the man had held on this long. That any of them had held on, really.

"Rodriguez –"

Rodriguez popped up and wiped his face in a rush. "Sorry, Top. I didn't mean nuthin'. I'm gittin' up."

Nunez wobbled to his knee, then his feet. As Rodriguez checked his mags, Nunez stepped to him and tapped his calf.

"Sit this one out, brother. You've earned a break."

Rodriguez sagged and closed his eyes. Nunez could see the wheels turn in his head: *I'm a soldier, I don't need no damn break.* But the weariness won out, like Nunez knew it would.

Tyler Rodriguez was a cowboy from Goliad, Texas. He was dark haired and dark eyed, deeply tanned from a life spent in fields and on horseback, and looked just like his *Indio* cousins in Mexico, but was such a Mexican country hick that his fellow troops nicknamed him "wetneck" and "redback." After a few raised eyebrows and one near-fistfight they changed it to "Mexneck," which everyone liked.

Rodriguez looked toward the enemy for a few moments. Then he turned, nodded in slow motion, and half climbed, half slid the few feet from the parapet to the trench floor. Nunez watched him gather himself, then patted him on the shoulder. Rodriguez took his helmet off and faced Nunez.

"Top, I ain't wussin' out, okay? I'll git back up there soon's y'all need me."

Nunez nodded and gave a faint smile. Rodriguez's eyes were bloodshot and red-rimmed, inside a face smeared with mud, blood, and oil. He reached out to gently grab Nunez's forearm. Nunez was almost sure he felt the man's hand shaking.

"It's jus' that," Rodriguez mumbled, "before we come out here, muh waff Brittney tole me, 'Kill whoever you have to. Them kids ain't like our kids, so don't worry about nothin' you do. Just come home to me.'"

"But Top," Rodriguez said, then swallowed and leaned in. "Before I shot the last one, I looked in his eyes through mah scope. He was cryin', and they was yankin' him toward us. He knew what that thing on his chest was, and he knew we was gonna shoot him before he got here. He was jus' a little boy, maybe fourteen. He seen all the pieces layin' everywhere, and he *knew* he was next. I ain't never seen a kid with a look on his face like that. That lil' boy was scared out his fuckin' mind, Top. Scared cuz' he knew I's 'bout to kill him."

Rodriguez squeezed Nunez's forearm. "Brittney was wrong, Top. That boy din't look so different from mah son. An' he was jist as scared as my son woulda been."

Nunez grabbed Rodriguez's hand. "Rodriguez, when you get home, tell Brittney that. Tell her you love her, but she was wrong. And the only reason you did what you did, was to protect her and your own kids. But you never thought their kids were less important than yours."

Rodriguez exhaled slowly. "Top, don't this shit bother you? I know you's a daddy. And I watched you pop a coupla them kids earlier."

195

"I'm not letting it bother me. I'm busy, I'll think about my kids later. And when I get home I'll try not to remember what we had to do here."

Rodriguez looked down. He swallowed hard, closed his eyes, and nodded. Then he let go of Nunez, sat in the mud and settled back against the trench wall. He stood his carbine against the trench beside him, dropped his helmet into the mud, wrapped his arms around his knees and hung his head into his hands. And never opened his eyes, while doing any of that.

Nunez climbed to Rodriguez's spot on the parapet and looked through his ACOG toward the enemy lines. Nearly 400 meters distant, he saw the line of attackers, chained together, plodding toward him. The line sagged in spots and formed a peninsula in others, with the points jutting toward the Texan trench. They were the fifth wave, coming out of an unseen staging area in distant low ground.

Nunez started on one end and counted. It took a couple minutes, but there was no real rush; previous waves, between having to wake up kids who passed out, or stopping and being forced to start again by warning shots fired by their own side, or recoiling in horror upon seeing what was left of the previous waves, had taken as long as sixteen minutes to reach the trigger point a hundred meters from the Texan trench.

Under ideal conditions, the Texans – infantrymen of Alpha Company, 4th of the 112th Infantry Regiment, 36th Infantry Division, who had come to call themselves the "Free Texas Army" – could have easily started hitting targets and detonating vests at 300 meters. But some soldiers were wounded, some were concussed, and all were dead tired, mud-drenched, nearing mental exhaustion, and nowhere near as accurate as normal. On top of that, some optics lenses had been cracked or shattered, forcing men to dump them and switch back to irons. But mostly, nobody wanted to shoot until they were absolutely sure the attackers wouldn't turn back. Until they had no choice.

Nunez put his carbine down. Rodriguez had been off, there were over seventy attackers this time. This was maybe the

196

second biggest group so far, chances were they'd take their time getting to the trigger point.

Lieutenant Waldron climbed to the spot beside Nunez. "How many, Top?"

"Seventy something, sir. Seventy-fiveish."

Waldron squinted into the distance. "They singing yet?"

"Not yet," Nunez muttered. "I'm sure they'll burst into a rousing rendition of *Staying Alive* before they get here."

"A rousing rendition of what?"

Nunez rolled his eyes. "Fucking millennials. Don't know shit about real music."

"Yeah," Waldron laughed. "Reminisce about grandpa shit later. You hear the news?"

Nunez turned to Waldron and shook his head. "What news?"

"Brigade fucked off and quit talking to us. Terrel's been calling for over an hour and can't get anything. It's not his battery, and he function checked his radio twice. We sent two runners back, and guess who they found?"

"I probably don't even wanna know, sir. And I think I know the answer anyway."

"The Azovs. Brigade is gone, and the fucking Azovs occupied brigade's position afterward. We don't have a clue where they went."

Nunez exhaled, and looked downward. "An hour? And why didn't anyone tell me?"

"You were asleep. And we haven't told anyone. No need to drop anyone's morale lower than it already is. Not until we've figured out what the fuck is going on, anyway. Besides," he said, gesturing with his head toward the enemy position, "one problem at a time."

Nunez turned away from Waldron and grunted. Yet another ridiculous disaster, in a deployment full of them.

One day earlier Nunez's company, in country only a few weeks, had been tasked with occupying trenches recently dug by Saudi engineers before they retreated, against orders, in the face of a slow-moving Iranian advance. A Saudi line unit had occupied the trenches, but they were so understrength and poorly trained they were practically a tripwire defense whose only job was to notify their superiors before dying martyrs' deaths. The Texans were supposed to convoy through Regular Army positions, dismount where the road ended at the edge of rocky, impassable ground, move the last three kilometers on foot and take over the almost-empty trenches before sunset. The Regular Army brigade commander's intent was clear: by nightfall, be fully established on the position and ready to fight.

The Texans considered it a near-miracle that they had gotten any real missions at all. The Regular Army troops had been openly hostile toward the Texans even before the flight from Joint Base Lewis-McChord. At least, the leadership was hostile; lower enlisted and more than a few senior NCOs were generally friendly, and some made comments like "Secede, brothers!" But those comments were from a distance, and didn't stop the leadership from screwing the Texans at every turn.

This wasn't surprising, considering the growing division between the Texas governor and US president. In the years since the cartel/jihadist incursion across the Texas border, the federal government push to jail the Guard troops who'd been hit hardest, and the uprising that had very nearly ensued until the president backed off, the Texas Military Forces had been about one boot step from revolution. From the moment of their arrival at Lewis-McChord the Texas troops had followed orders with a barely-concealed *fuck you* undertone toward senior leaders, and had even replaced the American flags on their shoulders with Texas flags. If Texas was on the verge of open rebellion, so were its sons in what they almost considered foreign lands.

But when they landed in Saudi Arabia, the Texans paid the price for their hostility. When the planes landed and cargo had to be offloaded, the Regular Army officer in charge put the Texas troops on the work detail. When the regulars were put up in temporary buildings, the Texans got stuck in torn, leaky tents. If the Saudis asked for manpower for the perimeter or Joes to burn shit from latrines, the Texans were voluntold. As requests came in for American units to plus up defenses at outposts, RA units were kept intact while their commander tried to part out the Texans in squads or even as individuals. The Texan commander, Captain Little, put his foot down at that; as a result, the Texans sat on a boring, empty, sweltering Saudi logistics base for almost a month, doing nothing but PT, drills, weapons maintenance, shit details, and going crazy with boredom.

But orders finally came through, for a company to pass through Regular Army positions and help defend a trench. Those orders reached Nunez's company by 1300. The Texas troops cheered at the order, and ran around like happy children spreading the word and rushing to ready their gear. Their ride would be Egyptian Army trucks, which presented its own problems. On top of that, when the Texans rallied up, mounted the trucks and moved to the fuel and ammo points they were told the Saudis hadn't allowed resupply to come through yet but it was expected within the hour. About half the company managed to refuel and load up, the rest of them waited. And waited. For three hours.

The fuel and ammo trucks finally showed up. It was almost 1700 before the company was ready to roll toward the Regular Army position. Getting close took another hour because troops at a Saudi Army checkpoint refused to let them move for almost twenty minutes, until someone called on the radio and screamed at the checkpoint commander. Then when the company made it to within ten klicks of the Regular Army's reported position, they were stopped at another checkpoint. Except this time the checkpoint wasn't full of confused Saudis; it was manned by about a platoon's worth of Ukrainian Azov Division fighters hired by the Saudis to fight the Iranians. Nobody had mentioned Azovs, and Captain Little, the Texan company commander, sure as hell never expected to see them anywhere near American troops.

The Azovs were poorly-regarded brawlers, a mishmash of Ukrainian nationals, European volunteers and a smattering of Australians, Americans and South Africans, bonded by a willingness to fight Russia and celebrate or at least tolerate the blatant white supremacist ideology of their leaders. But the Azovs hated Russians, and Russians liked Iranians, so Azovs hated Iranians, and ergo the Saudis found them useful.

Little radioed brigade. He was told to move through the Azovs and link up with brigade as ordered. Little approached the Azov in command and made his orders and intent clear. The Azov leader told him to fuck off. Little considered his options, nodded, and walked back to the convoy. He called his platoon leaders, First Sergeant and platoon sergeants together for an old-fashioned leaders meeting at his truck. Little was not unwilling to listen to subordinates, and his subordinates were unanimous: fuck the Azovs. They'd stand aside or get mowed down as the company punched through them.

Little didn't want to go down that path just yet. He called brigade again and explained the situation. He was told that only under the most dire of circumstances was he to engage the Azovs. The American position in the shaky coalition against the Iranians was far from secure, no actions likely to jeopardize the alliance were permitted, and the brigade's Saudi liaison officer would handle the problem. Until that happened, hold in place.

Little asked the Egyptians to pull 500 meters back, directed them to coil up and had his Joes set a perimeter. That took half an hour. He gave every platoon leader clear guidance on what to do if the Azovs showed even a hint of hostile intent, and ensured every Azov target was identified and prioritized. That took another half hour. As he completed his tasks, he expected the radio call telling him the problem had been resolved and he could Charlie Mike. It didn't come. So after his security was set, he waited. And waited. And waited.

Periodic requests for a SITREP produced the same answer: *We are working the issue.* Bored Egyptians kicked off their boots, smoked, crawled under trucks to nap, tried to start conversations about movies and Taylor Swift with the Texans, and left their weapons laying around unattended. Little kept being told to stand by until almost midnight, when he was finally given the all clear to move out.

Cursing Egyptians struggled into their boots and clambered into the cabs while bored, frustrated Joes mounted up in back. The coil unwound back into a column on the highway, with Little in the lead. They made a slow advance toward the Azovs, half expecting a firefight. Instead, through their night vision they saw the Azovs pull barricades aside, sit back on boxes and old lawnchairs, light up joints and toss back beers. As Alpha slow-rolled through the checkpoint the Azovs laughed, pointed fingers, and flipped the Texans off. The passing grunts saw graffiti on barricades proclaiming *White Jihad!,* in English, alongside an SS skull and crossbones.

Little ignored them and pushed on, finally reaching the American brigade HQ at almost 0100. Surprise number two awaited him: the place was in complete disarray. Little walked out of the brigade commander's tent half convinced that the entire HQ was about to pull up stakes and haul ass. Iranians were on a slow approach from the east, a pathetically thin line of half-trained Saudi conscripts faced them, and the brigade commander was not at all convinced they'd even be a speed bump. He urged Little to hurry the fuck up and occupy the trenchline. Little check/roger/hooahed and moved out, and the company hit the dismount spot a few minutes later.

The Texans dismounted, formed up, and moved out on foot toward the trenches. Less than two hundred meters later they felt the wind kick up and saw flashes in the sky. Three hundred meters later the wind gave way to rain, which gave way to veritable cloudburst. And instead of smartly crossing broken but fairly open ground on a cool night, the troops were suddenly drenched, freezing, barely able to see each other in the pouring rain, and struggling through what had become a sea of mud.

Men stumbled and fell, struggled to get up, and when they finally regained their footing discovered that the man they were following had disappeared. Huge gaps opened in the columns. Squads and platoons veered onto different paths. Officers and

NCOs wore themselves out running up and down the lines in a futile quest to keep the company together. Little ordered the troops to slow to nearly a crawl, everyone was reconnected and pushed back into their columns, and the company almost resorted to having each man hold the pack of the soldier in front. By the time Little halted the company a hundred meters short of the trenchline, it was almost 0300. Then he, a small security team and an Arabic-speaking grunt moved forward to make contact with the Saudis. And, of course, the Saudis opened fire on them.

Little and his Joes hit the mud. The interpreter screamed in Arabic for the Saudis to cease fire. Commands were lost in the rain and wind. Tracers flashed so high over the Texans that even if they'd been standing tall they'd have been untouched. A sharp boom sounded from the trench and an RPG sailed so far overhead it may as well have been aimed at an imaginary helicopter.

Little radioed back to his troops to ensure them everyone was fine and called back to brigade to tell them to tell the Saudis to cease fucking fire. As he strained to keep his voice even and calm on the radio, the rain softened from "flood-producing deluge" to "just enough to piss a soldier off." Eventually, after a couple thousand rounds, the Saudis stopped shooting. And after a few minutes of shouting back and forth in Arabic and flashing strobes, the interpreter managed to convince the Saudis that they were Americans and not to shoot anymore.

Little moved his troops up. In the dark, they could hear the banging and shouting of the Saudi troops as they collected their gear and pushed north and south to neighboring trenches. No Saudi commander stayed behind to brief Little, or even to make sure they were really Americans. They just grabbed their gear, left behind heaps of trash, piles of shit and dozens of piss bottles, and hauled ass. The Texans pushed into the trench, which was an early World War I-style affair of two sections, each a hundred meters long, with a dogleg to keep one artillery round from taking out a company.

Little had started the mission with a grand plan to properly clear the trenches, assign sectors of fire, select target reference points and pre-plot targets for supporting arms. Instead he struggled to supervise a company-minus of soaked, exhausted Joes cursing under their breath as they slid down slick, muddy grooves in the trench wall or just tumbled from the lip of the trench to the bottom. The rain started again, and Little angrily demanded accountability from harried platoon leaders who then berated their platoon sergeants who then cursed their squad leaders and demanded that every Joe be physically touched to ensure nobody had been left behind or drowned in the muck. Nobody was missing, and by some miracle nobody had suffered anything worse than bumps and bruises.

As officers and NCOs forced order from chaos, and the company began to look like a disciplined, cohesive unit again, Captain Little and his First Sergeant walked all the way to the north end of the trench. He ensured the northern flank was covered by a gun team, then moved south to pat every single soldier under his command on the back and assure them that the situation would be better when the sun rose. 1$^{st}$ platoon sergeant Jerry Nunez was the last man he patted before disappearing around the dogleg. And then the southern section of the trench was torn by sudden, deafening booms.

The earth shook. Nunez ducked. Mud and debris dropped from the sky around him. Shrill screams sounded from the southern trench. Nunez swore some of them sounded like children, but that couldn't be right.

Men in the north trench ran to the dogleg and stopped, unsure whether or not to go around the bend. Nunez held them back, mostly because he wasn't sure what the hell to do either. Then two soldiers ran around the bend right into him, screaming in terror or agony. Nunez grabbed one of them, and something splashed onto Nunez's face. Blood, spraying from the stump of the man's severed arm. Nunez yelled "TQ him!" to the nearest man, but by the time the TQ was out the wounded man was down. Nunez couldn't waste any time on him.

Gunfire rang out in the southern trench. A short burst, followed by a long one. Tracers ricocheted off metal and bounced upward. Nunez jumped onto a firestep on the parapet and started to climb, hoping to see what the hell was going on. Blinding flashes and earsplitting roars beat him back down to his knees. He screamed at the cluster of troops near him to stay down and cover the dogleg. Nobody could hear him. He turned around to look for his platoon leader, just as a panicked soldier fired a burst into the dogleg. Nunez whipped around and saw a sprinting Texas soldier lurch forward into a shivering heap.

Nunez went deaf. He could feel himself breathing so hard he was nearly gasping, but couldn't hear it. Then Waldron was suddenly by his side, lighting himself with a red flashlight and mouthing *Let's go.*

Nunez shook his head to clear it, then jumped to his feet. He grabbed two men, even though he didn't know who they were, and said "Follow us" into each man's ear. They nodded, trying to make their mud-spattered, terrified faces look calm.

The moment they hit the dogleg a blast knocked them backward. Nunez fell into the mud, stunned. He felt a succession of thuds. When he finally forced himself to think clearly, he looked for Waldron. The lieutenant was sitting against the opposite trench wall, holding his ears. They looked at each other, and just waited. Neither moved until it was all over.

When the booms finally ceased, Nunez listened for anything from the other side. First he thought his eardrums were just too concussed, then realized there was nothing to hear. No agonized screams, no shouted orders, no calls for medics. Nothing.

Nunez and Waldron led a small team into the other trench section. They found mud-and-blood-coated body parts, mangled M4s and SAWs, rifle-protective plates blown from body armor and impaled into the trench wall, punctured helmets surrounded by Kevlar confetti, and heads. Tiny heads ripped at the throat, with blank or horrified expressions. Dozens of them, slowly sinking into the mud, blood and slime.

Nunez gave himself a moment to be in shock. Then he went back, made sure security was set, and grabbed a few Joes for a detail no soldier would ever want any part of. He made them drag all the bodies and parts to the back wall of the trench, collect and stack what was left of weapons, and gather any serviceable ammo. Then he led roughly a platoon's worth of Soldiers to the south leg of the trench and set security. Once that was done, Nunez began assessing casualties.

Captain Little and the First Sergeant were gone, along with two lieutenants and one platoon sergeant. The company executive officer had stayed behind with part of the headquarters platoon so the company hadn't been completely decapitated, but it had been effectively halved. And there were no wounded; every last Soldier in the southern leg had been killed. Multiple simultaneous suicide vests detonating in an enclosed space left no survivors. As a final insult, but by the time Nunez and Lieutenant Waldron got everyone organized they realized the Saudis on their flanks had fucked off and left them alone.

Nunez, who was now the First Sergeant, Lieutenant Waldron and the one remaining platoon sergeant had a quick huddle and realized they were stuck. They couldn't leave their dead behind, and they couldn't carry them. They needed help, from aircraft or troops in vehicles, so they could both hold their position and evacuate their dead. And they still had no idea the strength of the enemy force they were facing. Waldron ordered the one remaining radioman to contact brigade, as everyone else prepared to repel another assault.

Four hours and three suicide wave attacks later Nunez found himself standing in Rodriguez's spot on the lip of the trench, watching another wave of children coming, knowing he would have to kill them soon.

Waldron had wandered off, probably going down the line checking on everyone. For the tenth time that morning Nunez checked the tightness of the screws on his ACOG mount, ensured his magazines were all rounds-down and facing right in their pouches, tapped the TQ in his ankle pocket, made sure his radio was off to save the battery, and patted the laminated picture of his wife and children taped to his SAPI plate inside his plate carrier.

As the line of weighed-down, terrified children staggered forward, Nunez reflected on the most important piece of wisdom he'd ever learned in the military: *Things never suck so bad that they can't suck worse.* But short of having the entire company wiped out, Nunez had a hard time imagining how much worse it could get.

Twelve minutes later, when the kids had closed to less than two football fields, someone slapped Nunez on the calf. Too exhausted to be startled, Nunez gave a laconic look over his shoulder. A smiling Waldron and the company's dour-faced radioman stood by his feet.

"Hey Top," Waldron said. "Guess what?"

"Let me guess," Nunez said. "An entire division is on the way in helicopters to relieve us and take us straight back to Texas."

"Close," Waldron said, still smiling. "Brigade told us to go fuck ourselves. They're not sending anyone."

Nunez stared at him. Waldron just kept smiling. The radioman looked downward, eyes red, seeming near tears.

"You're fucking with me."

"I wish," Waldron said, finally dropping the smile. "We finally got them to answer the radio. They said, and I quote, 'We can't send anyone. Good luck.'"

Nunez frowned. "What the fuck does that mean? Are they that mad about the Texas flags on our uniforms?"

Hillegeist, the next infantryman down the trench, snorted without looking up from his weapon. "Hey guys," he laughed, "maybe we finally seceded!"

The radioman jerked his head up and looked at Hillegeist. Waldron and Nunez turned to him as well. The sudden silence made Hillegeist lift his head and meet their eyes.

"Geez, sir," Hillegeist mumbled. "It was supposed to be a joke."

Nunez looked at Waldron. "Well sir, did we?"

"How the fuck should I know? I've been busy here with you."

A voice down the line yelled, "150 meters! Get ready!"

206

"You know," Waldron said, "if they keep this shit up long enough, we're going to run out of ammo. And then we either go hand to hand with suicide bombers, or abandon our dead and run away to the Azovs, or the regular Iranian Army dickheads in that low ground hit us hard. And we lose."

"God damn it," Nunez muttered, turning toward the enemy. "This is not how Americans are supposed to fight wars. I was told we'd always have the advantage, or some shit like that."

He looked through his ACOG and couldn't quite make out faces yet. But now that he was paying attention he heard a few notes of off-key singing, much quieter than last time, barely audible for a moment before being carried away by desert wind. He watched them march closer, the eager ones out front yanking the reluctant bombers forward. After another minute their song was easy to hear but not understand.

Then Nunez could make out their faces through his scope. Then the kids realized what the ragged, charred lumps scattered before them were. The singing abruptly died down, a few wails and shrieks broke the chorus, and terrified children recoiled from the carnage. Nunez scanned the line, hoping they'd break and stagger-step backward, all the way to the depression they'd come from.

*Just turn back,* Nunez thought. *Yeah, your handlers will probably shoot you, but at least I won't have to.*

What sounded like angry Persian curses sounded from bound children. Nunez searched left and right until he found one of the cursing voices; a taller teenager, arms stretched backward in a V as he pulled the others forward, face an infuriated red mask. Nunez lifted his head from the scope and saw many others, maybe twenty, doing the same thing. The line wavered, then advanced into the minefield of body parts.

*Motherfucker.*

"First Sergeant Nunez!", someone yelled from down the line. Nunez recognized Sergeant Berisha's stilted, formal tone and Balkan accent. "Shall I try to frighten them away with warning fire?"

207

"Don't waste your time!" Nunez yelled back. They'd tried it once, and it hadn't worked. "After I fire the first shot, everyone pick a target and shoot!"

Now he had to follow his own orders. He didn't want to deliberately shoot a scared kid, at least not a specific kid. Not again. Nunez looked through his scope again, closed his eyes and pivoted his muzzle left.

*Whichever one is in my sights when I open my eyes, that's the one I hit.*

Nunez opened his eyes. Just off center from his crosshairs was the face of a little girl, maybe thirteen, eyes wide with fear. He hesitated a moment, then moved his sights onto the boy to her left.

"Less than a hundred meters!" someone yelled.

*Leave me the fuck alone,* Nunez thought.

Behind Nunez, Waldron yelled, "I don't know what the fuck you're talking about! We've lost almost half the company KIA and y'all need to send reinforcements and evacuate our dead! You copy, or what?"

Nunez didn't bother turning around. Someone was talking to them on the radio again, not that it would help.

"85 meters! Are we gonna shoot, or what?"

Nunez looked down into the dirt and bit his lip. Then he raised his eye to his ACOG and laid the crosshairs just below center mass on his chosen target, trying to keep the boy's face out of his scope. He took a deep breath, let it halfway out, held it, and squeezed the trigger.

Just before the trigger broke, he closed his eyes. He just didn't want to see it again.

# Baizuo

## Larry Correia

The dog went nuts, barking at something.

It took me a minute to wake up. There was someone knocking on my door. But not the front door. The back door. The sliding glass one to my fenced in backyard. I grabbed my phone. It was just after two in the morning. The knocking and barking continued. Only a crazy person or a criminal would be in my backyard at 2 AM.

The protests had turned violent, surely spurred on by right-wing agitators who had been bussed in. After the looters had run out of stores to burn, they'd started hitting houses. Who could blame them? After years of living under an oppressive system. I was worried since I was old and sick, they'd probably assume I had a cabinet full of pills to sell. They'd be wasting their time; the pharmacy hadn't been resupplied since everything had fallen apart. Their shelves were as bare as my medicine cabinet, another failure of capitalism.

I thought about calling 911, and even started dialing, but stopped. Cell phones had stopped working weeks ago. Besides, even if I could get a signal to ask for help, nobody would come anyway. Not anymore.

At least the lights worked. The power had been out more often than not lately. It took me a minute to get into my wheelchair because everything ached. While I struggled into the scat Carl ran off to bark directly at the back door. Maybe the sound would scare them off? Doubtful. Carl was a Shih Tzu. He was more yap than bark.

My grandson had tried to talk me into having a gun in the house. When I'd told him that guns only made things worse, and I wasn't one of *those people,* he'd tried to give me one anyway, saying that the world was going to hell in a handbasket. He was right. The sorry state of things was obvious to anyone with a brain and an internet connection. But I was stubborn. What he was saying went against my identity. Ben, my sweet boy, love him to death, had turned into a right-wing nut job. I'd told him to leave it to the professionals. I'd be fine. The government was there to protect us.

Until they weren't there anymore. And right now, I wished I'd listened to him.

So, I rolled out to see who had hopped the fence into my backyard, defenseless except for ten pounds of agitated Shih Tzu. There were two men on the porch. The light above them was out, but from the shapes it looked like they'd given up knocking and started trying to pry the door open.

"What do you want? I don't have any money! I don't have any pills! Go away!"

The reply was muffled by the glass. "Grandpa! It's me."

"Ben?" It was hard to tell, because it had been a whispered hiss, trying to keep his voice down, like he didn't want to wake the neighbors. "Is that you?"

"Yeah. We need help."

That sounded like him, but I'd not seen or heard from my grandson in years, not since he'd had a falling out with our family. I'd figured he'd gotten caught up in all the chaos of the crash and gotten himself killed or arrested. He'd always been a hot head, and it would be just like him to survive Afghanistan to get murdered in Portland.

"Hurry, please. It's an emergency."

As I unlocked the door, I realized that there were bloody smears and handprints on the other side. Someone was injured. The glass slid open, and two figures stumbled through, one of

210

them holding up the other. They were both dressed in dark, dirty clothing, but were wearing those tan Army vests with all the pouches on their chests. Ben had a very frightening looking black assault weapon dangling from a strap around his neck and shoulder. The other young man might have had one behind his back, but I was too distressed to notice, because I realized he was bleeding all over my kitchen floor.

"Ben? What's going on?"

"I'll explain later." He helped the stranger limp toward the kitchen sink. "Shut the door, Granpda, please."

I did. "Has he been *shot?*"

"Repeatedly," grunted the newcomer. "You got any bandages?"

"I've got bath towels and paper towels."

"Awesome." He winced as he sank into one of the kitchen chairs. There was a rip through the thigh of his blood-soaked jeans, and a bunch of deep lacerations on his hard face. "And would you please shut that little dog up?"

"Carl!" Ben snapped. "Zip it."

My dog immediately stopped.

As I got the package of Costco paper towels from the pantry, Ben opened up one of the pouches on his vest thing and expertly pulled out what I assumed were medical tools. Despite the situation, my grandson seemed eerily calm.

"Relax, man. It missed the artery. You're going to be fine."

"Fuck! Fuck that hurts!"

Ben had joined the Army, which had enraged most of the family. We were a proper Portland family, from a long line of educators and social justice activists. Ben had assured us that he'd joined only to pay for college. Even back then I'd known that was a lie. Ben had always been a confrontational sort. That violent, sexist, ableist lifestyle had surely appealed to his base nature.

"I've not seen you for years, and you just show up at my house in the middle of the night with a man who's been shot! What's going on?"

211

"Sorry. There was trouble, I needed somewhere to hide, and you were close."

Carl whined, then went over and licked the wounded man's bloody hand. He responded by absently scratching behind Carl's ear. Some guard dog he was.

"We need to call the police," I said. "You need to get to a hospital."

"No," Ben said softly, distracted as he worked. "That's a bad idea."

"Yeah, who do you think shot me?"

*"What?* You were shot by the police!*"*

"Listen, Grandpa, I'll explain everything, but right now you just need to trust us. Every cop who was worth a shit either bailed to get their family out of the city, or they've thrown in with us. Anybody who is left is either a dupe or a quisling fuck, and they're making up the difference with PRA thugs. The mayor and most of the local government have sided with the Chinese."

"Commies gonna commie," said the wounded man.

"But they're on a humanitarian mission!" The internet had been down for weeks, but the local NPR station was still reporting. "The Chinese are not military. They're private aid organizations here to help after the crash, to make sure people have food, and water, and medical care! That's why they seized the port and the bridges."

The wounded man snort laughed. It turned into wheeze. "Man, I thought you said your old hippy grandfather would be cool?"

"He's the best of the bunch... But he was a professor. He's pretty liberal."

"Gullible you mean. Humanitarian mission, my ass. Never did see a 'humanitarian mission' that needed IFVs at every corner around the port!" exclaimed the stranger. I didn't know what 'IFVs' were, but they sounded military. "America is blacked out, at each other's throats, on the verge of civil war. So, the Chinese are here securing a beachhead and using the local useful

212

idiots to round up anybody who might cause them problems. They're disappearing troublemakers."

"People are dying out there," Ben said sadly. "That's why we were in the neighborhood, to try and stop one of their kill teams. It didn't go so great… Sorry, I didn't want to involve you in this, but we had nowhere else to hide."

What they were saying didn't make any sense. This was like some crazy nightmare. But I sat there in my chair, clutching paper towels in my bony hands, while my grandson sewed up a gunshot wound in my kitchen, and realized this was actually happening.

"Hate to break it to you, Grandpa, but we've been invaded."

\*\*\*

After Ben had gotten his leg and face stitched up and bandaged, the wounded man had taken a bunch of painkillers and then limped over to the couch to take a nap. I was amazed that he was able to fall asleep so quickly.

"Practice," Ben explained when he saw me staring. "Do you have any bleach? Before we go, I can at least scrub the place clean."

He wasn't trying to be polite about making a mess of my kitchen. "You're destroying the evidence."

"For your sake more than mine. They aren't in control enough to do house to house searches… yet."

I showed Ben where I kept the cleaning supplies. He immediately started wiping down everything. Luckily only the bedrooms were carpeted. The kitchen was Linoleum. "You owe me an explanation."

He paused, thinking over what to say, but then talked while he kept working. "We were on our way out when our car got hit. Jo—" He started to say his friend's name, and then caught himself. "He got shot. The engine was damaged, but I shook the pursuit. I managed to limp the car a few more blocks before it died, and then we ran for it. We needed a place to hide, and you were close. Sorry to drag you into this."

"Drag me into what exactly? What were you doing with all these guns? You're in America! You can't play soldier here!"

Ben sighed. "Ain't nobody playing, Grandpa. This is the real thing."

"You were breaking the law!"

"Law?" Ben snorted. "Have you looked outside lately?"

"That's different! That's an oppressed people rising up against the injustice of a crypto-fascist police state. Riots are the language of the oppressed. They have no choice!"

"Oh not this again," Ben muttered. "Do you even hear yourself? How can you spend your whole life simultaneously saying the government is evil racists *and* we should put the government in charge of everything *at the same time?"*

He'd always been the contrarian hot head in the family. We'd had this argument many times when he was younger, and to be fair, I recognized that I was just reflexively saying the same things I had always said. It was becoming increasingly difficult to defend the ideals of democratic socialism the closer the fires got to my own house. Regardless, Ben was being infuriating. "You know what I mean!"

"Yeah, and Orwell had a word for it. Look, I've been part of a… group that keeps up on this stuff. The crash, the grid going down. Word is that was a cyberattack, followed by a coordinated series of bombings to utterly gut our infrastructure. It's chaos out there. Most of the country is dark or in flames and the rest of the world is taking advantage of that. It's popped off in Europe, the Pacific, and India, and if the reports we just got are accurate, they're straight up dropping artillery on LA today."

"Impossible. That sounds like military industrial complex propaganda and—"

Ben held up one hand to stop my knee jerk response. "Cut the party line bullshit, Grandpa. We're way past team sports here. You need to get out of town. Most of the roads are blocked for *public safety,* but I know a couple routes that are open. Go east. The further you get from the city, the safer you'll be."

"Are you coming?"

He shook his head. "No. I'm needed here."

"To do what? Shoot Chinese people?"

"If necessary."

"That's racist!"

"Holy shit, they're literally assassinating people right now!"

If true, he had me there. I just wasn't used to thinking of communists as bad guys. Sure, they did some bad things, but their overall philosophy was one of helping the masses. China was a success story, of bringing billions out of poverty through central planning, or so I'd always taught. It was one thing to give a lecture about breaking a few eggs to make an omelet, until you were one of the eggs.

"Look, Grandpa. I know what I'm doing. When the military moves in, and they will, they're going to need eyes behind enemy lines. You need to stick Carl in his crate and get out of town."

"But this is my home," I sputtered. "I taught here. I retired here. I've spent my whole life here. I intend to die here."

"Oh, they'll help you with that for sure. Basically, you and a couple hundred thousand other civilians are being held hostage and you don't even know it. If the Army moves in, the Chinese won't hesitate to burn this place to the ground. The longer they hold this point, the more resources they can move in. When the Army eventually get orders, and they will, Portland is going to turn into a warzone. And I'm not talking the brick and Molotov version you're used to either."

This all sounded so insane. "You're talking about foreign aid workers from private organizations and peaceful protestors—"

"An unknown number of Chinese nationals got off an unknown number of freighters armed with a shit ton of heavy ordnance, and immediately teamed up with thousands of local assholes who are way past breaking the windows in Starbucks and fucking about in Guy Fawkes masks. I'm pretty sure they didn't do all this to distribute food. They've taken control of all the important infrastructure. This is a major, crazy ambitious op."

"I just can't believe that."

"Believe it. The PRC is making its move."

"Surely we brought this on ourselves with all our meddling in foreign affairs and—"

Ben sighed, and in that moment, he just looked really tired. "Spare me. It's the fucking apocalypse, you can put down your virtue signal. Please just listen. I don't want you to get killed."

I'd always been Mr. Give Peace a Chance, but my barbaric knuckle dragging grandson had brought this madness into my house. "Then you need to get out. I'm not going anywhere. I'm not supposed to drive anymore anyway, but my Prius is still in the garage. The keys are in the cupboard. Take it and go. Get out!"

Ben slowly nodded. He had learned a long time ago it was impossible to win an argument with me. No use wasting time. "Okay. But things are going to get worse before they get better. I saw how scared you were when you came to the door. I want you to take this." He pulled a large black pistol, sleek and dangerous, from his belt. "It's real simple. No safety. Just point and pull the trigger. Here. Take it."

"I could never hurt another human being."

"Oh, you'd be surprised what you can do when the chips are down." But when I didn't say anything for a long time, Ben relented and put the scary thing back in its holster. "Fine. Let me just clean the glass and we'll be out of your hair."

Ben went outside and worked in the dark. I sat there. Scared. Thinking about what he had just told me and wondering how much of it was true. What he was suggesting was so outside my belief system that I was having a hard time accepting any of it. We were always the aggressors. We were always the selfish, greedy ones. America didn't get invaded. We did the invading.

What if Ben was telling the truth? What if I was wrong? What if I'd been wrong my whole life? No. Never. Even if I was, I wouldn't admit it to my grandson.

I was out of meds. Pain meds. Heart meds. My oxygen tank needed a refill. I was old, crippled, and falling apart. Ben hadn't been wrong about me answering the door scared. I was terrified of every sound, every distant gunshot, every whiff of smoke, and sick to death of living in fear. Maybe I should have taken that offered gun, but Ben would only need to leave me one bullet.

Only I couldn't admit that either.

The wounded man was asleep on the couch. From the look of them, they were both exhausted, mentally and physically, like they had been run ragged for days on end. His armor vest thing was sitting there on the floor, resting against the wall, from where Ben had helped him out of it to tend his injuries. I rolled over to the vest and discovered it was far heavier than it looked. There were several pouches on the side, filled with something terrifying, that I'd only ever seen in the movies.

When I heard Ben coming back, I rolled my chair away from the vest so he wouldn't see what I'd stolen. "Done?" I asked him.

"Yeah. We're out of here." Even though nothing remained of the curious yet combative child I'd known, and somewhere along the line he'd turned into a killer, his melancholy was obvious. No matter how hard one was, it was always difficult to lose family. "I wish you'd listen to reason."

"I said the same thing to you when you enlisted. I suppose stubbornness runs in the family."

\*\*\*

Emotionally exhausted, I slept in late the next day. I bolted awake when I realized that there were people breaking into my house.

They kicked in the front door and swept in with guns.

"Public Safety Committee!" someone shouted. "Don't resist!"

217

They were tromping about, tearing through my things. Ripping open cupboards and dragging out the contents. There was one uniformed policeman, but the others helping him were very young, white men. Their only uniform was black hoodies.

Two of them came into my bedroom and pointed their terrifying firearms at me. I lifted my trembling hands to cover my face. "Don't shoot! I surrender!"

"Shut the fuck up, traitor!" one of them screamed, spit flying from his lips. And I truly believe he wanted to kill me.

An Asian man, probably about forty, and the only one not obviously armed, walked into the bedroom. He calmly placed one hand on the kid's gun barrel and gently pushed it down. "It's fine," he said with a slight accent. "He's harmless. Leave us."

The other two immediately did as they were told and went out to help rip my house apart.

"You need a warrant!"

"I'm sorry, but we do not. The mayor has declared a state of emergency."

Could he even do that? I had no idea, but I'd voted for him. "Who are you?" I struggled to sit up in bed. "What are you doing in my home?"

"I am Mr. Liu. I am merely an advisor to the Portland Public Safety Committee." He seemed rather innocuous, more businessman than secret police, in his khakis and a polo shirt.

"Are you one of the Chinese aid workers?"

"Yes. I am only here to help your fine city through this time of crisis. And now, you can help me, professor."

He knew who I was. How did he know who I was? Then I realized I didn't hear barking. There should have been barking. "Where's Carl? What've you done with my dog?"

Mr. Liu spread his hands apologetically. "I am terribly sorry. He acted in a very aggressive manner toward the safety officers and had to be put down."

I was stunned. Carl was my only friend. "You shot my dog?"

He didn't answer my question. I hadn't heard a gunshot, so they'd probably just stomped the poor little guy. There was one chair in the room, usually used only by my home care nurse, though I'd not seen her for weeks. Mr. Liu pulled the chair next to my bed and then sat down.

"Forgive my bluntness but time is of the essence. We have reason to believe that terrorists sought shelter in your home last night."

"No, of course not, never." I tried to sound indignant. "That's absurd."

"Please, professor. Think carefully before lying to me. I am trying to help you. Harboring criminals is a terrible thing to do, but if you were coerced or threatened into doing so, then the committee will understand, and be lenient."

"I don't know what—"

The uniformed cop appeared in the doorway. He held up some bloody gauze for Liu to see. Ben had tried to clean up, but they'd been in a rush. He must have missed that piece. Or maybe Carl had run off with it when he'd been distracted. Mr. Liu nodded. "Take it for DNA testing." The cop left. Then Liu turned back to me. "You were saying, professor?"

He had me. "They were injured! They needed help. I tried to call the police, but the phones were down again."

"Of course, of course. There is a vehicle registered to you, but your garage is empty."

"They must have stolen it."

"To go where?"

"I don't know." But I did know one thing for sure, and that was that they were going to kill my grandson if they found him. "They said something about driving to Beaverton."

Somehow, he knew I was lying. "I see…" Mr. Liu took out a pack of smokes.

"Don't do that! I have to use oxygen."

He ignored my protests and lit the cigarette anyway. His demeanor had changed, almost like a switch had been flipped. This wasn't an advisor. This was a commander, used to holding lives in his hand. He took a long drag, then suddenly changed the subject. "I am familiar with your work, professor."

"What?"

"I have files on all the faculty and staff of the various local universities, active and retired. I myself attended UC Berkeley on a student visa."

"It's a nice campus."

He leaned in close, lowering his voice. "It is a den of self-righteous hypocrites. Useful idiots. Short sighted, short tempered, spoiled, perpetually outraged hedonists advocating for their own destruction. Fat and slothful wretches who are inexplicably proud of their self-loathing. It has only gotten worse since. I was in the College of Engineering, which was not as bad, comparatively, but the rest…" he shrugged. *"Baizuo."*

"What?"

"'White Left.'" Liu blew smoke out his nostrils, and then laughed at me. "You are your own worst enemies, professor. You claim to be the party of science, yet set policy based on emotions. You possess the absolute certainty that you are the sole owners of morality, while in reality your philosophy changes faster than the wind. You claim to care about the future, except exist in a perpetual temper tantrum. Your weakness disgusts me to the very core of my being… And yet we couldn't have done this without you. A fact which amuses me to no end."

"Do what without me? What are you talking about?"

"A house divided cannot stand." Liu leaned back, chair creaking. "How can a society teach its children to hate everything about it, and still expect to survive?"

Ben had told me. I hadn't wanted to listen. "This is an invasion."

"It is a beginning. Unlike you morons, my people know the value of patience. Now tell me everything you really know or else." He didn't specify what the *else* meant. He didn't need to. He just let that hang there, like the smoke from this cigarette.

I was terrified, but behind that I was angry. I'd been trying to make the world a better place, really I had. It wasn't my fault someone like this had taken advantage of it. "Get the fuck out of my house!"

"So be it." Mr. Liu stood up. "Take the old man to the station for interrogation."

The young men came back in to grab me. The cop came to the bedroom door to watch. He was probably the supposed supervisor, but it was clear who was really calling the shots.

Except Mr. Liu was wrong. He wasn't calling shit. I'd put the stolen hand grenade beneath my pillow. I hadn't been kidding when I'd told Ben I expected to die here.

As the thugs descended on me, I pulled out the deadly little bomb, not much bigger than a baseball. My arthritic fingers barely had the strength to pull the pin, but who cared if the bones snapped? I was all out of fucks to give.

Mr. Liu's eyes widened when he saw the grenade. The cigarette fell from his lip.

"You shouldn't have hurt my dog."

# She Wore a Yellow Ribbon

## Jonathan LaForce

"Fire mission! Platoon adjust!" the field phone shrieked tinnily.

It had already been a hard half-day beneath an unmerciful California sun. Even though the brilliant sphere was now at its zenith in the midday sky, calls for fire had not slacked.

"Again?" Private Gonzalez-Peña whined abjectly from where he lay in the shade of the Paladin's bulk, struggling to stand up."Haven't these assholes heard of siestas and shit?"

"Shut up Gonzo!" Sergeant Ben Rogers yelled as he watched his gunners spinning their hand wheels in rapid time to lay on the azimuth of fire.

The soldiers had been stuck in this place, sucking up water greedily and wishing for rain or a good breeze to alleviate their suffering. Three long days of waiting.

"Shell HE! Lot Alpha Hotel!"

"Charge 5!"

"Where's my powder Gonzo?" Rogers bellowed as the tired private ran forward with five tan propellant units in their plastic sleeve.

Service to the artillery is hard work at the best of times. Slaving away beneath a blistering heat wave could hardly be called "The best of times." It was made worse by the fact that all three Paladins were parked across the width of the I-5 and I-14 freeway interchanges, just north of Los Angeles. The asphalt was

223

hot enough to cook meat and the interior of the all-metal self-propelled guns was an oven.

The men belonged to 3rd Armored Brigade of the 1st Armored Division, Fort Bliss Texas. They'd come to California for a rotation at the National Training Center. All of which ended when the Comm networks went down.

*Chaotic* had been a mild way to explain the nightmare which followed. Rumors reached them that Chinese occupiers had landed on the coast. Colonel Harper, the brigade's commander, took a gamble rather than wait for more bad news, rolling his men south and west. In the event he was right, his armor, artillery and mechanized infantry would be perfectly placed to prevent breakouts into the open area of the high desert or the Central California plateau.

That had been two days ago. Two very quiet days, and they'd seen nobody. The infantry dug in, enfilading the roads they blocked. The engineers even had time to dig revetments where there was dirt rather than asphalt or concrete. Men swore as they worked, cursing their sergeants and corporals as good troops should.

All of which changed just hours before sunrise. Rousted out of their fart sacks by the clarion call "Fire Mission!" the cannoneers began throwing rounds downrange. Missions came in spurts. Two rounds here, 4 rounds there. 5 another time. But it never stopped. And they could hear other guns firing. Rumor from Battery Fire Direction Center said the entire battalion, 3 firing batteries of 18 guns, were being fed fire mission data from somebody down in the LA Valley.

Whoever it was, they must've gotten it stuck in good and deep. Battalion Supply had already run convoys of propellant and rounds to each position, with more reportedly on the way from Fort Irwin.

"2 rounds in effect!"

BOOM!

"Shot 2."

Gun Two, on Sergeant Roger's left, had sent the first adjusting round downrange. Based on where that round fell, the observer would either make adjustments and call for a second adjusting round or call for the rest of the platoon to open fire.

Their field phone crackled. "Platoon! Fire for effect!"

The gun line sang as brass obturating bands rammed into steel breeches with ringing finality followed by large increments of powder. Breeches swung up, interrupted screw threads locking. The Gunners were checking their sights as Section Chiefs looked to their Number One man.

"Standby… Fire!" Rogers barked.

Specialist Cowley, the ever reliable Number One Man, pulled his three-foot length of worn cotton lanyard, and the guns of Charlie Battery 4/1 began to talk once more, booming out for all to hear as the sun continued across the clear blue sky.

\*\*\*

Los Angeles was a warzone. These last three weeks had been marred by more than just stray gunfire in the night. Fires had broken out across streets and neighborhoods in dozens of locations. Were Lucifer Morningstar and his minions to have transplanted the 7th circle of Dante's Hell into the Greater Los Angeles Metro right now, they would not have seemed out of place.

Scott Gambier knew all this. He had gone to college at UCLA, been stationed at Fort Irwin early on in his Army career. Looking down across the city from Angels Point, he felt as if the fabric which bound this teeming city of millions together was being ripped apart.

Three weeks without power had caused tempers to flare as that same sunshine poured down relentlessly, uncaring and unsympathetic of the Los Angelinos plight. Tempers which only got worse as Chinese troops had swarmed over the docks at Long Beach, disrupting the natural order of the port. Now these same Los Angelinos were fighting in the streets, as often against each other as they were the PLA.

"Sir?" The voice came from behind him. Tom Jeffries had been a Marine platoon sergeant, back in the day. Now that they were both Triarii, the former Marine SSgt was his right-hand man.

"Yes, Jeffries?"

"Situation in dispatch. You're needed."

"Dispatch?"

"Aye sir. It's a nasty mess."

Scott had been sent here to organize the resistance in LA. Santiago knew at some point, the PLA would use the PRA to try to seize the LA Valley for themselves. It was too rich of a target not to. They already owned the port facilities, but the railheads, and hundreds of miles of paved roads provided a logistician's dream come true for supplying a land army far from home.

*All of which makes me wonder why I'm going down to dispatch rather than heading out to deal with that.* Scott asked himself as he and his subordinate strode down the hill toward the ad hoc dispatch center. LAPD had rigged it up from spare parts and old equipment stashed in a warehouse. *Exactly what is so damn important I have to go fix it?*

"And I'm telling you he's not one of ours!" a woman in LAPD blue shouted.

"Then why does he have access to your comms?" a man demanded of her

"I don't know!" the woman confessed. "I'm running off my gut!"

"That's not good enough! How can you trust him?"

"It's worked so far ain't it?" the woman demanded.

"And you're positive he's not with you?" The man's voice asked.

"Utterly." That flat deadpan belonged to one Isaac Newton, Gambier's very capable ops chief. Taciturn by choice, he was a highly capable asset whom Gambier relied upon.

"Sounds like Newton's having a grand old time sir!" Jeffries jested as they paused outside the door of the LAPD dispatch center, looking inward.

"Smart money says he's weighing the pros and cons of shooting whoever that is" Scott remarked dryly.

"That would be the problem sir."

"Which is?"

"A Captain Orial, sent up from the 1st Marine Division to coordinate artillery."

"I wasn't aware there was anything to coordinate."

226

"You and me both, sir. Seems somebody started calling for fire over LAPD comms. LAPD passed the buck up to Ft. Irwin, who apparently has been in peaceful communication with 29 Palms. So, they sent what few Comm Marines from 29 they could spare, with a Divisional FDC from Irwin."

Scott held up a hand. "Go back to the part where the Army and the Corps are getting along."

"Yes sir. That's true."

"Will wonders never cease?"

"That's not even the best part sir."

"Oh please. Don't wait. I can see your grin from here Jeffries."

"They ran slash wire from the dispatch center to an old VHF antenna up the hill, then back down to the FDC Bubbas and started getting rounds downrange. Boys've been calling for fire since."

"On what?"

"Apparently, the Chinese. And anybody who forgot that if you don't start none won't be none."

"So, the ChiComms made their play for LA, during running gang wars, ran into somebody who knows how to call for fire and has the tubes in support to make it happen?"

"Yessir."

"They're popping ChiComms, plus any gangbangers who think they're hot shit. And the PRA twinks."

"Yessir."

"Jeffries, when we get done sorting out this mess, remind me to find a chaplain, make my confession and participate in Communion properly."

"Of course, sir." Jeffries chuckled and Scott looked at him.

"What's so funny?"

"Blessed is he who, in the name of charity and goodwill, shepherds the weak through the valley of darkness, for he is truly his brother's keeper, and the finder of lost children."

Both men shared a look and laughed.

"Thank you, Jeffries. I needed that." Scott breathed in a lungful of air, then sighed.

"Now that we've got God on our side, why don't we go settle things in dispatch before somebody decides to help Captain Orial meet God?"

"I like this idea sir. Cleaning up blood is a pain in the ass," Jeffries admitted.

*** 

"Attention on deck!" Jeffries bellowed as Scott stepped over the threshold and into the dispatch center.

Everyone not seated at a workstation stopped what they were doing and jumped into the position of attention, something the military and police had in common. It took most of them a moment to notice that Scott wasn't actually an officer anymore. Most of them sat down sheepishly.

In the center of the room, a policewoman in blue faced down a red-faced Marine officer, while Newton stood in his tans to one side, his arms crossed. Scott still found it slightly amazing that they were getting as much cooperation from LAPD as they were; California authorities were not exactly what he'd call level-headed, and most of the police forces had been purged a long time ago. *Maybe having a few of them ambushed and massacred really does have a way of focusing the mind.*

The veins on Newton's neck and forehead stood out far enough Scott could see them across the room, and he was rapidly becoming concerned about his ops chief. He looked towards the woman who was facing down the Marine captain and felt his surprise grow.

She was gorgeous. Not just oh-look-at-her-she's-cute, but a real woman, with curves no uniform could hide, a delicately boned face with very full pink lips and gleaming sable hair. Gorgeous all around. There was about her an air of competence and capability. *Best to mind my manners with this one* Scott told himself. *I need her on my side.*

"Ma'am, what seems to be the issue?" Scott asked her.

"This wo-" Orial started.

"Did I ask you?" Gambier asked firmly.

"No but-"

"I don't give a good damn what you want. I asked her to talk. So, you're going to shut the hell up until I speak to you. Understand?" Scott demands

Orial's face flexed. His dark skin flushed as Scott stepped in close, voice dropping.

"Do. You. Understand. Me? Or shall I call General Davies and tell him that the man he sent me is a pig ignorant dumb shit and shouldn't be allowed to command a chow hall detail in hell?"

"Yes. Sir."

"Very good." Scott stepped back, then looked at the woman. "Ma'am…?"

"Officer Megera Darke sir."

"Thank you Officer Darke. Now what is going on?"

"Several hours ago, the Chinese started pushing out patrols all over the valley. Sometime before dawn we got a call over our rebuilt radio net. Callsign "Habu Viper." Once the soldiers and Marines got here, we were able to speed up the turnaround time. Sergeant Richardson has been super helpful. We also moved them onto a separate VHF freq so that their calls come in clear and uninterrupted."

"How many missions has this 'Habu Viper' person called?"

"I don't know sir. I haven't kept track," Darke admitted.

Scott looked towards the Marines clustered in the corner. "Oh, Sergeant!"

"Already on it, sir! Shiver is counting 'em right now." Richardson declared.

"And sir, it's a three-man team," Darke added. "Part of why we asked the Triarii up here. We wanted to know if it was your people."

"What makes you say that?"

"Habu Viper is not on any of our records as a legit callsign. We've also heard different voices calling in as 'Habu Viper-Two' and '-Three'."

"Makes sense. Sergeant, what's my count at?"

"Eighty-seven, sir," Shiver declared.

Scott whistled appreciatively. "Busy fellas. Is that map what you're using to keep track on, Marine?"

229

"Yes sir. They're all over the place," Richardson acknowledged.

Scott studied it diligently, noting how the pins covered multiple spots across the Greater LA Metro. "What do you think Newton?"

"Looks like they've been hitting problem spots across the valley. Look at East LA and cross check it to previous incident reports. I'll bet it correlates to gang territory."

"Jeffries, go find me some guys familiar with the gang culture around here would you?"

"Yes sir!"

"Officer Darke, where did they begin?"

Darke appeared at his elbow. "They started up here in the San Fernando Valley, on the north side of the city." Her finger brushed the map, tapping a spot near Van Nuys airport.

"Where did the next one come from?" Scott inquired.

"Burbank. They called more along the way to this point, then turned right and got busy." One neatly manicured French-tipped nail traced a trail that ran south over the eastern flank of the Hollywood Hills, down through Chinatown, before heading back west toward the ocean.

"I wasn't aware we had units that far north to shoot for us."

"3rd Armored Brigade down from Fort Irwin," Newton volunteered. "The brigade commander deployed troops into blocking positions. Nothing can go north without hitting his troops."

"What about the 11th ACR?" Scott asked.

"I can go query FDC, but I haven't heard anything lately."

"Thanks, Newton. Richardson, how long do these calls usually take?"

"Not long sir. Even with the change off between comm sets we're staying under three minutes. These guys are pros, right down to detailed BDAs after every mission."

"What's the farthest south they've gone, Miss Darke?"

"Redondo Beach. The last transmission had them somewhere in this vicinity." She tapped the map for emphasis.

Scott considered his options.

"Captain Orial, are there any drone assets available?"

"Not at the moment. The Chinese appear to have pushed some serious countermeasures out throughout the city. The last couple lasted about twenty minutes before they went dark."

"Has anybody laid eyes on the harbor in the last three weeks?"

"Not that we know of."

"I don't know how they could," Darke bit her lip. "It's hazardous down there right now. We've lost at least three patrol cars down there. Possibly more."

"Noted. When they call again, can you get them to stay on the line and talk to me?" Scott asked.

"I'll certainly try."

"Thank you, Officer Darke." Scott swiveled his gaze to Orial. "Captain, let's go make sure chow is laid on for these hardworking marines and the soldiers outside."

Turning on his heel, Scott marched out of the room. Orial followed in his wake, face flushed, not noticing how Newton stayed only a couple steps behind him, hand never leaving the grip of his pistol in its holster.

The door swung shut behind the men and a semblance of calm returned to the area.

"Ya know, I'm starting to think the Triarii ain't such a bunch of right-wing assholes after all," a dispatcher declared.

"Who cares so long as they're our right-wing assholes?" another suggested.

"Settle down," Darke ordered. "We gotta get this whole city back online."

***

"Well, I will have to give Redondo PD credit" a stocky young man with a heavy beard declared as he cheerfully stepped into the Ford SUV he and his friends had been riding around all day in.

"Yeah, for what, Eddie?" The driver asked.

The driver was older than his passengers, curly black-and-silver hair clipped short, skin the color of dark aged teak from years of earning his living in the bright sunshine. Unlike his passengers, he wore a proper uniform- dark blue wool with a

231

polished black leather duty belt and combat boots. Somewhere amidst the disaster he'd even found time for a proper shave.

It didn't matter that three weeks prior his world had turned upside down. Officer Jaime Kopa refused to be anything other than professional in his conduct and appearance. He had patrolled these streets far too long to do otherwise.

His passengers wore no discernible uniform, but they were not given way to sloppiness either. Oh sure, a Sergeant Major looking them over would've complained mightily about the beards all three wore, and in Eddie's case the curly black locks which fell past his collar and onto his broad shoulder blades. A wise observer might've identified them as comfortable. Ballcaps from three different baseball teams, jeans, tee-shirts, and well-broken in tan rough-suede boots. The rifles each of those three carried were comfortable too, held in knowing hands.

"Well" Eddie continued, "not only are they hospitable, they let us take what we wanted of their pogue bait."

"It's not exactly like you gave them a choice" Kopa cautioned.

"Eh, they had choices. Just none as appealing as surrendering to my charming personality" Eddie replied from his spot in the shotgun seat.

"Please, tell me more about this charming personality. I want to know where you suddenly acquired it," the tall good-natured man in the back declared. Ricky Lee wore his Angels ballcap backwards as he shoveled a hot dog slathered with mustard and relish into his mouth.

"Eddie, you've got charm like I've got cans of Rip-it" the fourth occupant, Raymundo Iglesias declared.

"I'll have you know that I'm very charming, Iglesias!" Eddie said with a smile. "Just ask my girlfriend."

"For the thousandth time, you cannot marry your Ka-Bar!" Iglesias replied.

Lee, just behind the driver's seat, snorted Red Bull onto the plastic floorboards. "Dude! That freaking burns!"

"So where do we want to go from here?" Kopa asked with a smile.

Despite having been shot at and a series of running gun battles, morale was still high. The three former marines riding with him were good company as he desperately tried to keep order in a city dying by degrees

Eddie examined the map spread out across his knees. "We've seen ChiComm infantry squads at Van Nuys, Burbank, Glendale, and LAX."

"All of which we whacked" Iglesias reminded.

"Between us and the cannon cockers, yeah."

"Don't forget Little Tokyo."

"Yes, because I'm going to forget watching yakuza take katanas to ChiComms."

"Still not as funny as the Korean girl with a Hello Kitty AR. Blew that Lieutenant's head right off in the middle of his speech!"

"Thank God for Rooftop Koreans," Lee intoned.

"Back off, Lee," Iglesias ordered. "I'm the one with yellow fever, remember? You need some pumpkin-spice snorting basic white girl in Uggs."

"So long as she's an Angels fan, I don't care," Lee replied.

"Ya know" Kopa said suddenly, "I'll bet this close to the Harbor they've secured Torrance and Long Beach airports."

"Why does that matter?" Lee asked.

"Flights," Eddie declared. "Easy money says John Chinaman is flying in troops. He can land armor in the harbor, but you don't need troops onboard ship to move it. And keeping them pre-positioned in China near airports is easier than dealing with four weeks of seasickness."

"Imagine all that barf everywhere?" Lee surmised.

"Yeah. You can move troops from the airports back to the harbor in APCs and commandeered cars if you need to."

"If their officers are anything like ours, they'll march them back."

"Right? Friggin' Hudson's dumbass woulda done that without even thinking."

"Imagine all those troops in the open," Lee said softly. "Airbursts and willie pete. All over the street. Just thinking about it is giving me a chubby."

233

"Don't wait that long, hit the airplanes on the tarmac as they're getting ready to offload. That aluminum skin won't hold up to steel rain from on high."

"Either way, we get T-72s rolling down Wilshire Boulevard." Kopa added, trying to get the conversation back on track.

"I… yeah… that sounds nasty" Iglesias agreed as he struggled for words.

"LA becomes Stalingrad," Eddie said.

"Are we talking Enemy at the Gates?" Iglesias asked.

"Uh huh," Kopa confirmed.

"And how do you know all this?" Iglesias queried.

"Wild-assed guess. But why else go for the harbor?" Eddie declared. "It's part of why we took Anzio in World War II."

"Only one way to find out," Kopa said.

"I think we need to tell dispatch what we're doing," Eddie said.

Iglesias eyed him critically as he reached for the radio mike. "Dude. Bee Ess."

"Whatever for?" Eddie asked.

"You just wanna hear that dispatcher's voice!"

"So? Can't do any more harm than you running out the gate to Kin Town just to watch your favorite Mama San make Taco-Rice-and-Cheese all night."

"Yeah, Iglesias, how is Baby Mama-san doing?" Lee asked cheerfully.

"Oh frack you! I know that card came from you assholes!"

"What card would this be?" Kopa asked curiously.

"The damned Father's Day card I got while we were at 29 Palms, written entirely in Japanese. Complete with a sonogram and some random ass baby pics."

Jaime laughed at this. "Jeez Louise! Somebody really wanted to make you miserable."

"That somebody also told me the Yankees had been sold and were moving to South Dakota." Iglesias glowered at the other occupants of the car. "While I was stuck in the middle of Helmand. With no internet."

Lee and Eddie were howling by this point as Iglesias leveled a finger toward his friends. "*Rabiblancos chingaderos pendejos*! I spent weeks mourning my Yankees, until the next package showed up and I found out it was a damn joke!"

Jaime looked over towards the Marines still convulsing with laughter. "Y'all needs Jesus. And counseling."

"I agree. But first, let's call dispatch," Eddie rasped as he clutched his rib cage.

"Fine, fine. Go call your girlfriend."

*** 

"Dispatch this is Habu Viper, how copy?"

Darke replied easily, having been looking forward to the call. She took all of their traffic now, to keep it simple.

"Habu Viper this is Dispatch. Read you loud and clear. Do you have time to talk?"

"Dispatch I have all the time in the world to hear your lovely voice."

Darke blushed. "Habu we have a Vee Eye Pee on deck who'd like to speak with you about your activities."

"Sounds good."

The door opened to admit Gambier, who headed straight for Darke's desk.

"Habu Viper this is Triarii Tree Alpha."

"Triarii Tree Alpha, we hear you."

"Good. Any chance you'll be visiting other points today?"

There was a long pause. *Good* Scott told himself. *They know the Chinese might be listening in. Please let them be thinking of some clever way to say their destination.*

"Triarii Tree Alpha, this is Habu Viper. We think we're gonna follow the sage wisdom of street knowledge."

"Habu Viper, what is that advice?"

"Keep on cruising. Cuz it Ain't nothing but a G-Thang baby. Habu Viper out."

The radio fell silent and Scott looked around the center. "Somebody please tell me what the hell he just said."

One of the marines, a corporal by his chevrons, was muttering to himself before his eyes lit up. "Sir, it's in the first verse!"

"Huh? What's your name son?

"Hurt sir, The song is 'Nothing but a G-Thang.' It's a collab between Dr. Dre and Snoop Dogg."

"So?"

"Gimme the microphone first, so I can bust like a bubble. Compton and Long Beach together, now you know you in trouble."

"Ain't nothing but a G-thang baby." Three other voices declared in chorus.

"So, you think he's headed to Long Beach like we need?"

"It's possible sir."

"Good answer. Cuz we aren't psychic and we're having to do this all by ear."

***

"Have we heard from the Habu team at all since noon?"

Master Sergeant Grimaldi shook his head. "No sir. Not a peep."

"I'll give them credit" Captain Santochena said. "They've gone further and farther than anybody else we've had on patrol."

"Helps when you're dropping heavy artillery on the heads of everybody who looks wrong at you, sir." Grimaldi declared.

"I try to think of it as a 155mm Auxiliary Riot Control Agent Dispersal Projector," Santochena replied.

"Ahh, I see the wisdom in this."

Behind them, the tent flap opened.

"Gentlemen, there's somebody here to speak with you," Jeffries announced.

"Who's that?"

"They claim to be the Habu team."

The first man through the doorway was a bored looking Latino, followed by a much taller white man, and then a broad Polynesian in LAPD blue.

"Kopa, it's been you running around with these hooligans!" Santochena declared in surprise.

"Yes, sir. Have been since I left rollcall."

"Good on you, though we were expecting your report sooner."

We got caught up in traffic," Officer Kopa declared.

236

"Traffic?" Santochena asked.

"PRA *putas* decided they wanted to play roadblock for an ambulance," Iglesias said sullenly.

"And?" Scott pressed.

"Stinking *cabrones* won't be doing that ever again."

"Are you sure?" Scott asked.

"Eddie makes it a point to pay the insurance." Kopa said.

"Even if Somebody had already power slid through the mob and pimp slapped them with his SUV," Iglesias explained.

"The way of the sinner is hard Iglesias," Jaime replied as he flexed one massive hand.

"I like this man, where's he at?" Jeffries asked.

"In dispatch making his manners to the folks over there" Officer Kopa declared.

"Is that what they call flirting with the dispatcher these days?" Iglesias asked sarcastically.

"Officer Darke is a very lovely woman," Scott admitted. "Now, what can you tell me about the harbor?"

***

As bleak as the situation had appeared that morning, Scott felt like he was getting a handle on things. Master Sergeant Grimaldi was an adept hand at planning, as was his boss, Major Bachus. Between the three of them, and the information provided, Scott saw a plan coming together.

"Has anybody seen Captain Orial?" Scott asked. "I just realized we haven't had any input from him on this."

"No sir. Last I heard he had grabbed a couple privates and was headed to chow hall then dispatch with chow and coffee for the folks up there."

"Did you say Orial?" Iglesias asked, an odd note of worry in his voice.

"Yeah, why? Is that somebody y'all know?" Jeffries asked.

"What's his job here?"

"Coordinating artillery with us and 1st Mar Div."

"Has he said anything about being an Anglico or a JTAC?"

Grimaldi scratched his chin. "Now that I think about it, maybe twice."

"Oh shit!" Lee and Iglesias ran for the door as if trying to outrun Satan himself.

They hadn't made it across the parking lot before a man's body launched itself out of the building where dispatch had been placed. While he wasn't totally certain, Scott was willing to bet money it had to be Orial. He tumbled down the steps and into the parking lot with a complete lack of grace as a figure came stalking through the doorway hot on his heels.

"Run Dean! Run for your life you cowardly cur!" the stalking figure roared.

"Jeffries, I have a feeling there's a history there," Scott remarked, trying to remain nonplussed.

"What gave it away, sir?" Jeffries asked, joining him at the door to watch the spectacle.

They watched Orial run toward the security checkpoint. He didn't stop though, arms and legs chugging in a down-hill sprint as he turned left, taking Academy Road headed east.

"Mano, you good?" Iglesias asked aloud.

"Yeah, we all good."

"Was that really...?"

"It was him."

"Well, when you're ready we're putting together an op. Could use some help."

"I'll be there in a second."

"Sound good, mano."

Turning, Iglesias and Lee strolled back towards the FDC tent, chuckling quietly. As they walked away, Eddie stripped off his sweat-stained tee shirt and began mopping at his face, bronze back bare to the sun.

*Might as well go introduce myself and see what this was all about* Scott decided. Snagging a water bottle, he made his way over, noticing idly how a good portion of the dispatch center and many others were still watching.

"You the man in charge around here?" Eddie asked when he got close

"Yeah." Scott held out the water bottle. "Scott Gambier. Formerly Major Gambier."

Eddie took the bottle, studied him. "Well sir, you gonna arrest me?"

"Why'd you do that to Orial?"

"His name was Johnson," Eddie said darkly, looking back over his shoulder down the hill as he did so. "One of my boots. While I was downrange on a last-minute deployment, Johnson was found dead in a heroin den. It was labeled 'accidental overdose' but I found out the truth."

"Which is?"

"Boot got in trouble. Dean kicked him out of base housing, refused to let him live in barracks. Punished anybody who let him even sleep on their floor. Poor kid committed suicide because he thought he'd been abandoned."

Their eyes met, Scott watching the younger man deflate as he came down from the combat high of hormones dumping through his system, drinking greedily from the bottle's open mouth.

"I didn't murder him." Eddie said as he upturned the bottle over his head and let the water wash away his perspiration.

"I know."

"I made a martyr out of a craven coward."

"So long as you're done, we're good. You done?"

"Yes, sir."

"Good. We have a plan, you in?"

"If it involves killing the ChiComms who invaded my country, count me in."

Scott turned to leave, while Eddie made for the doorway where he'd left his rifle behind. The crowd parted for him, uninterested in finding out if he had properly calmed down yet.

"Before I was interrupted, who's the dispatcher I've been talking to since this morning?" Eddie asked as he threw the sling over his head then checked its rest.

"That'd be me" Darke volunteered, more than a little confused as Eddie stuck out his hand.

"I came by to say thanks. You're a professional over the hooks. Made my job a lot easier."

239

"Oh." His words took her back and she smiled. "You're welcome."

"You have the most beautiful voice I've ever heard over a radio. Angelic. And you're even lovelier looking than you sound. I think you're gorgeous."

Turning on his heel, Eddie left behind a crowd of knowing glances and a woman furiously blushing.

*** 

Peizhi Zhiqiang refused to smile as the *Stratidore's* bow swung across the length of the breakwater, guided by tugboats. He had a scowl on his face every bit as happy as the Grecian captain's.

*We're almost done* Peizhi told himself. *And instead of just sailing us in, he has to insist on using harbor pilots and tugs. With all this tech, you are going to tell me this is harder than parking my car? You just like making me suffer.* He looked out across the harbor to where the yellow-on-red starred emblem of the PRC snapped and popped in the breeze. Ostensibly marking the People's Republic's "humanitarian aid mission" to the stricken United States.

*I hate this damn boat,* Peizhi told himself.

4 weeks at sea, came down to these last few minutes. *Now to get ashore for a proper meal and feminine company. Surely there's now places where a member of State Security with good yuan can get what he wants.* Peizhi was tired of boats, of rocking around with every wave, the filthy Greek accommodations, dirty looks from the crew. He was sick of it all.

He and the platoon of MSS agents onboard were here to ensure that the crew kept to the letter of their contract, namely the delivery of 4th Armored Brigade's lead units to American shores. No ammunition stolen, no vehicles pawned off in cocaine deals to Colombians or RPGs sold to Al-Qaeda operatives. 4th Armored Brigade had been marked for the initial occupation of Los Angeles, and every second day new ships would make landfall. After a week, the entirety of the brigade would be ashore and expanding the beach head.

*I miss real food, cooked in a proper wok. Not this gyro and goat cheese.* He sighed. *If I have to eat lemon rice one more*

240

*time, I am going to start beheading people.* Peizhi sighed again, *I hate this damn boat.*

6 feet away, Captain Cyrus Korba heard the Chinese Colonel sigh unhappily. He knew the Colonel was tired. *God help me but I'm tired of hearing his whining. They kicked half my crew off in order to make room for their goon squad and expected us to keep up appearances? Fecking idiots.*

Cyrus hated everything about the Colonel. His tone, his mannerisms, his seeming disdain for all things Greek. *God willing, the impertinent swine will trip and fall down the gangplank breaking his damned neck along the way.* It felt strange speaking to a God he had not worshipped since boyhood, but it certainly made him feel better. Still, there were appearances to maintain…

"It never gets easier," Cyrus said in his British-accented English.

"What never does?" Peizhi replied after a moment.

"Having to let another take control."

"Ah."

"I go through this argument every time we come into any port."

"How do you deal with it?"

Cyrus smiled broadly. "I remember that I'm getting properly compensated for the work I perform. Better to surrender control for a few hours and get paid well than to not and never see a penny."

"A very capitalist outlook."

Cyrus shrugged. "Perhaps. It is very easy to starve on principles though."

*Capitalist swine,* Peizhi thought with a sigh. *But this is what we have to work with.*

*Go fuck yourself you slanty-eyed asshole* Cyrus told himself at the same time. *If the Japanese lost in the Pacific to the Americans, what makes you think you will do any better?*

"I wonder if there will be any good restaurants open when we arrive?" Cyrus asked casually.

"One can certainly hope."

\*\*\*

241

Three kilometers away as the seagull flies, Eddie looked down through his binoculars once more, seeing something which he despised. "Oh, those assholes."

"What?"

"Iglesias, tell me what you see just to the right of that gantry at 3 o'clock, on top of that building." Eddie handed him the binoculars, and waited while his subordinate looked for what Eddie was talking about.

"Is that-?"

"Uh huh."

Iglesias peered again, then swore something particularly vile in Spanish.

"Ya know, I normally hate to ruin a good ambush" Iglesias muttered.

"You and me both."

"But that has to come down."

"Agreed."

Iglesias stared up at his friend. "Hey mano, you remember how many batteries we got attached to us for this?"

"I'm thinking it's two."

"Well why don't you call your girlfriend and find out?"

"Huh." Eddie stroked his goatee. "What if…"

Iglesias held up the handset. "Call her, you doofus."

The history books would tell the tale of what followed in the long minutes. How one tentacle of the first invasion of American soil in nearly a century was repelled at the Long Beach docks, and the men who had made it happen. Those books would recount how off-target the first volley of artillery fire had been, going wildly off target. What those books could not have ever considered, was that the opening salvo went precisely where it was supposed to.

In that fiery conflagration, a red banner decorated with 5 yellow stars was torn down from the pole upon which it waved. The master smith before his anvil needs only a single strike where others need more. Iglesias had been precise in his instructions, and Master Sergeant Grimaldi equally precise in his calculations. Even as the salvo traveled that short distance between the foothills and the harbor, gun barrels swung towards their new target, leaving only devastation where they had spoken.

"Lee, how we doing?" Eddie asked nonchalantly as the rumble of artillery and secondary explosions reverberated through the concrete jungle with echoing finality.

"Camera crew is getting all of it and the colors are ready."

"Good."

Eddie's voice took on its professional tone once more, coldly dispassionate.

"Corporal Lee!"

"Yes, sergeant?"

"Uncase the colors, show these bastard whoresons who's sending them to hell!"

"Aye aye, sergeant!"

Turning on his heel as if standing on a parade deck, Lee looked over at the quartet of troopers from the 11th Armored Cavalry Regiment whom they had yanked up for a 'special duty.'

"Detail, atten-hut! Loose the colors!"

Heavy cotton and polyester fabric clutched in their arms spilled out over the edge of the skyscraper's uppermost crenellation. These soldiers had run cords from one end of the rooftop to the other, checking and double-checking their knots, just to be sure of this moment. Now their precious cargo caught the evening breeze, rippling as it settled into place.

***

A scream of incoming artillery rent the sky, splashes appearing in the water before something rocked *Stratidore*. Chunks of metal bounced off the bridge superstructure and *something* slammed into the forward window, shattering the pane of glass. Peizhi heard the screams of men around him, cut by flying glass.

*How did I end up the floor?* He asked himself. *I do not remember falling.*

Smoke billowed into the bridge as more rounds screamed out of the sky and into *Stratidore's* long deck with slamming finality.

*Is that artillery?* Peizhi wondered as he started to his feet. Hammer blows rocked the vessel again, tossing crewmen to and

243

fro. Something whizzed through the air, burying itself into the bulkhead behind him and he slowly turned, spying at last a chunk of jagged white-hot steel buried a handspan into the wall. He turned about, eyes tracing its flight path.

To his horror, the helmsman was now dead. Where once his too-large head had sat perched atop his gangly neck, now only a bloody stump remained, red fluid pumping out as the body slowly slid down and to the right, while his head rolled left.

*Tā māde niǎo!* Peizhi cursed as he watched the bow swing about to port as the sailors called it. They were still a good kilometer or more from the docks. *But we've made it to the inner channel. I'll bet if I speed us up and get us straightened back out, we can run ashore before we take too many more hits.*

His mind made up, Colonel Peizhi charged forward on his hands and knees, trying hard to avoid the broken glass and arterial fluids leaking out across the thrashing steel deck. *Three meters, two meters, one meter. I made it!*

Coming up just high enough to see the control panel, he grabbed what he dimly remembered as the steering wheel used by the late helmsman and cranked hard right. *I'll have time to correct if I need to, and besides, this beast takes forever to turn.*

The engine pods were controlled just forward of the helm in their own station. Keeping one hand on the wheel, Peizhi darted around the pedestal to reach for the engine control lever. *It doesn't have to be neat, it doesn't have to be pretty! We just have to get... out of the killzone!* He ran the lever forward. *Artillery can't move fast enough to stay with us! They wouldn't dare risk the docks!*

*Stratidore* bucked. Thrown off his feet once more, Peizhi clung to the ship's wheel, feeling so much like a rat caught in a terrier's mouth as the ferry ship. Outside, more plumes of water fountained upwards.

Elsewhere men screamed and the klaxons blared out that the ship was on fire. Peizhi could smell the smoke, even from up here. He felt elated though, as the rumble of surging engines could be felt through the deckplates. *Now to get to shore...*

He came off his feet again as something collided with *Stratidore*, and this time Peizhi was thrown across the bridge. His head slammed against something, and the world went dark.

244

"Add 100, left 100." Iglesias had watched, waiting for the cargo ship's turn to starboard to finish before he applied the next correction.

"On it."

Behind him, Eddie spoke into the mic with a special venom. "FDC, direction 2400. Add 100 left 100."

Across the bay, in the foothills of the Palos Verdes Peninsula, gun barrels rose steadily. Colonel Kaag had scrambled to round out his 3rd Squadron before he left Irwin. At first, it had looked like artillery would not be happening. The nominal artillery battalion under his control was a national guard unit whose gun crews were scattered all across the LA Metro.

Instead he'd received two batteries from the 3rd Armored Brigade, and thanked his lucky stars to have at least this blessing. It had taken a miracle to get the guns up here, and he had no plans to leave before the job was finished.

Gun 4, Battery C, in the dead center of the gunline, rang out with a chest-compressing BOOM that made Kaag smile. He should've been in his command track, but if he was gonna stick cannon cockers in a dangerous position, he'd join them himself.

"Shot 4" the field phone announced.

"Splash out."

"Splash over."

A pause.

"Fire for effect."

Above the diesel engines' rumble, Kaag could hear whooping and screaming as the cannoneers went about their work. He'd made sure to tell them what they were shooting at, and why. The planned-for "fire for effect" was 18 rounds apiece of high explosive M795 shells, followed by 2 rounds apiece of M110 white phosphorus. Every round had been fuzed point-detonating. Now the gun crews raced to see which gun could fire 20 rounds the fastest. Somewhere, the manual said 6 rounds a minute was the best Paladins could do in rapid fire. *Bet the boys can beat that today.*

***

Peizhi blinked eyes opening slowly as he struggled to remember where he was. The ground beneath him was shaking, alarms were ringing, and was that smoke he smelled? Why was there a corpse lying nearby? Two even. One of which looked like that annoying Greek captain.

*That is right, I am on a ship! This is a deck! What hit us? A torpedo?* His blood ran cold at the idea of being targeted by an American Navy submarine. But he was not a coward. Not even in this moment. Grasping a station by the edge, Peizhi hauled himself upwards, hand over hand, determined to head toward the helm so he could finish guiding the ship to-

"*Tā māde niǎo.*" Peizhi blurted out.

In his desire to put the ship back on course, Peizhi had overcorrected. Combined with his revving the engines up to full power, the *Stratidore* had run aground! His brain scrambled as it tried to figure out what to do.

*Silence.*

Why had everything gone silent?

Shrill screams could be heard. Not of men, but a daemonic freight train ripped loose from the deepest depths of hell. A sound which tore apart Heaven. Moloch in the fullness of his fury and uncaged. A howling, raging Baal come to claim his offerings…

Peizhi saw the center of the ship bend inwards as a hurricane of fire wreathed the top deck. Explosions rocked the ship as smoke filled his view. The last sight he saw before the bridge superstructure collapsed in on itself with a scream of tortured metal, was a massive American flag, rippling on the breeze as its brilliant red fabric caught the twilight's last gleaming.

*\*\*\**

Megera Darke was enjoying a delicious bowl of cherry pie a la mode when Captain Santochena and Officer Kopa approached her table.

"Mind if we join you?"

"Not at all gentlemen."

"You did good on the radio today Darke," Kopa complimented. "My son really thinks the world of the job you did. Says he wishes he was sticking around so he could send you more calls for fire."

"Your son?" Meg asked.

"Eddie," Santochena explained. "Edward George Kopa."

"Oh. I hadn't thought about that." She looked around trying to spot Eddie.

"Ya know Jaime, I remember when he was little. Weird seeing him all grown up," Santochena continued

"Yeah, but they can't stay little forever."

"No disrespect Kopa, if he shaved that beard off, he'd probably be even more handsome," Megera admitted.

"Told you daddy!" Eddie said sarcastically as he sat down nearby, followed by the other two Habus.

"Now you've gone and done it" Kopa proclaimed, looking at Darke in frustration. "He's gonna be insufferable for hours!"

"What did I do?"

"You fed the Marine's ego! Big mistake!"

"Nonsense, I am not some vain petty creature given to delusions of grandeur and arrogance," Eddie declared. "I am the very model of humility, like every other Marine I know."

Kopa snorted. "Son, you are a delusion of grandeur."

"I'm still trying to figure out where he gets off thinking he's charming," Iglesias snorted.

"And handsome, don't forget handsome!"

Darke blushed for the second time that day, thanking her good fortune that not all of the lights worked in here.

"So, Eddie, what're you gonna do now?" Iglesias asked as the Habus dug into their food.

"Honestly, I'm going back to Texas come daylight. I did what I came here for."

"I thought you were born out here man?" Iglesias asked curiously.

Megera felt her face fall for a moment, wishing she was wrong. Eddie was a handsome man, and given that he wasn't LAPD personnel, there were no professional obstacles to dating him...

Eddie finished his burger in Marine-like fashion then looked up at Iglesias as the other man cut his own swath through a pile of enchiladas and rice.

"Brother, I was raised here. Cali and I still don't get along," Eddie admitted.

"You sure about that?" Iglesias asked. "Bet we could make ourselves useful."

"Spaniard, I hate this damn place." Eddie polished off the last fries on his plate and drank from his glass, swallowing quickly. "Maybe 10 years ago, it was worth a damn. Now I don't know. Ain't nothing to keep me here anyways."

He stood to his feet and nodded at those nearby. "I'm gonna go clean my rifle in the smoke pit. Daddy, I'll see you in the morning."

"See you son. Get some sleep."

"I will." Eddie paused for just a moment. "Love you, daddy."

"Love you too, boy."

Eddie never noticed the man who sat in the corner watching him with a very keen interest. Of course, that was exactly how Scott Gambier had wanted it to go. He needed to make a judgement about a man.

***

In the smoke pit, Scott found the Habu team, relaxing as they enjoyed the breeze blowing through in the darkness. Iglesias and Lee both held cigarettes while Eddie ran a rag down the barrel of his rifle. They wouldn't likely have seen him in the cafe, positioned as he was in the corner.

"So, Mister Kopa, I've been listening, and I still can't figure it out," Scott confessed.

"Figure out what?"

"Why do this? Why come back? You said it- you hate the place. So why are you here?"

Eddie spat out another empty husk of a sunflower seed. "I was all of four years old when Daddy started with LAPD. He spent most of that on graves, working overtime, and trying damned hard to care for us as a family. I was there with him at the beginning, and 30 years later I'm here at the end to make sure he sees his retirement."

"Did you expect this to happen?"

"No. Not really. Lee and Iglesias tagged along because we kinda naturally roll that way. We had originally planned to shadow him in a rental car."

*Crack-crunch.*

"Sure didn't expect John Chinaman to do all he did." His tongue moved around his mouth, cracking a shell before he spat it onto the cement. "Sides, sir, this is my city. I grew up here. Ain't letting nobody take it from me." *Spit.*

"Fair enough." Scott pondered what his next move ought to be. *We need men, and there's no time to pull them back for 6 months of training. But... Ya know, when I think of it that way, it's much easier. Yeah, we'll go with it...*

"Kopa, while you might not have anything to tie you here, I think you ought to reconsider."

"Why's that?"

"You've taken a bit of a shine to Officer Darke, and son, I saw the way she looked at you."

"So?"

"Woman don't look at a man like that unless she wants him around. Been there done that."

"I'm a crippled 0861 on partial VA Disability. What the hell do I bring to the table? No woman worth a damn wants that," Eddie said bitterly.

"Gents, I represent the Triarii. You may have heard of us?"

"We have, sir," Eddie assured.

"I need local guides who are familiar with the area. I'm happily willing to pay top dollar, in cash. Don't suppose you know where I could find some motivated locals do you?"

The gleam in their eyes told him all he needed to know.

"The time on deck is 2056. Grab some shut eye, tomorrow we go hunting. And welcome to the Auxilia."

"OORAH!"

*God help me, I love happy, violent Marines,* Scott told himself as he walked away.

\*\*\*

Gravel crunched against the asphalt beneath Megera Darke's boots as she walked up the slight incline to Dispatch.

*Between the Army and DWP we've at least got hot water for showers. Thank God.*

A good meal and 8 hours of uninterrupted sleep left her feeling much improved as she savored the quiet summer morning. Rumors in the chow hall this morning said LAFD had even managed to put out most of the fires during the night. *We might actually be able to save this city* she told herself with newfound optimism.

In the parking lot and on the side roads around the Elysian Academy, she saw cav troopers moving around their vehicles. The 11th Armored Cavalry Regiment had bivouacked here last night. Now they were preparing to head back out into the city

"Four."

Eddie Kopa came off the pillar he'd been leaning against, stepping into Megera's path as he looked levelly at her with those intense dark eyes. He still wore field gear and a pistol, but he was in clean pants and a bright red aloha print shirt.

"Four what," Megera asked, as her mind raced to determine exactly why he was here.

"Four sons," Eddie said seriously, stepping in closer to her.

He'd shaved at some point this morning. The beard was gone entirely, taking years off that handsome, strong-jawed face. If anything, he looked younger than her. Even with a shower and shave, she could still smell spent gunpowder and hot brass on him, mixed with the scent of bore solvent. She paused. *Is that good cologne, too?*

"I want four proud, strapping sons to carry me to my grave. After a lifetime spent loving the woman who brought them into this world. The woman they call 'mama'."

She dared not speak, mind racing as she heard the words leave his mouth with rising surety.

"A tough, capable, compassionate, sensible woman, whose talents are rivaled only by her incredible beauty. And the two good-hearted daughters she brings into this world. Without beauty and goodness, there is no purpose in being strong."

Megera Darke looked into the eyes of a man who rode into her life with all the fury of a tidal wave. And it did not seem that he was interested in leaving her life just yet.

"What woman would give you that?" Darke challenged.

"I'm hoping you will. I don't have a ring I can offer, just the promise of one. What do you say?"

In the movies, women hemmed and hawed. Megera knew though, knew as surely as the sun set each day on the Santa Monica beach exactly what she wanted. And why.

"I know you don't love this city, but I do! I grew up here." She grabbed his shirt, hands clenching as she pulled him in close. "This is my home. Give me back my home and I'll raise every son and daughter you could ever want!"

He kissed her. No hesitation, no questions. No need. He kissed her with all the strength and passion he possessed. When they broke apart, lungs burning for want of air, she realized they were not alone. The soldiers behind them had stopped prepping their vehicles to hear them speak, and were now cheering them on! Heat rose in Megera's cheeks and she buried her face in his cotton aloha print shirt.

"You look so lovely when you blush," he complimented, a voice so soft only she could hear.

"You are mad," she told him without rancor.

"Aye. For you." He smiled. Far more gently than she had expected.

"What are you going to do now?" she asked.

"Go earn my wedding night. And every joyous memory we'll share from here to eternity."

He kissed her again and her heart leapt within her ribs, hammering against bone and muscle as her world coalesced into a singular moment of passion that overrode all other thoughts.

When they finally stopped, she realized that the entire dispatch center was lined up at the windows, lending their voices to the soldiers' cheers.

"It may not be tonight; it may not be tomorrow," Eddie said.

"I know. I'll leave the light on for you," Megera declared.

A quick kiss on the lips and then he was off, trotting towards the cavalryman's tracks with newfound enthusiasm. A song began amongst the cavalrymen as Eddie walked towards his track, grabbing his rifle from Lee with a smile. Megera touched her lips, the kiss lingering with it's scents and savors.

*"Around the block She pushed a baby carriage!*
*She pushed it in the springtime in the merry month of May!*
*And if you ask her why the hell she pushed it*
*She wore it for a young marine so damn far away!"*

Megera refused to take her eyes off him, from that moment until Second Squadron of the Blackhorse finally left the Academy grounds. Eddie had attached himself to an Abrams crew, taking a seat in the commander's cupola at the machine gun. He blew her a kiss as they rolled past. Then he turned his eyes forward, squaring his shoulders as he readied the crew-serve with a yank of the charging handle. The monstrous machine swept out of sight around a corner and he was gone.

She had no idea where Kopa the Elder had found the ribbon she now clenched in a fist. Just that he had pressed it into her hand as he gently told her, "You'll be needing this, Miss" then stood beside her, watching his son head off to war once more.

"Every man needs a cause worth dying for. Goes double for soldiers," he muttered as he stood beside her.

"Even Marines?" Megera asked.

"Even my damn fool Sergeant of Marines."

Fabric twisted in her fingers as she thought about the last 3 weeks, and all which had occurred.

"Does it ever get easier? Watching him go?" she asked.

"Not really. I prayed for him every time he went to Afghanistan. Prayed he'd be smart enough to stay away when things started going bad here." Jaime sighed. "Now I'm praying he gets to introduce you to his mother."

"I… I hadn't expected any of this."

"I know. Neither did he. We make the best of what we've got. I'm just glad he has something to live for again."

The last vehicle clattered out of sight, the rearing black stallion on a field of red-and-white popping in the early morning breeze from its spot on the whip antenna.

"If you'll excuse me, I need to go call his mother. Tell her what our only son has gone and done this time." Jaime said, then began making his way back up the hill.

She watched him leave, slow, stiff, trying to hold back the tears of pride. He had worked hard to make this city a better place, only to watch his son head into it aboard an Abrams tank and dressed for battle. *But we endure,* she told herself.

Reaching up, Megera tied the precious ribbon into her bun, then resumed her walk into the dispatch center, to wait for her man.

*Around her hair she wore a yellow ribbon!*
*She wore it in the springtime and in the month of May!*
*And if you ask her why the hell she wore it*
*She'll say it's for that young Marine so damn far away.*

# Chopper Was a Dolphin

## Mike Massa

"Never thought I'd see the day that flag flew over San Diego harbor." Bos'ns Mate Third Class Noah Zhang-Jefferson said wonderingly, trotting along at the rear of the formation of Basic Underwater Demolition / SEAL trainees as they passed the Naval Amphibious Base breakwater.

Across the flat waters of the bay and opposite N.A.B. Coronado, the scarlet national ensign of the People's Liberation Army Navy streamed from the mast of a warship steaming under the sky-blue arc of the Coronado Bay Bridge. Mostly out of sight from their vantage point, more warships and several Chinese cargo vessels were tied up alongside the old museum ships, adjacent to downtown. The remaining Chinese frigate was clearly visible, slowly steaming closer, framed against the shiny glass-fronted hotels that lined the harbor.

A few years out of his teens, Noah was just under six feet tall, but despite the broad spread of his shoulders, his build was more wiry than muscular. Still running, he took off a shiny green helmet liner emblazoned with the single chevron of his rank and the white numbers "452" on each side before scratching his scalp through his very short, wiry black hair.

"As fucked as this whole thing has been, I just didn't expect that."

"TJ, why are the fucking Chinese mooring at the cruise ship terminal and not 32$^{nd}$ Street?" Seaman Apprentice Billy Thibodeaux asked, running alongside Noah in formation. "There's better cargo handling gear and refueling facilities at the Naval Station, and there's fuck-all to stop them."

Both men glanced farther south, directly opposite the athletic field on N.A.B. Only a scant mile separated the Chinese ships from what had at one time been the headquarters of the U.S. Pacific Fleet, the most powerful collection of warships ever assembled. Now, under a hazy blue sky most of the piers were empty, populated by only a handful of aged Burke-class destroyers and various amphibious ships. All but one were missing the American flag, but they all shared the rust-streaked gray hulls, scaffolding and plastic sheeting used for long term storage and maintenance. The remaining destroyer had the familiar American flag at her stern, but no visible exhaust issued from her stacks.

"All of those are cold iron, Billy." Noah answered. "Everything that could get underway left two days ago, right after the EMP spike or whatever it was. But there's still a couple thousand sailors on-base and the fucking Chinese want to preserve the lie that they're here as guests, to help us after the *mysterious terror attack.*"

Noah emphasized the last three words by surreptitiously making air quotes.

"Does anyone really believe the Chinese just happened to be nearby when the lights went out?" Billy snorted, gesturing rudely across the bay where one particularly big Chinese ship was unloading vehicle after vehicle. "California politics have been effed longer than I've been alive, but I can't believe that the governor is really making nice with these assholes."

"D.C. is three thousand miles east." Noah said thoughtfully. "The governor has her own problems, and Sacramento's a ten-hour drive north – make that twenty plus hours now. The Chinese are *here* and anything happening *here* is up to local authorities, so..."

"Drop!" a bullhorn-amplified voice sounded behind the two trainees.

Instantly the entire class, all twenty-five post-Hellweek trainees, wheeled out of formation and assumed the push-up position as the white-painted electric Navy pickup truck eased quietly to a halt. Balancing on one hand, Noah hastily re-adjusted the helmet liner he'd barely gotten on his head on the way down to the pavement. A door slammed, and a newcomer approached, his already light tread silenced by the roadside turf. A dark blue t-shirt stretched across his muscular frame. The left breast was emblazoned with gold text: "UDT/SEAL Instructor."

"Zhang, running back from lunch is not a chance to grab-ass and shoot-the-shit." he stated matter-of-factly. "Now you can all push 'em out."

The entire class of trainees banged out thirty push-ups, a nearby few glaring at Noah.

"Again."

The class obliged as the senior officer trainee counted repetitions, sweating alongside his classmates.

"Class leader, I need a word with these two." the t-shirted man announced. "Take the rest back over the Silver Strand to wetside. I'll make sure they catch up. Ree-cover!"

"Hoo-ya, Instructor Hayes!" The class officer yelled.

Everyone jumped back into the standing position, shaking themselves back out into a column of fours on the run, eager to put distance between themselves and the clearly guilty. Noah and Thibbodeaux remained where they were, transfixed by the instructor's pointing finger, indicating that they should remain right where they were. They watched their class cross the intersection that divided the narrow peninsula of sand between the dry, or bayside of the base from the ocean side, home of BUD/S as well as the remaining two West Coast SEAL teams.

Class 452 turned the corner out of sight, safely away from the scene of the crime.

Minus the two students that had been caught talking in ranks, of course.

"Push-em out again, Chatty Cathies." the SEAL instructor ordered.

Noah and Thibbodeaux performed a third set of thirty. Noah strained to keep his form perfect.

"Hoo-ya, Instructor Hayes!"

"You assholes are going to be pushing them out until I get tired if you keep breaking the easy rules." Hayes said conversationally, crouching in front of the two students. "Imagine what happens when you get to the hard stuff."

"Hoo-ya, Instructor Hayes!" both trainees shouted again.

257

"Zhang, why were you out of uniform?" Hayes asked, folding his arms. A small red sealion tattoo smiled toothily from his left forearm, barely visible against the dark skin. "Did someone give you a chit to exempt you from uniforms regs so you could take your cover off?"

"No, Instructor Hayes!" shouted Noah.

"Did you remove your cover because you were overcome with emotion, busily admiring your countrymen unloading their tactical vehicles onto the sovereign land of my country, Zhang?"

"Fuck the Chinese Communists, Instructor Hayes!" Noah shouted, the cords standing out on his neck. "I was born in Utah and this *is* my country."

"Is that so?" Hayes asked, squatting down in front of the two trainees, his shiny boots inches from their eyes. "But you speak ChiCom, right, Zhang?"

"Hoo-ya, Instructor Hayes!" Noah yelled, suppressing the incipient flush of anger with the ease of long practice.

*One day someone is going to get creative when they try to provoke me. But not today, apparently.* "I speak it, read it, write it."

"Does my use of the term ChiCom offend you, Zhang?" the instructor asked. "Do you get all angry and bruised because of the sounds coming out of my mouth? Are you hurt at my spoken violence?"

"Negative, Instructor Hayes!"

*Word games, just word games. Always testing. The way I get to make a difference is by not giving them the satisfaction.*

"And why is that, Zhang? Did you learn Chinese so you could welcome our friends across the bay as they *assist us* during this time of emergency?"

"I learned it to better to understand our enemies, Instructor Hayes!"

"You *think* you have a poker face, Zhang." Hayes said after a longer than normal pause. He leaned into Noah's personal space, squinting speculatively between the two BUD/S students. "And you're better at it than this inbred, bayou-spawned Louisiana cracker next to you, but not good enough. One definition of combat is where you do everything right and still get screwed. If

258

you can't let words roll off your back, how will you deal with the stress of combat? Get me?"

"Hoo-ya, Instructor Hayes!"

"You've come a long way, Zhang. Don't screw it up now. When I tell you to recover, take your swim buddy and report to First Phase. Lieutenant Caravaggio wants a word." he said before pausing for several beats. "Tree-cover!"

The duo remained still, muscles quivering, heads up and backs straight.

"Hmmph." Disappointed, Hayes grunted and stood, forearms flexing as he placed his hand on his hips. "Maybe you're learning. Ree-cover!"

The two sprang to their feet, and immediately began running as fast as they could to catch up with their class.

\*\*\*

Noah leaned over from his position on the painted fins in front of the First Phase instructors' office, and carefully prepared to make his presence known. It didn't please.

He knew, as every SEAL trainee quickly learned, the best survival strategy was to be as invisible as possible. Standing in front of the open main entrance to the legendarily touchy First Phase staff's office was a great example of being highly visible.

Noah cleared his throat nervously.

*Being possessed of an obvious Chinese heritage while the PRC invaded your city was another form of non-invisibility, so screwing up the protocol for requesting entrance would be the icing on a PT beat-down cake.*

Before him, all polished brass and gleaming white ropework, was the legendary BUD/S bell. One way or another, it had been rung by every BUD/S student to ever attend the rigorous course. Most would do so upon dropping from the program, known as "ringing out." A lucky few would do so on graduation day. It also happened to be the doorbell for the Phase office. Since any ringing tone would be the start of an unpleasant hour or three for the trainee that screwed up the Phase "knock," there was a protocol.

With exquisite care, Noah very carefully placed his thumb on the rim of the First Phase bell before giving the clapper a single,

259

gentle swing. Dampened, the bell didn't ring, but produced an unmusical "clack" sound.

"Petty Officer Zhang-Jefferson and a party of one, reporting to the Phase Officer as ordered!"

A few moments later, another blue t-shirt clad instructor rolled backwards into view on an office chair. He briefly inspected Noah's appearance through the open doorway, and then glanced at Thibodeaux.

"Right. Go through to the Lieutenant's office. You're expected."

Noah doffed his helmet liner and held it upright on his palm, stepping through the door through in time to hear the instructor stop the second trainee.

"Not you, Thibodeaux." The mustachioed instructor said, raising his hand to spin the large, multicolored disk, labeled, "Wheel of Mis-Fortune," bolted to the office wall. "You can entertain me with your vast store of SEAL-trainee knowledge, in between sets of push-ups. Drop!"

Noah continued through to the inner office, hearing the clicking sound of the rotating wheel begin to slow as his swim buddy waited to learn his fate.

He paused in front of the next door. Navy officers and senior enlisted had the option of wearing khaki uniforms in garrison. Noah mentally cringed, seeing a room filled not only with the menacing yet familiar dark blue SEAL instructor T-shirts, but a veritable sea of khaki. Before he could compose a polite interruption, Lieutenant Caravaggio saw him.

"Come in, Zhang." the lieutenant said, almost conversationally.

Noah looked for an open spot against the way, but before he could slide behind a very tall senior chief, Caravaggio introduced him to the assembly.

"This is Petty Officer Zhang from Class 452." the Phase Officer stated. "His class was just about to go over to Second Phase. Since Second Phase staff decamped the 'Strand for parts unknown, the recent hiccup in the schedule is letting the First Phase students spend some more quality time with us. More to the point, the drawdown of the last decade has shrunk the Teams so

260

much that of our the deployment of Team THREE to Guam and the disappearance of ONE the same day that the ChiComs dropped our power grid makes Zhang the last fluent Chinese speaker left on the Strand."

Pinned by the appraising stares of more officers and chiefs than he ever wanted to see in one place, Noah stayed quiet.

"Zhang, tell us about yourself." Caravaggio ordered. "How did you come to speak Chinese and how well do you speak it?"

"Sir, we spoke some Chinese at home." Noah answered, trying not to gulp. "My grandparents lived with us. I graduated from high school early and took graduate classes in college. I can speak, read and write simplified Mandarin, traditional Mandarin, Cantonese and Hakka."

"What's Hakka?" asked the tall senior chief whose black plastic nametag read Rodriguez.

"My grandparents on my dad's side fled China in the early eighties, Senior Chief." Noah replied. "The Han majority gave the ethnic minorities, including my grandparents' tribe, the Hakka, the choice of adopting Han customs and language or being forced out. The Han pushed them out of ancestral lands in the north, and eventually out of China altogether. We speak Hakka to remember the old north, before the ChiComs made good on their promise to erase us."

Rodriguez grunted.

"Sounds like my cousins." he replied. "Once the Chinese took over the Panama Canal, they started pushing out anyone who didn't toe the line drawn by their government stooges in the new People's Panamanian Republic."

"Right, moving on," Caravaggio said rather pointedly, causing Noah to look back over at him. "Zhang, your instructors speak well of you. They say you've got a cool head, probably because you're a little older than the trainees that come straight from Great Lakes. We need a fluent Chinese speaker we can trust. The mission's high risk. It's also unauthorized, as we've been officially ordered to take no direct action against the PLAN units in the immediate area. That's all I can tell you at this time."

"Sir, what about my class?" Noah said, not quite

261

stuttering. Leaving his group could mean rolling to a later class, and even repeating some training.

"If we successfully complete the op, I personally guarantee you will rejoin your class without penalty." the Lieutenant said, studying Noah as he leaned back in his office chair.

*And if we don't successfully complete the op, graduation is academic. Right.*

Noah briefly glanced around the circle of hard-faced men. Mostly appraising looks returned his regard, but there was an angry stare or two. Noah had come to accept that. During the last forty years, hundreds of thousands of mainland Chinese students had flooded American universities, very slowly increasingly their levels of political activity as others carried on with their primary intelligence and industrial espionage mission. Cheap Chinese products, some produced by the equivalent of slave labor, had initially been a boon to cash-strapped Americans, but ultimately led to Americans exporting their own manufacturing capacity. And of course, Zhang's parents had lived through the Wuhan-Flu, which damaged economies world-wide. Then came the wholesale ChiCom take-over of Third World countries who could neither repay Chinese loans nor stave off the growing Chinese military.

The net result was skepticism of his bona-fides, because he happened to be an American with Chinese ancestry. The only ones who seemed to distrust him more than a certain inevitable percentage of his fellow citizens were the mainland Chinese he'd met during the only two years of college he could afford. They called him an American Born Chinese. It wasn't a compliment.

However, Noah barely hesitated before simply answering. "I'm in, Sir."

"Glad to hear it, Zhang." Caravaggio replied. "Looks like you get to meet Chopper."

***

"Aw shit!" Instructor Hayes said, heartfelt emotion audible in both bitter syllables. "I hate working with this asshole."

"What's wrong, Instructor Hayes?" Noah asked, walking behind the instructor towards the pier. Hayes' reply was mostly inaudible expletives. Back on the dryside portion of N.A.B., Noah

262

and Thibodeaux paced their instructor as he strode forcefully through an open chainlink fence and led them between low, tan painted buildings towards the many piers that jutted out into the bay. The cove alongside the base was a civilian pleasure boat anchorage, and beyond sailboats that swung to anchor, the Coronado golf course gleamed emerald, an incongruous background to base. Striding quickly to keep pace with his annoyed instructor, Noah glanced around at his immediate surroundings. He saw Thibodeaux notice as well. The import of the mostly empty boat slips, open equipment lockers and scattered piles of various supplies was plain. A lot of people had left in a hurry, and no one was left to clean up. Hayes' voice became intelligible again.

"Nothing is wrong," grumbled the normally taciturn instructor. "As long as you're into working with psychotic marine mammals."

"I heard that, Instructor Hayes." a short, cammie-clad man announced, standing up from a chair that had been placed in the shade of the nearby building. His nametag read Wilson. His baseball-style cap sported the fouled anchor of a Navy chief, above a patch with the words *Explosive Ordinance Disposal, Mobile Unit THREE*. "I think you might be a bit prejudiced. Some might say that SEALs are the original psychotic marine mammals."

"Chief, I got the word that EOD is collaborating with Center on our little plan." Hayes explained, ignoring the jibe and shaking hands with the shorter man. He gestured towards the two BUD/S students. "These two chuckleheads volunteered."

"Petty Officer Zhang-Jefferson." Noah said, suppressing a wince as he shook hands in turn. The Chief's grip was hard and calloused. A lunchbox sized cooler swung from a strap negligently looped over one shoulder.

"Seaman Apprentice Thibodeaux."

"My name is Chief Petty Officer Bob Wilson," the man answered, releasing Thibodeaux's hand. "But you can call me Chief. Let's introduce you to your new swim buddy, Chopper."

"Aren't any of the other systems up, Chief?" Hayes asked, falling into step with the chief as they strode out onto the nearest pier. "Chopper's not quite right in head."

"There aren't any other systems." Wilson replied in a lower tone of voice, making Noah strain to understand. "Like the rest of this base, all you have to choose from are the left-overs, like me and Chopper."

The Chief looked over his shoulder, catching Noah looking at Thibodeaux with one eyebrow raised. The Chief scowled suspiciously before turning to walk towards the waterfront. The sunlight struck highlights from the light chop on the bay, making Noah squint as he hurriedly composed himself. Thibodeaux was right behind him as Noah followed the two older men along the pier, and then out along a narrower floating extension. Each side of the finger pier had four adjacent enclosures, each about thirty feet square. He looked into the first one he passed and could make out what looked like underwater fencing extending downwards, but nothing else.

"What Chopper is, is all we got left." Chief Wilson said, coming to a halt at the end of the pier. "The very last of the Mark Six systems."

"What he is," Instructor Hayes muttered, "Is one dirty fucker. Why not just release him?"

"Captive dolphins can't hunt normally. Then PETA got laws passed and now Chopper gets better medical and dental benefits than you do." the chief said, waving his hand at the furthest pen. A sharp whoosh of exhalation and bit of spray arrested Noah's attention. The water swirled and a dorsal fin cut the water in the square open area. "Besides, he likes it here. So, there you are boys, meet Chopper. We retired the program a few years back. Gave the animals away to marine aquariums, since we couldn't just turn 'em loose and it was too expensive to retrain them. Old Chopper is a special case and we couldn't... persuade any of the parks to take him."

Noah focused on the animal in front of him, something he'd only seen at a distance during a Sea World visit. The dolphin was easily twice as long as Noah was tall, with dark countershading on it's, make that *his*, flanks. Chopper made easy circles around the periphery, and Noah watched as the sleek animal turned to watch the humans. His movement made the floating walkway bob gently.

"Why wouldn't they take him, Chief?" Noah asked, captivated by the graceful movement of the big dolphin.

"Because he's fucking nuts, literally." Hayes observed darkly.

"Well, Chopper is... a bit off." Wilson said, tilting his cap back on his head while he surveyed the pen with a proprietary air. "Mission capable, mind you, but not really suitable for swimming with park guests or doing tricks in front a glass wall for the kiddees."

"What's a Mark Six system, Chief?" Thibodeaux inquired, beating Noah to the question.

"These boys got a clearance, Hayes?" Chief Wilson asked, ignoring Thibodeaux.

"Negative."

"Huh." The chief rubbed his forehead with his free hand and then looked more closely at the two trainees. "Tell me again why we're using BUD/S students."

"One is a fluent Chinese speaker, the other is his swim buddy and a convenient object upon which to visit my wrath."

Used to Hayes' acerbic manner, the two trainees didn't even blink at the implied threat. They looked expectantly at the EOD chief, instead.

"Alright, listen you two." Wilson said, popping the lid open on the cooler. "Here's the UNCLAS version you can find in Wikipedia. The Mark Six is a Force Protection system designed to safeguard our harbor facilities as well as ships that are moored or anchored. Like I said, the Navy couldn't afford to fund everything anymore, but back when it could, the Six was trained to detect and mark the location of enemy swimmers that might threaten friendly forces."

"How do they mark them, Chief?" Noah asked. "Wouldn't the enemy divers object?"

"Son, you're what, six foot tall and about a buck seventy five?" Wilson answered, squatting on the dock. He fished a metal device out of his pocket that resembled a bottle opener and then clipped it to a wrist lanyard. When Noah nodded, the Chief continued. "Chopper here's a thirteen feet foot long bull Atlantic

Bottlenose dolphin and when he's been eating his face off, which is usually, he tips the scales at eleven hundred pounds. If you're in the water with him, you ain't got no say about him doing whatever the hell he wants."

"Unless you got a concussion grenade and you don't mind turning your own guts into fish food." Hayes said, his eyes tracking the dolphin like a gun turret.

"Hayes, you got to let that go." the chief stated pointedly. "It's been more than ten years and Chopper didn't mean nothing by it. Speaking of which..."

The chief dipped his free hand into the cooler and withdrew a limp, silver fish slightly longer than his hand. Then he lowered the "bottle opener" into the water and did something that produced a loud, metallic double click. The dolphin immediate drifted over and lifted its head out of the water. Chopper alternated looking first with one glittering black eye, and then the other, his open mouth affording Noah a great view of twin rows of conical, ivory teeth.

Wilson tossed the fish towards Chopper, who expertly fielded the snack and swallowed it whole before immediately returning to his position, awaiting the next fish.

"Chopper's unusually smart, even for his breed." the Chief continued. "He recognizes people. Take a mackerel from my cooler and when I make a double click, toss it to him."

Noah hesitated, then reached into the cooler and withdrew a slippery baitfish before promptly dropping it on the dock. Chopper momentarily thrashed, following the motion of his tasty snack dropping out of reach. The water roiled, making the narrow floating pier buck as the bottlenose rolled over onto its back. The move exposed a much lighter gray abdomen and a...

"Holy shit!" Thibodeaux said. "Is that what I think it is?"

Chopper rolled sided to side, inverted. An enormous, bright pink and white dolphin organ was exposed for all to see. The shallow "s" shape, more than half as long as man's arm and easily as thick, tapered to a blunt point. Noah involuntarily took a half a step back as he watched Chopper's pride and joy wobble menacingly back and forth. He bumped into Thibodeaux who was swearing softly.

"Fucking hell, don't push me in!" his classmate blurted, balancing on the edge of the pier.

"Watch your step, Zhang." Hayes growled, reaching out to steady the other trainee. "Neither of you want to fall in, trust me."

As Noah watched, even more of the alarming appendage appeared.

"...and that's why couldn't give him to a marine park." Chief Wilson chuckled, making two clicks again. Instantly, Chopper rolled back over and stuck his head up. "No need to freak out, he's just showing off half a chub, friendly-like."

"Don't make him wait!" Instructor Hayes cautioned tersely. "Give him the damn fish. You want the great big psycho to think of you as the kindly bearer of treats, not a target or toy."

Noah nodded but turned to the Chief.

"Do hurry up, lad." Wilson said. "You don't want to make him frustrated."

As soon as he heard two clicks repeated, Noah tossed the fish towards the big dolphin, who snap rolled upright and deftly snatched the bait out of the air. Then the burly marine mammal waited expectantly. Noah took a few more fish and repeated the procedure. Chopper's aim was excellent.

"So, what happens if Chopper thinks you're a target or a toy?" Thibodeaux asked worriedly.

"Not good things." Hayes said grimly. "Not good things at all."

Chief Wilson just smirked.

"We'll just make sure that he knows you're one of the good guys, Zhang." he added. "Now all of you grab another fish. You too, Hayes."

***

Four days out from the power grid's collapse and most of the San Diego skyline was still dark, including the Coronado Bay Bridge arcing over the bay. With the engines off, the loudest sound coming from the mammal support boat was the lapping of the small, wind-driven waves against the gray fiberglass hull. Nearly thirty feet long, the unarmed boat was moored to another pier, this time on Harbor Island. Clearly, the choice of location was designed to hide the boat among the thousands of pleasure craft in the bay, and the use of a Boston Whaler permitted anonymity that would have been impossible in one of the SEALs' go-fast gunboats.

The novelty of wearing civilian clothes as well as the pre-mission excitement had worn off and now Noah looked around the city, trying to make out landmarks in the unaccustomed blackness. The darkness wasn't complete, thanks to the quarter moon overhead and the occasional hotel or business ashore that was running generator-powered lights. Every so often he'd hear the Chinese dock workers on the radio, and he'd write down the conversation for Instructor Hayes.

A scant thousand yards distant, portable dock lights and the illumination provided by the Chinese ships lit the cruise ship terminal with puddles of urine colored light. "COSCO" was easily legible in twenty-foot-tall letters across the red-painted side of the nearest cargo hull. The ship was a car carrier and a giant ramp led from a large opening in the ship's side, angling down onto the pier. Noah watched from the bow of the Whaler as periodically another green or white truck would trundle down the ramp, swaying a bit, and then move towards the partially full parking lot at the foot of the pier. No civilian car traffic was evident on the normally crowded Harborside Drive.

The headphones Noah wore spat another partially garbled conversation. He used the tiny sliver of green escaping a taped up chemlight to scratch a rough translation across his notepad.

"Instructor Hayes?" Noah whispered.

"Yeah, Zhang?" Hayes answered softly.

"The Chinese stevedores are still bitching," Noah said. "They're re-arranging cargo and they're bringing up more trucks. They say they're having problems maneuvering the trucks and still keeping something they're calling *liangqi tuolaji* belowdecks."

"What the fuck is a langee tuasomething?"

"I think it means amphibious tank, Instructor Hayes."

"Anything else?"

"The other channel only has intermittent bursts of static."

"That's their encrypted military stuff." Hayes said. "Our gear is still a lot better; you wouldn't even hear the static."

Hayes suddenly held up one hand, motioning for Noah to shut up while the instructor spoke in a low voice on his own radio. Noah listened to him relay the BUD/S trainee's report back to the mission commander. Somewhere nearby and out of sight, Caravaggio waited with the dive team. There was a longish pause and then Hayes spoke again.

"Ok, Sir." he said, consulting his watch "The handler reports we can stand by for another hour and twenty."

After a few more moments, he replaced the radio in his belt and picked up a pair of binocs to scan the harbor.

Noah tried to emulate his instructor's insouciance, but curiosity gnawed at him. He hadn't understood half of what LT Caravaggio had said during their mission brief but hadn't dared to respond to the call for questions that marked the end of the presentation, preferring to allow any of the fully qualified SEALs present to speak up. None had.

*Apparently, everybody but me knows exactly what's going on.*

Noah didn't feel like disturbing his instructor, so he eased further aft, and found the EOD chief. Wilson was sitting on the edge of the diver access door, cut into the side of the Whaler, apparently watching the dark surface of the bay.

"Chief Wilson, can I ask you a question?"

"Sure thing, kid." Wilson whispered, looking up briefly before returning to his study of the water.

A whoosh of exhalation signaled Chopper's presence, though the animal was invisible.

"Why does Hayes hate Chopper so much?" Noah asked.

A low chuckle answered his question. Noah heard, rather than saw Wilson make the double click, and then Chopper appeared, his beak and forehead emerging from the black water to rest on the edge of the hatch. The dolphin opened his mouth and Wilson gave him a fish before patting the animal on the head as it slid back into the bay.

"It's like this," the chief answered. "There used to be lots of different mammal systems. Mark Fives we still have, but they're our object recovery sealions. They help us recover practice ordinance as long as it isn't too deep. Back in the day, you also had

269

your basic mine detection systems, the Mark Fours and the Mark Sevens. Those were dolphins too. We got rid of 'em since the robotic systems have improved so much. Then you had your Mark Eights, dolphins again, which we used to scout for underwater obstacles. Finally, you got your Mark Sixes. Like I started telling you before, the Six can find divers that might be attacking our ships. They're, uh, dolphins of a different color, you might say. And Chopper here, he's a bit more... different again."

"So, Chopper is going to use his sonar to find Chinese divers?" Noah asked.

"Your SEALs are going to mine the Chinese ships so they can't offload any more equipment." Wilson said. "Divers only survive if they're undetected, so before they head in, we're going to make sure that any ChiCom divers are highly motivated to get the fuck out of the water, but do it without making the enemy suspect our SEALs are getting ready to sink their ships."

"So, if Chopper finds the divers, then what?" Noah asked.

*I'm clearly missing something. How is a dolphin going to make any Chinese get out of the water? It's a dolphin. It's not like a shark that can bit the divers, right?*

"You wanted to know why Hayes hates dolphins and Chopper in particular, right?" the chief answered testily, yet keeping his voice down. "I'm getting to it."

Noah kept his silence, feeling rather than seeing Wilson's glare.

"Well, just like you used to be able to read on the Navy's own website, the way the Mark Six marks the target is to bump into it from behind, the same way they'd stun a prey animal, but instead of chowing down, the system attached a location device to the diver's back. Then the system comes back and performs a behavior, like a head shake, to indicate it found and marked a target. Then, and only then we give him a treat. But dolphins are smart *and* lazy, just like humans. They just want the treat and they want it *right now*. So, say a system comes back in less time than I know it takes to find the target and still performs the *"I found it, Dad!"* behavior. I know he's lying. I give them the repeat command and no treat, which makes them actually go work. Of course, if they really did do their job, not getting a treat really pisses them off, so they go mark the target again, but they're pissed, right? So, they *mark* harder."

"Chief." Instructor Hayes materialized next to the pair. "Go time. Send him out."

"Roger that." Wilson said, Noah temporarily forgotten.

The chief used the clicker to make the now familiar sound, and gave Chopper a fish. Then he used the clicker to make a short but distinct series of clicks and paused before repeating it. Chopper slapped the water with one pectoral and vanished.

"System is deployed." Hayes said into his mic, before resting his hands on the railing next to Noah. "Zhang, anything else? Any mention of divers?"

"Negative, Instructor Hayes." Noah replied. "Just updates when they're about to move a truck down the ramp and they need to switch drivers."

"We'll know soon enough, Hayes." Chief Wilson said. "Chopper will find the divers if there's any in the water. I was just telling your boy here how it works."

"Did you tell him about Chopper yet?" Hayes asked darkly.

"I'm getting there, I'm getting there." the chief replied. "Remember how I said that if I tell a system to re-mark a target without giving them a treat, they get angry and do it again, even harder? Well, what if the handler denies them a treat a few times in a row? Imagine getting tagged by an angry dolphin..."

"Two things you're leaving out, Chief - three actually." Hayes interrupted. "Number One. I know what I'm talking about because when the Navy had more mammal programs, EOD would ask the Teams for volunteers to swim against the systems in-training. New guys, like I was once, thought swimming with the dolphins was a good deal. Number Two. It is *not* a good deal, because the asshole EOD-types, including the occasional BUD/S dud that decides to go EOD instead, like to fuck with the SEALs by telling the dolphins to re-mark targets."

"Now, Instructor Hayes, surely you don't think it was personal, do you?"

Noah could hear the grin in chief's voice.

"And by the way, the dolphin gets the best sonar return

271

off the airspace in the target's body, so when it *bumps* you it tends to aim for the lungs or your sinuses." Instructor Hayes went on, ignoring the EOD man. "Only, it goes faster each time, till you're getting nailed from behind at fifteen miles an hour by an aggravated half-ton self-guided missile. Over and over again. Fucker broke my nose and busted two ribs. But that's not all."

There was a splash and a whoosh. Chopper had returned. Noah watched as the dolphin made an odd jerking motion to one side, like a lopsided dance.

"He says he got something," Chief Hayes said. Then he slapped the water with his palm and thrust his arm out, just like the trainers at Sea World. Chopper repeated the dance, but the Chief didn't relent. Finally, the dolphin slapped the water with its flukes and disappeared.

*Did the chief just send Chopper out to re-mark a target? Oh, fuck!*

"Sierra Six, possible contact." Hayes said into his mic, then nodded to Wilson.

"We can't release dolphins back into the wild not only because they can't hunt for themselves," Chief Hayes continued. "but because by dolphin standards, they're not quite right in the head. You might say that working with humans gives them bad habits that other dolphins, which are already fucking crazy mind you, find even crazier. Chopper dials that up to eleven. For example: it's not unusual for several wild male dolphins to gang up on a single female to, uh, impregnate her."

"Oh, Chopper doesn't insist on *female dolphins*..." Hayes began just as Noah's earpiece sounded again. It was his turn to hold up one hand while he scribbled with the other.

"Some excitement." Noah said. "The stevedores are talking about some kind of emergency, that the soldiers are excited and running to the base of the pier."

"Sierra Four to Six," Instructor Hayes said into his lapel mic. "Contact confirmed."

Then, to Chief Wilson.

"Go on, tell him the rest, or it doesn't make sense."

"Chopper really likes his fish," Chief Wilson said. "But if you don't give him a treat, he might just take something else he wants. Usually, it takes three times for him to get really frustrated."

Right then, the water swirled again. Chopper was visible at the boat door and he repeated the odd, one-sided jerking motion.

"Wasn't that kind of quick?" Noah asked, fascinated.

"Chopper's pissed off." Wilson said over his shoulder. "He's swimming faster, see? He wants his goddamned fish."

At the same time, the chief shook his head and slapped the water before thrusting his hand across the harbor. Chopper repeated his dance hard enough that water splashed into the boat, causing Noah to cover his notepad with one hand. Finally, Chopper disappeared, and boat rocked from the water displaced by his powerful flukes.

"Ha, he's riled up now!" Chief Wilson crowed.

"You're a sick fuck, Chief." Instructor Hayes said, smiling wryly. Noah saw Wilson's answering smile gleam in the dark.

"I was on Number Three, Zhang." Hayes addressed Noah directly. "Remember Chopper's little display back on N.A.B.? Well, Chopper takes that mating behavior and applies it to any old thing he happens to find. And it turns out that Chopper thinks that neoprene wetsuits feel really, really good."

"Instructor Hayes, this sounds a lot like the dolphin version of something that GWOT-era science fiction writer would come up with." Noah said. He was a bit of a pop-culture geek. "Remember, 'Oh no, something-something?'"

"Doesn't ring any bells, sorry." Hayes answered. "But what I'll never forget was when I was suckered into my little experience. Ole *Petty Officer Third Class* Wilson here made Chopper re-mark me four times. I'm bleeding from my face, my mask is shattered, I can't breathe for shit on account of my ribs being broke, and then that dirty fucker pinned me to the bottom in thirty feet of water and stuck his big old dolphin dick into my armpit before spinning in circles for a subjective three or four hours before swimming off, smoking a goddamn cigarette. Most terrifying moment of my life, and I've blown out parachute canopies, been blown up by Iranian IEDs and charged by a thousand screaming Venezuelans."

"The best part, the be..." Chief Wilson said, stuttering

oddly. It took Noah a second to recognize that the Chief was stifling giggles. "The best part was when we picked you up. *Seaman Apprentice* Hayes, you were covered in..."

"Yeah, yeah, it was a real laugh riot, Wilson!" Instructor Hayes said grudgingly. "Better those ChiCom divers than me."

"And when you tried to walk across the deck you slipped because it was so slimy and busted your ass again!" the Chief tittered, his shoulders shaking again."

"You mean, right now, Chopper is..." Noah began before pausing. His headphones began going nuts and Noah had to scribble furiously to keep up.

"Instructor Hayes, the stevedores say the soldiers are pulling some divers out of the water." he reported. Noah was grateful for the darkness, because it would mostly cover the look of dumb amazement that he could feel spreading across his own face, as he prepared to finish his report.

*This is crazy. We sent a psycho dolphin to have carnal knowledge of enemy divers in order to clear the way for a SEAL op.*

"The stevedores are repeating the divers' warnings. They're reporting a *kǒngbù de yěshòu* – the best translation is scary sex beast. The stevedores are calling for an ambulance!"

"Sierra Six, this is Four." Hayes said into his radio, after Noah's last statement. "Contact neutralized. Charlie Mike at this time. I say again, Charlie Mike."

The divers were just doing their job." Hayes continued meditatively. "The best they could. Sucks to be them."

"Right about now, those Chinese are trying to not tell their bosses exactly what happened." Chief Wilson said, his chuckles almost back under control. "Instead, they'll report a shark or something, since everyone knows the U.S. Navy doesn't have mammal systems anymore. And now your boys can get on with their mission, right?"

Chopper announced his return with a sharp exhalation before performing the now familiar dance.

"Good boy!" Chief Wilson said. "Have a fish. Have two! How was that ChiCom diver pussy?"

\*\*\*

The sun beat down on the back of Noah's neck. He, Thibodeaux and the rest of 452 were enjoying the *hospitality* of the Third Phase staff at San Clemente Island. Inevitably, the class had made an error during Land Warfare training, but the punitive exercises had a friendly, if grim quality. The staff recognized that the BUD/S forge had beaten the scale and clinker off the class, and now the goal was to mold them into the shape of a useful weapons system.

"This class needs to concentrate on the task at hand." the Phase Officer was lecturing through the bullhorn, his words drowning out the rasping exhalations of the class as they all rested in what might charitably be called the position of attention. "Don't think ahead to the war. The ChiComs will still be there when the survivors of this class graduate. Focus on learning what we're teaching so you're an asset, not a liability, to my beloved Teams!"

Any moment, the PT was going to start again so Noah tried to surreptitiously un-kink his neck. Jumping jacks weren't a high impact exercise. Then again, Noah was wearing a seabag that contained sharp-edged ammo cans of gravel, and they'd all been sprinting to the surf in between sets. Noah blinked the sweat out of his eyes.

*At least there aren't any of those First Phase pricks aro...*

"There's a special treat for you, 452!" crowed another Third Phase instructor. "Since you can't seem to get your shit in one sock, we got the band back together. One of them is especially looking forward to meeting the class hero!

The instructor affected a horrible Asian language accent that was more Japanese than Chinese.

"Wheh ah yoo, Mistah Hee-roh?"

"Hoo-ya, Instructor Strangelford!" Noah yelled, noticing the sliding doors on a Navy van slide open. His heart sank and a ripple passed through the class' ranks as they caught sight of the familiar, hated dark blue T-shirts of the First Phase instructors. Noah watched as the men shook hands with the cammie-clad Land Warfare staff. A familiar face materialized in front of Noah.

The man's cover bore the fouled anchor of a Navy chief, not the first class crow that had decorated it previously.

"Well-well, Petty Officer Zhang-Jefferson!" Chief Hayes

exclaimed jovially. "We heard that 452 was screwing the pooch, so we decided to come help out. How's the ChiCom hee-ro of the Battle of Coronado Bay?"

"HOO-YA, Chief Hayes!" Noah shouted as loudly as he could, while in his peripheral vision, the other three blue-shirted staff selected their own targets.

"Was that a 'happy to see you' hoo-ya or a 'fuck you' hoo-ya, Zhang?" Hayes asked, stepping closer. "Are you all busted up inside because I reminded everyone of your ChiCom family and your boo-hoo sob story of escaping China?"

*This again? When will I have done enough?*

Noah schooled his face into impassivity, watching a familiar, aggravating grin spread across his old instructor's visage.

"Or are you just irritated that this training is getting in the way of you banging some ChiCom broad," Hayes went on, his booming voice carrying across the little courtyard of the SEAL training compound. "and making more little infiltrators?"

"AS MAY BE, CHIEF HAYES!" Noah heard himself yell just as loudly as before, his voice reflecting from the buildings that surrounded the grinder. His treacherous mouth went on, unbidden. "AT LEAST MY GIRLFRIEND SPEAKS MANDARIN INSTEAD OF SQUEAKING LIKE A DOLPHIN AND RIDING ME LIKE A RENTED MULE, CHIEF!"

*Oh God, what did I just say?*

A sudden hush fell over San Clemente Island, or at least Noah's little part of it. His fellow classmates were actually holding their breath. The story of the Battle of Coronado Bay had passed into legend. Noah's role was well known, as were the roles and *history* of the other members of the mission, including Chopper. And then-Instructor Hayes.

The SEALs had planted mines on the two ships actually off-loading cargo. Months later, those ships still rested on the bottom, their uppermost decks even with the piers, and their cargo of partially unloaded light armor and other rolling stock remained underwater. The rest of the Chinese had pulled out and the only warships in the harbor flew Old Glory.

But, here and now, Noah shivered, unable to believe he'd actually said the thing he was thinking.

*Shit. Shit-shit-shit.*

Like sharks that had scented a blood trail, the other blue T-shirted staff circled closer to see what was next, their own victims forgotten. One file over, Thibodeaux spared him a single horrified glance.

Chief Hayes, his face set like a thunderhead, leaned in so close to Noah that his hat brim nearly brushed Noah's face. The BUD/S student, just weeks from graduation, fought to show no emotion.

A long moment passed. Another.

"Not bad, Noah." Hayes said very, very quietly, peppermint breath wafting across the infinitesimally small space between them. He smiled quickly, almost invisibly. "Not bad at all. You're setting the bar pretty high for the next American with Chinese ancestry that shows up at BUD/S, you understand. That's the right thing to. Of course, doing the right thing can still get you screwed. But even though I may have to beat everybody in your class for that remark, it was still solid work. Carry the fuck on, frogman."

# The Battle of Liberty County

## Mike Kupari

There was a girl, walking alone, along the side of the highway. It was unusual to see someone this far out of town and by herself. The nearest town, Filbert, was another eight miles down the road. Occasionally you'd see joggers and hikers out (not nearly so often as before all the troubles began), but this girl didn't look like she was out for exercise. She wandered along, slowly, as if she were exhausted. It was a cool evening on the prairie, and she was dressed only in jean shorts and a tank top. Something was wrong.

"Damn it to hell," I muttered to myself, hitting my truck's emergency flashers and slowly pulling over. This stretch of Highway 25 didn't get as much traffic as it used to, especially not since things started to go to hell nationwide. This girl looked like she was in trouble, and it might be a while before someone else came along, much less someone else willing to help. People were a lot more suspicious than they used to be, and were a lot less inclined to get involved in other people's troubles.

The girl paused as I brought my tractor-trailer to a stop, but she didn't turn around. The air brakes hissed loudly as I engaged them. Shutting the engine down so she'd be able to hear me talk, I climbed down from the cab and approached, slowly.

"Excuse me, miss?" I asked. "Are you alright? You broke down or something? You need me to call somebody? I got a CB radio in my truck and a satellite phone." Cell phones didn't work so well out here on the prairie, especially not lately.

She turned around, then, facing me for the first time. She was young, probably early twenties, and pretty. Elaborate tattoos covered parts of her arms and legs, and her hair was dyed a violet color. She was fair-skinned and freckled, but the most noticeable feature on her face was the bruise around her left eye. There were more on her arms and legs.

"Jesus Christ," I muttered to myself. I held my hands up so she could see them. She'd obviously been assaulted, and I didn't want to spook her. She watched me nervously as I approached, her eyes flicking down to the big, stainless steel .44 Magnum I wore in a holster across my chest. "Listen, I don't mean you any harm. I only stopped because you looked like you were in trouble. Nearest town is a ways down the road and it'll be dark soon."

"I...I tried to flag down a ride," she said, weakly, "but nobody would stop. I got lost. I think I went in a big circle."

"What are you doing out here? You're not from around here, are you?"

She shook her head slowly. "Can you give me a ride to the next town?"

"Sure, kid," I said, trying to sound soothing. "No problem. Where are you trying to go?"

"My grandma lives in Omaha," she said. "I guess I'm trying to go there. She's the only family I got. Do you...can I have some water?"

"Yeah, sure. Come on, get in the truck. I can take you as far as Jefferson. It's about twenty miles from here. I live there. I'm headed home."

"Thank you for being nice to me," she said, obviously trying to hold back tears.

"It's no trouble, really," I said, leading her back to my truck. "Look, I'm not trying to pry, but what happened to you? Who did this to you?"

She was quiet for a moment. "I was living at the communal farm up in...well, it's not really in a town. North end of Liberty County. You know it?"

280

"Yeah," I said, my eyes narrowing. I lived in Liberty County, South Dakota. Everybody in the county knew about that damned farm. The owner had passed away a couple years back and it had sat empty until a bunch of kids from Minneapolis came down and took it over. Word was they were communists, People's Revolutionary Action sympathizers. They mostly kept to themselves, so the locals left them alone. "Wait here."

Leaving the girl by the side of the truck, I went back to the driver's side, climbed in, and secured the door behind me. Moving across the cab, I shooed my dog out of the passenger's seat, undid the combat lock on the passenger's-side door, and opened it. "It can't be unlocked from the outside once it's secured," I explained, reaching a hand down to the girl. She hesitated for a moment then climbed the steps and took my hand.

"You have a dog," she said absentmindedly, as my road buddy came over to greet the new person.

"His name is Zeke," I explained. He was a big, burly German Shepherd and Pit Bull mix. "He looks intimidating but he's a big baby."

"I love dogs," the girl said, petting him gently. Zeke licked her hand then rested his chin on her leg, tail wagging.

"Sorry about the dog hair," I said, apologizing. The passenger's seat was covered in a blanket that itself was covered in Zeke's brown fur. "He's blowing his coat out this time of year."

"I don't mind," she said, smiling for the first time as she continued to pet Zeke. "I love dogs. Thank you for the ride."

"Oh, hey, you wanted water, right? Here." I reached into my electric cooler and handed the girl a cold bottle of water.

"Thank you," she said again. She still sounded woozy, but took the water and drank half the bottle. "Sorry, I'm really thirsty. I been walking for a while."

"I bet you have," I said. The farm she said she came from was miles up the road. "Hey, what's your name?"

"Stacy," she said after finishing the bottle. "Sorry, I'm just really tired."

"Tell you what, you can go lay down in my bunk back there." I pulled the heavy curtain back, revealing the sleeper portion of the tractor's cab. "It's only about a half hour drive, but you can take a nap if you want. You look like you need to rest."

She nodded slowly. "That sounds good."

"If you need more water just help yourself. If you feel sick or anything and need to stop you let me know, okay? Oh, my name's Alex, by the way."

"My name's Stacy," she repeated, seemingly forgetting that she had just told me her name. "I'm going to lay down."

"Sure, kid, get some rest." Zeke jumped on the bunk with her and curled up, protectively, by her feet. I pulled the curtain closed, buckled myself into my seat, and started the engine. Before pulling back onto the highway, I checked my phone. I had signal enough to send a text to my wife.

*I picked up a girl walking along the side of the road. Bringing her to town. She's from that communal farm the commie kids took over. She's covered in bruises and I think she's been drugged.*

My wife responded a few seconds later. *Is she okay?*

*I think she will be,* I replied, *but she's been walking for miles. Call the sheriff. I'll see you when I get to the house. I love you.*

***

There was quite a welcoming party waiting for me when I got home. Isaiah Freeman, the Sheriff of Liberty County, had personally come to my house with one of his deputies, as did an ambulance from the county volunteer fire department. Technically I lived outside the limits of the town of Jefferson, but the on-duty Jefferson City policewoman was there as well. In the midst of all this commotion was my wife, Sarah.

My home had once been an active farm, and the main plot was big enough to not only park my tractor-trailer, but to turn it around so I didn't have to back down the driveway when I left. I wouldn't be able to make the turn-around tonight, though. The four emergency vehicles, lights flashing, were blocking too much of the driveway. I didn't mind. I had been on the road for six weeks and I was scheduled to be home for all of seven days. I had been driving for hours and was just happy to be home.

My wife came up to my door as I shut the truck down. "Hey, you," I said, opening the door, managing a smile for her. Zeke, realizing we were stopping, had nosed his way through the curtain and come up front. He was standing by my chair, excitedly wagging his tail, waiting for me to get out of the way so he could greet Sarah.

"How's the girl?" Sarah asked, a concerned look on her face.

"I think she's still asleep," I said. "I'll unlock the passenger's side door and check on her if you want to send the medics over."

"Okay," she said. I stood up and got out of the way so Zeke could jump down to the ground. She led the happy mutt off as I went back into the sleeper cap to check on my passenger.

Turning on the light, I was able to get a better look at Stacy. She hadn't awoken. Her breathing was a little ragged, but she was breathing. Her violet-colored hair was splashed over the pillow, hanging across her pretty face. The bruise around her eye was a deep purple color, and I noted a bloody crack on her lip as well. Little red dots could be seen on her arms in several places. There were bruises around her wrists and ankles, as if she'd been tied up...or held down, forcefully. I unconsciously ground my teeth a little.

As gently as I could, I reached out and put a hand on her shoulder. "Stacy," I said, softly, "we're here. Wake up, kiddo." There was no response. I shook her shoulder a little harder. She grunted but still didn't wake up. I looked up then as someone knocked on the passenger's side window of my truck. The sound was muffled through the armored glass.

"Hey fellas," I said, opening the door. Standing on the ground were a couple of guys from the volunteer fire department. They had a stretcher with them. "She's breathing but is still unconscious. I tried waking her up but no dice. I don't know if she's just exhausted from walking or if she's blitzed out on drugs."

"You think she's overdosed?"

I shook my head. "I don't know. She's got what looks like needle pricks in her arms, and even when she was awake, she seemed kind of out-of-it. I gave her water, but I don't know how long she'd been out on the road. She might be dehydrated, too."

The fireman nodded. "We'll get an IV in her when we get her in the ambulance." He climbed up the steps into my tractor. "This is pretty high off the ground. You mind giving me a hand getting her down?"

"No problem," I said, beckoning him to come into the cab. "Watch your head."

A short while later I was standing next to my truck, speaking with Sheriff Freeman about what happened, as the sun sank below the horizon and the sky darkened. Stacy had been loaded into the ambulance and driven off to our little county hospital. I brought the sheriff up to speed on how I'd found the girl on side of the highway. When I was on the road, I had a pretty strict policy of not talking to the cops unless absolutely necessary. Things were dangerous and unstable out there, and oversight was decidedly lacking in many jurisdictions. Sheriff Freeman was a good guy, though. He'd been an infantryman in the Army, with multiple combat tours overseas. He retired from the Army as a 1st Sergeant, settled in Liberty County, and ran for Sheriff the next year. He was notable as the county's first-ever black sheriff. His election campaign literature had included several references to *Blazing Saddles,* which had been enough for him to earn my vote.

He didn't even care that I was still openly carrying a gun. South Dakota is a Constitutional Carry state, in as much as such things are even enforced these days, but a lot of cops still get nervous around any non-cops who are armed. Not Sheriff Freeman.

He took a long drink from his thermos, shaking his head as he swallowed his coffee. "That damned farm," he said. "I knew something like this was going to happen sooner or later. People come and go from that place all the time. Between you and me, I think some of the political extremists from up in Minneapolis come down here to lay low."

"That's the rumor. Far be it from me to tell you your business, Sheriff, but why haven't you sent them packing? They've got to be squatters, and that's trespassing."

"They're not," he said, much to my surprise. "Believe me, I checked when they first started showing up. The property was purchased at auction by a group called the *Center for International Solidarity*. It's basically a front group for the People's Revolutionary Action, but they are the legal owners." He frowned. "They're just a bunch of punks, but they know how to play the system."

"I don't know," I said. "There are places out there I won't go, even in this thing." I rapped on the armored door of my truck. "The PRA *owns* parts of some cities. The cops don't go into those places. Hell, even the mail doesn't get delivered to the no-go zones anymore."

"I know." He sighed. "You know, I don't like to be heavy-handed. I grew up with stories from my dad, talking about how you always had to be scared of the police if you were black. Now that I am the police, I don't want to turn around and make people scared of me."

"I appreciate that, Sheriff."

"We've been getting more and more complaints having to do with that place, though."

"If what she told me is true, somebody up there roughed her up pretty good. Did you see the bruises on her arms and legs? I'd bet you she was raped."

"I did," the sheriff said. "I can't comment on that while the investigation is ongoing, but if things like that are happening up there?" He shook his head again. "Not in my county. I won't tolerate it."

"Thank you for coming out, Sheriff."

He nodded, then paused, looking up at my truck. "I remember seeing trucks like this overseas," he said. He knocked on the door panel. "That's some heavy armor on there."

"It's a Navistar/International MV-5000," I said proudly, resting my hand on the fender of the huge, white truck. "Full armor package. Fuel mileage suffers for it, and the extra weight limits what loads I can take sometimes, but I wouldn't want to be out there in an un-armored truck these days."

"You make enough money driving a big rig to be able to afford your own up-armored truck?" he asked. "Damn, I'm in the wrong line of work."

"I picked this up at a government liquidation auction. It was like new, part of some foreign contract that fell through. Had to take out a big-ass loan and spend half my savings, but so far, it's been working out. You could make good money as an owner-operator even before things fell apart. Now? Customers will pay big money just to get their goods delivered, and so many drivers have quit in the last few years. The big trucking companies don't pay well enough for their fleet drivers to be willing to risk going to a lot of places. A lot of truckers are getting armored rigs now, but I was lucky enough to get my foot in the door early. These days, a truck like this would go for probably double what I paid for it."

"That bad out there, huh?"

"It can be. This thing has already saved my life a couple times. The farther you get from the interstates, the less likely there is to be any highway patrol presence at all. There are a lot of motor bandits out there. Some of them will try to force you off the road. Others will just try and shoot the driver and loot the truck after it crashes."

"Unbelievable. I hate that it's come to this."

"It's a damned shame, isn't it? Anyway, if that's all you need, I'm going to head inside. I've had a long day. Please let me know if there's anything I can do to help."

\*\*\*

One of the things I like about living in the country is having a piece of land big enough to shoot on. My wife and I owned 20 acres a few miles outside of Jefferson, and that was more than enough to build myself a nice little range on. Our property was surrounded by nothing but farm fields for miles, and I had a local with a front-end loader come in and build me up some berms for the backstop. The range was only 100 yards or so, but there were rifle ranges I could go if I wanted to shoot farther than that.

I was out there with one of my rifles, a Savage MSR in 6.5mm Creedmoor, with the variable scope dialed back to 1x. I had steel targets set up at different distances and was practicing transitioning between them as quickly as I could, offhand, from the standing position. No one would ever mistake me for a pro competition shooter, but I did alright, considering how infrequently I got to practice.

It was relaxing, being on the range, concentrating on what I was doing instead of all the insanity going on in the world. My wife was at work, so there was no one home to be bothered by the noise except Zeke. My intrepid mutt wasn't bothered by the gunfire if he was safe in the house.

"Good morning, Mr. Kowalski."

Surprised to hear someone address me, I turned around to see Sheriff Freeman standing behind me. Between being absorbed in what I was doing and my hearing protection, I hadn't heard him approach. His OD-green uniform was immaculate. His badge, fastened to the left breast of his body armor vest, gleamed in the morning sun, as did the sheriff's star on his brown cowboy hat. His pant legs were neatly bloused into spit-shined combat boots.

"Good morning, Sheriff," I said, taking out my earplugs. I safed my rifle and slung it over my shoulder. "Am I in some kind of trouble?"

"What? No, not at all. I actually came to see if you could help me with something.

Normally when you tell someone to *let you know if there's anything you can do to help,* you don't expect them to actually come to you for help. It's the sort of noncommittal pleasantry that gets freely tossed around up in the Midwest. "Oh! Okay, what, uh, can I do for you?"

"That girl you brought in? Stacy. She told us a lot about what's going up at that farm."

"Really? Like what?"

"Like people being held against their will, assaults, possible murders, harboring people unlawfully in the country, and drug distribution."

"Murder?" I asked, incredulously. "Drug distribution? Seriously?"

"Chinese fentanyl."

"Holy hell. Okay, what do you need from me?"

"I got a warrant to raid the place, finally. The girl's testimony was enough to convince the judge. Problem is, according to her, there are almost a hundred people there, many of them armed. I have all of seven deputies in my department, barely enough for our day-to-day operations. I was able to pull in a few more officers from towns in the area, but they're all short-handed right now, too. The Highway Patrol told me they can't spare anybody. I even tried calling in the Feds. The FBI and the DEA both basically told me to pound sand. That doesn't leave me with a lot of great options. I need more men. You seem like you know what you're doing. If you're interested, I'd be willing to deputize you to assist with the raid. I can't pay you, unfortunately, but I could really use your help."

"Sheriff," I asked, cautiously, "are you recruiting me for, like, your *posse*?"

He sighed. "If that's what you want to call it—"

"I assure you, that's what I want to call it."

"Fine. Yes, I'm asking you to join my posse. There is one other thing, though. Do you think we could use that armored truck of yours?" He spent a few minutes filling me in on everything Stacy had told him and laying out a strategy, one that centered around using my truck to get his people onto the property without giving the squatters time to prepare or destroy evidence. It was like something from an episode of *The A-Team*, but I thought it might actually work. I was already convinced, but there was just one hang-up I needed to address first.

"I need to talk to my wife about this," I explained.

He nodded. "Oh, I understand that. If you don't mind me asking, what does your wife do?"

"She's a microbiologist. She works at the Prairie Technologies Group lab over in Madison. They make vaccines for livestock, mainly."

He raised his eyebrows. "Is that right?"

"Yeah, and she married a trucker." I grinned. "I'd tease her when we were dating, tell her she was slumming it with a blue-collar Joe Sixpack who dropped out of college."

"You haven't lived here for too long, have you?"

"Only two years. We moved here when she got the job. I had been driving for about a year at that point, and being a trucker means you can live anywhere. Her last job was in Atlanta and she really wanted to get out of the big city."

"I was in the same boat. My last assignment was Fort Bliss. Things are pretty bad down in the border country these days. My wife wanted us to get out, raise our girls someplace far away from all that."

"South Dakota is pretty far from El Paso," I agreed.

"Forgive me for not remembering," he said, "but you're a veteran, right?"

"I am. I did eight years in the Air Force, then another four in the Reserve. I was in an AGR slot at Dobbins Air Reserve Base in Atlanta when I met my wife."

"What was your MOS? You seem like a shooter. Were you Pararescue, TAC-P, something like that?"

"What?" I chuckled. "Oh no. I was in Civil Engineering, 820th RED HORSE out of Nellis, while I was on active duty. I got promoted to Tech Sergeant in the Reserves and spent most of my time flying a desk."

"I see. You every deploy?"

"Oh yeah. We deployed a lot. I spent six months in the Balkans and went to Africa twice."

"Good to know. You seem like you can handle yourself. I'm not going to lie to you, this might get a little dicey."

I shrugged. "I figured. Like I said, I'll talk to my wife. If I get the okay from the boss-lady, I'll let you know."

Sheriff Freeman nodded. "I'll be on my way, then. Please let me know what you decide. Time is a factor, here, so I would appreciate it if you could get back to me as soon as possible. Thank you for your time."

"Sure thing. She gets home a little after five. I'll talk it over with her and give you a call."

***

"He wants you to do *what*?" Sarah looked at me incredulously, her arms folded across her chest. The redhead was coming out and I had to tread carefully.

"He wants me to join his posse," I explained, "for a raid on that farm the commie kids took over."

"His *posse*?" she repeated. "This is crazy. You're not a policeman. Why doesn't he call the state?"

"He did. They refused to help. He also wants to use my truck."

"Your truck? What for?"

"I guess there are a lot of guys up at that farm, and a bunch of them are armed."

That statement did not help my case. "What? No. Alex, no. What is he going to have you do, crash the gate and go in guns blazing? You're going to get yourself killed."

I put my hands on her shoulders and looked down into my wife's eyes. "Listen, hon. He's got a pretty good plan. My job will be to just drive the truck. The crew he's putting together are going to be hidden in the trailer. I'm going to pull up to the farm like I'm making a delivery, and tell them I got the wrong address when they stop me. They'll probably tell me to drive in so they can loot the cargo. When they open the trailer, surprise!"

Sarah still wasn't thrilled. "And what if they just shoot you in the head so they can steal your truck, too?"

"They won't," I said. "Motor bandits will do that, but guys like this? The authorities might ignore a trucker being robbed, as bad as things are right now. They won't ignore one being murdered, and they have to know that. Organizations like the PRA know when they should and shouldn't cross those lines."

"Right. I'll make sure they engrave *they probably won't shoot me* on your tombstone."

"I won't do this if you say no," I told her, "but this is important. That girl I brought in, she told the Sheriff all about what's going on up at that farm, and it's bad. There are people being held against their will there. They're distributing fentanyl."

"How does she know all this?"

"Seems her ex-boyfriend is up there, and he's PRA. She watched him execute a federal agent, in cold blood, up in Minneapolis. He brought her there against her will to lay low. I guess she told him she wanted to go home, and he turned on her. She's was drugged and raped, but a friend helped her escape."

I could tell this bothered my wife as much as it bothered me. She was the analytical sort, though, and was cautious by nature. "Okay, that's what she says. How do you know any of this is true? Maybe she's just a lying junkie trying to get revenge on her ex."

"That's a possibility," I admitted, "but the raid is going to happen one way or another. The Sheriff got a warrant. He's got his entire department on board, one of the Jefferson City cops, and a few volunteers from around the area. This thing is going down and I feel like I should help. This is our home. These people are our neighbors. We need to be able to depend on each other, as bad as things are right now."

Sarah tried to choke back tears. "I know. I'm just scared. We left Atlanta to get away from all this. You remember what it was like."

"I remember, baby. That's why I need to do this. We came up here to start a family. This place won't be safe as long as those lunatics are holed up at that farm."

"Please be careful," she said, holding me tightly.

"I will," I assured her.

\*\*\*

My home was in a relatively remote location, away from any prying eyes the PRA might have in town. It was agreed that everyone involved in the raid would come to my place in the predawn darkness. We had a mission briefing, then the Sheriff formally deputized us volunteers in a brief swearing-in ceremony. He handed out high-visibility armbands which said *POLICE* on them, so we'd be able to tell who the friendlies were, and we began to load up.

The empty trailer I'd brought home was a 53-foot refrigerated unit (or *reefers*, as they were known in the industry). I was scheduled to pick up from food distribution warehouses and deliver to stores across the Midwest when I went back on the road. Trucks routinely visited farms to pick up fresh produce, and that was the pretext I would use for stopping at the occupied farm. I was to pull up to the place and explain that I had gotten the wrong address. When the opportunity presented itself, I was to open the trailer. The Sheriff and his best men were hidden behind a wall of empty cardboard boxes. More would be waiting down the road, ready to roll in as soon as the raid started. The Volunteer Fire Department was on standby with their trucks and ambulance. The PRA militants wouldn't know what was happening until it was too late.

That was the idea, anyway. Alone in the cab, driving toward the occupied farm, I dwelled on all the ways this could go wrong. They might make me drop the trailer and leave without it, for one thing. The trailer couldn't be opened from the inside. The posse would be trapped until someone let them out. Fortunately, it wasn't too warm out in the early autumn, and the trailer was temperature-controlled regardless. The dozen men inside wouldn't have to worry about being cooked to death in a hot trailer, at least.

There was also the possibility, however much I had downplayed it to my wife, that they would just kill me and try to steal my truck. The PRA could probably use a rig like that for their own purposes, and if not, it would fetch a pretty penny on the black market. They may be communists, but their so-called revolution needed financing all the same.

*No sense in what-iffing it to death,* I thought to myself, as my truck rumbled down the highway. I was being honest with my wife when I told her my reasons for wanting to do this. Liberty County was our home, and I would be damned if I was going to let a bunch of militant fanatics set up shop in it. Given how screwed up the justice system was, I found myself grimly hoping that they wouldn't let us take too many of them alive.

It took me the better part of an hour to get close to my destination. Liberty County, as sparsely populated as it was, was the biggest county in eastern South Dakota. As I drew close, my grip tightened on the wheel. I grabbed the radio the Sheriff had given me and let them know that we were close. After that, I turned it off and hid it. I didn't want to look suspicious. Taking a deep breath, I hit my indicator and made a slow, wide turn off the highway, onto the gravel road which lead to the occupied farm.

I made my way up the drive slowly. It hadn't been maintained or properly graded in some time, and my tractor was particularly heavy from all the armor. The place had once been a huge farmstead, with a large main house, a smaller guest house, three big silos, and a bunch of outbuildings. Now it had fallen into disrepair, but the place was clearly occupied. Many vehicles were parked on the property. As I drew closer to the entrance, I could see people milling about. I guessed that some of the outbuildings had been turned into makeshift housing for people. South Dakota winters were too brutal for a tent city to be practical.

An old metal gate blocked the main entrance to the farm property. Several people gathered there as I approached, and some of them were carrying weapons. My heart was racing. *This is it.*

Three guards, dressed in black, approached my vehicle as I came to a stop. I rolled down the window and shut off the engine.

One of the militants, wearing black fatigue pants, a black hoodie, a black face mask, and a cheap nylon shoulder holster, climbed up the steps on the side of my truck so that he could talk to me. On the ground, behind him, two of his compatriots stood by. One and an AR-15 and the other had an AK. "What are you doing here?" he snarled, through his mask, staring at me with bloodshot eyes.

I had my hands raised where he could see them and tried to act scared. (It wasn't difficult, as my heart was pounding and I knew that I could get shot at any moment.) "Whoa, hey! I don't want any trouble! I must have the wrong address!"

"What are you carrying? Why would you come here? Are you a cop?"

"I'm not a cop! I haul produce," I explained. "I pick up from farms and bring it to distro centers. That's why I have the reefer trailer."

"Give me your paperwork," the man in black demanded.

"Look, I'm sorry, okay? I'll back out to the highway and be on my way. I don't want any trouble."

The guard fumbled at his holster for a second and drew his pistol. He stuck the Glock in my face, holding it sideways like he was in a rap video from the 1990s. "Give me your paperwork," he repeated, "or I'm going to shoot you in the fucking head."

"Okay, okay, holy shit!" I reached to my dashboard and grabbed the fake bill of lading I had typed up for just this purpose. It listed a variety of food vegetables like carrots, celery, potatoes, and corn. "Here!"

"Don't move," he ordered, taking the paperwork and hopping down. He stepped away from the truck and pulled out a radio. The other two guards, the ones with the rifles, watched me closely. I kept my hands on the steering wheel and made no sudden movements. After a few moments, the young man in black returned, and climbed back up to my window. "Here's what's going to happen," he said. "We're going to open the gate, and you're going to pull the truck in. You see that big building there, the one that looks like a garage?"

"Yeah, I see it," I said, not making eye contact with him.

"There's enough room in front of it to turn your truck around. Back it up to the big door on that building. We're going to open your trailer there."

"Open my trailer? Why?"

"We're seizing the food you're carrying so that we can distribute it to our community. The corporate pigs you work for don't have a right to sell the labor of the working class."

"Whatever you want. I don't want to get shot for vegetables. Take it. Just let me go."

"It hasn't been decided what will happen to you, yet. Cooperate and you won't be harmed. Try anything and you're dead. You understand?"

"Yes! Just don't shoot!"

"Good." He drew his pistol once again, holding it in his right hand while he gripped the door with his left. "Pull forward when they open the gate. I'm going to stay right here so you don't try anything stupid."

The PRA militant clung to the side of my truck as I pulled forward. The gravel road was bumpy; I hoped that if he fell off, he wouldn't accidentally shoot me as he fell. As instructed, I drove toward the large garage. More black-clad guards, carrying rifles, were posted by the entrance to the building. They watched disinterestedly as I swung the truck around and backed up closer to the building. More people appeared, dressed in normal clothes and not carrying weapons. They slid open the doors to the garage and stood by. I could see into the garage in my mirrors, and it was obvious that they were using it for storage.

The young man hanging off my door seemed satisfied with my backing job. "Shut off the engine," he ordered, yelling so he could be heard over the roar of the diesel engine. I cut the ignition and the truck shuddered to a halt. "Now give me the keys," he said. Without arguing I handed them over.

"The trailer is locked," I said.

"It won't be," my handler said. In my mirror I saw a young man approaching with bolt cutters. He looked back at me. "Get out of the truck. Don't make any sudden movements."

"Okay," I said, unbuckling my seatbelt.

"What are you doing?" he said, sticking the gun in my face again. "I said get out of the fucking truck!"

"I can't get out with you hanging on the door, man!" I said, holding my hands up as if they would stop the bullet from hitting me in the face.

"What? Oh. Right." The PRA kid actually chuckled at himself as he jumped down from the door. Knowing the communist fanatic waving a gun in your face is also an idiot is not a comforting feeling, but at least he had a sense of humor about it, I guess. In any case I did as I was told, climbing out of the truck and handing him the key. I had a spare in my pants pocket anyway. It was getting warmer as the sun came up; he pulled back the hood of his sweater and revealed a head of unkempt blonde hair.

I watched, tensely, as the workers cut the padlock off my trailer. My handler, somewhat distracted by it all, was watching them, too, and not me. After a few seconds of fumbling with the latches, they began to open the trailer doors. *This is it.* The doors were swung open and I held my breath. Nothing happened at first. Seconds ticked by but they felt like minutes. A bead of sweat trickled down my forehead as I waited.

"Liberty County Sheriff's Department!" Sheriff Freeman shouted, his deep command voice booming. "Drop your weapons and get down on the ground!"

The people who opened the truck froze for a couple seconds, surprised and obviously unsure what to do. "It's the cops!" someone shouted. The two armed guards who had been standing by at the garage doors rushed toward the back of the trailer. Then the first shots rang out.

The young man guarding me, the one with the blonde hair and the Glock in a shoulder holster, froze for a second, his eyes fixed on the source of the gunfire. His pistol was drawn, but he seemed unsure what to do with it. More importantly, he wasn't looking at me. I reached into my front pants pocket, my hand wrapping around the boot grip of the little revolver I carried there. I drew the piece, a Ruger LCR, and pointed it at the side of my captor's head. His head snapped to his left, eyes wide, as he realized that now he was the one with a gun in his face.

I squeezed the trigger. *BLAM.* The ugly plastic-and-aluminum .38 recoiled in my hand. My captor crumbled to the ground with a bullet hole between his eyes. Gunfire was erupting from the garage now as the Sheriff and his posse unassed the trailer. This was good, they'd be fish in a barrel in there and they needed to get off the X. People were running everywhere now, including a whole bunch of black-clad men and women carrying guns. I stood there for a moment I didn't have, eyes affixed on the man I'd just killed. I'd been shot at before, and I'd shot back a few times too, but this was different. I'd blown the kid away. His blood was on my face. *Holy shit. Holy shit.* I looked up. Armed men were headed my way. I had to move. I had weapons hidden in my truck cab, I just had to get to them. *Move, goddamn it, move!*

Finally able to will my legs to move, I scrambled back up into my truck and closed the door behind me. Turning into the sleeper cab, I dropped to my knees, set the .38 snubby on a shelf, and reached for a latch under my bunk. The bed rested on the lid of a storage compartment, and that's where I had my gear stashed. I reached for a set of electronic earmuffs and put them on. Next, I grabbed the plate carrier I'd brought and slid it over my head. I secured the Velcro straps, then grabbed the chest holster with my Redhawk .44 in it.

As I snapped the holster's buckle into place, I heard someone opening the truck door behind me. I pulled the big revolver and turned around just in time to see one of the black-clad militants in my truck. He was hunched over, trying to step over the driver's seat, an AR-15 slung across his chest. He wasn't wearing a mask and I could see every feature of his face. He was young. His long hair was jet black. His eyes, also bloodshot, went wide when he saw the big, stainless steel gun in my hand.

"Get out of my truck!" I shouted. The gun bucked in my hand as it roared. The fat slug struck the intruder square in the chest, but he was wearing body armor. He stumbled backward at the impact, hitting his head and sliding to the floor. I raised the revolver, putting the green dot of its reflex sight on his face, and pulled the trigger again. *BOOM*. The armored glass spider-webbed where the bullet it, surrounded by a splash of blood and brains. It was horrific, but I was over the initial shock. I didn't have time to screw around. I re-holstered the pistol, reached back into the storage compartment, and grabbed both my Beretta 1301 Police shotgun and a bandolier of buckshot.

Hunched forward with the shotgun shouldered, I kept the weapon trained on the open driver's side door as I moved to the front of the cab. Gunfire and police sirens echoed across the farm. The air in my truck stunk of burnt powder and blood. Movement! Someone else was climbing into my cab! My finger moved to the shotgun's trigger.

A deep voice called my name. "Mr. Kowalski! Are you in here? Are you—holy shit!" Sheriff Freeman froze when he saw the shotgun pointed at his face. Realizing who it was, I lowered the weapon. My heart was beating so hard it felt like it was going to burst out of my chest.

"I almost shot you!" I shouted.

"Calm down," Mr. Kowalski," the Sheriff said, looking at the dead body in my cab. "Are you hurt?" I shook my head, jerkily. "Okay," he said, his voice calming in its authoritativeness. "I can use you outside if you're up for it. You good?"

"I'm good," I answered.

"Excellent. Come on, then. You're with me."

***

The *Battle of Liberty County*, as the incident came to be known, lasted less than an hour. Sheriff Freeman and his posse of deputies, area law enforcement, and citizen volunteers took on a force of armed PRA militants which outnumbered them three-to-one. The firefight was as intense as it was brief- five members of the Sheriff's posse were killed, including two of his deputies, a

298

Jefferson City police officer, and two volunteers. At least nine others were wounded, including the Sheriff himself.

It was the biggest battle to take place in South Dakota since the Ghost Dance War of 1890, between the US Army and the Lakota Sioux. The incident briefly made the national and even the international news, but with so much going on in the world, it wasn't long before it disappeared from the news cycle. Hundreds of people, from all over the state, would turn out for the funerals of the five local men who were killed in the raid. A small memorial was erected in their honor.

The People's Revolutionary Action militants fared much worse. In total there were no fewer than ninety-two of them at the site, though most of them weren't armed and didn't participate in the battle. Of those that did resist, twenty-two were killed. Some attempted to flee but most surrendered. Stacy's ex-boyfriend, a 31-year-old from Minneapolis named Reza Caine, was among the dead. He was wanted for the murder of an ATF agent and was suspected to have been involved in several other violent crimes.

As Stacy had said, the farm itself was a hotbed of illegal activity. Millions of dollars' worth of fentanyl, guns, ammunition, and explosives, most of it believed to be imported from China, were seized. Of those arrested, nearly two dozen had outstanding warrants for a host of crimes. Six people on the property were found locked up and were being held prisoner by the PRA. These people were freed and returned to their homes.

The FBI, ATF, and DEA later tried to say that Sheriff Freeman had jumped the gun and the raid was poorly executed, but no one who was there thought that. The Feds hadn't wanted anything to do with it until it proved to be a success, and then they were mad that they couldn't take credit for it. Their reaction to the incident didn't do anything to improve the people of South Dakota's confidence in the federal government.

The whole thing seemed crazy, like a story out of the wild west, but it really happened, and I was there. At the time it seemed like the whole country, hell, the whole *world* was falling apart. In such times it's always tempting to stay out of it, to just keep your head down and hope the whole thing blows over. It would have been easy enough for Sheriff Freeman, hell, for *all* of us, to do just that. A bunch of country hayseeds taking on an internationally-funded terrorist organization on the word of a drugged-up girl found on the side of the road? It sounded insane, but that's just what we did, and somehow, we prevailed.

As for Stacy, the troubled girl who was the catalyst for all this? Thousands of people donated money to cover the medical bills for her stay in the Liberty County Hospital. When she was released, my wife and I loaded up the Toyota and took her to Omaha. She's been living there ever since, taking care of her elderly grandmother and staying out of trouble.

There were rumors swirling about that the People's Revolutionary Action would retaliate against Liberty County. Sheriff Freeman, in his re-election victory speech, told them that if they tried, we'd be ready for them.

They never did turn up again.

# Spiritus Invictus

## James Rosone

**0230 Hours**
**Near Seattle, Washington**

Major Josh Pillonato commanded A Company, 2nd Raider Battalion, and he'd been the "Skipper" for just shy of six months. Currently his company was at Fort Lewis, Washington, training with 1st Special Forces Group. Officially, they were cross training with their Army counterparts. Unofficially, they were there to break things and kill people.

Pillonato had started out enlisted in the Marines, before he'd had the wild idea to become mustang officer. During his enlisted years at 1/5, he had learned to become a dragon gunner. Then he'd gone on to become a Marine scout sniper, earning the coveted 0317 MOS. After that, it only seemed natural for him to try out for Force Recon. After a winding road that included four years in naval ROTC, he'd come back to the Marines and survived the grueling Raider selection process as an officer.

Looking back on all of that, Pillonato realized it that was practically a lifetime ago. Everything had changed since then. He didn't even know what to think of the current situation other than he was having a hard time recognizing the country he'd devoted his entire life to serving and protecting.

Washington state had been plagued by radical groups since the election of 2016. Since then, the world had gone from chaos to explosive diarrhea. Add in riots, IEDs, a terrorist attack that had knocked out most of the US power grid, and Communist Chinese Special Forces, and this freak show was quickly turning into a full-blown cluster mess of epic proportions. The only upside to it was that the A Company had been given a blank check to locate, close with, and destroy the groups or people providing the IEDs to the various radical groups using them.

The Chinese had made their move, and the world was feeling the heat from the Dragon's breath. Pillonato hated home games—fighting on your home turf. However, it did at least give them home field advantage. Unlike Iraq, Afghanistan, Syria, and a few of the other places he'd operated in over his career, he knew these streets, people, and cities. This was home.

The Chinese weren't stupid, though. They had been using the Port of Angeles to bring supplies and personnel covertly into Washington almost daily. It was kind of an open secret; most people knew it was happening, but the politicians in Washington weren't willing to put a direct stop to it—not with the world on edge and a direct war with China hanging in the balance.

Pillonato's unit had been getting their intel from 1st Group. They had A-Teams all throughout Seattle in civvies, collecting info on the ChiComms and their useful idiots in People's Revolutionary Action. The Chinese knew how to play all sides of the brewing conflict, and they were equal opportunists when it came to providing IEDs and weapons. All they cared about was sowing chaos and growing the domestic terrorist groups, or separatists within the US.

Since China failed to see the light after a few soft and direct diplomatic efforts after the dustup down in San Diego and LA, a few discreet military units had been given permission to make them feel the heat. They kept insisting that only PMCs were on the ground, and that none of the unrest was Beijing's fault. Hopefully, this would get them to return to the negotiating table.

1st Special Forces Group had gathered enough intelligence on the movements of the Chinese and their allies in Seattle and the surrounding areas that the brass and the politicos in Washington felt comfortable with a limited kinetic operation. It was hoped that once the ChiComms had gotten their noses bloodied again, they might realize the US was on to them.

\*\*\*

Pillinato had broken his company down into their Marine Special Operations Teams, or MSOTs; they each had a target they were going to strike simultaneously for maximum shock and awe. If Murphy's Law didn't kick them in the ass, they'd blend back into the night and regroup for round two.

Pillonato would be with Team One—their target was in the heart of the port, a Chinese merchant ship that 1st Group had positively identified as holding weapons for the various separatist and domestic terrorist groups. These groups had been actively used to foment hate and discontent against the federal, state, and local governments, when they weren't busy going after each other.

Team Two was going after an IED factory in an old warehouse on the outskirts of Seattle. Surveillance had identified a platoon of Chinese Special Forces operating out of the warehouse for a couple of weeks. They had also spotted as many as three dozen separatists coming and going from the building.

Team Three was tasked with killing the IED emplacement teams along a stretch of highway intersecting Highways 101 and 112. Their job was going to mostly consist of sitting in hide positions and waiting to see who would come along to bury some IEDs along the heavily traveled road.

Team Four had the fun and difficult job of blowing up the FedEx Shipment Center at William Fairchild International Airport. The Chinese had taken over the facility and were using it to store explosives for the separatists and PRA. It needed to be taken out, if nothing else, to deny the Chinese its use.

The attacks were all being timed to take place at precisely 0300 hours; Pillonato's instructions to his Marines had been to use maximum violence of action on the objectives. Aside from Team Three observing the highway and the intersection, he wanted his teams in and out in no more than fifteen minutes on their objectives.

What he hadn't said out loud, but he knew had been understood, was that there were going to be American civilian casualties. Then again, those civilians had declared themselves enemies of the Republic. A Company's mission was straight direct action, and when it came down to it, Pillonato was sure that not a single Marine or sailor involved had an issue with the mission order. Radical anti-American separatists had been allowed to terrorize, destroy, and cause chaos wherever they could for far too long. Tonight, for the first time, *they* would feel the heat.

***

Team One began their dive, launching into the cold water from the zodiacs in the channel. Even with his dry suit on, Pillonato felt the chill deep in his bones. As they approached their target, he could see that she was fully loaded; her beam was low in the waters of the port. She was far too big to dock so she was anchored just outside the port, while her supplies were ferried off daily.

In order to maintain stealth as they approached the Chinese-operated ship, the Marines wore Drager rebreathers. Because these specialized rebreathers didn't expel bubbles as they swam, they didn't have to worry about giving their location away to any People's Liberation Army Navy patrols that might be standing on deck, watching for divers.

Every other Marine in Pillonato's team carried a limpet mine. Each of the nine swim pairs was given a portion of the ship to emplace their mine for maximum damage. With that many explosions, there would be no way for the Chinese to seal off enough compartments to keep the freighter afloat.

Pillonato's swim buddy was the company First Sergeant, Tom Draney. He was a former Force Recon Marine who was plucked early in MARSOC's infancy. He was a seasoned warrior and one hell of a diver; between the two of them, Draney carried the mine and Pillonato was on the compass board. Their job was to place their mine on the screw shafts. The team leader and the team chief were placing their mine on the opposite shaft.

The team operations sergeant and the assistant operations sergeant hovered just beneath them. They were all operating the close contact underwater diver system or CCUDS, which would alert them to any divers in the water. 1st Special Forces Group had suspected that the PLA had deployed the Sea Dragons on the "special freighters" and were operating on the ground amongst the Chinese American population. The Sea Dragons were the Chinese equivalent to Marine Raiders, and they posed a legitimate threat to this operation.

The CCUDS acted much like a radar and a sonar, but on a much smaller scale. Pillonato blinked instinctively as he tried to make out the faint glow of the screen. Although the specially designed face masks gave them almost a 360-degree picture of their battle space, in a way it was more of a feeling than actually sighting it. Pillonato's mind started to play tricks on him. He checked his watch; based on how much time they'd been under the ship, the rest of his Marines should have all placed their mines by now.

First Sergeant Draney tapped Pillonato's arm, giving him the signal that the mine was placed. Before Pillonato could acknowledge, the alert sensor in his mask went off. A rapidly blinking red dot appeared before his left eye. There were enemy divers in the water.

*Things just got real*, he thought.

At dive school, there were Vietnam-era Recon Marines that had told them stories about underwater combat. It had been brutal, up close, and absolutely deadly.

Pillonato steeled his nerves. All of his Marines would have received the same alert.

*We've trained for this*, he reminded himself. They were about to join a very small group of men who'd fought to the death in hand-to-hand combat underwater.

***

Just under the bow of the ship, Staff Sergeant Sean Smith, Alpha Team element leader, had just checked to ensure that his mine was firmly affixed by giving it a slight tug. When he was sure that it was attached, he tapped his swim buddy, then pushed off from the bottom of the ship.

Just then, he heard a metal scraping sound. He immediately felt a burning pain in his forearm.

*Enemy divers!* he realized.

Smith's training kicked in and he drew his combat knife. Based on the displacement of the water around him, he could tell approximately where the enemy diver was, even if they didn't know where he was headed—he lunged his blade forward but missed. A searing pain rippled through his leg; the Sea Dragon had sliced through his dry suit.

Staff Sergeant Smith did his best to override the urge to scream and instead focused on the path of the enemy soldier. He dove forward and was rewarded by feeling the hoses of what he could immediately tell was a Chinese rebreather. Judging by the movement of the hose, Smith knew his opponent was angling away from him. Without hesitation, he lunged his combat knife again.

The blade pierced the soft flesh of his opponent until it hit bone. He heard a muffled scream as he twisted the knife inside the man before withdrawing to plunge it back into the enemy diver's body two more times in rapid succession. When Smith had twisted his weapon inside the attacker's body for the third time, he felt the man's body go limp. He knew he was dead.

Smith checked his face mask display to see where his swim buddy was, but he heard the fight before he could pinpoint where it was. They were close to the hull of the ship. Smith did a quick check of his depth gauge and saw that during his fight he had sunk to about 20 feet beneath the ship. He kicked like a mad man to reach his partner.

The water above him was frantic with action; he could hear knife blades hitting metal. Two dark shapes appeared just feet from him, but in the murky water, he couldn't tell who was who.

*Bam, bam!*

The figure closest to Smith kicked free. When he heard the shots, he knew right away that they were dealing with a Chinese variant of the Russian SPP-1 underwater pistol. At this range, the shots would be fatal. He swam up to the Chinese diver and wrapped his arms and legs around him. As the enemy soldier tried to wiggle free, Smith yanked the man's head violently to the side and drove his eleven-inch combat knife into the man's neck. As he ripped the blade free, it severed the air hoses from his rebreather, causing the man to spin uncontrollably.

Smith let him go and checked his face mask display. He saw where the rest of his MSOT was with respect to his position. The display indicated that there were at least seven more enemy divers in the water.

***

Near the center of the freighter's underbelly, Navy Special Amphibious Corpsman Paul Sampson watched the security monitor on his display. So far, the dive had been textbook; he was almost bored.

*Clang!*

Something metal was scraping the bow of the ship. Before he knew what was happening, Sampson's face mask display immediately began flashing a single red dot.

*Oh crap!* he thought.

As he prepared for the enemy divers, his senses caught on fire—he tried to will himself to see in the obscure waters. Sampson backed up to his swim buddy, who was also aware of the threat. While he was a seasoned Navy diver, this was a terror Sampson had hoped he'd never have to deal with. Sensing the danger more than seeing it, they both drew their combat knives and braced for what they knew was coming.

Sampson heard two muffled sounds and knew what it had to be—Chinese Special Forces. His swim buddy gave him the signal to move towards the stern of the ship where the captain was. They began to kick for all they were worth. When Sampson turned over to look back at where they had just been, he heard three shots. He felt three projectiles pass just above his head, zipping past them. He didn't have time to warn his swim buddy, he had to hope he heard them too.

Sampson spun to face the divers rapidly closing on them and developed a quick plan to try and take them out. He broke off from their current path and dove deeper. He wanted to try and get underneath the attackers and close on them so he could use his knife.

There was another shot, and he felt the bullet pass right through his calf. It was pain like he'd never felt before. It burned terribly, contrasting sharply with the cold water around them. On instinct, he angled back up and lunged his blade for the dark spot just above him. His body impacted with the enemy diver and his blade sank deep into the hostile's body. Just as he had been taught in training, Sampson twisted the knife and eviscerated the man.

Reaching out blindly along the man's body, he found the SPP-1 and cut the lanyard from the divers' wrist. While there was no doubt in Sampson's mind that the man was dying, he shot him in the face anyway.

*Screw 'em!* he thought.

Sampson felt a tap on his back—he almost fired the underwater gun before he realized it was his swim buddy. They managed to link up with the rest of the team, or what was left of it.

The fact that no more divers had entered the water meant that the attack had come from a routine dive to make sure that the ship was clear. However, it didn't mean those divers wouldn't be missed.

\*\*\*

With the immediate danger of the enemy divers dealt with, Major Pillonato felt a sudden urge to get the hell out of dodge. They needed to vacate the area and blow the ship before more divers were sent in to investigate why their comrades hadn't returned.

When the team had reached their underwater propulsion devices and transited back to their zodiacs, Pillonato got a head count and saw they were short three Marines. He knew they were not coming back. As angry as he was about their loss, he knew this wasn't the time to mourn them or do anything emotional. They still needed to get out of the area and hope the other teams hadn't run into the same kind of trouble.

Pillonato glanced at his watch; they had 30 seconds before the mines would blow.

"Look sharp Marines, we're about to blow up a ship."

As he hunkered down on the gunnel, he flipped up his night vision goggles and looked back towards the ship. When his watch hit 0300 hours and they didn't hear anything right away, he thought maybe something had gone wrong. Then they felt the rumble beneath their zodiac.

The Chinese ship exploded in a massive fireball. For a second, they were able to see under it as it lifted out of the water. Whatever the Chinese had aboard her was ignited by the mines. She ripped apart. From the size of the explosion, Pillonato figured she would be at the bottom in minutes.

"Hot damn, boss! What the hell was on that ship?" Sampson asked.

"Whatever the hell it was, Staff Sergeant, it was made in China and wrecked in America!"

As the engines on the two zodiacs turned over, they headed for their rally point. Pillonato said a silent prayer that the other three teams had succeeded in their missions.

***

Master Sergeant Willy Carlson, team chief for MSOT 2, was looking through his night vision goggles as two of his Marines crept into their firing position 25 meters in front of him. They were his sniper section, and they were packing the MK 13 Mod 7. These rifles packed one hell of a punch and it was his intent to use it to fight above their weight class.

They had been watching the warehouse since they had been inserted at 2300 hours. Even though he was African American, Carlson felt like the luck of the Irish was with them. The Chinese had only left a squad-sized element with a handful of separatists to guard the large facility.

They had spotted a large supply of explosives inside the warehouse and their Team Leader, Captain Jeremiah Johansson, wanted to make a statement with this mission. He'd made it clear that they were going to leave a crater where this building currently stood.

"Chief, we set?" Asked Johansson over comms.

"Affirmative, Skipper" replied Carlson.

"We go loud in three minutes."

"Groovy," replied Carlson in his gravelly voice. "Snipers are set, sir. The sentries are first, then Element One enters from the front, and Element Two enters from the side. They sweep, clear, set charges, and we get the hell out of the area."

"Copy that. I've got the ISR drone overhead at 1,000 feet. If anyone else comes to the party, Gunny and I have the back door covered."

"Copy that, Skipper. Let's do this."

"Leroy Jenkins!" whispered Johansson.

Carlson switched to his snipers and told them to start taking the sentries out in exactly 60 seconds. He then got the signal

309

from both elements that they were ready to go. Carlson smiled; he loved it when a plan gelled.

Checking down at his watch, he saw there were only ten seconds until 0300 hours. He looked through his own rifle scope at the two Chinese sentries outside the door of the main warehouse entrance. Carlson heard two simultaneous suppressed shots from the MK 13s and saw the Chinese soldiers collapse to the deck. As soon as they fell, both elements breached their respective entry points into the warehouse. Even though Carlson was on their comms channels, no one spoke. He did hear several suppressed pops and some shouting, but it was all over in less than a minute.

*That was too damn easy,* Carlson thought to himself.

"Chief, charges are set," reported Staff Sergeant Grady, the Element One leader. "We've linked up with Element Two. Twenty-one hostiles down—most of them were sleeping."

"Copy all. Conduct SSE and get the hell out."

"Aye Chief, we'll be out in three mikes."

\*\*\*

Two hundred and fifty meters away, Captain Johansson watched the video feed from the drone overhead. Off in the distance, he saw what passed for normal these days: houses with cars parked out front and the random stray dog. Out of curiosity, he switched to thermals. Johansson didn't see anything that caught his eye until he zoomed in. He stared at the screen for at least thirty seconds before it hit him.

He was looking at trails of broken gras—the thermal cameras on the newest drones were amazing. There were three trails and they were all vectoring in toward the team's backdoor and his position. Johansson leaned over and showed Gunny the feed. The Gunny spat a glob of tobacco on the ground, some of it landing on his sleeve.

"Well, crap, skipper. I was gettin' bored anyway." He flicked the selector on his suppressed MK 17 Mod 0 from safe to fire.

"Gunny, I see three trails moving towards us," Johansson clarified. "They must be wearing some kind of thermal shroud that masks them from optics." He wiped sweat from his nose then flicked the selector on his own rifle to fire.

"Sir, better let the chief know we are about to go hot."

"Good call, Gunny," Johansson replied before he filled Carlson in on their situation.

Both men lay absolutely motionless as they waited for what was about to happen. The night air was cold, so both men breathed into their sleeves so the vapor from their exhalations wouldn't be visible.

Their night vision goggles were next-gen and displayed vibrant color as if it was day. Their patience paid off as figures emerged from the woods. They waited until they could see all of them—they were heavily outnumbered. Even as good as they both were, once they started shooting, they'd be dead in less than twenty seconds. The enemy units were about thirty feet away and approaching cautiously.

"Hey, sir, remember that scene in platoon?" Gunny whispered.

"What?" Johansson whispered back in annoyance.

"Where Charlie Sheen wakes up and the NVA are right on top of them?" Gunny whispered again.

Before Johansson could reply, Gunny had pulled the pin on a grenade and risen to his knees. He threw it like a baseball— it was a line drive right into the chest of the closest Chinese soldier. The grenade hit the man so hard it knocked him back. As the enemy soldier tried to regain his footing, the force of the explosion threw his lifeless body into the man behind him with a sickening crack.

Before Johansson knew what had happened, Gunny had thrown two more grenades into the group of enemy soldiers before any of them had a chance to react. As they all dove for cover, the additional grenades detonated, shrapnel slicing through the air. The soldiers that had survived the surprise assault shouted in pain and agony.

In the midst of the confusion, Master Sergeant Carlson and the Assistant Operations Sergeant came rushing in from Johansson and the Gunny's right flank. The two groups of Marines had the Chinese in a classic L shaped ambush. The four of them made short work of the Chinese soldiers and their paramilitary trainees. The swiftness of the ambush and the violence of action

311

had caught them completely by surprise and overwhelmed them before they were able to organize a counterattack. The gun battle lasted less than twenty seconds before it was over.

"Clear!" Carlson shouted now that the shooting had died down.

"What the hell was that, Gunny?" Johansson barked angrily now that the threats had been neutralized.

"Sir, all due respect, Staff NCOs take care of our own. I sent the good Master Sergeant three chirps over comms, and well, he came a running."

"What do the three chirps mean, Gunny?"

"Three chirps…means we're screwed."

As the four men were about to laugh at the sheer insanity of what they had just survived, there was a tremendous explosion that lit up the night sky. They all whirled about, weapons raised, ready to unleash holy hell on whatever it was.

"Six, this is One," Staff Sergeant Grady said over the radio.

"Send it, One," Johansson replied.

"Um, charges blew early, boss."

"Really? We hadn't noticed," Gunny cut in, to the laughter of the guys around him.

"All right, boys, exfil. It's time to beat feet out of here."

As the team gathered back up, they made their way to their pick-up point. Operators from 1st Special Forces Group rolled up in a beat-up fifteen-passenger van, tagged with all kinds of kooky bumper stickers to make it look like some sort of PRA reject.

Johansson checked his watch, noting it was 0345 hours. It would take them about an hour to reach Fort Lewis. He looked at his Marines, most of which had already fallen fast asleep, he too, nodded off.

***

Captain Shane Scott was with Staff Sergeant Chad Evans and Element One as they sat in their hide sites, overlooking the intersection of Highways 101 and 112. The team was split in two separate hides—each with a view of a large stretch of the highways. Now it was just a game of wait and see.

They had sensors set up to alert them to an approach from the woods surrounding the intersection in case the IED emplacers were traveling by foot to reach the road. For added personal security, they had a small ISR drone overhead. It would loiter over the entire area keep a look out for any movement. Captain Scott's team chief was with Element Two; they had the newest members to the unit with them, so Scott wanted his most experienced NCO with that group.

Scott and his Marines had been watching two pickup trucks just off the highway, in what was probably some farmer's field; there was a group of what they assumed were local teens near the trucks, drinking beers. There was an old barn not too far away, so many one of the teens must have lived there and invited some friends over. They had a small bonfire going, and they were rocking out to music and generally acting like stupid teenagers. All the same, Scott had one of his Marines keeping an eye on them just in case.

Scott and his men had been in place since 0100 hours, and they were getting bored out of their brains at the lack of vehicle traffic. This road was usually bustling with activity during the day, but the later it got, the more sporadic the truck and car traffic became.

This mission was feeling like a bust. They couldn't know for certain if one of the insurgent groups would place an IED today, tomorrow, or five days from now. All they knew was this particular stretch of road had already seen two IED attacks and one foiled attack.

0300 hours was fast approaching, and aside from the teens breaking curfew and generally having a fun time, this seemed like a dry hole. Maybe that was a good thing. Maybe the insurgents were figuring out a lot of innocent people were getting killed by their actions.

Captain Scott didn't really buy into the whole Raider mythos; for him it was a job. He liked being an elite Marine well enough, but the whole sneaking around looking for bad guys to kill was starting to wear thin on him. Then the world went crazy, and his whole attitude changed. His team chief had told him he'd been born again hard. He wasn't sure about that, but he was definitely all in. He wanted his country to go back to the way it was before all this craziness.

"Skipper, the kids are up to something," Sergeant Wallace whispered to him.

Scott crawled over to him "What do you have, Sergeant?" he asked in an equally soft tone.

"Sir, I've been watching the kids and they all are doing the typical stupid stuff, but there is one who has been on a phone the whole time, and he hasn't had anything to drink. He's the odd man out."

"What are you thinking, Wallace?" Scott prodded.

"Sir, it's hard to tell from here, but he's built differently than the rest. He's lean, and he carries himself like…like a soldier."

Scott ran his gloved hand over his stubble. After giving the individual a bit more of a closer look, he was inclined to agree with Wallace. He looked down at his watch again; it was 0255 hours. Something needed to happen soon, or he would call it and they'd head back to Fort Lewis empty handed. Just as he was about to ask Sergeant Wallace another question, his Team Chief came over the radio.

"Skipper, we've got two trucks coming down the road. They're about a mile away. They are running dark, boss."

This made Scott perk up—that was definitely a sign of mischief.

"Chief, get your team close to those kids," Scott ordered. "If those trucks stop there, I want ears and eyes on them. If they turn out to be our IED team, then we'll smoke 'em!"

"Copy that, boss, we are Oscar Mike."

Scott and Wallace watched Team Two move like wraiths through the woods as they made their way to a position closer to the two trucks and the teens. One of the teens had walked down to the road and appeared to be waiting. Fortunately for Team Two, the music from the pickups aided in masking their approach.

The Marines arrived moments before the trucks came to a halt. As soon as the trucks stopped, one of the teens turned the music off while another doused the fire.

The man Wallace had glassed earlier as most likely being a soldier began issuing orders. From where he was positioned, the Chief could make out that the man was speaking Chinese. His lips curled into a preternatural smile. It was game time.

"Skipper, we've got ChiComms."

"Chief, game on! When you see them placing the IEDs or handing them off to these guys, I want you to execute with extreme prejudice. No prisoners, Chief. Understood?"

"Copy that, boss."

Scott watched through his night vision goggles as the trucks were unloaded and the teens and Chinese soldiers began to assemble a daisy chained IED along the intersection. Scott counted thirty-five people involved. It looked like there were roughly fifteen Chinese soldiers. The rest appeared to be locals, what the intel weenies referred to as UIs or useful idiots—people that could be manipulated to do certain tasks a more intelligent person would reject out of hand.

While Scott felt bad about what was about to happen, he knew this was a war, even if the politicians in D.C. hadn't come out and said it. It was a shame. But these individuals had made their choice, and war was an ugly business. Sadly, business was picking up. Would these UIs be remembered as malefactors or would anyone give a damn at all in a hundred years?

Scott blinked those thoughts away. Checking his watch, he saw that it was exactly 0300 hours. On the radio he clicked three times: the signal for the Chief to execute. As Chief's team rose to engage the Chinese, the quiet night exploded.

Green tracer rounds arced towards the Marines. Three of them were instantly cut down by the fusillade of incoming rounds. To their credit, the remaining Marines hit the deck and began to return fire at a murderous rate.

Captain Scott immediately had his team bring their M72 LAW rockets to bear. He wasn't sure how or what happened, but somehow Chief's teams had managed to walk right into an ambush. There had been absolutely no indication from their vantage point that the Chinese were even aware of their presence.

Scott muttered several curse words under his breath before he used the coms and barked, "Target the IEDs themselves!"

"Aye, sir!" three of his Marines yelled as they opened the LAWs and prepared to fire

"Back blast clear!" They yelled in unison as they depressed the firing plungers on the rockets.

*Swoosh!*

The three 66 mm rockets blasted from the tubes and raced towards the Chinese soldiers' position at a rate of 475 feet per second. The first rocket impacted a crate containing something flammable near the side of the road; the entire thing blew up in a spectacular fireball. The overpressure from the explosion instantly vaporized the five people near it.

The second rocket hit one of the trucks the Chinese had arrived in. The explosion wasn't nearly as big, but the fragmentation from the warhead's detonation ricocheted between the trucks, tearing into the insurgents who leapt behind them for cover.

The third rocket found its mark. It connected with one of the IEDs they had been daisy chaining together. Because the insurgents had wrapped the IEDs they were connecting with det cord, when the first one exploded, it caused a ripple effect, detonating all five of the IEDs. The blast that resulted from all of them going off practically at the same time was massive. It blew several of the vehicles the Chinese had arrived in over on their sides. Scott saw that one vehicle had been thrown entirely off the road.

\*\*\*

Before the debris had even settled back to the ground, the team chief, Master Sergeant Darnell Brooks, and his remaining Marines rushed toward the remaining Chinese and insurgents who had somehow survived the IEDs. Many of them were dazed, wounded, and dying.

The Chief was first to engage at point blank range. A Chinese soldier who was bleeding from his ears stared at him, unable to focus. His lips were moving, but no sound was coming

316

out. Brooks raised his rifle and shot the man in the face. As the man fell, a Marine yelled for him to take cover.

Before he could move, the Chief felt like a sledgehammer hit him in his back plate. Even at 210 pounds, the impact jarred him. Brooks spun on his heels to face the threat and fired before he even realized he was doing it.

The individual who had shot him in the back was a female who couldn't have been more than twenty years old; she practically seemed like a girl to him. Her body stumbled backwards from the bullets that had slammed into her. She dropped the rifle she had just shot him with and clutched at the hole in her stomach where a pair of 7.62 mm rounds had torn through her flesh as if she were made of paper. She slumped to her knees, coughing blood.

Brooks ran to her. "Damn it! Why did you do that?" he barked angrily.

"You... you shot me..." She said flatly, blood running down the sites of her mouth as she coughed. Her eyes pleaded for help.

He scanned her wound and knew immediately that the woman had minutes left to live. One of his Marines appeared at his side, looking first to the woman and then to him.

"We're clear, Chief. Site is secured."

"Check," Brooks said flatly. Without thinking, he raised his rifle and shot the woman in the face, blowing her brains out the back of her head. He didn't want to shoot her, but she was dying, and he didn't have the heart to let her spend whatever time she had left in agonizing pain like that. No one deserved to be left for dead like that. Shooting her in the face was the kindest thing he could do, given the situation.

"Marines, collect our dead and wounded," ordered Master Sergeant Brooks. "I want them moved over to that clearing for the choppers when they get here. I also want any and all enemy weapons and equipment piled up over there. When the choppers arrive, toss a couple of thermite grenades on them. We're not leaving anything behind for them to use against us or any other unit. Oh, and while we're at it, find a few of the insurgents, maybe a woman and a few men, and string up on those trees over there.

Place a placard on them with the words 'Traitors against America.' That ought to leave a solid message for any others who might think it's cool to take up arms against their country." Brooks was livid at how this whole thing had gone down.

Ten minutes later, the team climbed aboard a CH-47 after helping their wounded get on the chopper and making sure they had their dead and all their equipment. Before the last Marine climbed on board, Brooks tossed three thermite grenades on the pile of weapons and other equipment they'd pulled off the Chinese soldiers. Once that task had been taken care of, the chopper took off and headed back to Fort Lewis.

Captain Scott and Master Sergeant Brooks looked at their dead comrades laid out on the floor of the helo, covered in ponchos. Neither said a word. They just nodded at each other. Brooks looked at his watch—their portion of the mission had lasted only 22 minutes. He motioned for the Captain to send their SITREP back to the Major. It was a mission complete, but not before it cost them a handful of men.

* * *

Team Four had been sent to blow up the FedEx Shipment Center at William Fairchild International Airport. The airport itself was located within the city limits of Port Angeles, in Clallam County, Washington. It was a nice area, but with its close proximity to the ports, it had recently become a bit of a hotspot for the growing insurgency. A number of nature parks and public land nearby had also been turned into training camps—they had to get control of it before it got worse.

Staff Sergeant Juan Villarreal was a seasoned operator with this Marine Special Operation Team. This place was a long way from the East LA barrio he'd come up in, but in many ways, surviving that environment growing up had prepared him to survive anywhere. He'd been deployed to every major third world hotspot on earth during his military career. Never in a million years had he imagined that he'd be in an honest to goodness shooting war on American soil; it was the kind of garbage he'd read about in post-apocalypse doomsday books or watched in cheesy B movies.

318

His Team Leader, Captain Aaron Hammernick, had given his element the task of infiltrating the FedEx Building at the airport and verifying the intel 1st Special Forces Group had provided was legit. The Greenie Beanies had said was that this place was unwittingly or wittingly being used as a storage and transfer facility for military-grade equipment arriving from China, to be distributed to the various insurgent groups they were supporting and training. The PLA was supposedly somehow using the cover of FedEx shipments with legitimate cargo as a means of infiltrating weapons grade explosives, specialty components used for making IEDs and military rifles.

Worst of all, the shipment that had arrived yesterday was supposedly carrying ten FN-16 Man-portable air-defense systems or MANPADS. If that last part was true, then this would be a very dangerous escalation indeed. The FN-16s could not only knock down military helicopters, they could easily take down commercial jetliners.

Once the team was able to verify that the Chinese were in fact using this facility to store military grade equipment and munitions, they had been ordered to rig this place with enough C-4 to leave a 10-foot crater.

What Staff Sergeant Villarreal didn't like about this mission was the compressed timeline.

*How the hell are we supposed to make sure all this goes off simultaneously with the rest of the company?* he wondered. That was that kind of high-level officer crap that got Marines killed. In theory, Villarreal understood the Commander's intent. Simultaneity would ensure confusion and cause the Chinese response to be disorganized and chaotic—they couldn't send reinforcements to all four locations at the same time.

*Then again, I'm just a Staff Sergeant with ten years of experience*, he thought, popping his knuckles angrily. *Who am I to judge? I'm just a dumb grunt after all.* In the end, he'd get it done, timeline be damned.

Villarreal and the others had infiltrated the night before and had been laid up in some nearby harbor sites until the sun set. The airport was situated near the harbor, so it offered some good warehouses to shack up in while they waited for the perfect timing to make their move.

Villareal breathed on his hands to warm them. In a way, he was glad it was cold out. He could always wear more layers. If they had been hiding out in this place in the summer, they'd be baking in all their body armor and equipment.

The Marines in his element were annoyed that out of all the teams in the company, they had to be on station the longest for a mission profile that would probably only take an hour. They had done a map recon and rock drill of the facility. Luckily, the floor plans of the building and the airport were still available. The team had set up in the woods near Lee Shore Boats, off West Edgewood Drive.

Ordinarily, it would have been an easy infiltration. However, the Chinese had virtually taken over the airport, including trucks and cargo planes. They had convoys coming and going at all hours—not to mention the armed roving patrols. It was almost impossible to put an ISR drone over the airport due to the Chinese jamming the frequencies the smaller drones hopped through.

Their internal comms were going to be a no-go as well. They had been forced to fall back on using SMS messages via cell phones. Using military communications close to what in essence was a Chinese military installation would have made for a mission failure from the jump. As soon as the Chinese detected that kind of equipment in play, they'd know they were about to get attacked. Instead, the Marines did was they do best: improvise, adapt and overcome. Since their infil, they hadn't spoken above a whisper— even then, it was one or two words and only when it was necessary.

The first thing they observed about the airport when they arrived was all the add-ons. The Chinese firm that owned and operated most of the facility had nearly tripled it in size. Fortunately for the Marines, the Chinese had expanded it on the cheap. The new construction was little more than corrugated tin. Cutting through it would be simple enough, they just had to do it quietly.

320

Ever since the Marines had begun observing the airport, it had been nonstop with activity. Staff Sergeant Villarreal knew would work in their favor, though. Airport operations were controlled chaos—they'd just use it to their advantage.

Villarreal rolled over onto his back and looked up at the stars through an opening in the trees. He liked the Seattle area, or rather, he liked the view in this particular region of the Seattle area.

*Buzz.* His cell phone vibrated, and he looked down at the message.

"Come home, mom is pissed." The message from Captain Hammernick meant it was time to move.

"I'm with my friends, I'll be home in an hour," Villarreal replied back.

Whispering to his Marines, he told them it was time. He could feel the energy in the harbor site pick up immediately. These boys were action guys, and waiting was the worst. He sent one last text before he left the harbor site.

"Fine, tell mom I'm leaving now!!!"

He added the exclamation points just in case their texts were hacked at the data center. If they were being triangulated it wouldn't really matter; they'd all be dead in a few minutes if the Chinese knew they were here.

Their route to the FedEx center would take them through a lumber yard. Despite the early hour, the airport was well-illuminated. The shadows the operators craved were few and far between. Their movements would be a mixture of short flat out sprints, low crawling through brush, and slow deliberate movements through whatever patches of darkness they could find.

Once they reached the lumber yard, Villarreal had his Marines slow down and spread out. The yard was closed and there were no perimeter lights. Now it was more important to move cautiously and observe the perimeter of the airport a bit better.

It was essentially a straight shot across Fairchild Airport Road, and that's what gave Villarreal pause. There was a new fence installed all along the perimeter of the airport. Rather than attempt the direct route through the front door of the FedEx facility, Villarreal had instructed his Marines to move to the eastern edge of the lumber yard.

Once they got themselves repositioned, they would cross the road at the least covered area of the airfield, ready to cut the fence. They'd just have to hope there weren't motion sensors to detect if the fence had been tampered with. Then they'd sprint to the closest structure and hug the shadows along the backs of the buildings as they leapfrogged along until they reached the FedEx facility.

The plan was working well, and they were making good time, until Uncle Murphy struck. As soon as they reached the eastern fence line, a mounted patrol headed right for them with a spotlight turned on. The guards in the vehicle were using the light to pan through the parts of the buildings with long shadows. Villarreal told his Marines to hit the deck, eat dirt, and pray to the gods to make them invisible.

They had gone prone on a slight incline so as the jeep approached, the guards would be at an elevated position. The foliage was sparse, but it was better than nothing. The truck stopped above them and angled the spotlight at the fence line. Villarreal looked down the line of his Marines—to his amazement, the angle of the light actually created more shadow as it passed over them. After a long two minutes, the guards mounted back up and drove off.

Corporal Bosworth motioned to him and pointed at the entrance to a drainage pipe they hadn't seen on their map or recon of the airfield. Bosworth did a quick check and verified that it was open and free of any visible sensors.

Villarreal conferred with his assistant element leader and they both agreed it was promising. In true Marine Corps fashion, he called an audible. They would adapt to this apparent gift that fate had proffered them.

Donning their night vision goggles, the team crouched and entered the drainage tunnel. The tunnel was for the most part a straight line, although there were exits above them at about a hundred-meter interval with branches to the north that Villarreal assumed went the width of the entire airfield.

Suddenly, Corporal Bosworth halted the element and motioned for Villarreal to come to him. Even with the NVGs on, he could see Bosworth's gold tooth; he had a big grin on his face.

Villarreal shrugged his shoulders as if to say, "What?"

Bosworth pointed up. Villarreal followed the man's hand until he saw the purple and orange logo of FedEx. Then he too had a big grin on his face.

Using a pinhole camera, they surveyed the area. Villarreal couldn't believe it; they could come up right behind the building at a loading dock.

*Buzz*. His phone vibrated again, and he backed up further into the tunnel and checked the message from 'Mother.'

"Well?"

The Captain was starting to piss Villareal off. *If he's in such a damn hurry, he could bring his ass over here and take charge.* He took a deep breath and let it out before he typed his response.

"Traffic."

He checked his watch; it was 0218 hours. Villareal bit his lip. They would need to boogie if they were going to meet the 0300 hours time hack. He was going to have to "hasten slowly" as the saying went. Taking a knee, he huddled his Marines up and gave them the new plan.

"OK, boys, we are at the back door. Same plan: we go in, plant our charges and we ghost the hell out. Avoid contact if you can. If you can't…" His voice trailed off as he drew his suppressed MARSOC M45. With his free hand, he touched his combat knife. He looked them each in the eye, and they nodded.

Villareal approached the drain opening. Taking a deep breath, he slowly started to open it. It creaked.

*Of course!* he thought to himself. Despite the noises of the airfield, the creak echoed in the tunnel, and every Marine held their breath. Once he'd slowly closed the opening, Villarreal cursed under his breath.

"Anyone got any lube?" he whispered. Despite the obvious tension, he could see a couple of smiles on the camouflaged faces.

Villarreal saw Doc Kravitz dig into his aid bag and pass up a plastic bottle of something. When it got to Bosworth, Villarreal saw him mouth the word "Astroglide."

*Nunquam non paratus—never not prepared*, thought Villareal, suppressing a chuckle.

Moving back to the drain opening, he removed his left glove and squirted the liquid onto his ungloved hand. After smearing a healthy amount of the liquid onto the metal hinges, he returned the bottle to Bosworth.

Making a sign of the cross, he pushed gently on the hatch. This time, it made no noise. Villarreal moved quickly, ascending all the way out of the tunnel. Once out, he did a quick 360 scan with his suppressed M45. Then he advanced to the steps of the loading bay. The second he moved away from the opening, his Marines began climbing out of the tunnel and stacking up on the loading bay steps behind him.

Corporal Bosworth stepped around Staff Sergeant Villarreal and put the pinhole camera under the crack at the bottom of the door. He moved it back and forth and then pulled it back and stood.

Bosworth whispered, "Directly opposite us appears to be a receiving room. I also see a partition between that room and the loading bay door to our right. To the left is a dark hallway. Behind the receiving area, I see the main warehouse. I can see some movement, but it's at least fifty meters from us."

"Roger that, Corporal." Villarreal formed a quick entry plan in his head then gave the hand and arm signals to the Marines in the stack. Six simple hand gestures told every Marine where they were to move when they entered the room.

Corporal Bosworth knelt and pulled out his lockpicks. When he looked up, Villarreal tapped him on the shoulder. Bosworth went ahead and turned the knob, and the door opened. Bosworth looked down at his lockpick set and shook his head. Putting it away, he raised his M45 and entered the building.

Once they were all in the room, they knelt and stayed still for thirty seconds and just listened. They adjusted to the sounds in the building and were able to form a mental picture of where things were.

Villarreal motioned for Doc Kravitz and another Marine to remain at the entrance to watch their six. If need be, they would be first out if the team had to exfil under fire. As the element left the receiving room and entered the larger warehouse, he further split the team into two smaller elements. Villarreal paired up with Bosworth—they would set charges along the southern side of the building. The remaining three Marines would set charges along the northern side of the building. The two groups moved out low and fast.

As they advanced throughout the facility, they set charges along every other support beam. Towards the middle of the building, there were plastic crates with Chinese writing on them. Villarreal had Bosworth scan for any immediate threats, and then opened one of the crates. What he saw inside confirmed their worst fears—FN-16 MANPADs. There were five to a crate. Villarreal counted two crates that looked like they were carrying them. He closed the top of the crate then moved over to another crate opposite these.

When he opened this next crate, he saw something different—ammonium nitrate/fuel oil. The crates were stacked five high. If he had to guess, he estimated each crate could hold somewhere around 200 to 300 pounds. He did some quick high school math in his head. Slowly, he and Bosworth backed into a tiny alcove in the wall.

Pointing to the crates, he whispered, "This whole section of the building, all these crates are filled with AN/FO. That grouping of two crates over there, those had five FN-16s each. I made sure to snap a couple of photos and a short video clip of what I saw in each of them for the intel guys."

Bosworth looked puzzled for a second before his eyes grew wide with momentary terror at the realization.

"Damn, Staff Sergeant. If all these crates are filled with AN-FO, holy hell. If the Chinese supply this to the separatists..." He trailed off at the thought.

"Bosworth, we have to set these charges and get the hell out of here. We have to get back to the Skipper. When this place blows it's going to look like a nuke went off here."

As they rose to continue their work, Villarreal spotted the other element along the northern wall, busy setting some charges. They were also completely unaware of a couple of security guards that were less than ten feet from discovering them.

Without hesitation, Villarreal raised his pistol and fired a single shot. The round punctured a hole in the wall right between the heads of his Marines. They instantly raised their weapons just as the security guards turned the corner where they had hidden between the crates. Villarreal saw two flashes but heard no noise that rose above the background din of the warehouse. As the security guards fell, he saw his Marines drag them into the shadows, out of sight.

Villarreal knew the Marines on the northern side could see him. He held up a charge of C-4, pointed to the crates, and spun his index finger in a circle, which told them to hurry the hell up. He got a thumbs-up and he and Corporal Bosworth began placing their remaining charges.

Villarreal started to formulate a plan in his head on how they were getting out of here. This place was going to cause a massive explosion when it finally went off. In his own estimation, there were at least twenty tons of AN/FO in this warehouse. They'd need to get a lot further away from it than they had intended to before they set it off.

Running wasn't going to work—they wouldn't be able to get far enough away fast enough before they'd get detected. They needed a vehicle big enough to get the entire team away. He glanced at a large digital wall clock; it read 0237 hours. Villarreal realized he was starting to panic, and he had to take a few deep breaths and force himself to calm down.

The element regrouped back at the receiving room. He told Doc Kravitz and the other Marine with him to find a truck big enough for the whole team to fit inside. Bosworth was behind him—he pantomimed an enormous explosion. The two men left the room in a hurry.

Villarreal took the cell phone out and called the Captain. It rang once and in a terse whisper, the Captain spoke.

"What in the hell are you calling me for?" he whispered harshly.

"AN/FO. Get to the tertiary extraction now!" Before the Captain could respond, Villarreal ended the call.

He hoped the Captain would understand his tone and start running. As he placed the phone in his pocket, he heard a vehicle screech to a halt outside the loading bay. Bosworth gave him a thumbs-up and they all left the building. Apparently, Doc Kravitz had stolen the most obvious vehicle he could have, a FedEx delivery truck. The Marines opened the back and piled in.

Bosworth was climbing into the truck when he raised his rifle at Villarreal and fired on full automatic above his head. Instinctively, Villarreal turned and raised his rifle to fire. What he saw made his heart sink—the security patrol they'd seen earlier was barreling towards them. Before he could fire at them, he was yanked off his feet by Bosworth and pulled into the truck.

"Go, go, go!" he yelled. Their truck was already burning rubber.

The truck smashed into several staged pallets and parked cars as it gained speed. Bullets tore into the truck, striking Doc Kravitz and another Marine. As Villarreal looked out, he saw that two other security jeeps were now giving chase. Automatic fire was being traded back and forth between the vehicles. The smell of gunfire, blood, and burning rubber filled the truck.

"Frag out!" one of the Marines shouted as he hurled a grenade like a baseball from the truck. The weapon shattered the glass of the closest security jeep. A fraction of a second later, the front of the vehicle exploded as the grenade went off.

Villarreal and Bosworth both emptied a full magazine into the driver of the second jeep that had roared ahead to try and close the distance on them. The passenger in the vehicle was half hanging out the passenger side window, firing his assault rifle at the tightly packed Marines in the back of the truck.

As the shooting intensified, Villarreal and Bosworth both simultaneously shouted, "Changing!"

The two of them stepped back to drop their magazines and reload while two more Marines took their place. The other two Marines unloaded on the last vehicle still giving chase. Suddenly, the vehicle started to back off. Either the driver had been killed or they had decided that they had had enough. In either case, it looked like they were going to make it out of there.

"What the hell, man!" Bosworth yelled, pointing to his watch.

Villarreal grabbed Bosworth's wrist and saw that the time read 0248 hours. He ran forward to the driver.

"Speed the hell up and get us to our tertiary extraction site!" he yelled. The Marine nodded and stepped on the gas. Soon they were driving west, away from the airport on West Edgewood Drive at about 80 miles per hour, pushing the truck way past its redline speed.

They had to get to Dry Creek Grange to pick up the rest of the team. By his estimation if the Captain had heeded his warning almost ten minutes ago, they should be just about—

"Stop the truck!" Villarreal shouted as the headlights illuminated what looked like men running away from hell itself. They had nearly shot right past the rest of their team. The Marines stopped, turned around, and sprinted back to the FedEx truck. They piled inside, all gasping for air and drenched in sweat despite the cold outside.

From the looks of them, they had understood his call and had started running flat out. The Captain made his way to him, but before he could speak, Villarreal yelled to the driver, "*Go!*"

"How... much... time...?" Captain Hammernick asked between gasps for air.

"None." Villarreal started to explain more, but the night sky turned the color of day and then three seconds later, the sound and pressure wave from the explosion nearly knocked the truck over; the driver fought to maintain control.

The windows on the truck had blown out as the blast wave passed over them. As Villarreal looked back, he saw a fireball reaching at least 250 feet into the sky and climbing. As the sound from the explosion died down, he heard secondary explosions from the fuel farm at the airport going up.

Everyone slumped to the floor of the truck, glad to be alive. The Captain tossed his radio to Staff Sergeant Villarreal.

"Radio the Major and let him know we are mission complete," Hammernick muttered, almost too exhausted to finish his sentence.

"Yes, sir," Staff Sergeant Villarreal replied. He smiled at what they had just pulled off; they would live to fight another day.

Turning the radio on, he switched to the company frequency. "Six, this is Four Bravo. Mission complete. The facility is gone. Oh, and the airport too."

Without waiting for a reply, he shut the radio off. Within an hour they'd be at the landing zone for helo extract. Until then, he was done being a Marine—at least until tomorrow.

Abbreviation Key

| | |
|---|---|
| AN/FO | Ammonium Nitrate/Fuel Oil |
| PRA (extremist movement) | People's Revolutionary Action |
| CCUDS | Close Contact Underwater Diver System |
| EXFIL | Exfiltration |
| IED | Improvised Explosive Device |
| INFIL | Infiltration |
| ISR | Intelligence, Surveillance and Reconnaissance |
| MANPADs | Man-Portable Air-Defense Systems |
| MARSOC | Marines Special Forces Command |
| MOS | Military Occupational Specialty |
| MSOT | Marine Special Operations Teams |
| NCO | Noncommissioned Officer |
| NVA | North Vietnamese Army |

| NVG | Night Vision Goggles |
| PLA | People's Liberation Army |
| ROTC | Reserve Officer Training Corps |
| SITREP | Situation Report |
| SSE | Sensitive Site Exploitation |
| UI | Useful idiots |

# Afterword

I hope you've enjoyed these side trips to other parts and perspectives in the burgeoning global crisis that is the *Maelstrom Rising* series. Some will probably see some more development as the series goes on. Others might just be snapshots of a moment in time.

If you're new to the series, coming to this collection because one of your favorite authors contributed, I hope that you'll check the rest of it out:

Escalation

Holding Action

Crimson Star

Strategic Assets

And if you're an old hand, but have discovered an author here whose work you enjoy, please check their work out, as well:

Brad Torgerson

Steven Hildreth, Jr.

LawDog

JL Curtis

Mike Massa

Chris Hernandez

Larry Correia

Mike Kupari

James Rosone

The other two authors in this collection, sadly, do not have Amazon pages yet. Hopefully, that will change.